A.J. SCUDIERE

NightShade

FORENSIC FBI FILES ⟶ BOOK 4

ECHO
AND
EMBER

"There are really just 2 types of readers—those who are fans of AJ Scudiere, and those who will be."
-Bill Salina, Reviewer, Amazon

For *The Shadow Constant*:
"The Shadow Constant by A.J. Scudiere was one of those novels I got wrapped up in quickly and had a hard time putting down."
-Thomas Duff, Reviewer, Amazon

For *Phoenix*:
"It's not a book you read and forget; this is a book you read and think about, again and again . . . everything that has happened in this book could be true. That's why it sticks in your mind and keeps coming back for rethought."
-Jo Ann Hakola, The Book Faerie

For *God's Eye*:
"I highly recommend it to anyone who enjoys reading - it's well-written and brilliantly characterized. I've read all of A.J.'s books and they just keep getting better."
-Katy Sozaeva, Reviewer, Amazon

For *Vengeance*:
"Vengeance is an attention-grabbing story that lovers of action-driven novels will fall hard for. I hightly recommend it."
-Melissa Levine, Professional Reviewer

For *Resonance*:
"Resonance is an action-packed thriller, highly recommended. 5 stars."
-Midwest Book Review

ACKNOWLEDGMENTS

Echo and Ember is one of those stories that was in my heart even before it was Eleri and Donovan's case. I'd love to list the people who helped shape the story, but because it has been forming for so very long, it's hard to pinpoint that list. My time at the University of Tennessee in the Human Forensics Identification program has helped shape all these books and of course many thanks go out to the professors and the team there.

The usual suspects get the nod here. My kids, Jarett and January (you can email me or catch me online to ask which books which name came from!) are always at the top of this list. It's gotta be weird with a parent working on their computer all the time and commenting about killing people. My husband deserves a massive shout out. He deals with all of it, and does so with grace.

Then there's Eli, my partner in fictional crime. I would not be published without her. I'm just not organized enough.

And the best group of betas who keep this fictional world going 'round. They catch errors, tell me where I was unclear, and when I'm off my ever lovin' rocker. THANK YOU: Daddy, Dana, Eli, Julie, Laura, & Victoria. For everything!

One last shout out goes to my amazing Advanced Reader Team— my renegades are the best. Special thank yous to Felix Bearden, Dan Cox, Craig Fallon, Dacy Johnson, and R. D. Nyberg!

DEDICATION

I don't know how many kids remember the name of their junior high librarian. I do.

She was "Mrs. Ball" when the class was in, but after school or in the short time before classes started in the morning, she told me to call her "Jackie." She held books for me, even books that required a parent's signature. I have no idea how many new books at Jefferson Junior High went into my hands before they went onto the shelf, but it was a pretty big number. I was a voracious reader, and she fed my habit. There was always something waiting for me behind the desk.

She handed me my first Terry Brooks book. My son is named after a character in that series. My daughter is named after another book character. She put "The Clan of the Cave Bear" in my hands. Directed me to a Lois Duncan book I didn't know existed, one with a very enlightening ending. I read "Heart's Blood." I read mysteries. I read literature. I read everything.

She told me about S.E. Hinton—who published her first book, "The Outsiders," at sixteen. I told her that I wrote some and maybe I would do that. Echo and Ember is my eleventh book under the name A.J. Scudiere. I didn't do it by sixteen, but I did it.

Jackie Ball passed three years ago. And I'm so sorry I didn't look back before that.

This one's for you, Jackie! Thank you for everything.

"Our tales of monsters tell us more about ourselves than about the monsters."

—author unknown

1

Eleri stood looking at the pictures of the crime scene as she stared at the body in the morgue. None of the evidence lined up, but for the life of her she couldn't figure out why.

Maybe it was because she was distracted by Dana Brantley, Night-Shade Agent and higher ranked officer. The woman stood over the body wearing what looked like an FBI issued suit and a corresponding FBI issued sense of focus. Her dark hair hung in curly rings that seemed to understand even they should obey her. Something about Dana stuck out as being "off" or "weird." Coming from Eleri, that was saying a lot.

There was barely room around the body for all five of the agents, though they'd managed to flash their badges and run the medical examiner off.

Eleri watched as Donovan looked over his shoulder at the door. Through the window, the M.E. looked at the group of them as though they were going to chop up his dead body for steaks or something. Donovan and Wade could probably smell the man's suspicious thoughts from here.

"I remember that," Donovan muttered. He'd been an M.E. in South Carolina for a handful of years before getting recruited into the FBI. "Nothing sucks more than having your best cases pulled out from under you."

"Did you get tired of the standard gunshot wounds and murder-by-knife cases?" Wade asked with a small grin. His eyes didn't stray from the gray body on the gurney in front of them.

"GSWs are the worst. I was planning on researching an imaging system to be able to x-ray or PET scan the body and see the trajectories. I had the grants written and everything, but I got recruited," he commented as his eyes came back to the gray skin and the clearly dead man with no outward signs of murder.

"No, you wouldn't," Eleri said. "You would have had to talk to people to develop that."

"Shut up," Donovan returned.

"Shut up, both of you." Agent Pines added her two cents dead tone. "Dana needs quiet."

Dana Brantley was apparently communing with the body. Christina Pines was standing by. Though her suit was pale gray with pinstripes running through it, she looked like the other half of Dana Brantley's matched set. Pines had her blondish hair pulled straight back into a bun with nary a hair escaping. She clasped her hands in front of her as though standing guard.

Thus, it looked like Pines was functioning as Agent Dana Brantley's protector—or at least that was her only skill that Eleri had figured out yet. Still, Eleri shut up; Wade remembered Dana from his days in NightShade and spoke highly of her. Eleri decided to pin him down for clarification later.

She turned to Dana. "Would it be better if we left you alone with the body for a minute?"

"No, having you here is good." Dana spoke softly, as though even her own voice interrupted her work. "I'm getting things off the body and things off the handful of you—what *you're* getting off the body. So that helps. Just quiet . . . is good."

Eleri didn't respond, figuring what Dana most likely knew was that she—Eleri—wasn't contributing anything to this examination.

The man was dead. His skin was gray, he hadn't had a Y incision yet—Donovan was going to do that when Dana decided she'd had enough of speaking to the dead. So as of right now, they were investigating a murder that could have been a heart attack.

Only it wasn't a heart attack.

Eleri knew that for a fact—if only by the gathering of people around the body. Having her and Donovan here was enough to rule out any natural death. But her Agent in Charge had sent not only her and her partner, but he'd pulled Wade de Gottardi out of retirement again. "Retirement" was a strong word for Wade's gallivanting around the world and giving lectures on his latest research in the rarified world of sub-atomic physics.

Then, Westerfield told Eleri and Donovan that, for the first time, they would have another set of NightShade partners working with them. Enter Dana Brantley and Christina Pines.

Pines had no discernable skills as of yet. Eleri only had time to read the dossier on Dana during the quick flight into Wyoming. But since Dana could apparently get visions and read things—almost like Eleri did—Eleri was concerned that Dana was going to turn and light into her at any moment, telling her exactly what Christina Pines did for the NightShade division of the FBI.

Eleri pushed her thoughts back toward the case.

The man on the table looked like he might have suffocated. She wanted to say so. The blue shade of his skin didn't hit any one particular spot like a bruise. His lips didn't show signs of distress. His eyes hadn't shown any petechial hemorrhaging—bursting of the vessels in the eyes that signaled hard-end strangulation.

She turned her attention to the rest of him, even as she noticed both Wade and Donovan taking slow deep breaths. Since Dana said no one should touch him yet, they were smelling him.

Eleri did a full body scan of the naked corpse.

Healthy enough looking man. Mid-forties—she'd read that on his chart when she came in. But if she'd had to look at him and guess, that's where she would have landed. He had that look of a man who was working out and coloring his hair and realizing that time was moving him forward whether he wanted it to or not. He was fighting it every step of the way. His body—in addition to saying "dead"—said gym time.

His nails were manicured. Office job? Probably, given the corporate haircut and the shape of his feet. The curl of his toes indicated that he'd spent a long time in wingtips or something similar. Eleri had seen it often enough.

He didn't look like her end of the spectrum though, not her parents' kind of money. Those men looked only sun wrinkled, they usually didn't have the same urge to fight time—because time made them richer, thus they didn't have to be better-looking. Eleri felt the corner of her mouth pull at the thought. Still, she'd learned long ago never to judge a dead body.

"We need to CT scan him next." Dana finally spoke, her eyes open and darting around the room to all the rest of them as though she'd only blinked for a minute. "Anyone else?"

Eleri didn't know if Dana meant "Did anyone agree?" Or "Did anyone else want to contribute?" to what was rapidly becoming her one-woman show.

"He was afraid." Wade spoke up and Donovan quickly nodded in agreement. "My guess is that he saw his killer and he knew he was going to die."

"He was also surprised." That was Donovan's voice and Eleri was almost startled by his voluntary group participation.

"That's it!" Wade commented. He'd clearly smelled the same thing and couldn't place it. "I've been out of the smelling-bodies game for a bit. You don't get 'I see my killer' scent in the general population, you know."

Eleri almost laughed out loud, but this man had died a serious death. "What was surprising?" she asked.

"Don't know." Donovan didn't shrug with it. He was calmer, more withdrawn with the others around. It wasn't Wade, Eleri knew that. Donovan had been comfortable around Wade since he'd gotten over that two-wolves-pissing-over-territory thing they'd done when they met. The worst part was that she had been the territory, even if she wasn't the kind one would expect in that situation. She was Donovan's FBI partner, and his first real friend, though he was working his way up to three these days. And Wade was gay, so she wasn't ever going to be that kind of territory to him. But the two men had actually growled and almost gotten into a full-blown wolf-fight in the middle of Wade's sub-particle physics lab the first time they'd met. Now they were buds. She shook her head at the thought and picked up the chart.

She hadn't wanted to look at it at first. She wanted to make an unbiased assessment. They all had.

Dana looked at her. "What does it say?"

"Well, it says he wore wingtips to work every day."

Pines' eyebrows rose, though if that was her version of laughter or a comment that Eleri wasn't as funny as she thought she was, Eleri couldn't tell.

"He worked in a genetics lab—"

"Oh fuck." Donovan sighed. "Not again."

"What?" Dana asked, looking back and forth between the two of them.

"We just came off a nasty case with kids and genetic therapies," Eleri told her.

"Was that the one down in New Mexico? I heard hints," Dana commented and Eleri only nodded.

Turning back to the chart, she kept going, "His lab designed genetically based drugs for cancers and . . . Oh, that's lovely." She stopped and looked up at them. "He did classified work for several of the major pharmaceutical companies."

"Classified? As in 'government classified'?" Pines asked. When Eleri nodded at her, she responded, "I didn't know they did classified work. I mean sure, proprietary, but you're talking national security clearance, right?"

Eleri nodded again. She already didn't like this case.

Donovan looked at her and sighed. "At least we're indoors."

She grinned, thinking back to three feet of snow and riding ATVs through gritty desert winds. Inside was good. But she didn't think it would last long. Again, she turned back to the case at hand. "Forty-four years old, black hair, blue eyes, Burt Riser. PhD in biomedical research."

Dana grinned. She probably knew this guy, or at least his type. Dana had been a lab rat, from what Eleri had read on her. Well, the parts that weren't redacted for being above her pay grade. Dana was also the lead on this case—something Eleri still hadn't quite acclimated to. She was used to herself and Donovan being their own little world. They only had to answer to Westerfield. But apparently, Dana did, too. So at least they would stay roughly on the same track, even if Eleri was no longer the senior agent.

Pines grabbed the edge of the metal gurney. "Let's get him into the CT machine then and see what he tells us."

Without comment, they all put hands on the metal cart and got the body out of the room. They passed by the M.E., who was still eyeing them as though they were going to do some zombie ritual, and they headed into the biomedical scan room. They'd done a quick tour of the facility before they even looked at the dead guy for just this reason—they didn't want to tip the ME to what was going on even by asking for certain tests or options. NightShade protocol demanded it. So they closed the door and used the equipment at hand.

Eleri understood the man's ire. They came in, stole his case, and used his supplies to do it. Aside from the Federal Bureau of Investigation demanding that this case be remanded to a higher office than the local M.E., they were just douches. Pines might even be an actual one. The jury was still out on that.

Thirty minutes later, when they'd all gone through the hands-on manipulations of moving a dead body into and out of the machine and then printing out x-ray style films and stitching together all the smaller ones they had, they managed to make a good full body image. Casper, Wyoming was home to tech companies like the one Burt Riser worked for, but the morgue had yet to become state of the art.

Donovan taped all the scans to the wall in the shape of Burt Riser while the rest of them stood back. Shining light from the front wasn't ideal. Eleri was glad the wall was white. The only other option here was to put each film on the light box and trust their brains to put it together. They could do that later. Right now, they needed the big picture.

"I don't see anything," Eleri commented. Surely, she was missing something and one of them would say so.

But they didn't.

Donovan, fully in his wheelhouse, pointed. "Hyoid's intact. He wasn't strangled or if he was, it was an incredibly gentle job."

"It was probably gentle, whatever it was," Eleri commented, feeling more at ease as though she was only talking to Donovan. "His coloring doesn't show the mottling or bruising you would expect in a violent death, right?"

"Right." He turned to the other two, working harder than she was to be inclusive. "I was an M.E. for years. Externally, I see no defensive wounds, no indication of anyone with hands on the victim, and though he was afraid when he died and probably knew his killer, his death wasn't violent. Looking here at the skeletal structures—"

"He had bruises on his legs," Dana interrupted.

"They were older. You can tell by the color." Donovan didn't seem bothered by the comment. "They might not have even shown when he was alive. Sometimes they only appear after death when the blood flow changes. Honestly, it's consistent with him running into his coffee table repeatedly, or something like that."

Eleri looked at him. She loved when he talked about what he saw as an M.E. She couldn't distinguish scents like he did, and she would never gain that skill, but she could learn to discern bruising and tell what kind of things bodies had done. She had some of it, but her background was more skeletal and chemical than autopsy related. "How do you know?"

"The bruises were slightly different colors and sizes, but the marks all fell within a one-inch height of each other—which would be normal if he's walking near the same thing repeatedly in different footwear. Anywhere from barefoot to shoes. Plus, the marks are all horizonal—like a table edge—and have a distinct edge at the top, look."

He was pointing out the shape of the bruise on the body to Eleri, but all five of them were leaning over, listening. When he finished pointing, he said, "So that's it. Basically, all I can come up with is: 'he hit his shins lightly on something.' I'd want a tox screen, but I don't smell anything."

He said the last words cautiously, maybe because he didn't know how Dana and Christina would take it, but they didn't blink.

Wade spoke up then, "I don't have anything either. I don't smell anything—not that I'd know what I was detecting any better than Donovan. He's trained in this field, he knows these smells. But what I can tell is that there are no explosives. I know I smell smoke, but I think I may also smell synthetic smoke on him. Like something plastic or man-made burned nearby. There's a hydrogen buzz to him."

"That's hydrogen?" Donovan asked, suddenly nerding out with his werewolf friend. "I got that too, but I didn't know that's what the smell was."

"If you make water in the lab, you'll learn that smell real fast. You'll also likely lose your eyebrows, but it's worth it." Wade grinned as if everyone just blew up gaseous hydrogen and oxygen in the lab at some time. He then turned to Dana. "What did you get?"

"Nothing." She looked flummoxed. "That's the thing. I always get something. But he doesn't have broken vessels, there's no normal clotting cascade, so he wasn't bleeding even inside. The CT scan confirms that. No cancers, no immunological disorders—actually, he's disturbingly healthy."

"Sure, for a dead man," Eleri commented, then wished she hadn't.

"No, I mean when he was alive. Most people have *something*, and I can see it when they're dead. So, if you were, say, hit by a car, I could tell that you'd had bone cancer or fibromyalgia."

"So that's a real thing?" Eleri didn't doubt that fibro was real, but a lot of people did. Lacking a testable medical diagnosis, it left a lot of people wondering if the symptoms were all in the heads of the sufferers.

"Oh, it's real," Dana said. "But this guy—he has nothing. No GI problems, no back pain, no heel spurs. Nothing. He didn't die so much as he ceased living."

"With great fear." Pines put in.

None of it added up. Or if it did, Eleri didn't see it.

Just then, Dana's phone rang.

Westerfield. Eleri knew that much. She waited while the other woman had a very brief conversation with their boss and then pulled out a tablet. A few taps on the screen and Dana pulled up a picture and whispered, "Holy shit."

Then she looked at them. "Westerfield didn't want us to know this before the initial exam, but this was how our victim was found."

She turned the tablet so they could all see. Burt Riser was lying on the ground, his suit unrumpled and as pristine as a dead man's could be, not a hair out of place, but clearly dead. All around him, in a messy, almost-ring that somehow left him untouched, the apartment was burned to a crisp.

2

Donovan tried to scrutinize the alarming photo as Dana moved the tablet, giving them each a better, closer look at the crime scene picture for a moment.

Agent Christina Pines was last to see it and she only looked for a moment before she looked away, muttering, "Fuck."

Dana's eyebrow quirked up as though the two of them knew something. But Donovan knew it, too, and he didn't like any of it.

He didn't like working with all these people. He'd just come around to working with a partner, and to be honest, it only worked because the partner was Eleri. Despite their differences, she was more like him than not. Working with just the two of them was fine; five people on the case was simply more than he could handle.

He'd only recently accepted the idea that his own father and himself were not the only ones who could do what he could. He'd figured out—after meeting Wade, after learning about the existence of others like him, some truly awful, like the *lobomau*—that his grand-parents were the same. As a kid, he'd only known they were odd. He'd never seen them change, not like he'd seen his father do.

It had taken Wade pointing out that "wolf" didn't mean "bad" to start to convince Donovan there was more to it. Wade also told him there was a community of others like them, willing to let Donovan join if he wanted. The jury was still out on that. Just as it was still out on Agents Dana Brantley and Christina Pines.

Donovan had read through the background information Westerfield had given them about the other agents. Dana Brantley was some kind of death psychic. She could apparently see or feel damage to the body. She could then distinguish whether the person had been knifed, shot, poisoned, or more, though whether that came from her biomedical degree or some NightShade skill remained unclear.

Christina, on the other hand, was much more physical. She'd apparently developed a little of Westerfield's ability to move small objects around without touching them. The report called it psychokinesis; Donovan didn't really have a name for it. But Pines' major skill —probably the one that had gotten her recruited to NightShade—was much more in line with this case now.

Eleri looked around at the group. "This guy, Burt Riser, we think he's number four, right?"

Dana nodded back at her. "That we know of. I think our first order of business is to find out if that number is maybe higher than four—since serials don't usually start with their full complement of tricks but develop as they go."

The lead agent waited for a beat so Donovan nodded, assuming that was what she wanted. Eleri and Wade did too, and Dana went on. "Job number two is to figure out the links between the victims."

"They don't have anything yet?" Wade asked. Maybe he hadn't done all the reading. That was a petty thought, Donovan realized. Wade was no longer a NightShade agent. Though the Bureau had badged him and given his full credentials back, it was only for this case. Westerfield had plucked him from his research lab and brought him here. Whatever the Senior Agent in Charge told Wade, it had made him willing.

"We got nothing." Eleri shook her head. Donovan figured if there were connections, she would find them. Her frown made him worry. Three cases, three solves. It looked good in their record.

What looked bad on their record—apparently—were the "strays" they picked up. Senior Agent in Charge Derek Westerfield did not like the way they utilized civilians. First, they'd picked up Lucy Fisher— a.k.a. Walter Reed—when she outed Donovan as a wolf. "Picked up" was a strong term for GJ Janson. She'd glommed onto them to the point of getting herself arrested. But in the end, she'd been set free with no charges. Still, two strays in three missions? Maybe that was why they were working under Brantley and Pines on this case. Donovan shook off the negative thoughts. Maybe they were just working with the other agents because that's the way this case needed to be worked, not as some kind of punishment. Not that Westerfield would tell them either way.

"Wade and I need to go to the scene." The words were out of his mouth before Donovan realized he was going to say them. He was just grateful they made sense. He followed it up as though he'd meant to say that. "Should we split up, or all go?"

Dana looked around. "All of us. Let's finish up here and make that our next stop, while it's still daylight."

It was ten a.m., but Donovan knew how that could go. A seriously involved autopsy took hours.

"Shall we?" Dana looked at him, suddenly handing him the proverbial baton.

"Okay. All hands on." He coached them through pulling the body back onto the gurney and then he wheeled the guy back into the main room, passing the still disgruntled M.E. in his office. Donovan shook his head at Dana as she reached to help push.

The other four had wheeled the guy in here, not poorly, but Donovan hadn't touched the gurney then. This time, he did it himself, the sense memory of the metal handles under blue, non-latex gloves swamping him with a disturbing feeling of home. The heft of the body on the gurney felt right to him; even the scent of the morgue was comforting. He searched around, using Eleri as his assistant and talking the others through a few tasks so they didn't feel left out. Look at him, playing on a team.

With the scalpel firmly in his grip, the tip of his forefinger pressed against the metal as a guide, he made the first cut. Then the second. Then the third. Skin didn't simply lift, it often had to be cut and pulled away and Donovan went to work peeling it back. He wanted to see the ribs before he cut them. The lack of bruising made the likelihood of some traumatic chest injury low, but given the lack of anything else, he had to check.

Christina was the first one to get bored and turn away. Maybe she didn't know what she was seeing or maybe she just didn't care. She took Wade with her, suggesting they check victimology. For a moment, it looked like she was going to ask the M.E. to vacate his office for her—the ultimate insult. But she passed him by and led

Donovan's friend and new partner out, probably into the sunshine. Donovan reminded himself he liked it down here.

Dana stayed close, leaning over his shoulder and asking questions —her biology background making them relevant. A few times she prefaced her words with "I worked with mice in the lab, so stop me if I'm on the wrong track," but she'd asked solid questions.

The problem was, he was into the chest cavity and he'd found nothing. He weighed the organs. He sniffed them, usually able to smell that something had been used on the victim, if not exactly what. But there was nothing here. No reason to order any toxicology reports. The organs just smelled like a liver, a heart, what they were supposed to be. Not even like sick ones.

He took the bone saw to the victim's head and found a perfectly normal brain. Later, Donovan peeled the skin around the bruising on the shins and found exactly what he'd guessed before, even though by then he was praying to find an injection site for GHB or some other mind-altering drug, anything that would make this case more normal.

"Well?" Dana asked.

"It really looks like he just ran into his coffee table a bit too often. I got nothing either." He turned to his partner, almost calling her "El" before thinking something a little more professional was called for. "Eleri?"

"I looked. I don't have your eye for this or your nose, but I don't see anything either." She looked away, then back at Dana. "I want to suggest we exhume the others, though I'm damn confident we won't find anything there either."

"Might be worth it just to be sure. Then again, if we don't have solid evidence it's all the same killer, it will be hard to get warrants." The other agent seemed thoughtful, but she didn't offer a definitive answer. Then she turned back to Donovan. "So, it's official? He died of nothing? And he died while frightened and in the middle of a room on fire?"

"The fire would be scary." Eleri shrugged. "But people don't die of fright in fires."

She looked at him right as Donovan thought the same thing he saw go through her mind. He let Eleri voice the thought; he'd had too much interaction for one day already.

Eleri posed her question to Dana. "So, did he see the fire? Did it scare him? Or did it happen after he was dead?"

———

Eleri had never been so grateful to have a suite as she was at this moment. Normally, having Donovan in the room next door was plenty close enough, thank you. They lived in each other's pockets during cases; Eleri didn't think they needed to share a central room, too. Only this time, she was grateful.

She didn't have to walk down the hallway to ask what he thought. She didn't have to wonder if Christina or Dana would hear her pass by their room and realize she was . . . what? Passing notes? Cheating on them?

No.

But it would feel that way. This way, she was just passing time with her roomie.

Donovan walked out into the main room, barefoot in jeans and a t-shirt. His hair was wet and heavy. She almost asked if he'd scrubbed as hard as she did to get the autopsy smell to go away—it hadn't fully. Maybe he had a method. Screw it. She asked, "What am I doing wrong? I can still smell the autopsy."

"You know that stuff gets in your nose, El." He looked at her sideways and pulled a can of soda from the mini fridge.

She frowned. With his far superior nose, he must . . . "Do you just smell it *all the time?*"

"Kinda." He shrugged as he grabbed the pop tab on the can and made it hiss.

"Damnit, Donovan. I was resisting having a coke until you had to go and do that."

He didn't ask, just searched the cans and threw her one. Eleri glared back at him, set it on the coffee table and started tapping on the lid so it wouldn't blow up on her. Whether that really worked, she didn't know. The science was still out.

"You need a stronger smelling soap. Best bet is to mask it." He grinned and took a long drink.

"That's lovely." She sighed but didn't open the thrown can yet. "So, what do you think of the other agents?"

"I like that de Gottardi guy."

"Ha ha," she deadpanned. "You already know him. The others."

"I can't tell if Christina Pines is simply not talkative or if she has a stick up her butt." He shrugged as though he disliked saying it.

"And Dana Brantley?"

"Definitely alpha." This time no shrug, no wavering.

"I guess that's good, since she's in charge." Eleri finally popped the top on her drink, sighing in relief as it merely let out a slight fizz rather than attacking her with spray. She took a slug from the can and waited while the bubbles tracked down her throat before asking what she really wanted to know. "Do you think we're being punished?"

"Who knows? Westerfield seems more the type to just yell and demote us rather than saddle other agents with us if we're so awful."

"Or," Eleri chimed in, "he's come to the conclusion we just enjoy working with others and that's why we keep 'picking up strays.' Maybe he made us part of a legit team before we built one ourselves."

"That's more probable. You'll get a hit off of him before I do." He crushed the can in his hand—a pretty jock move for a nerd—and chucked it into the trash. At least he did it without yelling "two points!" Donovan sat next to her on the couch and waited less than a heartbeat before asking, "What didn't you tell the others?"

3

E leri sighed at Donovan. There was a certain comfort to being known and known well. At times, it also felt like a damned invasion of privacy. The man could smell her like a wolf—he often knew where she'd been by smells she carried with her that she wasn't even aware of. He knew if she didn't wash her hair that morning. Eleri knew that, while washing her hair was the best line of defense for any secrets she might have, it wasn't foolproof. He'd once said she smelled like she'd been on a plane. Never mind that he was right, what did that even smell like?

She looked her partner square in the eye and said, "I keep dreaming of Emmaline. I think that note from my Grandmere really shook me up."

Donovan frowned. "You don't think it's maybe the other way around? That something's up with your sister and you and your grandmother both picked up on it?"

"Maybe."

"Why not? Your Grandmere obviously has a tap into the other side." He was looking at her like she was nuts. Maybe she was.

"So, when I was a kid, we would spend summers at Grandmere's. My mother hated us being there, but my father said it was culture. She lives in the Lower Ninth Ward in New Orleans." Eleri punctuated her words and took a thought while she drank some of her soda. "Grandmere was just . . . Grandmere. People visited her all the time.

When I was a kid, it didn't really occur to me that she was running a voodoo shop from her home."

"Eleri, you're a Remy. The Remys are one of the best known in the whole U.S. I looked it up," he added, more as though he wanted to explain why he'd done that. "I just got curious after she kept sending us that stuff. She said Emmaline will be found soon."

Eleri nodded, taking it all in. She knew about the Remys. But she, too, knew from the internet. Her mother had denounced the religion, raised her girls to be good, rich, white *Southern Girls*. Only by pieces did Eleri find out that she wasn't really white. She was only rich from her father's side of the family. And she was Southern only in the fact that New Orleans was kinda considered the South. Her family's part of New Orleans was not the genteel southern part. She shifted the topic, not questioning why it all made her so uncomfortable. "Emmaline's been dead for years. If they find her, it will only be bones."

Donovan took a deep breath. "But that's what you do, Eleri."

She took another drink of the soda only to find it empty. Seemed like a fitting metaphor. She'd considered for years that she might one day lay hands on the skeletal remains of her sister. In fact, she kept track of found skeletons—checking teeth and sex and race to see if they might be her sister. Three had come close, but none had been Emmaline. Things like jewelry, dental records, and even time of discovery ruled most possibilities out. Emmaline was still out there somewhere.

Eleri shifted the topic again. "This guy, Burt, he's our current number four. But I don't think he's four."

"None of us really do. Dana made a good point. This is not the work of a beginner." Donovan took her soda can, crushed it and tossed it at the trash, missing by a wide mile. Popping up to get it, he excused the miss. "I ran track."

"No." Eleri was still focused off into space. "I'm trying to catalog how many there were. This isn't number four. I feel it. I *know* it. It's not just a theory." She couldn't put her finger on it yet.

Her first partner, an awesome cowboy of an agent, believed in her hunches. J. Binkley Ramer simply hadn't stayed with her long enough to see those hunches turn around and bite her in the ass. Her thoughts flitted to him and back. He'd taught her about working the scene, about absorbing the data and letting it sit. "Shit!"

Donovan turned from the trash can and looked at her as though waiting.

"That's it. These are all variations on a theme. As weird as that was —the fire around him that didn't touch him, and the non-existent cause of death—it took four deaths to link them because they aren't all quite the same. We have all the deaths with the odd fires. Well, we think we do, but we have to look beyond that. He didn't always use fire."

Donovan settled into the couch next to her. "The fire is weird, too. Not just that it burns *around* the victim and never touches him. It's weird in itself."

"What do you mean?"

He pulled out pictures from the printed files they were carrying with them. The FBI hadn't just made copies of local police files. When they'd taken this case, they'd taken all the paper and the bodies and the evidence. Now, it was in the hands of NightShade agents. By definition, it was weird, but Eleri still didn't understand what Donovan meant.

"There's no trace accelerant." He laid the pictures side by side.

"Matches," Eleri supplied. "Not every fire has an accelerant."

He pointed to the picture of the body, drenched from the firemen's hoses, putting out what had been a fully engaged house fire that somehow didn't touch the body—not even smoke stains.

"Look at the floor after the fire is out." He pointed again. First, he pointed at the flooring around the body, then he pointed to other rooms in the house where photos had recorded the aftermath and the damage. "See the alligatoring?"

He was referring to the cracks and crevices formed in the wood surface when fire burned it. The direction of the long lines indicated the direction of the burn. She didn't see anything odd until he showed her the floor around the body.

Donovan had hoped to get away from everyone for breakfast. It didn't work. He shouldn't have tried to get away from Eleri, because something worse had showed up.

"Morning." Christina Pines sat down opposite him.

Donovan blinked as he took a moment to place her. He'd recognized her by smell as he walked past. He hadn't thought anything of it, just headed to the small continental breakfast and fixed himself a waffle at the breakfast bar. He'd grabbed a set of plastic "silverware" that was way too flimsy to use on almost any real food, but by God, he was going to try. Peanut butter and syrup were the perfect things to eat on a waffle. Alone. Anyone else would think he was five years old.

So when Agent Pines picked up her plate and drink and walked over to sit with him, Donovan resigned himself to the company. "Morning."

He tried to speak the word with kindness, with welcome, with a smile he didn't feel. Pines looked very different this morning. In yoga pants and a long tee, she'd also not tied her hair back. The long straight locks revealed streaks of pink he didn't think he'd ever seen on an FBI agent. She'd looked professional enough yesterday, in her suit and bun.

"I know you and Eames didn't quite understand the wording in my file. Honestly, I didn't understand Eames' much either, though I have met a few like you." Pines took another bite of her toast. "I guess Eames just has hunches and they're real. Right?"

He nodded, but didn't speak. It sounded like she'd met more of "his kind" than he had.

"I figured it would be easier just to show you what I do," she volunteered, speaking more than she had the entire day before.

"Here? At breakfast?" He asked, eyebrows climbing.

"Actually, I already did it."

He was not impressed. She hadn't done anything. Donovan tried for tact. It was not his strong suit. "Is that all you're eating for breakfast?" He motioned to the toast she was just finishing. "Dana's got a big day lined up for us."

"No. I'm having oatmeal, too. I really like it with strawberries and brown sugar and walnuts, just like they have here." She smiled at him.

Donovan smiled back, wondering what in hell she was smiling about. He'd thought Eleri was weird when he first met her, but Christina Pines took the cake. "Are you going to go make it?"

"Donovan, look at your plate."

He looked down. A Styrofoam bowl of oatmeal sat in front of him. It was piled high with brown sugar, walnuts, and strawberries. A single plastic spoon poked from the lump he would never in a thousand years consider eating. Startled words fell from his mouth. "I made a waffle."

"No. You only think you did." She looked a little more solemn now. "I didn't want to waste food, so you made my oatmeal."

"While I thought I made my waffle?" His heart was thudding. He'd picked up two tiny tubs of peanut butter. But they weren't here. He *remembered* doing it. He'd grabbed two of the syrup packs—not the artificial sweetener, either. High fructose corn syrup all the way. He *remembered* rifling through the bowl to be sure he picked the right ones. He didn't even have the plastic fork and knife he'd played with while the waffle cooked.

But there was no waffle. No smell of it. Had there ever been?

"You wanted to know what I bring to the team. This is it." She reached over and pulled the oatmeal toward her, even as Donovan still blinked. "Don't worry. I won't do it to you again. I just figured it was better if you knew what it was before you saw it in action. We all need to know what we're dealing with." She dug in the spoon and took a bite. "You should go make your own breakfast now."

Woodenly, he stood up and headed back to the counter. Only this time, he questioned if he was actually doing what he thought he was doing. Or was Christina Pines playing him again? His thoughts bounced around in his head.

She could make people think what she wanted them to? He reached out to the waffle iron, getting close enough to feel the heat and wondering if it was worth the burn to know it was real. He decided against it but kept the thought in his back pocket for later, despite the fact that he didn't know if it would work.

Back at the table, he plunked down opposite her, not moving with ease given the simultaneous directions of his thoughts. He was still staring at his food when she spoke, "It's a real waffle this time, and it's getting cold."

After a pause, she continued, "It's my understanding that any illusion I give you is lacking. Unless I work at it, you may not have the right sensations for what you're touching. You may not smell the waffle cooking. That kind of thing. Also, if you pay attention you can feel a slight buzz in your brain."

Donovan was chewing his first bite—which tasted exactly like waffle with peanut butter and syrup, though he was still suspicious of its reality. He did have a buzz at the back of his head. He frowned.

Christina was looking down at her empty bowl before she spoke again. "I know most of us NightShade agents didn't have the most fun time growing up. It's not easy being a freak. But I was the most popular girl in school."

"Yay for you." Donovan let the words roll off his tongue with so little inflection that they may have sucked some air out of the room.

"I was prom queen. Dated the hottest guy in school who was also the quarterback." She paused. "He didn't earn it. I made the coach promote him over Shawn Measer—who actually deserved the spot. But I wanted my boyfriend to have everything he wanted."

"Let me guess. You made him quarterback and he dumped you." Donovan took another bite so he didn't mock her sob story outright. She didn't know anything. Eleri's sister. His father. That was some real shit. She'd been prom queen? Christina Pines could suck a bag of dicks.

"No. He couldn't dump me." She looked up now, her stare making it clear that he hadn't put two and two together. "He never really wanted to ask me out in the first place. But by the time I left him behind for college, he believed he was going to marry me. No one actually wanted me to be prom queen. No one even wanted to be my friend. It was exhausting."

"Poor you." His sympathy was about as low as his belief that he was actually eating his damn breakfast.

"No. I was awful. And I know it. But, what I didn't know was that I was sharpening my skills. I'm damn good at it now." This time she punctuated her sentence by standing. She finally left him to eat his breakfast alone, just as he'd hoped to in the first place.

Too late, Donovan turned to ask her a question. He wondered if he should warn Eleri or if it was already too late.

4

When Donovan returned to the suite, Eleri was gone. She hadn't left a note nor contacted him. So he didn't know if she was out getting her own breakfast or if she was getting Christina Pines' breakfast and the same treatment he'd gotten.

Shit.

Donovan texted her.

—Pines has some weird mind control thing.

That was it. Anything more and he'd sound too strange even to himself. The man who'd spent his childhood watching his father change form into a wolf and had even seen his father murder another man that way, thought Christina Pines was too far out for words. Eleri and her odd gifts had taken some getting used to. Pines was creepy, though. She made him question what he knew and he didn't like the feeling or the way it continued to crawl under his skin.

—Thank you. I read that.

Sure, she'd read the files same as him. It wasn't the whole story.

—She'll make you see things that aren't there. Think you are doing things you aren't.

—Thanks. I'll steer clear until I talk to you.

If you can, he thought. How would she even know if she ran into Pines and the woman made her forget it even happened? He fought the shudder that threatened to overtake him, but didn't win.

He wondered when Eleri would be back, but didn't want to talk more—even a few texts often pushed his limits for contact. He often maxed out given his close operations with Eleri, interviewing suspects and dealing with people involved in the crimes. He remained perilously close to overload a lot of the time. With very little down-time between this case and the last one and with the full team rather than the two of them, he was afraid he might explode.

He sat at the small table and pulled out his computer and his tablet and his phone. Only once he had all his screens lined up did he start working on what Eleri had suggested.

Unexplained deaths in . . . anywhere. With anyone.

Unusual strangulations. Unprovoked heart attacks. Spontaneous combustion—which wouldn't turn up in the same search as arson or fire setting deaths.

He put his head in his hands. Each search turned up pages of links to files that he couldn't begin to sort through.

Donovan weeded out the ones with multiple or linked deaths. He didn't think that was what the missing pieces would be. They would look like one-offs that didn't get connected to anything else. Then he keyworded in "weird."

That finally narrowed it down and Donovan started looking at the files in earnest. An hour later, when Eleri walked in the door, he had twenty-two flagged as possible related cases.

"Hi, El." He looked up, welcoming the break and finding he needed to rub bleary eyes. It was barely nine-thirty in the morning.

"Hey. I had to get out of the room to make my brain work while I sorted files." Eleri walked in with actual folders in her grasp. "What was that about Pines? I know she has some ability to make you change your mind."

"No," Donovan countered. "It's much bigger than that. I thought I was getting myself a waffle—cooking it at that little iron they have at the continental breakfast—and I was actually getting a bowl of oatmeal."

Eleri blinked at him.

"The whole nine yards. Not just one thing. I thought I was picking out syrup and getting the right plastic forks and what I was doing was all different. It's not small. She could make you murder someone and not know it." *That.* That was what he hadn't even thought to himself, what freaked him out so badly about Pines. Eleri was odd. Donovan was strong, strange. Pines was *dangerous*.

Eleri plopped down into the chair across from him, thinking for a moment before she finally spoke. "We can't judge her based on her ability. We have to judge her based on her use of it."

She set the stack of folders down, looking nowhere near as concerned about their new partner as he was. "I spent the morning in the local branch office. I pulled and copied files. . . . Well, I pulled them and made a clerk copy them."

"I went onto the server. Same thing."

They spent the next half hour checking files against each other and winding up with only two that both of them had flagged. Eleri looked at her phone. "We have to head out."

Making sure all his cases were marked accordingly, Donovan watched from the corner of his eye as Eleri gathered her papers, carefully stacking folders and pictures. She often used tablets and such, but sometimes she said she just liked to line up actual pictures. Made her think better.

They hit the elevators with Eleri holding on to her pages and Donovan wondering if he was really in an elevator with his partner or if he just thought he was.

Dana had reserved them a conference room in the hotel, claiming that the likelihood anyone here knew how to bug the place was incredibly low. Beyond that, no one would have the time or the knowledge to do it even if they could. She met them in the hallway, her arms full of folders too, and she eyed Eleri's stack as though assessing her more highly because of it. Donovan sighed.

Christina Pines followed along, her usual reticent self again.

"I think this is it." Dana pushed open the wide door to find Wade sitting in one of the large, cushy conference seats with a bag of Cheetos busted open and a can of diet coke sitting near his hand. He looked up as they entered and clicked off what looked like a cheap video game on his phone.

"Are you ready?" Dana questioned him, her eyebrows crooking with borderline disapproval. They'd been tasked with spending their mornings separately trying to find other cases that fit the profile— what little there was of it.

"Mmm-hmm." Wade seemed to think nothing of her concern, or else he missed her tone. Donovan guessed it was the second one. But it was Eleri who came to their friend's defense.

"He broke his key off in the ignition of his car two months ago.

Even the dealer had never heard of that. He thinks Cheetos dust defies Einstein's laws, and he may turn up wearing the same plaid shirt three days in a row. But Wade can look at a scene and tell you who the shooter was by the trajectory of a bullet. He's saved at least five men from jail or execution by *proving* they couldn't have committed the crime they were accused of, even though all the evidence pointed their way. And I'll bet he has a wadded-up paper in his back pocket with a list of the people whose files he pulled because he can't remember their names, but he'll be able to rattle off all the stats of each case by memory. He's ready."

As she smiled, Wade sheepishly pulled a crumpled piece of high school notebook paper from his pocket. A list of names was scrawled on the blue lines, probably with the mechanical pencil that peeked from his shirt pocket.

Donovan grinned. Maybe he would come around to Dana Brantley. Probably not Christina Pines. But he was realizing he loved Eleri. She'd become family—something he'd never known before, not really —and she would have his back, the same way she had Wade's, should he ever need it.

Donovan's heart bounced between the epiphany of having real friends in Wade and Eleri, and the constant state of the willies caused by having Christina Pines anywhere near him.

Dana was opening her mouth, but Donovan beat her to it. Turning to Christina, he asked, "Did you show Eleri and Wade what you can do? Because they should know."

"Not yet." She remained blank-faced despite his obvious irritation at her.

It was Dana who spoke softly to her partner. "You probably should. Get it out of the way." Then she looked up at the other three of them. "We don't work with other partners often. I think Christina's skill can be . . . disconcerting."

Donovan couldn't help the horse-like snort he let out. Disconcerting, his ass. Dana merely nodded slowly. "It's best that you know, because if she has to use it, you should know what you're dealing with. Go ahead, Christina."

Pines nodded at her boss and said, "It's a beautiful day."

Donovan frowned at her. Maybe Eleri had been out, maybe Christina had been out, but with the pile of homework they had, how was he to know—

He looked at Eleri, who was scanning the room with unseeing eyes. His heart thumped. "El."

Christina shook her head at him. He couldn't even talk to her?

"Donovan, where are you? I don't see you." She was looking directly at him, if she leaned any closer she'd feel his body heat, or at least his breath. But she clearly didn't. "Donovan?"

He held his tongue, though he didn't want to. His teeth clenched.

Christina spoke again. "Here's a file."

Both Eleri and Wade reached out to the table in front of them. Eleri managed to pick up one of the files in front of her, but the way she did it, the focus of her eyes, made it look as though someone had handed it to her. Wade picked up air. Just air. Unless he was a trained mime from France, he actually believed he was holding something.

"What does your file say, Eleri?" Dana asked this time.

Eleri began reading the name and information. Donovan didn't pay any attention other than to see that she was really reading what was on the page. Though when Christina asked the same of Wade, he began reading the air. Donovan almost vomited.

"You can't see the other agents but we're here," Christina told them. "Tell us what you do see."

Eleri looked confused. Then she began speaking as though they were idiots. "It's a forest. There are elm trees and low scrub brush. There's a trail. . ."

She went on about an animal track she saw. Wade mentioned the height of the trees, the number of ants in a typical colony like the one he was looking at. He commented on the sunlight through the canopy and the approximate temperature. Donovan had enough.

"Eleri! Snap out of it."

"Snap out of what? Donovan?" She still couldn't see him.

He glared angrily at Christina and Dana and tried another tactic. "Can you smell the forest? Do you hear the animals? Can you feel the sun on your skin?"

"What? . . . No. Now that you mention it, the feeling here is weird. I almost feel like I'm sitting, but I'm walking." She looked around as though trying to find her bearings, simply not seeing the standard, mid-level hotel conference room around her. Wade was conducting experiments on himself—plugging and unplugging his ears, touching his skin with different pressures then reaching out as though to press the back of his hand to something. He then reached out to Eleri.

"Eleri." He turned, his eyes finally seeing her. She looked at him and he spoke again. "You're the only thing real here."

That was it. Donovan almost dove across the table to strangle Christina. At least he hoped that would make her stop. It was Dana who held up a hand, signaling everyone to be still.

"What?" Eleri sounded startled, but this time when she looked at Donovan, she saw him. She reached out to him, touching his arm as he watched Wade knock on the table, then slide his hand across the surface until he ran into Eleri's hand. She grasped his, the three of them now making a chain.

"You might feel a very, very slight buzz in the back of your skull. But that's what Christina can do," Dana said it as though she'd slid a quarter across the table without touching it. Donovan had seen their boss, Westerfield, do exactly that, but this took the cake.

"That's not okay." Eleri glared, her eyes darting between the two other women.

"Which is why I don't do it unless I have to." Christina started back.

"No. No wars. This is on me." Dana held a hand out between them as though they were junior high girls fighting over a boy. Somehow it still worked, though Donovan was holding his jaw in, fighting the intense urge to roll his shoulder blades and pop them into his alternate form. He saw Wade was breathing heavily, too.

Dana spoke calmly and clearly. "She's done it to me, too. I know it's scary as fuck to realize you've been played and that it worked so well. But it's important that you understand it, too." She made eye contact with each of the three of them, clearly in charge. "If the time comes that she has to use this to subdue a suspect, you need to know what's happening. What that person sees and hears, how much they believe it, so we can all act accordingly."

There was a pause. Since no one else said anything, Dana filled it in, "We need to get to these cases. I'm sorry that had to happen, but you needed to know. Trust me, Christina has the utmost integrity. She doesn't use her ability unless she must. And she's only used it on me to show me what it was like, just like with you. She's never done it again."

Donovan felt the words escape, though he knew he shouldn't say them. "That you know of."

5

Eleri still felt her body buzzing by the time they broke for a late lunch, though she wasn't sure if that was an actual physical after-effect of being mind-altered or if it was psychological from trauma.

Dana was smart enough to split them up for the meal. She and Christina went off their own way, as though Christina might need comforting. As far as Eleri was concerned, she could just zap the two of them into a magical forest with a unicorn.

The other two left Eleri, Wade, and Donovan sitting at the table to determine what to do. Eleri couldn't decide.

Wade grumbled under his breath, "Christina can suck a bag of dicks," and Donovan exploded into belly laughs the likes of which Eleri wasn't sure she'd ever seen before.

Was it real?

She reached out and touched him even as he jerked away—a consequence of tear-forming guffaws. He wiped at his eyes and looked up to Wade. "That's *exactly* what I said."

Her stomach turned and her nerves buzzed. Eleri had seen a lot. Most cops and agents had. So had paramedics, firefighters. There were professions like hers where the daily plan was to see the worst of the worst. She hadn't thought she could still be flipped upside down. Hell, she was in NightShade. Nevertheless, Christina Pines had done a number on her with a forest and a path and a beautiful dapple of sunlight shining down.

Did it matter that the forest was the one the house was in? The house she'd been dreaming about for months. Small, square, with the door set at an angle into a porch at the corner of the front room. Had Christina pulled that from her head? Surely, she couldn't have just *invented* the exact same place . . . then again, maybe Eleri's memories had been altered. Maybe the house was different, and her mind was simply putting these things together now . . . She didn't know and couldn't even figure out how to figure it out.

"Eleri." Donovan's hand waved in front of her face.

"She needs food," Wade chimed in.

"I don't want to eat." She felt muzzy. Her lip curled at the thought of food.

"You need it. It's beyond disconcerting," Donovan told her as he pulled her up by the hand, brooking no disagreement as they headed out.

She probably did need food. At least she should have it nearby if she changed her mind, so she tagged along. Her voice stumbled over itself as she tried to put the pieces together. "It's not just that it's strange, it's that it's violating."

"That's it," both Donovan and Wade said together. Their stereo responses were starting to get on her nerves. Clearly, she needed food.

Not fifteen minutes later, each of them was feeding their faces with what must be a one-pound burrito and she was at least somewhat eating a salad she'd composed herself. It was a burrito salad, maybe not the best food option for someone who didn't want to eat, but neither of the guys seemed to notice.

Her stomach had settled by the time they returned. Christina seemed her usual reticent self, not contributing much. Was that all she did? Hang around and wait to override someone else's senses?

Okay, that was mean. Clearly, Christina had at least passed all the coursework at Quantico, just like the rest of them. She'd also started as an analyst and worked her way to agent. She must have some redeeming qualities.

Eleri pulled the second half of her salad out and set it on the table with the plastic fork and paper napkin she'd grabbed. Dana gave it one glance then decided to ignore it. Eleri ate.

"Are we ready to dive back in?" Dana looked pointedly at each of them, even her curls didn't move when she was in boss mode.

Eleri nodded and took a defiant bite. She was embracing her inner pre-teen but she didn't care enough to quit. Besides, they were already divided, Christina and Dana on one side of the table, Wade, Donovan, and herself on the other. Plenty of space between *them* and *us*.

They tried to discuss various files each of them made a case for, but the conversation was stilted. Dana put her face in her hands. "Look. I know it's awful when she does that, but she won't do it to you again."

Before Donovan could do more than lift his eyebrows, or before Eleri could huff out a breath, Dana spoke again, "I know it for the same reason you do. Her Extrasensory Altered Reality Projection isn't complete. There's always a sense or two missing. You can always identify it. So she can't trick you anymore. If you ever doubt reality, you can test the environment. Hers won't hold up."

The silence grew awkward. Again, Dana filled it. "And she's a damn good researcher. What's your next file?"

The conversation got better; Eleri could feel it becoming a little easier as they moved to a common ground—scientific analysis. Never mind that the analysis was of dead bodies, non-object-linked strangulations, fire, and a singular missing person under arson circumstances.

Her salad bowl empty hours later and her ass asleep, Eleri tried to sum up what they had. A handful of cases overlapped and deserved further research.

Body Number One—according to the original files—was Leona Hiller. She'd been burned. The fire had not stayed around her. But she also appeared to have been strangled. The odd thing—well, one of many, Eleri mentally commented—was that she had no hand marks on her neck. No ligature marks, no mechanical marks at all. The burned flesh made it difficult to tell and she'd later been cremated. But the M.E. on that case had gone above and beyond—finding a broken hyoid—crushed in five places. Which was odd as hell. Her findings indicated that Leona Hiller had been strangled by something like a corset for her neck. It put perfectly even pressure all the way around her throat—unlike, say, a hand or a garrote. And this thing slowly and uniformly cut off her air until she died. Her lack of smoke inhalation was what led the ME to check.

"She's good." Donovan had said of the report with an air of respect. Eleri had agreed, thankfully. The report was all they had with the body in ashes.

One of the "possible" cases had no fire but had a very suspicious and similar strangulation. It made the pile.

They also had four deaths with suspicious fires. What clearly looked like accelerant use but with no accelerants found at the scene in three of the cases. In the fourth, the fire was deemed to be caused by flashover—when the room became so hot that multiple pieces of furniture and walls just burst into flames—but it achieved flashover without the arson investigator being able to pinpoint the initial fire. He left it as an unknown, because no start point wasn't possible.

Dana rubbed her eyes. "We need dinner. I'd like to have it together. And with no work—not this case anyway."

It wasn't what Eleri would have chosen. She was looking forward to locking herself in her room and ordering room service. She hadn't planned on even talking to Donovan, but they had to make this team work. Using "Extrasensory Altered Reality Projection" on them was not the way to team build. Maybe Dana had missed that memo. Still, Eleri didn't feel she could say no to dinner. If this team fell apart, it wasn't going to be her fault. "Sure, but I have one more I want to put in the pile."

"Okay." Dana sighed. "Last one."

Eleri pulled out her paper file, enjoying the weight and objectivity of it. "No bodies."

"Then why . . .?" Wade asked.

She noticed Christina stayed mostly silent.

"Fire. Bookstore. Blazed through the place. Downstairs, upstairs, it started at the front door, though witnesses say no one was there to start it. Only the bookstore owner and two patrons were trapped inside."

"But no bodies," Donovan supplied. "Honestly, the neighbor's sun catcher could have focused light inside the front door. It would be just like burning ants. Boom. Fire. It was full of books and the people had time to get out."

"It's believed the patrons all made it out the back door, but everything was ash in a matter of minutes," Eleri commented.

"I don't get it." Dana looked at her oddly. She shook her head, the curls bouncing now, her authority having dissipated. She blinked as though her brain didn't work well.

"Books don't burn," Eleri said.

"Paper burns and burns well. Of course, books burn." Donovan sighed.

Wade's hand lightly slapped the table. "No, they don't." He was looking around the room, his eyes darting with the speed of his brain. "Fire is carbon based compounds plus oxygen. The book *is* paper, but you know—" he looked *at* them now, "when you kindle a fire with paper, you crumple it. You give it oxygen spaces."

Eleri nodded along. "A bookstore has books shelved side by side. Tons of paper, but no oxygen. The covers or the spines that show will burn. But if a book is closed, even if it's the only book on the table, it will be a long time for the middle to burn. Many books are even denser than wood and burn slower."

"But the place went up in a matter of minutes," Dana reiterated.

Eleri nodded. "Not a single book salvaged."

"Add it to the pile." Dana motioned to the "pile." Some of the files were just scraps of paper with the name of an e-file. Some were actual folders with documents and pictures that Eleri and Dana had brought. Christina—who had scribed most of the meeting on her laptop—gathered the "pile" and put it in her computer bag as they cleared out.

Dana told them where they'd be eating—didn't even put it up for a vote, but maybe that was smarter with five people. Eleri tried not to be petty. It didn't completely work.

This time she ate a burger with fries covered in parmesan and garlic. Normally, she tried to stay healthy but between the last case and this one, she was ready for red meat and fried food, because fuck a good diet. If this was what this case was going to be like, she was eating burgers and burritos the whole time. She'd supplement with biscuits and mac'n'cheese. She was going to need comfort food.

She cursed Westerfield for setting them up this way as she dragged her fry through ketchup. Quickly realizing she was starving, she'd eaten most of the burger at record pace. Apparently, sitting in a conference room and arguing about ways to die was heavy work. She smiled as Dana told about her childhood, growing up in a nice trailer park outside a town outside Knoxville, Tennessee. "My brother taught me to catch salamanders and frogs. Then he went into the military and I got a scholarship to the state university. I kept getting scholarships and by the time I hit grad school, the money I was paid to assist the classes was the best I'd ever lived. I kept at it."

"How'd you wind up in NightShade?" Wade asked as though she and her partner hadn't brain-whammied them earlier.

Dana talked about getting recruited as an analyst and doing that for several years before Westerfield approached her. Eleri was getting a picture that her boss carefully constructed his team, finding some odd skill and chasing the person down before convincing them they *needed* to be an FBI agent under his department.

She took another bite of the burger, the tail end of it dripping barbecue sauce on the plate. She'd never eaten so many burgers as she had since she met Donovan. She then dragged another fry through the ketchup and the pieces in her brain clicked.

She looked Dana in the eye. "We have to go to Burt Riser's house tomorrow. I need to see the scene. With the arson investigator. I finally figured out what's bothering me about the fire."

6

Donovan stood in the living room of what had been Burt Riser's home. It was still identifiable, but only barely. The overwhelming scent of wood, ash, and mildew almost forced him back, but he fought it. So did Wade, he could tell.

He opened his mouth a little. Though it helped, it wasn't quite enough. There were onions in the trash—now burned, wet, and rotting. Synthetic fibers had been used in the carpeting; they weren't mildewing, but remained acrid even after this time. The house had once been nice, if a bit over-designed. Not anymore.

Dana turned around to look at him, her eyelids blinking rapidly. She whispered, "Do whatever you need to do when the arson investigator isn't paying attention." She looked to Wade, too. "We'll cover for you."

He nodded, huffing out his breath as though that would help. It didn't. His sinuses still burned, his eyes teared, and he could taste some of it in the back of his mouth. Eventually, he gave up and pulled the front of his shirt up over his nose and mouth though it only offered a little respite.

Dale Dickens, the self-proclaimed "arson guy around here" led them through the burned-out shell of a house. He took point, automatically assuming that his job here was to give the agents a tour. He jabbed a fat finger at various burned pieces of wood, wall, and furniture as they passed. "These markings show the fire burned really fast. Strange one, that."

Donovan wasn't sure exactly what he was looking at, but he nodded dutifully.

At the end of Dickens' little presentation, the arson guy asked what questions they had, what they were looking for specifically. He stood there, facing them in what used to be Burt Riser's living room. Dickens put his hands on his hips as though convinced they couldn't possibly have any questions, he'd done such a thorough job.

Dana went first. "Why can't we go upstairs?"

"Well, ma'am," he started, but Donovan heard the tone of "little lady" slathered on thick. "The structure isn't stable enough to hold us."

Dana offered a slick-sweet smile in return. "Oh, I'm much lighter than you."

Apparently, she didn't like the "little lady" attitude, either. Donovan grinned under his shirt.

"Heh." Dickens brushed her off again. "It's not about weight, honey. It's about stability of the structure."

"Yes, that's actually why I asked in the first place." She turned and pushed on a load bearing wall. "The construction here is sound. I can see the drywall has been burned away, but in all cases, the center of the studs is still untouched, yellow wood. Also, if you look up, you can see all the burn marks on the ceiling, and it's disturbingly uniform—not a standard fire, even with accelerants or flashover— and you can still see that the original joists in the flooring are intact. So, I'm not sure why you didn't take us up there." She stared at him, her eyes boring holes in his soul, her lips forming an almost sugary smile as she dared him to speak to her as an educated human.

"You wanna risk your life and go up there, you just go ahead." He finally waved her by and Dana marched up the stairs, sticking to the edges of the steps where they would be stronger and avoiding the railing. Above them, she took a few tentative steps that Donovan could hear very clearly, then she began jumping.

"Totally safe!" she yelled down. "Not even fully burned up here."

But they'd known that from the report.

Donovan looked at Dickens. "What do you think was the source of the fire?"

For the first time, the man's arrogance drifted away. "I honestly don't know. It's gotta be some new accelerant. You can see the multiple start points." He jabbed his finger toward the floor, marking a darker ring where he appeared to be showing how the fire started. "But nothing shows on any of our tests. I notified the commission that we have something new in the game and we need to figure out what it is. I sent in carpet samples." He jabbed his finger another direction where several squares of charred carpet had been cut away.

Donovan was curious himself.

He decided that being male might work in his favor, not that Dickens probably thought too highly of him. The man had been looking at him like he was a pansy for not handling the stench very well. But right now, he was the only one left. The others had all run upstairs following Dana, their decorum just shy of thirteen-year-olds at a slumber party. He could hear them chattering but didn't bother to make out individual words.

"So, you think it started in this ring with an accelerant, then moved to flashover to get the whole room?" Donovan waved his hand around at the various bits of evidence as he spoke.

Dickens scratched at the back of his head. "Seems that way. Honestly, it's the best conclusion I can draw. Without the accelerant test, I can't close the case."

As if it was only the accelerant that made this one odd. Donovan didn't say that. Instead, he volleyed with, "I've seen the photos of the upstairs rooms. Some aren't burned. But the room down here where the victim was found was completely charred."

Dickens nodded. He looked uncomfortable. He seemed like a man who didn't like what he couldn't explain. "Yes."

"So, I'm not way off base suggesting it looks like the fire chased him." Donovan threw it out there as casually as he could.

"Now, that just doesn't happen."

Donovan waited for a "sonny" that he didn't get. While he understood the man's reasoning—it was an idea well beyond his realm of perspective—Donovan didn't fully agree. What he'd seen here, and at the other house, it did look like the fire was chasing the victims. It looked like whoever did it had full control of the burn.

He asked another pointed question. "Does it look like the accelerant went upstairs?"

Now Dickens was back in his world. "Sure, see?" he pointed again, running his aim all along a path to the stairs. "You can see the darker trail where the accelerant was used."

"But it's not as dark." Donovan frowned looking back and forth from the front room to the stairs. The shading in the pictures he'd seen wasn't as clear. He could hear Eleri in his head. "I hate pictures."

"Yeah," He scratched his head again in a serious tell and Donovan figured if the man played poker he lost often. "I just think it wasn't as close to the ground and not for as long."

"How is that possible?" Donovan frowned again, harder this time. "If you pour an accelerant, you could pour a narrower line or not soak the carpet, but how do you get it 'not as close'?"

This time, Dickens lit up. "You want my real theory?" When Donovan nodded yes, he continued. "Flame thrower."

Eleri's back hurt. Her head hurt. Her feet hurt, and she was wearing sensible shoes. Cute, but cushy. She shouldn't feel like she'd been walking barefoot on gravel all day.

Picking her way through Burt Riser's house hadn't been a walk in the park. The floor had been warped and buckled, rubble had fallen everywhere, and her cute but sensible shoes had not been made for that.

They'd finally left the property and Eleri had never been so grateful to get back into the SUV and not be driving. Of course she was in the back with Wade and Christina. And of course she was in the middle. And of course Dana chose lunch again and she chose another all-American, order-anything place. Dana apparently loved burgers as much as Donovan and Wade. Christina had remained silent all morning. Eleri reminded herself to ask Donovan later if he thought maybe the woman was a little simple, at least in comparison to the rest of the crowd.

Then they'd decided to see another house. This time Leona Hiller's house. Hers was the oldest case of the original four pulled. She'd been killed over two years ago. Eleri expected the house to be cleaned up.

It was more than cleaned up. As they pulled up, she saw that it had been completely re-built. Enough different from the house in the file pictures, it made Eleri blink for a moment as she saw the old house overlay on the new one. Whether that was the stress of a long day or an actual piece of intel she should use, she didn't know. She was too tired to decide.

What did bother her was the gate at the start of a long gravel drive. The house sat at the end, but so far away. Her feet protested, but Dana pushed the button on the comm system and spoke politely to the man on the other end. Unfortunately for Eleri's feet, he let them through.

Eleri walked the long gravel drive, trying not to let it show how ready she was to fall into a bed. But the bed was a two-hour drive away, and she would have the joy of occupying the middle back seat —*after* they looked at this house.

James Hiller let them in. Leona had been his wife until her murder. He merely nodded at them as he opened the door. Eleri vaguely cataloged his curt motion as the house blinked in and out of perspective for her. She tried not to look as though she was high on some weird drug.

He motioned the children away from the hallway behind him. "Go play in your rooms. Now."

They balked only for a moment, then shuffled obediently up the staircase. The second floor was part of the new design. The old home had been only one story, but more spread out. Transparent images of children ran through the space in front of her—a far greater number than the three children who'd gone up the stairs a moment before. She'd thought the Hillers had only two children . . .

It was the brunette child that stuck in her thoughts when James Hiller turned back to them, but stayed in the doorway. "FBI, huh?"

It was only then that Eleri realized Dana and the others had flashed their badges. She was slow on the draw, pulling it out even as Donovan elbowed her. Well shit, she was getting etiquette from Donovan. Things were not looking good. She smiled but was afraid it looked forced at best and freakish at worst. Hiller paid no attention to her.

"Y'all come around here every fistful of months, trying to make some sense of it." He looked at each of them. "All you do is upset my kids. I haven't heard dime one on what really happened to my wife."

It wasn't an invitation. Despite his surprising Southern drawl, he wasn't welcoming.

Dana talked her way in the door. It was a damned impressive feat given that there were five of them. Donovan, Wade, and Christina all looked slightly antisocial and Eleri figured she probably just looked high. She kept seeing random kids. Eleri knew they weren't real children—no one else reacted to them, for starters. Her eyes blinked as her brain told her what it was putting together.

The flashes of the old house were real. Her brain was trying to tell her something. There had been a lot of children here when Leona Hiller was alive. But why?

". . . your wife's murder has recently been linked to three other murders." Dana was telling him.

James Hiller looked shocked—his first genuine reaction to anything about their visit. Then he took a moment to visibly absorb the information. "That's the first thing that makes any sense. No one hated my wife. A serial killer—that's what you're talking about, right? —that's the only way someone would do this to her."

Eleri watched as Dana put on her best friend-of-yours face and wound up for the pitch. "I know you've answered so many questions before and I know it's hard to do, to dredge it all back up. But with this new angle, we feel we really have a lead—"

That was a lie, or at least a very bold stretching of the truth, but Eleri didn't interrupt. She didn't have the energy.

"—and now, we really think we might get somewhere. You can see —" she waved a hand at the group, "—the FBI has taken over the investigation and we have a full team on it. Anything you can contribute may be the difference in solving the case and bringing your wife's killer to justice."

That speech was so great, and so sincerely delivered that even Eleri felt like putting her hand over her heart and singing The Star-Spangled Banner.

Now he ushered them into the house, beyond the front foyer, and into a living room he didn't quite belong in. Then he left for a moment to settle the kids. Eleri took stock of the place; the room looked a little too formal, a little too unused. When James Hiller returned, he offered sodas or water and a few of them took him up on it.

Eleri spoke first. "When your wife was alive, there were quite a few children here. Is that correct?"

He looked startled. Then flustered. He blinked. "Yes, she often watched other kids for extra income."

"It was a daycare?" Eleri asked. None of that had been fleshed out in any of the earlier reports. As soon as the words were out of her mouth, she realized that's exactly what Leona Hiller had been doing. Only her daycare wasn't licensed. Eleri just needed to convince James Hiller that she wasn't trying to trip him up or shake him down. She only wanted information. Everything helped.

"Oh no, nothing as . . . *involved* as a daycare. Just some glorified babysitting for the neighbor kids." His halting cadence gave away the lie and his smile was forced. "No one asked about that before. Is it important?"

Dana launched into a "we need to just ask the questions" that was very kindly laid out. She even sweet-talked Hiller into being perfectly willing to answer any odd query any of them threw out, all under the umbrella of helping to find his wife's killer.

It was obvious that he loved Leona very much. Still, he was startled, embarrassed when a woman came through the front door.

"Lisa!" he popped up.

Eleri put the pieces together. The brunette child was hers. James Hiller was living with another woman.

It had been two years. Nothing fishy there, not in Eleri's mind. Only his reaction.

She looked up at "Lisa" and tried not to blink as the image of another woman, one with paler hair than Lisa's, overlaid the Lisa in front of her. But the woman wasn't Leona Hiller and it clearly wasn't Lisa.

Eleri couldn't identify the woman, but she did conclude that her brain had been right. The third child didn't belong. Other children were here often when Leona had been alive. And another woman, not Lisa and not the blond Leona, played into it.

Her head hurt too much to figure out how.

7

E leri walked through the forest alone. She'd been walking all day, only this time her feet didn't bother her. She didn't know why they didn't hurt, but she was grateful.

The forest was lit by a silvery full moon that gave her enough light to see clearly by, and she kept one foot moving in front of the other. The temperature was perfect and it was so nice to get out and away from the others, even if she should have been fully asleep. She didn't even remember escaping the hotel, only that she'd needed to.

Somehow, she'd made it outside with the heavy stock card in her hand. Her Grandmere's scrawl had written a single line in the middle of the card. Other than addressing the envelope to her, Grandmere had written nothing else.

Emmaline will be found soon.

Eleri's fingers involuntarily clenched at the card as though she could somehow hold onto her little sister. Emmaline had disappeared at age eight. The two girls had been out riding with their instructor and, skill by skill, he'd put them through their paces, with each horse and rider pair waiting while the other ran the course. When it had been Emmaline's turn, she'd simply been gone. Her horse had disappeared with her, too.

The FBI had gotten involved quickly. They treated the disappearance as though this could be no runaway, no simple case of wandering off. The rash reaction was as expected; Eleri's family was wealthy, it would be a high-profile case. They were certain—despite the lack of leads or information—that the girl would be found and brought home soon. The horse should have returned on his own if he'd been abandoned. He should have found his own way back. In fact, he hadn't been found for several years. And then, only on a chance encounter.

A friend recognized him at a farm he was buying thoroughbreds from. The Eames' had the horse's blood tested, and though they could never prove this was the horse that had disappeared with Emmaline, they did prove that he was bloodline of Banker's Sovereign, just like Emmaline's Silver Sovereign had been. The owner had no papers for him, though he was a well-bred show horse. The owners had been questioned by the feds, but they had no knowledge of Emmaline or her disappearance.

Eleri kept the cardstock note clutched in her hand now. She'd not been in touch with Grandmere about the note. The two of them were the only ones who seemed to have any idea what happened to Emmaline, though they'd never spoken directly of it. If Grandmere had a phone line, Eleri would have called. If Eleri had her phone on her. . . Her hand swiped at her back pocket. No phone, but she wasn't concerned. The night was just so beautiful.

The path opened up in front of her, the trees giving way to a little clearing, the moon shining on the sloped, square roof of the house. The porch was small, barely big enough to stand on; the white wood railing would contain a person with just enough space to knock on the door. It was set at a forty-five-degree angle across what should have been the corner of the house.

Eleri didn't knock.

Turning the knob, she entered.

Only this time, the rooms weren't empty. How had she not heard this noise from outside?

Children shrieked and ran about the room, playing tag, or blocks, or some odd form of patty cake. Some bolted by, yelling and calling to each other, shrill glee trailing them in sound waves Eleri could almost see.

She followed them around, knowing the house looped on itself. If she kept walking through arches and doorways she would wind up back at the front room. Were the old man and the old woman in the back again? Eleri couldn't hear with all the kids yelling and playing, but she didn't ask them to stop. She just walked.

In the back room, she found the woman.

Though she usually sat in a rocker, this time the woman stood. The rocker was gone. This room was quiet, no children entered, though Eleri braved it. The woman's eyes shot open as Eleri crossed the threshold. For a moment, it appeared she was angry, then she reached out and grabbed at Eleri, dark, thin fingers encircling Eleri's wrist in a strong grip before she could even protest. She pulled Eleri with her though her feet didn't move. Into the circle Eleri could now see on the floor.

Frantic, she looked around, unsure if the woman was friend or foe, though in the past she'd always seemed neutral. At the doorway, children stopped, looked in, but came no further, as though an invisible barrier kept them out. After a moment of watching the strange ritual, they would go on their way, back to playing.

Now, Eleri stood with the woman, finding herself in the middle of a circle with a five-pointed chalk star. The woman raised her hands to the skies and Eleri found herself following along. As she looked up, she could see stars punching through a moonless sky. Then everything went black.

Eleri's eyes fluttered. Light came in through the hotel window, a shadow blocking the direct beam. She rolled to the side, the hard ground grating against her hip and shoulder.

Ground?

Carpet.

She was lying on the floor. The shadow had been the high bed, the blinds letting the bright daylight seep in.

A knock came at the door. "El?"

"Donovan?" She asked it as though she were confused. And she was.

"Who else would it be?" There was a small pause. "I take it you're not ready?"

"Nope." She sat up, still on the floor, her elbows on her knees as she surveyed the mess around her. The card from her Grandmere lay stuck in the lush carpet mere inches from her, but didn't look as though it had been damaged at all by her odd dreams of the house. Eleri plucked it up, rubbing the heavy stock of the paper in her fingertips. She sighed. "I woke up on the floor."

With her declaration, Donovan pushed the door open. Maybe it was a bit too bold, but it was obvious he was concerned and nothing else. "You're okay?"

"Yup." She sighed again, not feeling rested enough for the night she'd spent.

"I got worried. You're usually up before me," Donovan commented as he scanned the mess of the room around her. He didn't say anything about it.

"Weird dreams. I'll be there in a bit." Then she paused, turning around to look at the clock she hadn't set, so confident that she'd wake up at a reasonable time. "Did I miss anything?"

"No, we have time for breakfast, but I want to go somewhere that Christina isn't." He'd said the same thing the day before.

"Call Wade," she told him, mentally preparing to get up off the floor.

"Already did."

He closed the door and the sound of his feet walking away let her know he'd declared her good enough and was waiting for her to get ready.

She frowned. The room looked almost like it had been tossed. Though she couldn't see the top of the bed from where she sat, it was clearly no longer made up. She'd climbed into it earlier. At some point, she must have climbed out, too. But she hadn't brought the covers to the floor with her nor even pulled them back up—not fully made, but not a tangle—like she usually did.

On the floor, assorted pieces of her clothing looked like they'd been pulled from her suitcase. It almost looked like she'd needed something at the bottom and rummaged through, simply throwing pieces over her shoulder as she rejected them. Also, not her style.

She frowned at the items and stood. Her joints protested, probably from sleeping on the floor. Only as she became fully upright did she see it wasn't random.

Only white shirts. Probably pulled from the hangers. Other white items were around the room, but the shirts defining the space around her were button downs, a t-shirt. It took a moment of squinting in confusion before she realized that the ones near her were all cotton. All white, and all cotton . . .

She turned.

Five pieces. Wadded up. Equally spaced around her with socks, underwear, and more in spots between.

In a five-pointed star.

Donovan looked at Eleri a little sideways during breakfast. The mess in her room concerned him, though he knew she was prone to odd dreams. Still, she'd been acting strangely this morning, even for Eleri. "Was there something you didn't say about the children you saw at the Hiller house yesterday?"

She shook her head. Dana had asked the same thing almost as soon as they got in the car yesterday. Eleri gave Donovan the same response she'd given Dana. He'd hoped she'd have something to add now that everyone else was gone. Clearly, she didn't.

"No. I just saw a bunch of kids in the house. It was obvious Leona Hiller ran an unlicensed daycare there. The way her husband bristled at the mere idea was a pretty sure giveaway that it was one. But that's all I saw. I have no clue what it means or if it means anything at all, other than that I was seeing Leona Hiller's life."

"It sucked that the house had been rebuilt," he commented around toast and eggs. Eleri had voted for a high-end breakfast joint and was eating some kind of banana bread French toast and cantaloupe with honeydew slices arranged like a flower on a pretty little plate. Unable to stomach a quiche filled with a bacon he still couldn't pronounce, he'd gone for a classic.

"It sucked for you. For us," Eleri commented back. "Honestly, my impression was that James Hiller was finally getting his life back together. I'm not surprised that he rebuilt the house differently." She paused a moment then added pensively, "Did you notice that his new girlfriend, Lisa, looks a lot like Leona?"

"She even has an L name," Donovan agreed. Yes, he'd noticed. He'd also noticed there were almost no pictures of Leona Hiller around the living room. A few of her with the kids—two of them—but none with James and none of just her. "They've replaced her pretty well."

Eleri shrugged. "They may have had to. How do you come home one day and find your house burned from the inside out and your wife dead? Then you find out it wasn't natural, that someone came in and burned her? Most people don't carry that well. Especially since the cops and now the FBI come back around every few months and make you dig it back up."

James Hiller had clearly been treated as a suspect for a while—which made sense. He had a good job, an at-home wife who wasn't a community pillar or anything, so no one knew or could say just how much the couple might have actually loved each other or how happy the marriage was. His good job had given them both solid, quality life insurance policies that paid out higher in the event of murder or death by random crime. It hadn't looked good for him.

His saving grace had been his bank statements, which had been steady-Eddie for years. He didn't even get bonuses at work, and he balanced each checkbook by hand to the penny. Then there was the concern that while no community members could vouch for the quality of the marriage, no one could speak against it either. Leona Hiller had been relatively quiet, but her few good friends said she loved "Jimmy" as she called him. His coworkers said James never had a bad word to say about his wife. She was polite and kind at work functions, and James gave a death glare and fired anyone who made misogynistic comments, faster if they were about his relationship or his wife in particular. No one could pin anything on James Hiller.

Donovan slid the last of his toast across the plate, cleaning the eggs with it before he ate it, a move that would have gotten him kicked out of Eleri's home. "Do you agree with Dana and Christina that he's as he appears?"

Eleri nodded, her mouth full, her plate still half covered with yet-to-be-eaten food. She checked the time and rolled her eyes.

Donovan almost grinned. "Well, you were the one who slept in. Not my fault this time."

They cleared out and drove back to find Christina and Dana waiting in the parking lot of the hotel, Wade just coming out the sliding glass doors looking down at his phone rather than where he was walking. Luckily, there was no traffic.

Donovan parked and he and Eleri practically fell out of their SUV, anxious to not appear late. He looked at Dana oddly. "Are we waiting for something?"

"Yes. Minivan." She looked to Eleri. "No agent should have to sit in the middle of the backseat. I'm sorry about yesterday. I . . . apparently, some days I can't count."

"I get the way back?" Eleri asked, using an odd term Donovan didn't think he'd ever heard before.

"Is that a problem?" Dana crossed her arms, clearly not liking having her nice deed questioned.

"Nope. Beats the hell out of the middle." She grinned.

Just then a minivan pulled into the lot, followed by a compact car bearing a rental logo. Inside three minutes, Dana had signed everything and pocketed the keys.

Donovan frowned. "We aren't going anywhere?"

Dana shook her head and started back inside, leading the rest of them like ducks. "Back into the conference room. I think I found something."

8

E leri was already emotionally done with the day by the time they'd settled into the conference room. Now they'd been cloistered in here for hours. They used a different conference room this time, to avoid "loss," as Dana called it. Though that didn't seem to be anyone's primary concern now.

Eleri watched as Dana put her face forward into her hands and breathed deeply. Dana was the only one who did it, but they all felt it. Between the lack of sleep and the panic attack Eleri had picked up from whomever had been in the SUV before her, Eleri was pushing herself just to maintain focus.

Wade had been looking at scenes, calculating burn temperatures. He kept saying "really damn high" which matched to some of the molars of the victims popping off. But it was inconsistent. There were other victims that remained untouched by the fire. Their intact teeth indicated their bodies stayed a reasonable temperature despite the extreme fire all around them. Back teeth exploded in the two-thousand-plus degree range. So that was something they knew. Or Eleri told herself it was.

Donovan was still trying to piece together the Riser fire—where the arsonist seemed to have chased down Burt Riser with a flamethrower. He'd tapped Wade to figure out where to stand and how to aim to make the patterns shown on the floor. They'd tried to determine the height of the attacker. They hadn't been able to make it work. Eleri had jumped in a few times, her physics skills nowhere near Wade's, but she'd tried.

"Wouldn't standing there make the accelerant trail veer to one side? I mean the flame-thrower would be aimed that way, not straight ahead." She pointed.

"Sure, but then he's standing *in* the flames he started a few minutes before," Donovan countered as Wade scratched numbers on paper. He would write frantically then spend just as much time erasing or scratching it out. Eleri gave up.

Pines was working her way through the medical examiner's reports—looking at them with a Bureau agent's eye rather than a medical/biological one. And Dana was examining method of death.

Eleri was tasked with victimology.

Leona Hiller was a stay-at-home-mom with two small children. She ran a daycare. Eleri ignored everything that had happened to her as she died—that was Dana's problem.

Marcy Davis, another probable victim, was a schoolteacher. That might be a link; both women worked with children. Marcy Davis had taught second grade—children older than what Leona Hiller worked with but still young. Eleri wanted to latch onto that. They lived about sixty miles apart. But with Leona Hiller not running a licensed center and with the house having burned down, there were no records to be able to cross-reference anything.

Any link between them would be great, except that Burt Riser was a geneticist—about as far from a childcare worker as one could get. He lived in a different city. He lived in a different tax bracket, for God's sakes. The man was wealthy as all get-out. Nice house. Gated division. Eleri felt a thought snake through her brain, but she couldn't grab it.

Riser worked in a privately funded lab. As far as Eleri could tell from the notes in his case, he didn't interact with much of anyone outside of work. If it wasn't a mouse or a lab assistant, he didn't even look at it. What could he have done to trigger this attack?

Her brain struggled with that. Maybe his case was the place to begin. He didn't fit the profile she was working up. Nodding to herself, Eleri decided this was the start point. Leona Hiller was a victim. Eleri could feel it. Burt Riser was clearly a victim. The third? It was only a maybe. Eleri concentrated on what they knew. Maybe someone was mad about a specific genetic development or lack thereof. But how would that get the target on *him?*

Eleri searched his papers but couldn't find anything. Burt Riser had few friends. Apparently, he had a girlfriend for a short while, but no one the feds questioned knew her. The other workers and scientists at the lab said Riser was friendly when he was paying attention, but mostly he had his thoughts on his work. At home, he didn't have a dog or cat or even a goldfish. So how would someone target him?

Her head hurt. She had nothing.

Dana had nothing. Christina kept making pained faces.

Wade and Donovan kept saying "no, that doesn't work" and erasing things.

Dana lifted her face from her hands. "We need a break."

Eleri refrained from using what was possibly her favorite phrase and saying, "No shit, Sherlock." She just nodded.

"It's early stages," Dana told them. "Something will come together."

They were agents, they didn't need to be told that. Eleri bristled for a moment, then thought, maybe it didn't hurt to hear it. As frustrated as she was, maybe she did need the reminder.

"Lunch," Dana declared, "but first, does anyone have *anything* to report?"

They all shook their heads then stared at each other as though it was someone else's responsibility to find the elusive connection.

Eleri shook her head too, and maybe it shook something loose. "Oh! I was wondering if there's footage of Riser's neighborhood. Of people who came and went that night. The neighbors all have alibis. Solid ones."

"Call that in before lunch," Dana instructed her and Eleri nodded, pulling up the number for the local police on Burt Riser's case seeing if they had the footage or could direct her how to get it.

In the background, she heard them discussing the other files, and whether they should travel to any of those scenes this afternoon. Eleri wished she could vote no, but she couldn't.

By the time she hung up, the local PD had promised to have an assistant email her the footage from the entry gate at Riser's neighborhood around the time of his death. They informed her that they had the footage because they'd checked it, but even their specialists had found nothing. The man on the phone gave her a "more power to you" that didn't hold much weight, but she thanked him and turned to the others.

"Food. Please."

Dana nodded. Eleri wondered if she could also ask for a nap. Sleeping on her floor and wasting her precious rest on that little house that seemed to mean nothing had done her no good the night before. She hadn't even mentioned the clothing to Donovan. She wasn't sure he'd recognized it for being more than just a mess. Besides, what would she say?

She didn't say anything now, either. Dana kept them all in a group, walked them through a vote on where to eat like they were on a high school field trip and then chauffeured them to the restaurant. At least she picked up the tab.

Eleri had learned a few things on the ride out. One—the family that had the minivan before them had small children in car seats. Four of them! And two—she'd picked up some awful thing that she couldn't define, but it was terrible. Blood everywhere. Dead parents or children or something. And for a flash of a moment, she'd been standing in the middle of it.

On the way back, she sat in the back of the minivan without incident.

Also, she had to admit that she felt better after eating a meal under a moratorium of "no work talk." Even Christina opened up a little. Though one of the few times she spoke, she stopped herself from telling a story because it was work related. Eleri began to wonder if she did anything else.

Finally fed and back in the conference room, they sorted the files they'd chosen of other possible cases.

Donovan pulled out one case he thought had potential—the others had the job of seconding the idea or arguing it down. It wound up as a mid-level possibility for a visit. The second file got put aside; it would take a full day or a plane flight to get to the location—which honestly also made it less likely it was actually related to these. This killer seemed to keep his work clustered in this corner of the US.

The third file was one Eleri put out, but Dana shook her head. "Too old. I don't think there will be anything there still to see. We got lucky with Riser's house."

That was true, though the FBI's version of "luck" meant that Riser was rich and had no direct heirs. His greedy relatives were still arguing his estate in court, which left the house and thus the crime scene, still intact for them to visit. In many cases, especially with fire, people tore down and rebuilt or remodeled at the least, like James Hiller had. With the death of a loved one, sometimes people just sold the land and took the money and left the bad memories behind. That meant no scene, no witnesses, no remaining evidence. Eleri didn't fight for it.

They were on file number four when Dana's phone rang. She stepped away, though she answered formally, putting Eleri, Donovan, and Christina on alert. Only Wade remained oblivious.

When Dana hung up she faced them. "Do you want the good-slash-bad news?"

They all nodded. Anything was better than the conference room with its pile of files and no leads.

"We have a new case."

"Linked?" Wade finally looked up from the case he'd been studying.

"Fire in a circle around the victim. Sudden death from no obvious cause. House is still hot—as in the fire department is putting out the last of the sparks and nothing has been touched except for that." Her eyes lit up and Eleri felt her own feelings spark. Something to *do*. A *real* lead. She had to remind herself that someone had died to give her that clue and her job was to stop it from happening again. Another death was both a lead and a failure.

"Where?"

"Louisiana."

Donovan watched the woman huddled at the edge of the scene. This was the part he hadn't had to do as a medical examiner. He couldn't say it was part of the job he liked: the crying wife, stunned, shocked, and shaking, was something he'd been happy not to deal with in his old life. Now, he had to look at her as a suspect.

There was nothing about her that said she had any hand in this.

She was yelling at the police. "I don't know!" then again, "I don't know!" and "Oh, my God. Oh, my God. Leroy. Leroy."

She pulled the blanket tighter around her despite the warm, heavy weather. Just outside Alexandria, which was just over an hour south of Shreveport, the air clung like wet felt and Donovan could feel the strain on his lungs just to breathe normally.

LeighAnn and Leroy Arvad had not lived a glamorous life. The house was a modest doublewide trailer—or it had been before it was burned. LeighAnn was still in a uniform that looked like it was ninety-eight percent polyester and two percent bacon grease and syrup. Leroy Arvad had not been killed for the inheritance.

The team packed their things with a speed known only to Bureau agents and wanted criminals. They'd hopped on a small private plane, the fastest way to get here when time was of the essence. Finding herself in another minivan, this time Eleri sat in the back with the luggage even though Wade had volunteered to take the spot. They'd come straight to the house to find Mrs. Arvad still watching the mess hours after it had been found and firefighters not letting her inside. They were still standing watch and dousing the occasional spark as the afternoon lengthened into a very bad evening.

Donovan breathed deep, taking the smell of burning synthetics into his nasal cavity and letting it sit. He let his senses pull out small particles and waited while his brain matched them to things he'd smelled before.

Wade spoke first. "Smells like the last guy."

It did, that hint of hydrogen as it burst hung in the air around the house. It was faint, but present. Donovan nodded, thinking how nice it was to have another nose around. Someone else to confirm. It wasn't that Eleri didn't believe him; she did, she supported him and followed what he said with no question. It was that when he questioned himself there was no backup. Wade was backup.

He did smell hydrogen. And that was odd.

Donovan turned to tell Eleri, only to find she'd wandered closer to the house even though the smoke was still wafting up in tendrils from the rubble. The trees still dripped, the humid weather doing nothing to dry out the thousands of gallons of water the firefighters had doused the place with.

Perhaps this was a good time to mend fences. Or to build bridges, or whatever the hell else he was supposed to do. Donovan had no clue how to interact with people—it was why he'd chosen examining the dead as his profession in the first place. Not for the first time, he wondered where he would be right now if Agent Derek Westerfield had not strode into his office almost two years ago and suggested Donovan Heath, MD become an FBI agent.

Donovan had laughed at the man. He'd laughed as hard and long as he could in front of a stranger. At least he had until agent Westerfield described Donovan's ability in detail to him, stopping him dead cold. No one knew that about him. No. One.

Now so many people did that Donovan figured he might as well wear it on a shirt. So it didn't matter that he turned to Dana and told her what he smelled. She would believe him, too.

"It's hydrogen—that buzz. Wade and I both smell it."

"Does that mean it's the same guy?" Dana looked at him, no question about what he sensed or how he got the information.

"Has to be, doesn't it?"

Dana shrugged. "I can't smell hydrogen burn, and I don't know how often you'd find it at a house fire. That's your call."

And so it was.

Donovan called it. "I've never smelled it at a fire before this case. This is our guy."

9

Donovan walked the scene, heading into the house despite the firefighters' warning that the structure wasn't cleared by the arson investigator yet. Donovan just nodded. Wade didn't even bother with that.

They stepped gingerly, listening for squeaks, creaks, or the sound of wood giving way. Several times Donovan jerked back, relying on his keen senses to keep him out of danger. Wade almost walked into the back of him.

"Sorry."

Donovan turned, looking at his friend. None of the women were in with them. None of them had the skills—except maybe Eleri—to walk through here without being more likely to get hurt than not. Heat still radiated from the frame of the house. In places, mist rose from charred wood and synthetics. Donovan wasn't sure if the mist was actual steam or not. He didn't check.

"Not paying enough attention," Wade offered by way of apology again. "This is weird. You could maybe pick it up at the last place, but here it's strong."

Donovan understood. He'd thought the same thing, but doubted himself. "I don't know why that is. I want to say the smell is stronger because the fire is much more recent. Still, I feel as if it's even more than that. I just haven't been to enough house fires to know just how likely that is."

"I have," Wade countered abruptly. "And it's definitely abnormal."

The smell of hydrogen was strong enough to buzz. The *feel* of something burning hung in the air, but Donovan couldn't place it. "I've never smelled a flamethrower before. Do they smell like this?"

"No, they smell like gas. Like ethanol. Like hairspray even. Depends on what you make them out of."

"Homemade flamethrower?" Donovan frowned.

"Absolutely. I've made a few myself."

Good to know, Donovan thought, though truthfully it didn't surprise him that Wade had simply made his own flamethrower. He'd probably thought one day, *I'd like to have a flamethrower* and just assembled one. Maybe his friend made his own bombs or fireworks. He didn't put anything past Wade.

"Thing is," Wade continued, "they don't smell like this. That pure hydrogen burn? You smell the accelerant in a normal flamethrower."

"So this is an abnormal flamethrower?" Donovan asked, but Wade didn't really answer, he'd already wandered off.

The body was in the middle of the main room. The front door had suffered in the fire, so they'd entered by way of the back porch. Once he saw the body and established a safe route to it, Donovan headed back for Dana and Eleri. He only nodded at Christina, who seemed to take the near-dismissal in stride. He didn't like her.

He spoke as he pointed out where to place their feet on each step. They were like clumsy elephants to him here. They didn't hear the wood straining, settling back in after expanding from the fire. They didn't hear the slight hiss of escaping gases or the constant dripping of draining water onto the dirt under the once-mobile home. "Wade and I both smell that hydrogen smell again. I don't know about it, but Wade says it's not normal. This means we've got some dude running around the country, killing people with fear and a flamethrower."

Dana tipped her head a little, considering that. "Maybe the fear is from the flamethrower. Maybe it's so scary looking . . ."

Eleri shook her head. "Wouldn't that give them a heart attack? Wouldn't that be something we'd see in autopsy or you'd sense? There was no physical sign of death in Burt Riser."

"Y'all done in there?" A heavy voice yelled in from outside the house. Donovan hadn't heard it before.

Dana yelled back, "No! It's our case."

"It's my case," the voice yelled back and Donovan heard Eleri muttering under her breath.

Dana just yelled it out loud. "We're the FBI. It's our case."

There was nothing Donovan wanted to do less than be involved in this argument. Who had the bigger dick? Dana did. She was FBI. Whoever this guy was, he was local and he was out of his league now. Donovan looked around the scene.

It wasn't to be.

Dana—exasperated when the argument continued—started toward the front of the house. She made it three steps with Donovan lightly dogging her before her foot went through a soft spot in the floorboards. She swore, picked herself up, swore again when she looked at her torn pants leg and blood on her shin, then she motioned roughly for Donovan to show her a safe path to the front of the house where she stuck her head through an exploded-out window and swore again.

"This is not your fucking scene! I'm FBI." She flipped open her badge and jabbed it at him even though there was no way he could see it from the yard. "I own this shit all the way up to the road and out to the property edges."

"My guys put this fire out." He put his hands on his hips, something about the gesture reminded Donovan of the last arson guy. But he was too busy watching Dana shift and making sure she didn't go through the floor again to think too much of it.

Dana's demeanor changed suddenly. "You put the fire out? Well, golly gosh, that makes the whole thing yours." She smiled. "Christina? Be a doll and get them all the paperwork from the four murders in three other western states. Explain to these nice boys that there's no known cause of death in two of the cases—now three, looks like—and that we've got ourselves a fucking serial killer on our hands. And let's us all go get a nice lunch now that these sweethearts have taken this shit off our little old hands."

She stared at the inspector.

He stared back.

But the game of chicken didn't last long.

"Suit yourself, missy," he told her.

"Fuck yourself, asshat," she replied back.

Dana's expression stayed flat. Donovan, on the other hand, was struggling to keep his face straight. If he laughed too hard he might not just reflect badly on the FBI, he might go through the floor. Dana had been lucky and not gotten very injured. He used to think he had a foul mouth. Dana made him feel like a rank amateur.

She headed back toward the body but her head clearly wasn't in it. She was like a dog that had just successfully defended its turf—the winner, but not fully itself again. It took her a few minutes of looking down at the body of Leroy Arvad before she could say anything.

Donovan looked, too. He didn't see much he could distinguish. Instead he listened to LeighAnn Arvad as the local police tried again to convince her to let them take her to the police station. No one was winning at that game. He smelled the room, the hint of ozone, the burn of hydrogen that he'd noticed before but was unmistakable here. He looked at the traces of burn pattern on the floor—they were sharper here and smelled stronger, too. He sniffed at the body, but aside from the scent that told him Leroy Arvad was scared enough to lose control of his bowels before he died, there was nothing to smell that Donovan didn't already know. Leroy had been terrified. He stank of the fear-pheromones a live person exuded with mortal terror.

Donovan looked at the body as a medical examiner. Parts intact. No obvious bruising. Though he paid extra attention around the neck, he could see nothing. The house looked much the same as Burt Riser's house. The main difference was that Leroy Arvad didn't run. The killer didn't chase him down with his flamethrower. Nope, good ole Leroy had stood in one spot, faced the man, died of fear, fallen onto his back, and laid there while the house burned around him.

"Nothing," Dana pronounced. "He died of *nothing!*"

Donovan concluded that wasn't a normal thing for her to find. Not before this case at least. She looked at him, "You?"

"Nothing we didn't already have, except that Wade and I have latched onto the flamethrower theory. We now believe that he's using some kind of homemade device."

"Which will only make it harder to trace." She sighed. "I shouldn't have been such a bitch. I shouldn't have said 'serial killer' and I should have let the arson guys take the case."

"Sure, but they'd have given it back when they realized what a shit show it is." Donovan offered what he considered consolation. "And by then, they would have screwed something up."

"Yay. Bitchiness wins," she said, but her tone didn't match the celebration of the words. "Tell me about the flamethrower. Maybe there's something about it that we can trace."

Donovan shook his head, but Wade jumped into the conversation. Thermodynamics and all, he was in his element.

"I don't even know that there is an accelerant. Honestly, I can't smell one." He shook his head. "It's as though the flamethrower creates instantaneous flashover—as though it's producing fire through heat alone. But I don't smell the remnants of a heating element, either. If I were making this, I'd use hydrogen and oxygen gas tanks and a mixture and ignition system."

"Would it get up to the temperatures we're seeing here?" Dana frowned, shook her head, and stepped to the side.

Reaching out lightning fast, Donovan grabbed her arm and stabilized her as another soft spot gave way under her foot. This time she didn't fall through. "Nice save." She looked at him appreciatively.

"I hear the floor groaning as you start to step on it."

She flattened her mouth, widened her eyes and gave a short nod. It took him a moment to realize he might have insulted her weight. He had no real idea though, so he kept his mouth shut.

"Well, he died before the house burned," she commented.

Donovan looked at her. *Shit.* She was right. "No."

"Yes," she responded. "No soot around the nose or mouth. No blistering. He didn't breathe in the hot air. Or smoke."

"No, he didn't." Donovan said. "But he *saw* the fire. Or at least he was alive when it was burning."

Without stopping to think if there was a better way, he pulled a knife from his back pocket. Stepping three paces, he stooped and sliced at Leroy Arvad's shirt, cutting a chunk from it. Standing, he held it out. "Wade! Smell it. Smell both sides."

Wade did, almost reverently, definitely methodically testing each piece. "It's through and through." He was nodding as he handed it back.

"What does that even mean?" Dana asked, looking back and forth between the two men. The two wolves.

"We need to change and we need to run the property," Wade said, but he was looking at Donovan. Donovan agreed.

"Keep everyone but us out. We need to check all the corners," he said, already looking for a place to change. He didn't think any of the rooms still had four standing walls to hide them as they altered.

Dana's hand landed on his shoulder, stopping his thoughts. "What does that have to do with him seeing the fire?"

"He saw it. The smells are mixed." That didn't help anyone who couldn't smell it. He tried again. "The scent of fear, of terror, and the smell of the ozone and hydrogen are completely mixed. The fire scents didn't get stopped by his sweat. They got onto his skin, mixed in. It was burning while he was actively sweating. So it was burning *while* he was alive."

Dana sucked in a deep breath and started out of the house. Her breathing had turned shallow while they stood there. She probably didn't handle the chemicals in the air very well. That was normal; it was Donovan and Wade that weren't.

She stepped carefully in the spots they'd walked in on, impressing Donovan that she'd been paying attention. Especially since she'd tried to go through the floor twice and had even succeeded once. She called for Eleri who was scoping out a back room and came out just as carefully planting her feet and paying attention to spots where Wade pointed.

Dana looked at Eleri with fierce eyes. "Touch everything. Get everything you can out of this place. Because according to Donovan and Wade, the fire burned around him. While he was alive, and yet somehow, the air around him didn't burn. It didn't even get near his mouth or eyes."

Dana shook her head. "I hate this case. Everything we find out is worse than the last thing. And this guy is out there with some home-made flamethrower and he's killing people. We already lost Leroy Arvad on our watch. We won't lose two."

Her conviction was admirable but misplaced, Donovan thought.

There was no way they were figuring this out before the flamethrower hit another person.

10

"Tell me about the flamethrower," Dana pressed.

Eleri shrugged. Though she'd touched what walls and pieces of furniture she could, she wasn't getting any impressions or information about the flamethrower.

"Was there a gas can? No—wait—a hydrogen tank?" Dana followed her, peppering her with questions.

Donovan and Wade had gone off to change, literally. Christina was nowhere to be found, and Eleri was wondering why she'd gotten duty with Dana. Here Eleri was told to "touch everything." Never mind that most of it was still on fire in its little wooden soul. Okay, she was bitter.

Eleri tried to shake it off.

She put her hand on a scrap she found and almost said, "This was the bedroom," but it was too obvious. There was no psychic ability needed to deduce that the bigger of the two rooms in the back was the main bedroom and that the soggy scrap she held in her hand had once been the comforter on the bed. It was probably acrylic, given the way the edges had curled and twisted. But that was deduction too, requiring no ability other than having working eyeballs.

"If we could find anything about the fuel source or how this guy was lighting the fire, that would be helpful," Dana pushed.

This time Eleri's tongue got the better of her.

"I've got nothing. Seriously, this is their comforter. Here's what

I've picked up so far: No one lived here other than LeighAnn and Leroy. LeighAnn desperately wanted to conceive, she even envisioned their life with the daughters she thought she should have had running around—" Eleri flitted her fingers by as though that might make her purely useless information more helpful. "—and they weren't able to have children at all." She paused. "That's it."

"Everything?"

"No. Leroy has a collection of lawn mower parts out in the back. He thinks he's a mechanic of sorts, but LeighAnn hates the parts rusting in the grass. LeighAnn had a doll collection. They cost about fifteen dollars apiece. She saved up for each and every one of them. And they're all burned now and the Arvads don't have fire insurance."

Okay, Eleri made that last part up—not the dolls but the lack of fire insurance. She'd bet she wasn't far off the mark though. Still, she'd learned a long time ago that trying to force something to come was as useless as heels on sneakers. No good could come of it.

"Dolls, huh?" Dana looked at her, disappointed, and Eleri tried not to be disappointed that Dana was disappointed in her. She didn't put stock in parental unit dissatisfaction anymore.

"I'll let you know if I get anything of value." Mostly what she had were LeighAnn's imaginings. The dolls. Dreaming of a baby. They didn't have the money to furnish a nursery for a baby they didn't have, but LeighAnn dreamed. Little blond girls running around the place, and LeighAnn brushing their hair, feeding them peanut butter sandwiches, showing them the dolls. Older girls, coming and going, getting report cards, learning to drive. Dreams of a family. Dreams that had literally gone up in smoke.

There was a lot more of LeighAnn than Leroy here. No surprise. She looked up at Dana. "Leroy was a long-haul trucker. He got back last night."

Maybe Dana already had that information. She had to have Christina doing something of value, right?

Just then, something wet nudged at her hand and she looked down to see Donovan standing at her side. He nudged her again and turned away.

Eleri looked up to Dana and said, "That's my cue."

Dana was staring at the wolf, which Eleri found odd. "Have you not seen him this way before? I thought you knew about them." She frowned at her boss, who hadn't changed her dazed expression.

"I did," she stuttered. "I mean, I *know* about them, but I've never met one before. I—"

Eleri waited the full beat it took Dana to get herself together.

"—I understand the science. It's pretty sound, I've just never met one in the flesh." She knelt down and spoke slowly and tentatively. "Hi, Donovan."

Oh, shit.

"Um, Dana." Eleri waited until her boss looked up at her. "He can understand you just fine. Actually, his ears work better now, in this shape."

"Oh! That makes sense!" Dana said, but she didn't stand up. In fact, she was reaching out to touch Donovan's head.

"Dana." This time Eleri said it sharper. "You notice how I'm not petting him? Yeah, he hates that. He may bite your face off."

Dana jerked back and stood up this time, looking at Eleri in alarm. Eleri almost felt bad. But Donovan was nodding in agreement to her "bite your face off" statement. "He's still Donovan. He's still a highly trained FBI agent, and he hears and understands everything. He just can't talk to you."

Donovan nodded again and trotted off, his paws hitting the floor soundlessly and leaving paw-shaped squish marks in places where the soggy carpet remained. Eleri followed, glad to be out of that house, out from under the pressure of reading the sodden remains of what may have been a relatively unhappy life.

Outside, Wade waited.

Where Donovan's coat was almost fully black, Wade's was brown with a golden hint. His eyes were still green, less like an actual wolf's than Donovan's. Donovan blended better. Wade was the prettier of the two, though Eleri had never told either of them that. Both men pushed one-eighty plus pounds, making them incredibly large wolves and definitely frightening to any mere human they might come across. If they ran into anyone, it would be helpful to have her walking along with them.

Apparently, that wasn't really what the two men had in mind. Donovan nudged her toward the folded pile of clothing.

Eleri looked at him. "Yeah, it's your clothes."

He made a noise at her, then did it again before she understood.

"Wait, I'm your pack mule?"

He nodded as she muttered, "Screw you," but she picked up the clothes and folded them all into Wade's plaid shirt, tying them into one massive hobo bundle. "Am I just carrying this along behind you in case you need them?"

Donovan nodded again and trotted off, leaving her to figure out if she had any higher purpose in this jaunt. And she'd been afraid Christina had nothing of value to do.

Even that idea was put to bed not a few minutes later when they cleared the front yard, the two wolves sniffing their way around.

"My God, those are big dogs!" The male voice brought Eleri's head up sharply, though both the wolves managed to ignore him completely. They'd probably smelled the man from a distance and must have deemed him harmless long ago.

She was opening her mouth to answer when Christina beat her to it. "We use *bloodhounds* in a lot of our cases. Helps find leads in fresh situations like this."

Bloodhounds? These were clearly wolves.

Well hell, Christina was manning the perimeter, and she'd just used her skills to override that guy. He'd remember a bloodhound. She was much more useful than Eleri, it seemed.

Christina spoke again. "Sir, I've asked you several times to leave. I know you're an officer and I know you're off duty. But it's just a good time to leave, isn't it?"

"You know what?" he asked her as Eleri watched. "I think my wife and kids are probably waiting on me. I'll head out."

"You have a nice evening, sir." Christina smiled at him and watched as he walked away.

Eleri had paid attention throughout the exchange, then turned to catch up with the men. They'd sniffed the perimeter and were at the edge of the ruts that made up the driveway when they put their heads together and started making whining noises. She wished to hell she understood them.

Dana was looking for a gas can or hydrogen tank or something, hoping that if they knew what the flamethrower used, they could track purchases, or find a person capable of using it. "Is it from a gas can?"

They both turned their heads up and looked. Both heads said "no."

"Part of the flamethrower?"

Again, no.

Eleri was dead on her feet. Another long day, the sun was going down. She hadn't gotten any good impressions from the house and was fighting the overwhelming feeling of uselessness. The expression on Dana's face when she'd come up with nothing of value was wearing on her soul. Eleri had had enough of disappointing people when her parents decried her joining the FBI. Her mother still refused to acknowledge her work. Eleri got her appreciation from her bosses. She knew it, but it was still a sharp pain to see that look on Dana's face. Now, here she was, ferrying clothing for the guys and about three hairs short on her temper. Any moment now she was going to crack and ask them, "What is it, Lassie? Is it Timmy? Stuck in the well?"

She bit her tongue and followed them around the property. She high-stepped over the rusted engine parts she'd seen in her thoughts. The ones LeighAnn hated. Eleri felt some sympathy for the woman, clearly they were useless and he wasn't doing anything with them except keeping them. Hulls of lawnmowers hid nearby. These had been left so long the plant life had grown up around them. There was no swing set for the children LeighAnn desperately wanted and Eleri couldn't help the apt comparison to her own mother and father, who easily got pregnant each time they tried, who had money to raise the girls with the occasional nanny, summer camps, horses, lessons, and more. Yet her own family had suffered, too. A terrible loss that LeighAnn would never have to deal with, given her inability to conceive in the first place.

Eleri's maudlin thoughts had left her standing, staring into the weeds while the men wandered off. She could no longer hear their *wuffing* noises as they moved with their heads down, pushing through the tall grass, and catching whatever scents they could. For a moment, she stared at nothing, but this time she paid attention, training her ears even though they were no match for the wolves.

Just when she was ready to give up and holler for them, she heard the noise. Not that it did her any good.

"Eleri!" Donovan's human voice called out from the stand of trees at the back edge of the property. "Bring the clothes."

"Yes, sir," she grumbled. She may not be lead agent on this case, but she was *his* senior agent. She mocked his voice, "Bring me my clothes, Eleri." Then responded in her own voice, "No, you can run around naked."

Though it was all under her breath, the sing-songy tone carried well enough to the men with beyond-human hearing. She could hear Wade laughing. Then she heard Donovan, the breathiness of his voice indicating that he and Wade had both heard her loud and clear.

"Okay, we'll come out naked if that's what you want . . ."

She saw flashes of nude male skin through the slim tree trunks. While she oh-so-desperately wanted to see them change from human to wolf form or back, watching her partner walk out of the woods in the altogether was on her to-do list at about "never."

"Fine!" she yelled. "Take your stupid clothes and get dressed." She tossed the pile—poorly—in their general direction before turning and walking a little bit away. Her back turned, she waited, arms crossed over her chest.

It took only a few minutes of muttering, hers and theirs, before they emerged, fully dressed if a little askew.

"We're dressed. You can turn around."

"Dressed doesn't make you any better looking," she retorted, though she didn't know why. The day had gotten to her. Yesterday, too. She wasn't in charge. They had a dead body and some sick fuck out there, tormenting people with some kind of hydrogen flamethrower, and she had nothing other than the fact that the dead man liked to collect old lawnmower parts and let them rust in the yard. She turned around though her attitude didn't improve. "Tell me you found where the dude stashed his gas can."

"There is no gas can," Wade repeated.

"Compressed flammable hydrogen tank?" She tried again. She was a biologist and a chemist with a specialty in human toxicology, but Wade's physics always seemed to be two steps ahead of her ability to grasp it. She could only get there when he dragged her along.

"No hydrogen tank." Donovan grinned, and before she could ask why, he glanced at Wade and back at her. "There is however, another person. Female. The hydrogen burn smell was clinging to her. So she was there for the fire, but she was alive and walked through the woods."

Eleri felt her chest compress. *"She escaped?"*

11

D onovan wanted a shower. Bad. He loved running in the woods. He loved running in new places. But he didn't like putting his clothes on in the woods. He didn't like putting clothes on over his freshly altered and un-showered form.

He missed his home.

He missed his backyard with the high fence and the safety of knowing that even getting a drone into his backyard would be difficult at best. He had a high fence and a covered porch. He would slip the latch at the back gate and run free into hundreds of thousands of acres of protected South Carolina forest.

Here, the grass was neither wild nor tame, just some weird overgrowth in between. The house smelled . . . not good. Donovan had asked Wade and apparently it was a wolf thing not to distinguish "bad" smells. Very few things made him turn his nose away, but there had been some mold in the house before it burned. Old food. It wasn't the fact that it was a trailer; he'd been in pristine ones. It was probably that the undertone of lack of care took him back to his childhood—that smell demarcated the time after his mother had died.

Eleri wasn't holding up, either. The days had run her ragged and Donovan had learned over the past several cases what that did to her.

"Is she okay?" Wade asked him, reaching back and adjusting something around his belt. That happened when you got dressed in the woods, and Wade had never been a black-suit type of fed in the first place.

Donovan didn't know what to answer. Yes, Eleri was okay because she was *always* okay. She'd been ten when her sister was taken from twenty feet away. And she was coming to grips with getting asked to use her skills on command, where in the past she'd always worked as though she just had lucky hunches.

But she wasn't really okay. She needed to be able to dive forward, to do *something*. She was nearly incapable of sitting back and letting someone else steer. Also, she had the added weight of her Grand-mere's note that Emmaline would be found soon. Eleri and Donovan were the only two who knew, so he wasn't ready to tell Wade about the note. That was for Eleri to decide. Her sister, Emmaline, had been alive for years after she'd been kidnapped, but had died at seventeen. Despite all Eleri's claims of only having hunches, she *knew* in her heart these facts about her sister. Emmaline had now been dead for over a decade, and still her parents met with the feds every year, reviewed the case for new leads, acted as though their daughter— now grown if she was alive—might come home one day. Eleri knew the truth.

It hit Donovan right then, that he was quite possibly the only person she'd ever told. So he didn't answer Wade's question of "Is she okay?" directly. He just said, "I've got her."

Wade let that answer stand as Eleri returned with Dana and Christina in tow. It was Christina's presence that bothered him. He turned to her, "Who's manning the perimeter?"

"One of the officers who came back." She shrugged.

"You trust them?" Donovan asked.

"Of course. He's doing what I told him to." There was a tone in her voice that made it clear she'd overridden him to make him follow along, and a nonchalance that told Donovan it wasn't hard for her to do it. He didn't like the way his stomach turned.

Though he tried to hide his dislike of that, Dana caught it. She looked at Eleri who also appeared a little disturbed by Christina's "methods."

"She's doing what I told her to do. If you have an issue with that, you take it up with me." She'd gone mother hen on them and all Donovan could do was nod. But Dana wasn't done. "When I met

Christina, she could make you think you were holding a baby dragon in your hand. Now she can make you think you're on a different planet. Like everything else, it's a skill. And you can have your issues with it, but we have to trust her integrity. She can get suspects to talk faster than anyone else, she can talk a jumper off a ledge every time, and she can neutralize a hostage situation faster than any negotiator."

Donovan felt his gut twitch at Dana's casual use of the word "neutralize." Did Christina just make the perpetrators turn and shoot each other, effectively ending the hostage crisis? He didn't know.

Dana caught his questioning look.

"You want to be upset, be upset. You don't like it, fine. But I'm standing over the body of a man who died on our watch. You want to question LeighAnn the usual way, then the next person who dies is on *your* head."

Well, fuck a duck, when she put it that way.

"Besides," her voice was softer now, "you can trust it. If she pushes you too long or changes too much, you'll start to notice the cracks. She can't override you if you're watching out for it."

That didn't quite match Christina's own story about having the whole school vote her prom queen or her quarterback boyfriend dating her for years, but Donovan held his tongue while his brain ran with the idea that Dana was taking up Christina's defense and maybe she didn't even know what her partner was truly capable of...

"So, tell me about this woman? Eleri said someone escaped?" Dana deftly changed the subject, and while it didn't alleviate his fears, his stomach did right itself.

"She went through the back woods here to get off the property." Donovan pointed into the trees at what could be called a "trail" only in the most generous of terms.

"She went quickly—hence the idea that she was escaping," Wade added as Dana frowned.

"Dumb question, but how can you tell she was moving quickly?"

Donovan watched as Eleri quirked a brow at Dana's question. Eleri knew the answer because she'd sat him down and asked it all before. Partly as a need-to-know about his skills and partly because she was just disturbingly curious about it as a scientist. She didn't answer the question though. Her phone must have pinged because she pulled it out of her pocket. The happy/disappointed look that crossed her face could only mean it was Avery on the other end of the line.

Springtime meant hockey playoffs and Avery Darling's team—the North Dakota Executioners—had made the post season. Just barely. Donovan expected to be watching Eleri watch the game that evening. If they could get past the case in front of them. Her face said she didn't expect it.

He turned his full attention back to his new boss. "The trail is more spread out. The smell gets thicker when a person pauses in one place. All that can be bothered by wind and time, but this one is relatively fresh and light. Also, being in the woods helps stop the winds from spreading it, but lets animals get at it and more smells interfere." He'd been rambling, so he shut up. Then he added, "She had the hydrogen smell on her. She was in there with the fire."

"Something's off, though," Wade added, "but my brain's not putting it together.

Dana didn't seem to care. "Tell me when you put it together." Turning abruptly, she started issuing orders. "We are heading out. Getting to a hotel. You two are showering." She eyed Wade and Donovan, then herself. "Hell, all of us are showering and reconvening about twenty minutes after we check in. I think I hear our CSI people pulling up. Then we'll go interview LeighAnn Arvad."

No one argued. Donovan, for one, was looking forward to that shower. What he found out thirty minutes later was that there were no hotels in any reasonable distance of this place. And that the motel they ended up at was only able to get them a chain of rooms at the far corner after cleaning a room that had been abandoned and not yet taken care of. Christina volunteered to take that room. Neither he nor Wade, with their extra sensitive noses, volunteered to take that burden off her shoulders. So it was that they spent twice as long waiting for the rooms they'd been promised as they got to actually get ready. Dinner didn't happen. Not then.

Donovan sighed and asked Wade if he'd ever put his finger on what was wrong with the scent trail in the woods. Neither of them had figured it out yet, but something was off.

Eleri's stomach was rebelling, even though she stood in a simple pose with her arms crossed. Even though she was watching the interview with LeighAnn Arvad and not even participating in it. Something about Christina's override made her gut churn. She didn't know if it was something left over from when Christina had done it to her, or if it was just about being in the room with it.

Maybe it was something a bit off in perception versus physiology —the way a person could get sick from wearing glasses that tilted the room. Or maybe her body was picking up on the override in some way and her stomach reacted. That was possible, Donovan had said he had it, too. Or maybe it was just the idea that what she was participating in was so vile and invasive that her stomach twisted. It was like having to watch someone get abused and doing nothing. She didn't have it in her to not jump in. But she was holding back now.

She was also extremely hungry.

She was agitated.

LeighAnn Arvad was not. Eleri told herself that the serene state Christina created in the woman was good for her, calming her blood pressure and all the physiological alterations that came with shock and sudden grief. At least, that's what she kept repeating in her head like a mantra.

LeighAnn Arvad, on the other hand, was telling everything. She told how they couldn't conceive. How sometimes Leroy drank too much but she loved him anyway because he's "a good man!"

It sounded like someone had been telling her he wasn't.

He was a long-haul trucker and she was a waitress at a local stop called the Waffle Pit. She recommended it. Eleri thought she'd do her best to avoid any food source with "Pit" in the title. But the longer the interview went on, the hungrier she got and the more she started considering it.

Dana leaned in, talking to Eleri in a low voice, despite the fact that they were beyond the two-way glass. There was no way LeighAnn could hear them. "Is she telling the truth?"

Eleri almost balked. She wasn't a human lie detector. Then again, Donovan kept telling her she was more than she'd thought. She was better at these things than she gave herself credit for. She changed the topic. "When do we get time off?"

"Two days, three from now? I don't know. Why?"

"My grandmother is just over an hour from here."

Dana took a look at her. Must have seen the wear on her and for once Eleri didn't bother to hide it. "We have a good team. We'll get you the time. Do you need to take Donovan?"

Well, shit. Eleri wasn't prepared for Dana to be perceptive and nice about it. "They've communicated before, but never met. It would be great if he could go."

"I'll see what I can swing. I mean there's five of us. And I'm hoping we aren't neck deep in the shit yet." Dana sighed.

Eleri held out what she had. "I'm pretty good at telling when people are lying. I don't think she is. You can also put Donovan or Wade in there. They can smell it."

Dana raised an eyebrow, then sent Wade in to literally sniff out the situation, before telling Eleri and Donovan to get the hell out. That was it. Just in a heartbeat, she had leave time to go see her Grandmere. And she found she needed it.

It took an hour to get a rental car, and the only place to eat while they waited was . . . The Waffle Pit. But driving to her Grandmere's house, Donovan reading and researching on his tablet in the passenger seat, already made her feel lighter.

It was close to midnight as they pulled up to the house without a phone. A rundown, older home in the Lower Ninth Ward, it was a memory Eleri hadn't visited in forever. She would have wondered if her Grandmere was even here, except she *knew* that she was. She was also relatively confident Grandmere had been expecting their arrival since the time it had been decided they would leave, maybe even before they knew it themselves.

Something in the air here felt right. She'd needed this.

As she unbuckled her seatbelt, Donovan did the same. He'd been watching the houses with fascination as they drove through the patchwork neighborhood. This area had been under more than ten feet of water during Hurricane Katrina. Some houses were rebuilt, though not most. Some lots hosted new, brightly colored modular homes on stilts. Those had been brought in by celebs and charities. Some lots were just eerily blank, while others had sagging structures still sporting marks from the immediate post-hurricane rescue work. The house next door to Grandmere's still had black words spray painted on the front, "Power and gass off." Eleri almost loved that "gas" was misspelled.

She stepped out of the door, breathing in the heavy air that felt like home. Her heart settled in her chest in a way she hadn't known was so necessary to her well-being.

Donovan stood too, closing his car door and looking at her over the top of the small SUV. He looked down at her—normal, given their height difference. "I figured it out. The woman in the woods. What was off. She wasn't escaping. She wasn't afraid. I think she's the killer."

12

E leri was still looking at Donovan, digesting the idea he'd just thrown at her, when she felt her Grandmere around her. Arms hugging her tightly, making a circle of safety and comfort and home. It wasn't the place so much as the woman.

"Grandmere!" Eleri turned into the hug, feeling like a kid again. She held onto Grandmere with everything she had, giving and taking in a way that was usually shut off to her.

"Hello, Donovan," Grandmere said over Eleri's head. No one questioned that Grandmere knew his name. She'd sent him gifts in the past, known things about him that Eleri had only just found out herself.

In a moment, when she and Eleri broke apart, Grandmere turned her immense personality on to Donovan. He was soon enveloped in a hug that he—unlike Eleri—resisted. She could see him stiffen as Grandmere held on tighter.

Eleri watched, wondering what would happen, but her money was on Grandmere. In a handful of tense seconds, that played out. Even Donovan broke and hugged the woman back, looking like he was melting into her hold. For the first time, Eleri put pieces together. His mother had probably hugged him, but she'd died when he was very young. His father hadn't touched at all, not in a positive way. From what she'd seen, his father didn't stay cold—no, he'd hit. Who told Donovan he was okay?

She'd done it some, but in an offhanded way. Not like this. Not like Grandmere had. She'd sensed he needed it and she delivered. As Eleri watched, the hug ended with Donovan looking decidedly more relaxed. Before she could think, her Grandmere turned to her.

"Where is the brown wolf? Why did you not bring him?"

Of course, Grandmere knew about Wade. Not that she'd ever met him. Eleri wasn't even sure if she'd ever mentioned him. "He's working with the team, Grandmere."

The old woman nodded, deep, dark skin showing lines but looking far younger than her actual years. Grandmere had to at least be in her nineties; Eleri was always astounded at the number when she tried to add it up. Grandmere was actually Eleri's great grand-mother. Her own mother, Nathalie, had been twenty-five when Eleri came along. Her grandmother—the first Emmaline—had been in her teens and left Nathalie on Grandmere's doorstep before promptly disappearing. That math put Grandmere possibly cracking the triple digits. She didn't look it.

There was a smile and a turn and a casual gesture inside. Donovan raised his eyebrows as Eleri grabbed her bag. She just nodded. He didn't know it yet, but he wanted to stay at Grandmere's.

Inside, the place smelled like her childhood summers, both before and after Emmaline disappeared. It smelled like comfort food and lemon cleaner and an underlay of scents Eleri could never fully place —herbs, fire, broken rock, woods, sun, and more.

She bet Donovan could pick pieces out of it. She didn't ask, just turned and watched as he took in the tiny house. It was cramped with furniture too old to be nice, but not old enough to be antique. Things came in shades of faded bright blues, oranges, reds, nature-style greens and gold. Somehow it all worked.

In moments, Grandmere had them sorted into the three tiny bedrooms the place sported, and Donovan didn't comment on the single, compact bath. When Eleri emerged from unpacking her bag into the drawer—a compulsion as she was probably only staying a single night—she'd sat on the end of the small bed and stared across the room. She'd done this every time she arrived. The other twin bed belonged to Emmaline. The other drawer, the lower one, also belonged to her little sister. Eleri had insisted she was taller and deserved the upper drawer. It had been bitchy, sure, but looking back through years of guilt, she could see that she had been a normal kid.

For years, she had stared at the other bed and known that Emmaline was out there. Eleri had believed the distance was temporary. But then, when she was nineteen, she'd woken cold in the middle of the night and seen her sister. Not a big deal, as she'd been "seeing" her sister all along.

But that night she'd known. What she saw was not a projection of a living Emmaline, but the end. Eleri had cried the next time she came here. Grandmere had held her. Neither had spoken but both had known. Now, she stared until she almost broke. The bed stayed empty, neatly made, somehow dust free. Her only recourse was to leave, the feelings were too powerful despite the fact that she'd sat there for only a minute or two.

She ventured into the kitchen, finding Donovan at the table with Grandmere. He ate a hearty beef stew and steaming bread despite the heat that pervaded the city. A tall glass of ice water sat by his hand. Grandmere ate only a buttered piece of bread. She stood when Eleri entered the room, acting as though it were merely noon instead of well past midnight. Without speaking, she served Eleri a much smaller bowl of the stew and a single slice of the bread then silently added another ladleful to Donovan's bowl.

Only as she sat back down again did she speak. "Your Donovan has been researching me." She ignored the choking sound Donovan made as he swallowed wrong in surprise. "Apparently, I'm on the internet. I didn't know that."

Eleri felt her eyes go round in surprise. Donovan got himself together.

It was Grandmere who spoke, asking him, "What did you do? Something like an ancestry search?"

"No, in Eleri's file. Her mother's name is listed and it has her maiden name. So I looked her up." He took another bite, though he still looked a bit disconcerted. "Nathalie Remy Eames pings a *lot* of charity connections, but it also links to Nynette Remy of New Orleans. That's how I found you, Mrs. Remy."

"Oh honey," the old woman put a hand on his arm, "you can call me Grandmere, too." Then she pushed her head out a little, sniffed the air at him a bit.

Eleri found that funny. Someone sniffing at Donovan for a change, but she didn't get to laugh. Grandmere was speaking to him.

"You smell like a wolf, and they aren't all decent people like you."

Her pause was brief and knowing. "You've met them. You knew that before you knew there were decent ones. Which makes your accomplishments all that much more impressive." She reached into her pocket and pulled something out which she pushed into Donovan's palm without revealing what it was.

"You carry this with you. It's not from me. It's from your people in Europe. One of them handed it to me about three years ago, told me I'd know who to give it to. I've known a while now, but I wanted to give it to you in person." She folded his fingers over it, preserving the mystery. "You keep it on you."

He nodded as though that wasn't as strange as it actually was.

Eleri remembered Grandmere was always giving or selling trinkets to people who stopped by. Sometimes she talked with them for hours, sending her granddaughters out to play. But she'd not given them to Eleri before. In fact, she'd rarely even spoken to Eleri about any of it.

Eleri frowned, then asked Donovan, "You're just taking a weird token from someone in Europe, through an old woman you've never met before?" Because when she thought about it that way, it was beyond odd.

"She's your family, Eleri, so it's not that strange. And she's not any old—" he stopped himself, "—she's not just anybody. You know this. She's Nynette Remy."

Sure, she was. Eleri nodded but didn't say anything and Donovan seemed to realize something. He spoke again. "Nynette Remy is considered the highest ranked voodoo priestess alive today in the U.S."

Eleri froze.

Sure, her great grandmother practiced the old ways. When Eleri was in her early twenties she'd looked up references to Aida Weddo and the prayers Grandmere had incanted over them. She'd thought it was much the same as the ones she got at church, just a different religion. Voodoo was something many people practiced, especially in New Orleans. And her mother had told her Grandmere was crazy, believing in things that didn't exist. Eleri had somewhat dismissed it. She'd floated between belief and the unquestioning acceptance that came from it being part of her childhood. It was just the way things were. She hadn't looked further.

"Eleri," Donovan spoke softly, his spoon no longer moving.

"You're the direct descendant of the Remys. The most powerful Voodoo family ever in the US. Stronger than Marie Laveau."

"She was all show," Grandmere scoffed, as though she'd been there.

Eleri looked back and forth between her great-grandmother and Donovan.

"Your talents aren't random," he told her.

"Oh, she doesn't know the half of it. Nathalie didn't want any part of it, so she raised her girls far away in a little white church and a big, sprawling house. But that didn't change what you are." Grandmere took her hand, the heat between them feeling stronger than before, though Eleri had no idea if that was real or her imagination.

She didn't know how to respond. She'd come here thinking she would relax for the night, be *home* in a way she hadn't been in a long time. She was not prepared for family secrets to come clawing their way to the surface. But they weren't secrets—it seemed everyone knew but her. She turned to Donovan, "You knew? You didn't say anything?"

"Why would I? I only recently put it together that *you* didn't. I didn't start digging until the notes came, until the second time your Grandmere pegged our operations. She was right. We needed to trust GJ. She helped crack that case."

Eleri nodded, her brain fleetingly wondering where GJ Janson had gone off to. Wherever it was, Special Agent in Charge Derek Westerfield was keeping tabs on her. He did not like that Eleri and Donovan had let the grad student get mixed up in their previous case, though Eleri thought GJ Janson had been at the heart of things even before they'd gotten there. GJ had tangled herself into things.

"You don't go blaming him." Grandmere patted her hand, bringing her thoughts back to the now. "It's time."

"Time?" Eleri asked. What had she walked into? Her only consolation was that she trusted her Grandmere.

"You're ready. You're here to pick up the pieces that your mother wouldn't. You have gifts she didn't."

She must have looked horribly confused.

Grandmere patted her hand again. "No, you aren't my successor, as much as I would have liked that. It should have been Emmaline. Instead, I have found another. You have cousins. One is powerful. He will follow in my stead. You are yourself with your own place in this world. You will help many. Save many. But it's time."

Grandmere popped up from her seat. "It's time for ice cream." She picked up the bowls in front of each of them and carried them to the sink, leaving Eleri and Donovan staring at each other as though the old woman was crazy.

"We always have ice cream after dinner," Eleri told him. It was inane, but the only thing she could think of to say.

Grandmere returned with a small container and three spoons.

"This isn't your usual brand," Eleri commented as Grandmere screwed off the top. The woman was a bit of a connoisseur when it came to ice cream. Maybe that was an element of living in the hot south without air conditioning.

"Oh, it's gelato. It's terribly expensive, but I'm living large in my old age." She smiled.

The three of them dug in, clearing the pint-sized container in no time. They ate as though her Grandmere hadn't just delivered a statement worthy of a prophecy. Standing, the old woman screwed the cap onto the empty jar and tossed it into recycling. Eleri wondered if Donovan was right, that Grandmere was some high-priestess. But that couldn't be right. Grandmere was oddly normal. She liked Magic Eraser sponges. She recycled. She didn't have a phone, never had. Never had air conditioning in the house and refused when Eleri offered to buy it for her. She wasn't some priestess—she was just your standard, eccentric old woman. Those were a dime a dozen.

Except she wasn't. In the next sentence, she proved it.

"I know it's time. And you do, too. You've been dreaming of the house, haven't you?"

13

Donovan pulled up in the rented SUV and parked near the minivan where Dana and the others were just exiting the vehicle. Eleri had slept most of the two hours on the way to Alexandria, Louisiana, forfeiting her right to the steering wheel. No wonder, she'd seemed a bit shell-shocked.

When Donovan researched her Grandmere, he found some very interesting things. But he thought she already knew them; he hadn't been holding out. Still, he'd gone to bed after the ice cream and the bomb Grandmere had dropped.

Eleri had mentioned repeated dreams about an odd house, but that had been a while ago. Apparently, she was still having them. Before he left the room, he'd leaned over and told his partner, "Be sure to tell her about the other night when you woke up on the floor with your white clothes in a pentagram around you."

Eleri glared at him. Maybe she thought he hadn't noticed at the time? But neatnick Eleri sleeping on the floor in a room that looked like it had been searched for cocaine? It had only taken a minute to realize she was sleeping in the center of a cleared circle with white clothes forming a five-point star. It would have taken more effort for him to miss that than to see it.

Now he reached across the car and pushed at her shoulder gently. "We're here. Time to get back at it."

Donovan didn't worry about the fact that she was operating on two or less hours of sleep. No one graduated Quantico well rested.

She looked up at him from where she'd curled in to the corner, using the tension of the seatbelt as a pillow. Her eyes were fuzzy, but she managed to get out a full-fledged "dammit" before she sat up and shook the rest of her clouds out of her brain. "I should have been reading up on the way here."

"No, you shouldn't. We'll go in cold, but we'll go in alert. That's more important." There'd been another murder. His heart sank each time he let himself think about it.

Each murder was a personal failure. Chasing serial killers put agents in the looney bin. Eleri had already been there once. He didn't think this was necessarily the best case for her. It occurred to him that might be the reasoning behind Westerfield putting them in such a big group. Serial killer cases needed as many brains working on them as possible. Anything that triggered a NightShade investigation needed more. Maybe it wasn't punishment that they were working under Dana Brantley, maybe it was protection. Donovan liked this vision of a kinder, gentler Westerfield. He just didn't fully believe it. And the painful twist in his gut didn't go away. Another person was dead.

For a moment, he thought about going back to being a medical examiner. He'd have to move somewhere new. His old position had been permanently filled. At least there he'd never been responsible for anyone's death. Now he was responsible for so many. He was tasked with finding justice for the dead, just like before, but now he also needed to keep the living alive. The race against the clock killed him. The clock had been turned on at Leroy Arvad's house, and it had just started counting faster.

He looked to Dana and stated facts, not excuses. "We got in the car as soon as you called. I was driving, Eleri was asleep. Her grandmother kept her up all night. Bring us up to speed?"

Dana only nodded. No berating them. "Body is in that apartment building there."

He saw a cluster of two- and three-story dwellings, but one had a fire truck and a handful of men in thick yellow pants milling around out front. One unit in that building had a doorway that was blackened almost to ash. Donovan shook his head. "Fire?"

"Yes. Somehow contained only to the apartment it occurred in.

Aside from some smell, there's not an ounce of visible damage in the surrounding units." Dana let that sit between them for a moment.

It was Eleri who asked the obvious question. "How is that even possible?"

Dana sighed. "I'm hoping you can tell us."

"No pressure there," Eleri muttered, but Donovan didn't think Dana could hear it.

Dana led them in, past the firefighters. Though they looked at her with questions, she stayed silent. Her closed lips and her lightweight navy, pinstripe suit declared to all the world that she was a fed. Christina came in behind her, dark pressed slacks, white button-down shirt, hair up, closed-mouthed, adding to that image. Then there was Wade—khakis (slightly not pressed) and a plaid shirt. Eleri at least always looked expensive. Probably from her upbringing. Even her white t-shirts looked nicer than anyone else's. Donovan, on the other hand, had worked hard to look like a professional. To not look like his father. Only in the later years did he realize it wasn't the dirt under his nails or the rips in his jeans that made his father look low-class. It was the way he carried himself, the unwarranted arrogance, the anger that radiated off him from the circumstances he'd never admit he created himself. Still, Donovan wore nice pants and dry-cleaned his shirts. Anything he could do to distance himself from his past, he would.

They climbed a single flight of steps, though the building went up to a third floor. The apartment that had been burned was sandwiched right in the middle of several others. How had none of the nearby units suffered fire damage?

Dana waited until they got inside the front door and snapped on gloves. She also pulled out a stack of face masks and started handing them out to the others. Donovan slipped the small nose and mouth filter onto his face, though it hardly accomplished anything other than looking like he was at least trying. He turned to Eleri out of habit, then reoriented himself to speak to Dana. "This is even fresher. How did they get the fire out so fast?"

Dana sighed the sigh of the weary. "That's just it. They didn't."

"What?" This time it was Wade asking even as he reached gloved fingers out toward a blackened wall. Slowly, he closed the distance and touched what should have been coal hot.

Donovan raised his eyebrows at his friend.

"Nothing." Wade shrugged, flattening his whole hand against the dead and almost crumbling ash of the drywall. "I mean it's *warm*—"

By then Donovan had both his hands on the wall and so did Christina. All were looking at each other in awe.

"—but it's not even close to hot."

Dana shook her head again. "The neighbor swears that Mrs. Orlov went out for groceries at ten a.m. Just like she does every day. She came back with three bags. Which the neighbor says is not normal— she usually only has one."

"That's why you think the neighbor is accurate," Eleri commented. "But the extra grocery bags make today unusual. She hit the store every morning? Who does that?"

"Old Russian lady," Dana answered without looking at Donovan's partner. She moved to a new section of wall, then another, touching each flat handed and still marveling that it wasn't hot. "Apparently, she's still in the habit of buying each day's supper on the day she makes it."

"So, that part's not unusual for her, except for the extra bags. Something big planned?" Eleri still wasn't touching the walls, Donovan noticed. "Guests?"

With a sigh of resignation, Eleri peeled her gloves and reached out to touch the wall for herself. This time, Donovan noticed as she stood there, waiting, the paneling wasn't wet. The fire department had found no stray embers, no sparks, no wiring problems, and stumped, they'd left it untouched for the feds. Though, clearly, they hadn't left.

Gennida Orlov's body lay untouched in the middle of the room. She lay on her back, eyes open, staring at the ceiling. Donovan looked at it, only half noticing Christina standing guard in the doorway, Wade sniffing his way around the room, Eleri walking slowly, touching everything that she could.

He checked the air, though he didn't need to.

"Smells the same?" Dana asked.

"Yes." He and Wade said it at the same time. It was Donovan who added, "It's got that hydrogen smell again. That . . . *fizz* of explosion. Though there's clearly no explosion here. This is as controlled of a burn as I've ever seen."

"Guests." Eleri said the one word as she touched what was left of the couch. It was outside the oval that protected Gennida Orlov. "She had guests."

Donovan ran back outside, subtly sniffing and checking the stairs. While the woman could have come up another set, he could tell Gennida Orlov used these stairs almost right up to her doorway every day. She'd done the same today, though she was alone.

The firefighters were watching the doorway—all that they could see of the burned shell of an apartment. They were probably just hanging out because of the complete oddity of the case. It took Donovan a moment to figure it out, but he decided to look like he was visually inspecting the stairs as that was plausible. He looked, too, but mostly he got his face close to the railing and while he tilted his head as though checking the light, he inhaled deeply.

He smelled firefighters—men, sweat, old gear with the scent of fires past—and residents. The residents were some older people, reeking of medications, and some younger. Some children. But . . . He stepped up a few more steps and got down on his hands and knees on the steps, then back up as though closely inspecting the handrail. She would have touched it probably, maybe trailed her hand along it as she climbed. Bare skin touching painted metal and leaving a trace of scent. And . . . there she was.

The woman.

Turning, feeling dumb for thinking of it so late, he scanned the crowd. He spotted a few women from other apartments. He called Eleri out and pulled her down as though showing her something on the staircase. "She was here. The woman from the Arvad house."

"You smell her?" Eleri looked at him sharply before going back to the game of pretending they were looking at the textured steps staring at evidence instead of old gum.

"Yes, she was here. And this scene is new enough that we need to keep an eye out for her. Arsonists often come back to survey their work." It was Arson 101 and he felt dumb for not checking faces better when they came in.

Eleri's hand touched his arm. "We didn't think of it, because we usually come in long after the fire's out. Any lookie-loos are usually gone. So don't beat yourself up, just tell me what you have."

He told her about the three women he saw in the crowd that might potentially be *her* and watched Eleri's face as she surreptitiously spotted each of them and nodded. He added, "We need to keep track of them."

"Let's go one better." Eleri stood up, motioning him to follow and headed down the stairs. They watched carefully but no one fled. It would have been a dumb thing to do and too lucky for them if someone did.

Eleri walked into the crowd and Donovan followed. She moved around, introducing herself and shaking hands and asking questions. She gathered the apartment dwellers and the watching crowd into a tight group, pushing the firefighters—probably not their suspect and not female—to the back of the crowd.

As Eleri asked them what they'd seen, if any visitors had gone into Mrs. Orlov's home or come out of it, Donovan followed along, slowly inhaling.

No one had seen anyone come in or out. One man had been sitting on the bench in the playground area that was visible to the front door. He'd even been facing it. Just sitting and watching his kids play on the jungle gym. He'd seen Mrs. Orlov. He even correctly answered how many bags of groceries she was carrying. Then he noticed that there was smoke coming out of her door. He called 911 and ran up the steps but the firefighters were already there, pushing him back. Telling him to let them do their jobs.

Eleri thanked the crowd as they'd gotten around to everyone. Then she turned to Donovan as they climbed the stairs, out of earshot of anyone but a wolf.

"I didn't sense anyone who'd been up here."

"None of them were her." He wanted to shake his head, but knew not to give away anything to onlookers. It was part of the steely demeanor that earned the feds their reputation, but it was based on necessity, not appearances, he'd learned.

Turning to his partner, he asked about the one man's comment. "He said the firefighters were already there when he got up the steps. He'd just called but there they were. That doesn't seem right."

"Maybe they'd already been called?" Eleri shrugged and he watched her play out scenarios. "Maybe he wasn't as brave as he wants us to believe, and he waited for them to arrive before making a show of running in. You're right, it doesn't add up, but it isn't necessarily sinister. He wasn't lying per se."

"They were all telling the truth as far as I could tell," Eleri added, also not giving in to the shrug he could tell she wanted to make.

He agreed and spoke as he crossed the threshold, past the door the firefighters had broken through to get inside. Dana looked up at his words.

"The crowd was excited, but not anxious, not the way someone gets when they lie." He looked at her. "We just checked the people out front. Our woman was here. She went up or down the steps, maybe both. But she's not here anymore and no one who is saw anything. Maybe she was waiting for Mrs. Orlov?"

"We've got a bigger problem here." Dana sighed. "I'm getting concerned that there's a poison we don't know about at play. Again, our victim died of nothing. She simply ceased to live. Just like the other one."

Donovan frowned at her, not putting together the pieces that were clearly bothering Dana. A lot.

"I'm starting to think it might be infectious."

Eleri sucked in a breath, then immediately regretted it. "That would mean we're all at risk."

14

Eleri paced the room, though "room" was a generous term. It was the biggest one the hotel in Alexandria had. Dana moved them from single rooms to a suite, claiming she and Eleri and Donovan had enough expertise in biology and medicine to keep an eye out for symptoms. She'd argued, "We all need to be together."

Eleri had responded with, "Why? Donovan has the most medical training and he prefers dead people. He is *not* the doctor you want watching over you."

After the words tumbled angrily out of her mouth, she winced. She turned to Donovan and the look of mirth on his face was the only thing that kept her from saying, "No offense," a term that literally meant the opposite.

Dana didn't budge.

They had quickly abandoned their old hotel rooms, Dana leaving strict "Do not disturb" orders and flashing her badge. She didn't say "infectious disease" but did everything she could to stop anyone from going in there. Then she said she was going to call Westerfield.

Eleri had jumped. "Wait. I know someone."

Dana raised an eyebrow. Christina just sat, taking everything in, looking as grim as the rest of them, but not saying anything. Eleri wanted to yell at her. At first it had been nice to have Christina stay quiet, but it was beginning to verge on creepy now. What did she know? What did she feel? Eleri wanted to shout, "Just say *something!*" but she held that in, too.

Instead, she focused on Dana, as it was her senior agent who needed convincing. "I know a pair of infectious disease specialists at the CDC. They can at least talk us through the early evaluation. Otherwise, Westerfield is going to call in a team and lock us down and test the hell out of us and the bodies. We don't even know if we're on the right track yet." She paused but clearly hadn't convinced Dana yet. "These two are CDC. Top national clearance. They hunt diseases."

She kept babbling in an effort to avoid the Westerfield/lockdown scenario. Westerfield had no medical background. He'd toss the key, hand the whole case to another team, and then apologize after three months of full quarantine when the five of them clearly had nothing. Eleri would likely have gone full Donner Party by then. The only question was would she eat Dana first or Christina? Eleri pushed the thought aside and ran her mouth. "I did an internship at the CDC with them. Two actually, as part of my graduate degree. I'm not an infectious disease expert by any means, but I don't think we need to do the full lockdown yet. I don't even think it's an infectious disease. Let's ask them before we go nuts."

Dana finally conceded to the phone call and agreed to follow expert advice.

So Eleri pulled the number and paced the floor with the phone to her ear. Of course it was after 5pm in Atlanta. Of course even when she got through to the office, they weren't there. No, she didn't want to leave a message. Yes, she wanted to page them. Yes, it was an emergency.

Then she hung up and waited while the rest of the group sat there staring at her. There was no need to explain. The room wasn't big enough for anyone not to have overheard exactly what she said.

She turned to Dana again. "They're very trustworthy. Best of the best. They almost converted me out of forensics and chemistry."

That was it. She was out of things to say—things that would help her cause, at least. Anything more she said would only make her look like an idiot. It took fifteen minutes for them to call back. During that time Dana orchestrated an order of Chinese food, paid by card and told the driver to deliver it to the hotel room and knock but just leave the food at the door.

Nope, nothing suspicious here. Move it along. Nothing to see.

Eleri was grateful when her phone finally rang. "Hello?"

"Eleri!"

"Jordan!" She was shocked by the relief coursing through her system just at hearing his voice. Dr. Jordan Abellard would tell them it was nothing. She believed that. "How are you? And Jillian? Is she with you?"

He laughed. "They rarely send us in different directions anymore. We're good." There was just a beat of a pause. "But you contacted us 'urgent.' What's going on?"

"A case." She'd stayed in touch with them enough in the intervening years. They didn't know about her stay in the mental hospital, but they knew she was an FBI agent. "This is high order clearance. Is this line secure?"

"No. Shit." She heard him talking to his wife, Dr. Jillian Brookwood in the background. "Give us five minutes."

He hung up. Eleri wasn't offended. He was right. There was nothing left to say if his line wasn't secure. Three minutes later, her phone rang again. "Jordan?"

"Jillian this time. Good to hear your voice." Eleri could hear the cautious smile. "We've got you on speaker. The line is secured and we are in a secured location. You?"

Again, Eleri breathed easier. In their lab, though she'd been a lowly grad student, they'd taught her everything they could in the two terms she stayed. She did chemistry panels for them. Ran toxicology tests. In return, they taught her to ID known infectious diseases and map their spread. They showed her what emerging diseases looked like when no one yet knew what they were. And when the budget allowed, they took her on field cases with them. She'd been a disease hunter for a short period of time, and it had been wonderful. The husband and wife team were excellent mentors. And now she needed them.

"We're okay. All physically healthy right now. No one has any signs or symptoms. And one of our team is an M.D.—though he's a medical examiner." She introduced the team, leaving out their skills. Drs. Brookwood and Abellard were not part of NightShade and no one beyond Westerfield's team knew what Westerfield's team was capable of.

She explained the bodies, the lack of cause of death, the fire exposure. Dana opened her eyes wide, as though Eleri might give away the details of the odd fires. Eleri had enough, her own eyes narrowed in response, but at least Dana sat back a little. She sighed. "We've ruled out just about everything else. Infectious disease is what we have left."

"You have a killer using a disease to take people out?" Jillian turned it over. Her tone gave away her skepticism and for that, Eleri was grateful. "That seems unlikely." She paused. "What's the time-frame for the death?"

Eleri looked around at everyone, but no one knew. Finally, it was Dana who spoke.

"Hello, Agent Dana Brantley speaking. It's fast, whatever it is. And I don't have any evidence that it's a disease, but we also don't see any evidence for anything else."

"How fast?"

Eleri grinned. That was just like Jillian, such a logical mathematical mind. They all shrugged until Dana said, "Probably a matter of minutes. Thirty minutes at the high end. But that's a guess."

She paused and said, "We really have no idea, but it seemed safer to quarantine."

"It's always safer to quarantine," Jillian replied, the words rolling off her tongue as though she'd said them a thousand times. Eleri imagined she probably had.

There were murmurs on the other end of the line and Jordan came back on. "Sit tight. Follow quarantine, and we'll be there tomorrow by two. Is that okay?"

Eleri was starting to answer him when a knock came at the door.

"What's that?" Jordan asked.

"Chinese food."

"I thought you understood how to run a quarantine," he chided her, but Eleri laughed.

"It's all set up. No contact, we won't open the door until he leaves. He can pass germs to us, but not the other way around. And we get dinner."

"All right. Hang on to that. We'll be there tomorrow."

They quickly said goodbye and hung up. Eleri watched as Dana began parsing out too many food containers to fit on the table. That was probably fine, none of them fit in here anyway.

Dinner was a quiet affair—no one wanted to be stuck and

everyone was trying to be polite until 2 pm the next day, and it was already difficult.

Dana had sorted them into the two bedrooms. Wade and Donovan in one, Eleri and Christina in the other and Dana on the pull-out couch in the middle. Eleri stayed up late, forcing herself to seem awake so she could talk to Dana without the others around. Probably they all realized what she was doing, but did they know why?

"Dana, what safeguards do you have on Christina?" Eleri asked point blank. She wasn't excited about having the woman as a room-mate, but she tried not to let that get in the way.

"Same as the rest of you." Dana had enough nerve to look a bit offended.

"You need more." Eleri stayed on point despite Dana's narrowed eyes. "She can convince you she's here and walk right out the door."

"She won't." Dana seemed very assured.

"That's good. You've been through quarantine with her before then?"

"No, but—"

"That's the problem. Quarantine is scary. People crack—"

"She won't crack. She's one of us, despite the cold shoulder you all have been giving her." Dana's lips thinned.

"People crack," Eleri repeated. "Good people crack. People you would least expect it from, they crack. So we watch them carefully. But we can't really watch her, can we?"

Dana paused. To her credit, she thought it through. She was rigid, but not completely inflexible. Eleri was coming to appreciate that. "Not entirely. There's a certain element with Christina, you just have to trust her."

"And you believe she's trustworthy?"

"Yes." Dana was adamant.

"And *you* believe that you actually believe that?" Eleri pressed, making her point.

"I do." There was no hesitation. "If you let her work you over— and I know, it sucks—you'll start to find the loopholes. She's good. Very good, but it's not complete. Any time you get stuck, any time you wonder, stop and see if the smells are right, quickly check a texture, a taste, she'll have missed something."

Or you'll think she has. Eleri didn't say it. She only nodded. There were loopholes in Dana's loophole theory. But Eleri believed strongly that terrorists rarely happened on their own; they were made. It was hard to convince a reasonable person to actively turn against another unless that other had instigated something in the past. Eleri wasn't going to do that. She only thanked Dana for her time and headed into the room, trying to figure out how to be friends with the reticent Christina. She had to figure out how to do it sincerely, too.

In the room, Christina lifted her head and asked, "Did you get what you needed?"

So, not that subtle after all. "No, not really," Eleri answered truthfully. "I'm sorry but I'm not tired, and it looks like Dana is. I can be awake out there with her, or send her in here so you can both sleep, but I don't—"

"She won't do it. She's standing guard." Christina sounded fully awake.

"That's what I thought." Eleri sat on the bed. "I'll be quiet."

"No worries, I'm up anyway. Hard to sleep when you think you might be dying of a deadly disease."

"I honestly don't think we are," Eleri offered. "It doesn't make sense. I think Dana's just at the last thing and has to rule it out."

"Really?" Christina sat up, her fear seeming to overtake her no-talking-unless-spoken-to rule.

"Sure. Whatever it was, it killed them pretty fast. Faster than eight hours—which is how long it has been since we stood over today's body. Plus, we stood over previous bodies, even cut one open, and didn't catch anything. None of us." The relief that grew on Christina's face kept Eleri talking. "Dana's only real point in favor of disease is that if it was delivered in some form that killed them. Thus we may have gotten smaller, non-lethal doses and be carrying it. For example, maybe the victims had to inhale it and we only touched it. Or it's possible that it's highly transmissible, but their death killed it too, or the fire did. The odds are pretty low on this one."

Christina was nodding, color coming back into her face and for the first time, Eleri realized it had been missing. She offered some reassurance. "It's going to be okay. All my money is on that. Donovan, too. Do you not know this?"

Christina shook her head. "Nope. All you science geeks out there confuse me."

"You're not a science nerd?" Eleri was shocked. Well, shit. She should have paid more attention. The quiet Christina had been riding the assumptions Eleri and Donovan and Wade had been making about her.

"Math and Business," Christina volunteered, making Eleri wonder if it was the first thing she'd volunteered ever.

"You should have a good time chatting equations with Wade, then." Eleri paused. "Was that enough information to help you get to sleep?"

"Nope. I'm awake now." Christina shrugged.

"I have video from the gate at Burt Riser's subdivision. Do you want to watch hours of unimportant cars wait while a gate opens? A second set of eyes is always helpful."

"Sure. Sounds super exciting. Do you want chocolate? I have a stash."

"Well, well. Still waters," Eleri commented. "And yes, I want chocolate."

Christina was doing better. Eleri continued to hold her tongue that Dana knew all the things Eleri did about infectious diseases. So why was she quarantining them, despite Eleri's clear argument against it? They were losing investigation time, just when things were rolling. Was Dana doing to her what she'd just done to Christina? Doling out facts but holding back the real opinion?

Because Dana Brantley could touch a body and *feel* what was in there. What did she know that she wasn't saying?

15

The next morning, Donovan sat through the most uncomfortable round-table he thought he'd ever been at. And he'd sat at tables where medical examiners had been raked over the coals for missing a murder, or accusing parents of abuse that hadn't happened. This was simply more awkward.

Five adults, two bathrooms, one tiny living area with a table not big enough for all of them, a mini-fridge, a microwave, and a coffee pot. Plus, they were all squirrely about whatever Drs. Brookwood and Abellard might find.

Dana, of course, would not just let the morning roll by. No. They had to have regimented time. Donovan reminded himself he was not in charge. In fact, he hadn't been in charge since the day he left the M.E.'s office. While that job hadn't been any carte blanche situation, it wasn't Dana's preschool time schedule either. He spent only a brief moment appreciating Eleri's leadership style before he was told it was his rotation for the shower and that he should eat breakfast thereafter. He was given three options for food.

Fighting the urge to put his fingers in the air in the "I'm listening, teacher" signal, he tamped down the accompanying sigh and took his shower. He was grateful that, at least there, he got to be alone.

After he'd milked that time as much as he could, he emerged to find that the overpowering smell of Chinese food wasn't just from not being able to throw out any trash last night. Eleri was microwaving wonton soup for breakfast. Christina was right behind her, looking skeptical as Eleri seemed to walk her through it, but almost smiling. Donovan blinked. Had Eleri made a friend? Out of can't-tell-if-reality-is-real Christina?

He'd opted for breakfast sandwiches. Three of them. And a large orange juice. It wasn't his favorite—fruits and vegetables generally weren't—and he told himself his differing physiology made his bad diet acceptable. He wasn't up for milk, though. Didn't want coffee. Wonton soup was not his liquid of choice, probably ever.

Dana accepted two deliveries at the door the same as last night—a knock and leave them by the door. Tip was delivered over the credit card, nothing they touched would leave the room. In fact, none of them even stepped foot outside. They broke quarantine only long enough to reach an arm into the hallway and grab the food bag. That happened only after Donovan or Wade listened at the door and made sure the hall was clear. It wasn't a true quarantine, which actually reassured him, but didn't do anything to get him out of this room.

He sighed as he opened the bag of biscuits filled with bacon, ham, cheese, and eggs. The smells co-mingled with the Chinese in an odd way. He was grateful that smells weren't "bad" to him; it was probably a pretty off-putting mix otherwise.

Wade reached into the bag even before Donovan could and stole two of the biscuits. With a coffee in hand, he returned to his spot, never having spoken a word. Donovan went back to his seat, too. He ate first, knowing that biscuit crumbs and computers didn't mix. It was a realization Wade came to too late if the mild swearing and brushing at the keyboard was any indication.

Donovan would have wanted to sit back, eat, enjoy the flavors—even though they ran a little to the plasticky side—and smell the air. He would have liked to go out onto the balcony. He would have liked to be anywhere but in this stuffy room, where Dana had to be talked into using the thermostat. Wade had to explain the closed air system, how each room could control its own temperature and so on, before she would agree. None of it mattered in the end; he was still uncomfortable. So Donovan ate quickly, the tightness in his chest not easing as he opened his files and tried to find connections. Taking a note from Eleri's playbook, he pulled up a pad of paper and started making spider maps of any connections he could find.

An hour later, he had lots of circles, but no more than a few lines connecting them.

Eleri and Christina had tapped out for a mid-morning nap, claiming they'd been up late watching video. They watched it all again this morning and—bleary-eyed—declared it no more helpful than before.

Neither Leroy nor LeighAnn Arvad connected to anything in the other cases. Nothing. Not a relative, not a former job, nothing. The only thing Donovan could find that came close was that Leroy ran a delivery line that went from a city that was about two hours from the general area of the country that the first four deaths had occurred in back to Louisiana. That was it. It was nothing.

He told Dana exactly that.

What he didn't tell her was the feeling that Leroy Arvad was incidental. He was starting to think that the long-haul trucker had been used for transport and that the other victim in the area, Gennida Orlov, was the real intended victim.

He had nothing to tie this together, nothing he could put a finger on, anyway. Also his theory had a lot of holes. He played it out.

"Hey, Wade." He waited until the other man looked up. "How big would this flamethrower be?"

"I was actually just calculating that . . ." He tipped his head side to side as he looked back down at the page. Donovan had no doubt it was covered in equations and conversions he'd looked up online. Probably how much hydrogen was necessary to convert to a certain quantity of heat. Wade had probably calculated a per BTU number.

"I've got another question. Could it be a person? A skill, like we have?" Donovan felt the room go cold. Had no one else considered that?

Everyone stopped, only Wade stayed in motion, tipping his head back and forth a little as though that helped the thoughts roll around. "I mean it *could* be."

Dana was on her feet, as if that was necessary in the tiny space. She asked contradictory questions all at once. "It could? But why not?"

Wade sighed. "Well, I've met a lot of NightShade agents and I've never heard of it." He paused, more thoughts rolling through his head. "It could be a skill, but it could be a real flamethrower. I think I can build one. And while someone with this skill could exist... I've never run into them. I don't see people with Eleri's skill out there committing crimes. I don't see people like Christina robbing banks. We're weird, so we work really hard to stay under the radar and blend in. This is the opposite of blending in. And I think it's like Occam's Razor, too. The simplest explanation is a flame thrower."

Dana seemed to accept that and sat back down.

Donovan nodded, as did Eleri and Christina.

Wade went back to his calculations. "I'm guessing it's about the size of a leaf blower."

He kept going. "If the fuel was hydrogen, it would probably need some delivery system. An air mix, something. And a propulsion system. Carrying enough of it—compressed—would mean a tank of some kind."

"Like a scuba tank?"

"Exactly." Wade was nodding. "So this is no handheld device. Given the size of the fires we saw, I would guess it's pretty big."

Dana jumped into the conversation again. "Couldn't you just use a small one to start the fire? After that, the house itself is the fuel."

"That's true." Wade leaned forward, in his element. "But we saw the burn patterns. This wasn't an issue of starting a fire, it was about leading the fire and controlling it all the way through. Hell, it seemed to chase Burt Riser up the stairs. It was controlled enough that a few of the others had a relatively clean circle around them. So it was burning the provided fuel, *not* just starting, then burning up the house."

Dana nodded. "So how big, really?"

"Big leaf blower," Wade told her.

"Then how does he—she—" Donovan corrected himself, "—get it into Leroy Arvad's truck?"

Dana blinked at him. "You think the woman was in the truck? You're sure it's the woman?"

"I'm as close to sure as I can be. She ran away. She had the smell. She wasn't afraid—she was *excited*. That says 'killer' to me," Donovan argued.

"Alright then. She." Dana motioned with her hand. "So, you think she rode with Leroy Arvad?"

Another shrug. "It's the best I've got. The only connection from Leroy to any of the other bodies is that he drove a truck between the general areas they were in. That's it."

"What about Gennida Orlov?" Dana was asking if he was connected to the newest victim. She was the one physically closest to Leroy Arvad.

"I've got nothing between them, and I'm running into a blank connecting Gennida Orlov to anyone else, either." Donovan worried his hands together. "She was an old woman who knew all her neighbors' names and not much else. She didn't get out much. Didn't even go to church. So her connections are scarce. Now, this is where it gets interesting."

Dana leaned forward and so did Wade. For a moment, Donovan felt like he had something, only when he tugged on that string, it just yanked loose and seemed to lead to nothing. "She has only one living relative, a daughter. The daughter is Wilemina Orlov. Both of them immigrated together about twenty years ago. The daughter—Mina—was in her mid-teens at the time. They came as asylum seekers from Russia, but the reason for seeking asylum is redacted."

"Chew on that," Dana marveled. "That must be something important."

"And," Donovan added, "Mina Orlov later married one Peter Aroya and settled down in Casper, Wyoming. No one can find them. I set some analysts to finding the couple. At the very least, Mina Orlov needs to be notified about her mother. But Casper is close to Rosedeer."

"Where Leona Hiller was found," Dana mused. "What are the connections between them?"

"Nothing easy to find. The—"

"—analyst is on it," she finished for him, nodding.

It made sense. But Donovan thought it wasn't much more than a hunch without some evidence.

"Gennida Orlov was the intended victim." Eleri propped herself in the doorway to make her declaration. She probably looked rumpled there at the border of her bedroom and the main room. Surely, she looked as though she'd napped, which she had. However, it seemed her nap had helped the case more than it helped her. "All I know is that when Gennida Orlov died, it was purposeful. Leroy Arvad was a side gig. The last words he heard was a woman saying, 'I'm sorry.' So yes, Donovan, I think the killer is a woman, too."

"Let's work with that . . ." Dana then led them through trying to figure out how to get that damn flamethrower into Leroy Arvad's truck cab. Could it be done without him noticing? Could it be dismantled and reassembled?

"Can she just build a new one?" Eleri asked. All eyes turned to her.

But it was Donovan who picked up the thread. "You're suggesting she throws the old one out each time. And because she knows how to build one, she gathers the materials and does it again?"

This time, all eyes focused on Wade.

"I'd have to try it to see."

"Well, you have a fun assignment when we get out. You get to build a flamethrower. Donovan here gets to smell the truck to see if the woman was in it. Then he gets to check the path behind the Arvad house and see if we can follow it all the way to a discarded flamethrower." She turned to Eleri, "What did you and Christina get?"

"Well, first we watched the footage from Burt Riser's community around the nights he died. We looked at all the cars going through the gate. Watching paint dry would have been far more exciting. Nothing was out of the ordinary. So we checked all the license plates on the cars and mapped them to houses in the neighborhood—to see who should be closest to Burt Riser's house."

"That's a good idea." Dana smiled and Eleri was disturbed to feel the faint praise in her heart.

"Well, only three of them went close to his house in that time frame. Despite him being there for a while, you may have noticed that not all the lots are sold yet. He apparently got in early. So not too many neighbors out in his neck of the suburban jungle. Again, nothing out of the ordinary."

"Can you see who is in the cars?" Dana asked her and Eleri nodded yes. "Then follow up and match the people to the houses."

Sure, why not? She thought it sarcastically, as if she hadn't had a boring enough assignment. She didn't get a chance to respond because a knock came at the door. In an effort to keep her tongue in her head, she went to answer it, speaking *to* the door rather than opening it.

"Who is it?"

"Jordan." The familiar voice came, filling her with warmth and relief. She had once admitted having a bit of crush on the guy, though she would never have acted against Jillian and it had passed. But damn, she liked that guy.

"And Jillian!" the crisp southern accent chimed in beyond the lock. This time Eleri smiled. That accent hid a razor-sharp mind that had little time for the social frivolities her voice called to mind. This pair would have them out in no time.

"It's so good to hear your voices." She didn't open the door. "What do we have to do so we can prove we're clean and get out?"

16

Eleri wound up doing Donovan's blood draw. She hadn't wanted to do it, as her medical training was minimal. He wasn't comfortable sticking the needle into his own arm, to which she told him, "Why not? You're used to sticking dead people."

It wasn't funny.

Her smile had felt tight since she'd woken up. She was a grown woman, a professional, an agent for the Federal Bureau of Investigation, and she was sharing a bed.

Jordan and Jillian had executed protocol—aside from skipping putting "Quarantine" tape across the doorway—and passed a cooler with supplies in and out. Eleri was confident they bagged the cooler in biohazard plastic before they even touched it. Then, her brief interlude with old friends was over and she was left, still stuck in this room with four other people.

It took three hours before Jordan called her. Eleri answered the phone with a calm-sounding "Hello," that covered all the panic in her. What if Dana was right? She shouldn't be. It was just an overkill precaution, but what if she was right?

"You're clear." Jordan had done this before. He knew the best "Hello" was an "all is well."

"Me or all of us?"

"All of you, though Christina has a high white cell count and may be coming down with something. But there's no evidence of anything nefarious." There was a smile in his voice.

"Hallelujah." She transferred the information to everyone else, though they had already deduced the good news from her reactions. "We can leave?"

"We are standing right outside the door."

Hanging up, Eleri threw the door wide open and hugged first Jordan then Jillian. One deep breath later, she noticed the others shaking hands—that was probably the more professional thing to do. She didn't care.

Eleri turned to Dana. "Can we get them to check the bodies? We don't have anything but we should still find out if the bodies did."

Dana was nodding. Better to have the CDC on it than to try to run complex and expensive tests at each region. Eleri already had her bag packed and knew Christina did, too.

"Thank God," Dana announced skyward before rounding Drs. Brookwood and Abellard up to check out the bodies. Then she told her team they all had two hours to themselves before they had to regroup. Eleri spent five minutes moving her things back into her old hotel room. The one she had by herself. All by herself. Just setting down her bag felt good. Then she walked right out the front of the hotel into the sunshine, the rest of them be damned.

She needed to untangle her brain.

Grandmere said the house she dreamed of was a common dream for those who were called. Though for most, the house was empty. Donovan had filled in a few gaps for her too, since he'd been googling Grandmere, thinking he was gathering information Eleri already knew.

She hadn't.

Grandmere was just Grandmere. She made biscuits and beans in the middle of summer, somehow never breaking a sweat over the oven despite the lack of air conditioning. Grandmere was the one who gave the best hugs. She was better than Eleri's own mother at soothing a scraped knee or a bee sting. She had old quilts and old furniture, beds and floors that squeaked, and a room filled with knick-knacks.

Only they weren't knick-knacks. As Eleri opened her eyes to all the things that had been filed away incorrectly by her childish brain, she saw the voodoo high priestess for the first time. Donovan had a better grip on her Grandmere than she had. Slowly, pieces were falling into place, the family stories fleshing out.

Grandmere's daughter, the first Emmaline, was missing. She was a drug addict who'd brought her infant daughter—Eleri's mother, Nathalie—home and then disappeared. Grandmere had raised Nathalie as her own. To this day, Eleri's mother called Grandmere "Mama." But the first Emmaline wasn't just a druggie who'd disappeared. She was a daughter of the Remy line, drunk on her own magic and mixing it with heroin and hallucinogens. Grandmere believed she was dead, because she'd felt Emmaline's power slowly fade away over the months after she'd dumped baby Nathalie and run off. That had all been news to Eleri.

Nathalie had denounced the family magic, but according to Grandmere, she carried it in her blood and there was nothing she could do about it. It was in the second Emmaline, Eleri's little sister, that Grandmere found her successor. Apparently, she'd questioned that possibility with Eleri, but knew it for a fact the first time she held baby Emmaline. Nathalie had given her the what-for when Grandmere had asked to train the girls.

All of this was news to Eleri. At thirty, she was only just now learning about her heritage. Grandmere had waited for her to ask and Eleri wished she'd done it sooner. It had all poured out as they walked through the neighborhood. Somehow the Lower Ninth Ward looked beautiful and necessary through Grandmere's eyes. Though Grandmere loved Nathalie, she laughed at her too.

"That girl was always trying to be normal. Hair like this. Clothes like that. Then she went off and married Thomas Hale Eames. Man, she stepped in it with that move! Thought she got herself a nice, normal man. Instead, she doubled down on you girls." Before Eleri could ask what that meant, Grandmere continued. "She has no clue. But you have to come to this on your own. It can't be forced or even given. It must be taken. Are you ready?"

It was the strangest question Eleri had ever been asked, and she'd spent time in a psych ward. But she trusted Grandmere and answered a clear, "Yes."

She'd been confused when Grandmere had simply nodded. No great wise advice. No beginning of an education. Only the simple words, "It will come to you now. You already have some, but you have only the very beginnings. You have threads. You will inherit a tapestry. You have much to do."

It was then Eleri realized that they had walked a loop and were back in front of Grandmere's home. Back to the tiny shotgun house where Donovan slept. Each time Eleri started to ask a question, Grandmere told her something else.

"There's lobomau in these parts. Your friend doesn't know enough of his history to stay away from them. They smell it on him. He's a target." A sage nod of her head set Eleri as Donovan's protector.

Again, as Eleri opened her mouth, Grandmere filled in the words. "It's in our blood. Can you feel it?"

And she did. It felt as though her very circulation had a mild electric charge. In the psych ward, the therapists told her it was delusion —the idea that her thoughts might mean more than just an active imagination. They told her the zing of recognition was a misfiring of nerves. Now here it was, and Grandmere asked her if she felt it. Eleri did.

The call had come in before she could do any more. Then the quarantine. Then Jordan and Jillian, and more questions pressing on her. She dreamed of the house again when she slept those brief hours in quarantine. She dreamed of Leroy Arvad. As though she stood where the killer was, she heard the words, "I'm sorry." She'd heard the killer's voice.

Her feet moved under her, walking through the small town of Alexandria. Her stomach grumbled and she got dinner to go, eating something she didn't even taste as she walked back to the hotel. Despite the humidity, it felt far too good to be outside and free. If she hadn't been so caught up in her thoughts, she might have enjoyed it.

With an active effort as she approached the hotel, Eleri turned her brain back to the case. Despite thorough investigations of all the cars and license plates entering Burt Riser's neighborhood, nothing seemed out of place. The plates were registered to homeowners, except for one evening when a handful of non-local plates came up. But they all turned into one particular driveway or parked along the street within the boundaries of the entry camera. A house on the main street was having a party. So none of them went up the street and around the curve toward Burt Riser's house. Five cars did go that way—three with single men in them, one with a single woman, one family with two children in the back, the one visible through the window was a blond girl. In each case, the name on the plate matched the name of a homeowner in that area of the subdivision. They'd even checked driver's licenses and pulled pictures to match to the drivers. Everything checked out. So how had someone gotten into Burt Riser's home?

Pulling her phone out of her pocket, she broke down and called Donovan. She'd sworn she wasn't going to speak to anyone during the break, but here she was, already back on the case.

"Why are you calling me?" Donovan's voice rang over the line. Apparently, he'd had the same thoughts as she had.

"Because I'm an agent to my very core," she sighed. "We need to figure out how she got into Burt Riser's house. Nothing shows on the video from the gate. We also need to check with the other homeowners in the community. It's pretty ritzy. We should see if anyone has their own security cameras."

"Who would still have that footage?" He asked her, into the conversation now. Maybe he was an agent in his bones now, too—his not-quite-human bones.

"A place like that, your neighbor goes up in flames, you never know. Someone may have kept something." She shrugged to herself, almost back to the hotel, her food trash still dangling from her fingers. "I'm thinking you and I do it. Jordan and Jillian can finish testing the bodies with Dana."

It was a nice idea, but she was no longer in charge. Still, she was a toxicologist. Eleri had a chemistry component to her degree, but this wasn't a poisoning, it was a possible infectious disease. And honestly, she was convinced Dana was chasing her tail on that angle. But Eleri was used to being lead, and as such, sometimes you chased your own tail just to cover your butt.

Donovan had been silent on the phone, but just then he spoke. "Oh shit. I guess I'm like you, too. I'm out on the back patio—being outside—but I'm reading what came in from the analysts. You have to come back here. They found something."

17

"You aren't going to believe this." Donovan stood up as Eleri came into the pool area. The place was empty, leading him to think he could have had his unnecessary quarantine outside at least. His only consolation was understanding Dana's need to not be responsible for spreading a deadly infectious agent. Drs. Jordan Abellard and Jillian Brookwood were already at the morgue locally checking on that.

"What am I not going to believe?" Eleri walked up, clearly her break had come to an end too, even though the clock told them they had more time. The job got to you that way. She shoved her trash into the can as she walked by, not even looking at it.

"The analysts found a connection to Gennida Orlov. Remember her daughter lives out in the general area where the first bodies were found?"

Eleri nodded and even recited the daughter's name. "Wilemina Orlov Aroya." The case was definitely getting to her.

"Well, she's married to one Peter Aroya. They married twenty years ago. He's a bit older than her. We're still pulling up records of whether they have kids. It initially appeared they did, but the records on the kid isn't panning out."

Eleri crossed her arms. He understood. He hadn't gotten to the good stuff yet.

"Peter and Mina Aroya? They're missing."

"What?" Her head tipped forward. "Have you told Dana?"

"No. It just came in before you got here."

"Shit." She shook her head. She swore a lot for a rich Southern girl, but he liked it. It made her more human. "Let's go."

He agreed, but shuddered at the thought of heading back into the hotel. Or maybe it was about heading back under Dana's thumb. He didn't dislike her so much as he simply didn't know her well enough to like her, and the situation sucked ass. He and Eleri had been in high pressure situations before, but there was something about following a serial killer, about not knowing the why, or the where, that ate holes in his stomach.

"We still need to find out how she got into Burt Riser's house," Eleri commented as they climbed the stairs, a silent, mutual agreement keeping them away from the elevator.

Dana wasn't in either the suite or her original single room.

"Maybe she managed to take her break seriously," Eleri mused.

If she had, then she was better at it than any of them.

Christina was walking up to the door of Dana's old room. Wade appeared down the hallway, heading their way.

"Looking for Dana?" Christina asked.

Donovan refrained from saying "no" just to be ornery. Instead, he nodded.

"Me too." Christina missed any expression he might have made and just launched in like they were friends. Then again, maybe she was Eleri's friend now. "We need to check out how she got into Burt Riser's house."

She kept her voice low, in case the zero other people in the hallway could hear her. Eleri didn't manage to cover her surprise.

"I thought of the same thing."

Christina shrugged. "It's logical. If the cars all check out, then either one of his neighbors did it or our suspect got in another way."

"I can't make the fire work," Wade announced, not keeping his voice low.

Donovan held in a snort, but asked, "What do you mean?"

"I'm having a mathematical problem with it. I can't get the fire to burn as hot as the markings suggest it did without hitting the kind of flashover that burns everything." He shook his head as he talked. Donovan thought there might not be anything Wade liked better than a puzzle.

"Are you sure?" Eleri looked at him closely, as though she might read it off him.

"Yes. No. I don't know. Fire's not my thing."

Christina looked at him oddly and Wade continued, "I do kinematics. Some sub-atomic physics. Nuclear. Lots of trajectory work. I do thermal systems—I mean they apply, but only a little, in the case of actual house fires."

Christina looked more and more confused as Wade kept trying to list something to make her understand. Eleri hopped in.

"Christina's a math and business person." Then she turned to Christina. "He studies mechanics mostly—where would a shooter be if a bullet wound up where it did at the angle it did. How fast could a bomb go off and how much of a building could a certain chemical mix take out. But he doesn't calculate burn rates."

"Not on natural and exposed multi-synthetics."

As Donovan watched, Eleri gave Wade the you're-not-helping stare.

Jumping in, Donovan tried to put it to rights. "You still can't get it though?"

"Not accounting for the fact that I don't know how the fire was started—"

"Hydrogen," Christina said.

But Wade shook his head. "Smells like it. But I can't come up with a reasonable system to have that be the fuel. Not in a hand-held or backpack style container like this. And I can't figure out how to get it so hot in some spots and yet not catch the things next to it on fire."

Dana walked up behind them then and Donovan checked the time. She was on the dot. It was clear as they headed into the room that the feeling of it bothered all of them.

Dana closed the door and announced, "Drs. Abellard and Brookwood have done some preliminary work on the two bodies we have here and it doesn't appear there's any infectious disease at work."

"Wouldn't you have sensed it? Isn't that your thing?" Wade asked her, making Donovan glad he hadn't been the one to ask it.

"One would think." Dana inhaled deeply. "But since I didn't sense *anything*, I was concerned. I don't like these bodies."

As if anyone did.

It was then they all jumped on her, the four of them suddenly shoving ideas at her of what each of them thought needed to be done.

Dana held her hands up and for a moment Donovan saw her as a mom, calming her brood. "Okay, Christina and Donovan head off to check the truck and the woods."

Donovan frowned, thinking he'd be paired with Eleri or at least Wade.

"You need Christina." Dana looked at him pointedly. "What if someone sees you? Eleri can shoot them, but Christina can erase it." Then she turned to Wade. "You and Eleri are heading to Wyoming to check out back yard access to Burt Riser's house. I want you to try to break in, then do some knock-and-talks in the neighborhood this evening. See if any of the neighbors remembers seeing or hearing anything."

Dana looked pointedly at Eleri. "See if you sense anything." Then she turned to Wade. "Sniff around. The two of you see if you can get us something we can use." Then, before anyone could say anything, she continued, "I'll stay on the lines with the analysts. Donovan got a connection to Gennida Orlov's daughter in Wyoming. She lived close to the bodies, you say?"

Donovan nodded, pulling out his phone. "She has lived in both Casper and in Rosedeer."

He watched as Dana almost gasped. Leona Hiller's house was in Rosedeer. Burt Riser was from Casper. And there was someone in the "maybe" list, a schoolteacher who'd been killed over a year ago, who was also from Casper, Wyoming. No coincidences there.

"Are we looking at Mina Orlov as our killer?" Dana asked him.

"I don't see how we can't be," he answered, feeling like the case was finally coming together.

Eleri had managed to sleep on the small, chartered plane that had brought her and Wade here. Leaving before the crack of dawn hadn't changed her attitude about the case. She stood at the back of Burt Riser's yard, thinking how she hated tall, wooden fences. Chain link was at least climbable. Had they found chain link, they would have declared it a done deal—at least a possibility—and left it at that.

Nope. No chain link for this neighborhood. Not even the adobe-esque cinderblock that was more common out west. She could pop up and over that. This place went with wood. Who had wood in this humidity? It was already starting to give way and Riser's house wasn't that old.

"Shit." Eleri felt her hands fist and perch on her hips. The bugs were trying to eat her, and she was grateful it was too early in the season for a full insect-fest, but there were enough to be annoying. She waved her hand in front of her face. "We should have interviewed the neighbors first. We're going to look like we were breaking into someone's home."

"Technically, we are," Wade pointed out even as he reached out and tried one of the boards of what had to be a seven-foot fence.

It was the same fence that was behind all the homes on the street, or Eleri would have questioned the choice. It was solid pickets, no spaces to peek between. If it hadn't been rotting away to the point they could pull one of the boards aside and see the back of the house, they might have mistakenly broken into the wrong one. The houses did all look a lot alike.

"We have to try. Our killer wouldn't have given up because the fence was tall. We're just going to have to clean up before we knock on doors." The woods behind her had been a bitch to get through. There was no easy parking, and they'd had to go through the gate of another community, flashing badges, *oh joy.* Then they cut through the remaining trees to this.

Walking the perimeter of the fencing, they decided that *through* was better than *over*. Over didn't look like much of an option. "How would she even get over this?"

"Well," Wade thought for a minute. "She jumps a little or maybe she just reaches this cross piece." Wade pointed to the brace between the fencepost that all the boards were nailed to from the other side. This fence was "pretty side" in. "A hundred-to-one it's over her head, and fifty-to-one it's significantly over her head. So she muscles herself up. But the picket tops are about six inches above that, with no spaces. So she needs more strength to get over that."

"She drops to the ground on the other side," Eleri finished. "All with this flamethrower, what? On her back? Could she toss it over first?"

Wade gaped at her in horror. "No. The danger of breaking something, causing a leak and burning herself . . . way too great."

"Can she have it in parts and throw the parts over?"

"Sure, if she wants a hole in her line that might make her blow up.

The hydrogen tank shouldn't break, but you don't fucking throw them."

"*Ooooh-kayyy*," Eleri conceded. "So she didn't throw it over. She carried it. But we get the same issues when she jumps to the ground. A twisted ankle or a mis-step and she's damaged her clearly-highly-flammable equipment."

Wade agreed. "Plus, how would she get back out? The fence is sheer on that side."

Of course it was. "Then we go through."

They spent the next thirty minutes weaseling their way between the boards of the fence and back out.

"Well, that was for shit," Eleri declared. She'd barely been able to squeeze through. "I would never have been able to get that equipment through. Unless you're way off about the size and weight, this is a no."

"I'm not. And that's assuming a minimum size," Wade commented easily. "Also, remember, the fence was newer then and in better repair. The boards wouldn't have moved so easily."

Eleri sighed. Wade was an excellent agent. She reminded herself of this. But if the boards wouldn't have moved even as much as they did now, then she hadn't needed to crawl through, had she?

"I'm cranky," she declared. "Let's find somewhere and shower, then come in the front gate and knock on some doors."

It was two hours later that they'd checked into a hotel and simply cleaned up. It was another half hour before they were passing through the big metal gates at the main entrance to Burt Riser's subdivision. As Eleri looked, she realized they weren't wrought iron. Instead they were a cheaper, lighter metal painted black. It made sense, but it got her wondering if the neighborhood maybe only looked nice on the surface. She'd let Wade drive, thinking she might let her own mind wander more, and something hit her as she headed through the gate. Something about Wade showing his badge and ID that made her pause, gave her a tiny sense of Deja vu that she knew was not her own.

In a moment she said, "She came through the front gate."

18

E leri watched the man standing in his own front doorway, waiting for any tells. He didn't give any. He wasn't lying. Wade nodded sagely, which Eleri could tell was an act. He was hardly paying attention; he was mostly trying to smell anything that might be worthwhile.

"I'm telling you," the man said from the oversized arch. His arm rested on the jamb and he had no compunctions about talking to the FBI. "It looks like suburbia, but it's not like the old school. We don't know our neighbors. I mean, my wife does a little bit, but I don't."

"Is she here?" Eleri smiled as nicely as she could.

"She's at yoga or something. You can talk to her when she gets back, but it's . . ." He looked down at a very shiny watch. "It'll be another hour, at least."

"Do you remember anything from the night Burt Riser was murdered? Or anything from around that time?" It was the same question she'd asked each of the other neighbors. This guy was the only one to say it, but he was right—it was *not* old school. None of them had seen anything or even appeared to care. The house across the street had a murder and it was as distant to them as if it had been in another town. There seemed to be some iron-clad belief that if they didn't bring evil in, it wouldn't find them. Eleri knew otherwise, but she kept her smile in place.

"I didn't see anything. My wife said she saw a couple kids walking down the street just before it got dark. Said she didn't recognize them. She told the police."

Eleri wanted her ears to perk. Wanted to believe it was anything other than what it was. But it was just more nothing. She nodded, though that information hadn't been in the police report. Clearly, the police had dismissed it. Probably they were looking for a man. Then her brain perked. "Could one have been an adult? And your wife just thought it was a kid?"

"It was kids. Cops asked the same thing." He didn't move from his spot in the doorway, apparently happy to talk to them and tell them what he knew. He still wasn't going to invite them in and offer them tea or anything. No one here had.

Eleri tried again, "Do you have any home security?" She'd noticed the camera facing the front stoop when she came in.

"We do now. No camera toward the street, though." He nodded when she started to frown at his forwardness. "Cops asked the same thing. We got the camera at the front door and wired the windows and doors. Your neighbor gets murdered and you notice."

Funny, Eleri would have thought exactly the opposite given the way none of them had known anything. "Thank you for your time."

She walked back to the rental car with a confidence she didn't feel. She was dead on her feet again, despite being clean. As she slid into the car beside Wade she asked, "Did you get anything?"

"Nope. Everyone smelled normal. Second house over eats Indian food. But that's not surprising as the woman who answered the door was clearly Indian. The fourth house had a fire pit out back, the dad had been using it. And the last guy wasn't lying. But that's all."

"Well, that was useless."

"No, now we know that our killer clearly flew through the front door without picking the lock, Mary Poppins-style, while no one saw."

"Yeah. That." Eleri moaned. She needed sleep.

Donovan spent far too long working out his signals with Christina. Had Eleri been here, he could have simply walked into the woods and gotten started. As it was, he'd spent the morning sorting files, and then he had to spend time explaining to Christina where he would leave his clothes, that she should pick them up and carry them, what one bark would mean, or two. He generally hated barking.

He also hated that he felt this way about the assignment. He was an adult. An agent trained to work in a team or solo. He should be able to play better with other adults. But he didn't want to.

He stood in the woods naked, his ears perked, knowing Christina held her ground in the distance. He didn't like when people saw this. Only Walter/Lucy had, and that had been a fluke. He still wasn't sure what to make of it, though it had gotten them in bed together. He pushed that thought aside—no use running around in the woods like that!—and started his work.

He pulled his shoulders forward, hunching his back, moving his scapulae in place to shift over a bit, almost like dislocating a shoulder. His ribs contracted, sliding a little between the muscles. His attachment points were different than normal. He had a medical degree; he'd checked.

He heard the slight *pop* as the bones in his face pushed out. Each time he did it now, he thought about GJ Janson asking if his maxilla and facial bones were not fused. Luckily, she seemed to have no clue what exactly he was, only that he was different and that he was part of some group she had seen skeletons for. He pushed his left heel out and rolled his foot forward, shifting those bones, feeling the muscles slide as they moved into place.

His skin prickled, the sensation of the hair sliding out—almost like when he got goose-bumps in his normal shape. It was both familiar and disturbing.

In his new form, he tested four paws on the ground and rolled his head side to side, taking deep breaths. This time, when he pricked his ears, it changed what he heard. He listened backward, toward where he'd left Christina standing guard, and heard her humming tunelessly to herself. He gave one sharp bark, indicating he was ready then waited, wishing again that it were Eleri with him and wishing he didn't care.

Christina came through the woods to him, "Are you ready?"

He gave a one-motion nod and started off. She walked behind him, her footfalls heavier than they should have been for a woman her size. He guessed she didn't spend much time out in the woods. He'd been spending a surprising amount out and about—breaking into, searching, investigating—all kinds of places. More than he'd expected when he took the job. It seemed it wasn't just him. The NightShade division wasn't shy about making use of their agents' special skills.

They'd agreed ahead of time to check out the truck first, the woods were just a convenient spot to change. Changing at the hotel brought the risk of discovery. Plus, he liked the dirt under his feet, the smell of trees, even the thick air here. It was certainly closer to home than Wyoming had been.

He trotted a little too fast for Christina to keep up, but it didn't matter. They both knew where the truck was, and she was just his handler. It was his nose and his senses that were checking out the truck. It came into view and the overgrown yard tickled at his feet as he pushed through. The grass scented up at him, green and lush and untended.

Within the minute, he was at the truck. The closed door presented a problem in this form, so he began on the outside. Christina would be here soon—he could hear her hustling to catch up. Though he supposed it was possible to work the door open himself, it would be a bitch. Besides, door-opening fell to the person with the human hands as did peeling back the "Crime Scene" tape that had been put on the truck earlier.

He'd worked his way around to the passenger side by the time Christina made it. The driver's side door was covered in Leroy Arvad —fingerprints that were most likely his and a scent that definitely was. There was a variety of other scents that weren't Leroy himself, but were associated. Donovan could pick up diesel, fast food, and a chemical smell he'd had trouble identifying on the body. The woman? He couldn't be sure.

"Would you like me to open that for you?" Christina now stood behind him, pointing up at the cab door.

He stared for a second, his best attempt at sarcasm, but it went past her. Then he realized he was being an ass. What if he didn't want the door opened yet? She was being nice, smart. He offered one bob of his head and she hauled herself up and grasped the door with a gloved hand—she must have put the latex on before even asking— and he felt like more of a heel. She carefully pulled back the yellow tape, then when the door opened, the scent hit him.

Her.

Eleri had been right. She'd been in the cab. As a passenger. And she'd been there for a while.

He was up and into the space despite the awkwardness of it. He snuffled frantically, letting the smells come in and out of his nasal cavity quickly, rather than lingering.

Having to back down was hard and he tried not to make an ass out of himself.

"Was she there?" Christina hadn't picked up on that answer by his movements or at least she wasn't willing to guess.

Donovan lifted his head and dropped it in his facsimile of a nod. It wasn't comfortable in this form, his chin didn't go up and down the same way; he was actually bobbing his whole head from the neck. But he did it three times for emphasis. *Hell yes, she was here.*

"Do you need more?"

No. This time side to side and he let her close the cab back up and replace the yellow swaths of plastic that should help them preserve the evidence. He was off again, the tall grass clearing the scent of Leroy and the woman from his nose. This time he inhaled deeply and headed into the woods.

He kept a much slower pace here, allowing Christina to stay right behind him. It was getting darker and the terrain in the woods was rougher. No point in doing a search and rescue on his own partner. Also, she had his clothes.

They already knew the trail contained the scent of the woman and he didn't have to go more than a heartbeat into the trees to catch it again. The wind and thick air had already begun to scrub her residue from the grass, but in here, it lingered almost in globs, catching on trees and bushes she'd brushed against.

This time he would follow it to the end. The slower pace forced him to be more careful and he noticed things he hadn't on the quick first pass with Wade.

She didn't leave the trail, no wandering into the woods. She had scent low and high, putting her walking upright—not crouching, crawling, or trying to hide. At one point her trail split, giving him two distinct paths to follow. He doubled back and wondered if she'd done the same.

All the while, he watched and sniffed for the flamethrower. Had she chucked it to the side? Did she make a new one each time? Had it brushed against *any* of the plants in here?

How could that be possible?

The woods ran out, dumping him and Christina at a sharp dirt embankment leading down to a road. The woods continued on the other side and Donovan watched for traffic before heading across.

He spent fifteen minutes trying to pick up her scent, but he couldn't. Christina had turned on her flashlight in the deepening dusk, picking her way along behind him. At one point, a driver came by and spotted them on the side of the road and slowed to a halt. Donovan didn't stop sniffing around, but he listened.

"You stuck out here, ma'am? Need help?"

"Oh no. We're training for search and rescue. We have to practice in the dark, you know." Christina rattled off the lie smooth and pretty. Better than he'd expected of his mostly silent new partner.

"Oh, you do good work!" Though he didn't look up, Donovan could hear the smile in the man's voice. "That's a big dog you got there. Is he part wolf?"

"No." She said it as if it had been a good question, but simply wrong. Donovan tried not to go still, act odd, or as if he'd been paying attention.

Christina continued, "He's not that big at all. Just average German Shepherd size."

Donovan heard the slight edge in her voice. The man wouldn't remember the large black dog. He might remember Christina, but it would be a standard search dog he recalled later.

"Well, keep up the good work!" He drove off into the night as Donovan wondered if Christina's talent hurt her or drained her energy or if it was just as normal as breathing to her.

For his part, he had nothing. No scent of the woman in the woods on the other side of the road. So he called off the search and led his partner back across the street toward where they'd started.

Back near the Arvad's house, he gave two short barks with a long pause between.

"What do you need?"

Frustrated, he did it again. He hated barking like that.

"Oh!"

Yes, he thought, it was their pre-planned signal that he was ready to change back. She hadn't remembered it the first time. He fought the sharp sigh that wanted to huff out.

But she neatly set out his clothes and walked a decent distance away out to stand in the grass behind the Arvads'. LeighAnn wasn't there. The house was now a burned hull and Donovan remembered the woman left to stay with her sister.

He rolled his shoulders, curled his back and rotated his ankles back into place. His face was more difficult, and he pushed his chin down, getting the muscles and bones in the right place to slide back to human. His sense of scent diminished, his hearing dulled, and the hair had already pulled back into his skin leaving only the thicker than average, but relatively human-looking, hair on his arms.

Kicking into his clothes, then quickly donning his sneakers, he checked out the night around him for any last clues then went out to find Christina.

"Well?" she asked.

"She was there. She went all the way to the road and then disappeared."

"You think she hitched another ride?" Christina was tilting her head, looking at him oddly as he nodded. "Then what?"

"There's no flame thrower. She didn't throw it away in there."

"So she took it with her." Christina shrugged, even though that didn't really make sense. How would she ever get a car on that back road to pick her up if she had a damn flamethrower in her hand?

"No," he answered, "she didn't take it with her. It was never in the woods at all."

19

E leri dreamed of the tiny, square house again. This time she walked the woods behind the Arvads' mobile home, into the trail she'd followed Donovan down.

Glimpses of white ducked in and out between the tree trunks, staying just ahead of her as she picked her way along the path in the dim light. The moon was visible through the branches above, which somehow seemed so much further up than they had before. The path was wider, gentler, and though she thought of it, she didn't worry about messing up the scent trail either Donovan or Wade might need to come back and follow.

She wandered for a while, the young woman in the white dress just ahead of her. After a little bit, Eleri became frustrated and sped up, stepping faster, catching her toe on a vine, stumbling, but not caring.

"Eleri." The woman turned.

"Emmaline." She smiled at her sister. Stuck now, forever seventeen, while Eleri grew and changed. "Emmaline."

"I'm being helpful." Her little sister smiled. Then stepped out. Her left foot moved left. Her right foot moved right, and she split. For a moment, she hovered in a double image, making Eleri wonder if her eyes had gone nuts. But everything else was stable, only Emmaline made her blink.

Another step and Emmaline was back to being one clear image.

She then smiled and faded into nothing, leaving Eleri staring at the house again. She was facing the door—the odd front door set at forty-five degrees into the corner. Emmaline's image had been just in front of the tiny porch when it disappeared.

Had she just not seen the house because she was watching Emmaline?

Eleri didn't know, but she pushed her way inside.

Again, children played in the front room, only this time they were eerily silent. They stacked blocks that somehow didn't click. They played with dolls, but spoke no words. Even the crayon pressed hard on paper that ripped made no sound. The only noise was Eleri's feet on the floorboards. Each step seemed to echo though it didn't disturb the children.

She didn't think of it, didn't recognize it at first, but the sound of her gasp brought all the children to stop what they were doing and look at her. Tiny, dishwater blond, blue eyed, all of them. Identical faces. She tried to count but couldn't keep track, her brain fuzzy though the children were stationary and it should have been an easy task. Suddenly scared, Eleri walked past the creepy, silent children, all the while telling herself it was just a dream.

She passed through the arch into empty space she assumed was designated for the dining room. The next room was the kitchen, but she didn't notice it yet. As she passed through, she looked back to see all the children were gone. The toys, too. The front room was empty, as though they had never been there. When she stepped into the next room, she felt the heat and air push at her, almost moving her backwards as the walls caught fire around her.

The middle of the room pulsed with heat, but the flames stopped in clear lines, making a path through the space into the kitchen. The heat made it hard to breathe, but Eleri needed to look around.

Over her head, the flames danced in pretty patterns. They intertwined and fought, reaching out to each other but never down to her. At her sides, the flames burned bright hot blue but the walls didn't blacken or crackle.

Breathing became more difficult. The hair on her arms stood up, but it didn't singe or curl. Despite the strength of the fire, Eleri didn't burn. She knew she wouldn't. She didn't understand how or why that was, but she knew.

As she started to move forward, a familiar looking woman

stepped into view through the archway that led to the kitchen. Wiping her hands on a towel tucked into the pocket of her jeans, she motioned to Eleri to come forward. Into the kitchen. Where it was safe.

She didn't say any of the words. Eleri just understood. The kitchen was safe.

The flames didn't pass the doorway and Eleri felt the heat behind her as she walked through. Out of curiosity, as she entered the cool kitchen, she turned and looked back, to see the other room now fully engulfed. The fire must have followed her. But the woman at the sink, despite her motion and indication of safety, seemed to have no real awareness of the flames. Or maybe it was so common to her that it didn't bother her anymore. Eleri couldn't tell.

With a smile and a nod, she returned to the sink full of dishes and began washing them. The sink sat under two windows that came together at the back corner of the house. The sink was set at a forty-five-degree angle into the corner leaving a deep, triangular shelf, where the woman stacked dishes.

Eleri examined the design, thinking it mimicked the odd door on the opposite corner. But as the woman brushed back a stray strand of hair, Eleri caught something in the gesture and recognized her.

Leona Hiller—the dead woman from Rosedeer, Wyoming. The at-home mom whose husband had rebuilt the house and found another woman who looked remarkably like his wife. As Eleri remembered that she'd been strangled, bruises bloomed around the woman's neck, but she put the last dish in the drainer then turned to a row of tiny bowls on the counter. Holding a bag of carrots, she counted a few into each bowl, then went back with another veggie, some kind of bean and counted those, too.

The daycare. The one she unofficially ran in her home.

As Eleri remembered that fact, the woman looked up and moved her hand, this time ushering Eleri away and into the last room. Eleri turned and headed through the next doorway, where once again she found the old woman in the rocker. Her black hands had worn knuckles that somehow still were graceful as she stitched a thick thread into a doll.

Eleri looked more closely. Something about the woman looked like Grandmere. Something looked like Emmaline. Like Eleri. Like their mother. The woman didn't look up, just kept to her stitching.

She'd thought the woman to be Aida Weddo, but had she been wrong? The woman was now clearly an ancestor. One whose genes had run strong in the family, one whose blood flowed through Eleri all her life though she'd known nothing of it until just recently. Was she also the great Aida Weddo, High Goddess of the old religion Grandmere practiced?

Eleri looked more closely, trying to get a better view of the woman's face.

In a blink, too fast to have humanly moved, the woman was staring at her. Eleri's saw her own eyes, the green deep and unending.

The mouth said, "Wake."

"No, Donovan, it was Leona Hiller. I'm sure of it." Eleri had peeled herself off the floor, cleaned up, and waited until it was late enough that Donovan would be awake. Then she showed up, knocking on his hotel room door and telling him everything. About Emmaline leading her on the path. About the house, the fire inside, the creepy little kids who made no sounds, and the woman she'd thought was Aida Weddo but now reflected herself.

"It means something," he stated as though she needed to hear it.

"It would be nice if that meaning were more damned obvious." But it wasn't. "I've been seeing Emmaline more lately. It stopped for a while, you know."

"But you said it happened that way. You wouldn't dream of her for some months, then she'd come back."

"I know. I can't help wondering if she's back this time because she's back, or because I need her, or because Grandmere told me they would find her and I'm conjuring her up." Eleri paused with the same pinch in her heart each time she thought of Grandmere's words. Her mother, Nathalie, had never let go of the idea that her daughter was still out there and would be found some day. Over the years, she'd made off-hand comments that had begun as "your sister will be safely returned." Now, Eleri was pretty convinced her mother thought her sister had been brainwashed into believing she was another person. Living her life under another name and not remembering the family she was born to. When the time was right, Nathalie would welcome her daughter home like a lost princess. Some kind of

Cinderella story where Nathalie was both the loving parent and the fairy Godmother.

Her mother would be devastated when Emmaline's bones were found. By now that was all that would be left of her daughter. Eleri knew that in her heart as well as by fact of her education. The worst part would be that the bones would match, but they would be almost ten years older than when Emmaline went missing. Eleri knew this. Grandmere knew this. No one else knew it. Ten years they might have found Emmaline alive. Ten years they had missed.

"I woke up on my floor again." She changed the topic in her head, though she wasn't sure this one was better.

"Another pentagram?"

"Yup. This one was paper, though. At least it was easier to clean up."

"Did the papers say anything?" Donovan looked at her as though she were omitting vital information.

"Yes," she deadpanned. "One said 'faith be unto Satan.' And another said 'no Eleri, only Zuul.'"

"Fine. Be that way." His mouth quirked though. "What was the paper, then?"

"Those little tear-off sheets of hotel stationery. So it had the hotel logo at the top, but otherwise they were just small rectangles." She shrugged. "I was just grateful not to have to put my suitcase back together this time. Can you make heads or tails of it?"

She sat in silence while he thought about it, then shook his head.

"I'm afraid." She tried to say it clearly, boldly owning her fear, but it came out as a whisper. "I'm afraid it will mean something and it will only be obvious when it's too late."

"Don't worry about it, Eleri." Donovan put his hand on her arm in a rare gesture of actual human comfort. He'd been a little clingier lately, making her wonder if he appreciated their partnership more after having been shoved into this team. "These things turn up. As we gather more information, you'll put the pieces together. You always do."

"No pressure there," she sighed.

Their phones beeped in tandem and they looked at each other. Dana wanted a meeting. Eleri had come back late and gone to bed tired after Donovan and Christina had returned. She'd been talking, not listening, so she didn't know yet what they'd found in the woods or at the truck.

Already up, Eleri and Donovan grabbed their things and headed out the door, but Eleri's brain nagged at her. There was something in that dream that she needed to see. Sooner rather than later. Or someone else would die.

20

Donovan stood at the picture window and looked out over the rolling land before him. Dana had given them a break. Nothing had happened and nothing had come together, so she'd set them free. They all knew it could end at any moment. Now, he stood here and watched the tall, green grasses at Bell Point Farm sway in the light breeze. In the far distance cows roamed, but they couldn't get close. Not here. The estate was obviously a toy farm, a plaything for the wealthy to pretend they farmed.

"Does this place make any money?" He asked over his shoulder to his partner and hostess.

"Yes," Eleri replied seamlessly. "It makes any money."

Then it wasn't dead weight, but it clearly wasn't the height of farming cash.

She spoke again and he could hear her buttering toast. It was a lush potato bread baked by a professional whose building was on the far opposite side of the property, where actual work occurred. The butter was churned on site, also far from the house. The knife scraped the perfectly browned top of the bread as Eleri sat at the very expensive hand-hewn farm table that occupied a space bigger than the last home Donovan's father had parked them in, though "home" was a strong word there. "Bell Point Farm could be completely self-sufficient if it needed to be."

"But only if you could get to the actual farming from the house," he muttered under his breath.

"Touché," she replied easily. She knew. She knew he'd lived in trailers that made the Arvads' place look neat and homey. She had to know that his father only quit hitting him when he got big enough to hit back, and not because his father had found any kind of god or become any better of a man.

Eleri had grown up in this kind of place. Not just here, but in several homes as lush as this one. When she was younger they'd spent more than just vacation time at FoxHaven, their home on Avon Island off the Carolina coast. But she said she'd mostly grown up around Patton Hall, their other home in Kentucky. That was because her sister had disappeared from there and her mother had refused to leave the area for years in case Emmaline came back.

Hardship came in a variety of forms.

Still, Donovan thought of toaster ovens that had only "cold" and "burn" settings. He thought of the smell of old dishes in the sink—one of the few smells he actually classified as "bad." He thought of rooms that had holes in the ceilings and walls from something the previous tenants must have done, and black mold he could see if not smell.

One thing that bothered him about Bell Point Farm was that he hadn't earned it. It was too big, too old, too rich for anything he knew.

"You don't have to stay." She seemed to read his mind. And who knew, it might be one of her talents, not that she thought so. "It just seemed easier to stick together until Dana needs us again."

Though all five of them had finally achieved a first-name-basis, Eleri had not invited Dana or Christina to spend their time off at Bell Point Farm. The land sat outside Charlottesville, Virginia, an almost too-charming town that barely achieved city status and was home to one of the oldest universities in the country. Eleri had driven them through town on the way up. The university itself was over two hundred years old and some of the buildings in town were older than that. Donovan suspected that the floor he was standing on had seen blood, death, birth and possibly centuries. It had seen slavery and freedom. And now it saw a man who was at least part wolf and didn't know what to do with himself.

Eleri calmly ate an artisan breakfast at an artisan table that was made to look rustic. "I thought you might like to run the place. The land the house sits on is relatively isolated. And I put out word that I brought two big dogs with me. No one is to shoot."

"Well, that's comforting."

"It's the best I can do." She shrugged as he remained feeling out of place.

Wade was off somewhere on the property trying to build flame-throwers. He could claim he was working, but it was easy to see he was simply intrigued by the challenge of making it the right size. Not that he could solve the puzzle of where it had gone. It wasn't in the truck and it wasn't in the woods, but it had been in the house.

Donovan didn't like where that thinking led him and he tried to turn his brain off. He changed to a more mundane subject. "Is Avery's team going to make it to the playoffs?"

"Yes!" Her tone changed dramatically and Donovan wondered how far this relationship would go. "His team won their series and pretty quickly, too. He has almost a week off. Of course, their 'break' only means three days, but he'll be here this afternoon."

She almost buzzed with excitement and Donovan thought of Walter Reed. She was Lucy Fisher when she was coming on to him. And he wanted to see her again, but he didn't have Eleri's buzz. Should he? Was that the mark of the "real thing"? He had no idea.

"Seriously, Donovan, go for a run. It's some beautiful land, and you're my guest." She stood up. "Eat whatever is in the fridge. Sleep when you want. As long as Wade isn't running around shouting 'Eureka!' that is."

"Does he do that?" Donovan frowned, having a hard time imag-ining that was how Wade reacted to solving a problem.

"I wouldn't be surprised," Eleri countered as she stood and cleared her plate and crumbs from the table. She put her dishes into a slick machine hidden behind a cabinet panel. Like everything else in the kitchen, it was oversized, yet somehow the tiny Eleri fit in just fine. It was Donovan's bulk that didn't.

Eleri disappeared into other parts of the house. Donovan hadn't yet gotten lost per se, but he'd had his moments. He looked again out the window, realizing he wasn't yet ready to go out and let go. He was too moody, too stuck. It didn't help that they all were.

The case had gone cold.

No one had located Peter Aroya or his wife Mina Orlov Aroya. So no one had been notified of the death of Mina's mother, Gennida

Orlov. They'd questioned the apartment building residents again and the stories were even hazier than the first time. Donovan talked to one neighbor who recalled seeing Gennida Orlov that day, but this time the neighbor squinted her eyes and looked up and right as though struggling to remember it correctly.

"I think she might have had extra groceries that day. Though that would have been odd."

Donovan remembered this woman and he was growing confused, too. The first time, just a few days ago, she'd said that Gennida Orlov *had* carried several bags of groceries and that it *was* odd. Now she acted as though being asked about the events leading up to her neighbor's house fire was like being asked if she'd gone to the bank on a particular Tuesday seven years ago.

To make it worse, several of the eye witnesses were now reluctant to commit to their stories. With the apartment complex pushing for a hasty clean-up, it felt like this part of the case was simply disappearing from under them. He'd never seen such terrible witnesses. Most people wanted to tell you *ev-ery-thing.* Down to what socks they'd been wearing and what coffee they'd ordered at the shop that morning.

He and Wade had gone back to the Arvads' home—at least no one was pushing to clean up that crime scene—and found . . . nothing. Just more of the same. So the flame thrower didn't just have to be portable, it had to be scent-free and able to be picked up by a random person on the road. For a moment, his brain wandered again to the possibility that there was no flamethrower. Then he reminded himself that Wade thought there was. Donovan turned back to the hitchhiking theory. He couldn't imagine what kind of man picked up a woman carrying a flame thrower! For a moment, he wondered if she was beautiful, if that was maybe the trick. Often people got stupid if they thought they could possibly have something they believed was beyond them. He knew. He'd done it enough in high school. Until he learned he couldn't have things.

He wandered the long hallway in the house, the floor more visibly worn along the center where feet had tread since long before their grandfathers were born. Tables and the occasional sideboard lined the hallway, because it was wide enough for that. Paintings of Eleri's ancestors hung on the walls, oils old enough to need serious care.

He stopped and looked at one.

Thomas Hale. The painting was so old as to clearly be from another era. Though the name plate revealed no more than the first and last names, the signature on the painting said 1643. Had he been drinking something, Donovan would have spit it all over the canvas.

He looked at the other paintings as he went. John Hale. Sarah Hale. Rebecca Eames.

Did the names just sound familiar because he knew Eleri's father was Thomas Hale Eames and the first names were all common ones?

He looked further.

One grandmotherly person was Eleri Llewelyn Hale.

He couldn't shake the nagging feeling. Pulling his phone from his pocket, Donovan began typing in the names. It was only a moment before he was looking over his shoulder.

Llewelyn was the family name of probably the most prominent family in American Witchcraft.

Seriously? Eleri was running around acting like her hunches were luck, yet she had this family lineage. He blinked. Grandmere had said Nathalie—Eleri's mother—had run from her heritage in New Orleans and had run "right into it" with Thomas Hale.

But it was all here on the internet. Had Eleri never checked? Did she not know?

"Donovan!" Eleri's voice rang out, bouncing off the old lathe and plaster walls.

"Yes?" He tried to sound normal.

"I'm heading to Charlottesville to run a few errands and then pick up Avery. Do you need anything?"

He needed so many things, but he said, "No, I'm good."

He'd talk to her when she got back. *Damnit,* she'd have Avery with her. That wouldn't do. Donovan turned to the next painting and put "Thomas Hale" into his phone.

The Hale family was a first family of Massachusetts—Eleri had mentioned that before. Donovan's heart rate slowed. "Llewelyn" had to be some odd coincidence, right?

"Rebecca Eames" loaded on his screen. His heart kicked. There was a famous Rebecca Eames—convicted but not put to death in the Salem witch trials.

Massachusetts. Paintings from 1643. He turned and looked down the hallway as though the ghosts would come for him. He looked at the next painting, unsigned. Undated. John and Sarah Hale.

John Hale, minister of a church in Beverly, Massachusetts. Donovan pinpointed it on the map. Near Salem. Sarah Hale, accused of witchcraft late in the Salem trials.

Holy shit.

Eleri had to know.

Or did it just not register because she never looked? He'd never questioned his grandparents until much later. He'd never thought his father was different until it had been pushed in his face. Was it possible Eleri didn't know?

Now, he itched to run.

The combination of not knowing enough about the case with now maybe knowing too much about his partner begged him to change. He needed the fresh air. He needed the scents of grass and dirt. He needed to get out of this house of witches.

He'd made it as far as his room. He grabbed his small pack, stuffing extra supplies in it and mostly leaving it empty so he could put his clothing in, tie it in a tree, and disappear as the wolf for a while.

He was stepping out the back door and onto the wide patio when his phone rang. He cursed it. For as much as the house resembled Monticello, they must have their own damned cell tower. His lack of ability to escape signal was the most modern thing about the place.

No name popped up and he didn't recognize the number or even the area code. He shoved in back in his pocket.

He was crossing from marble tile to the neat green of the too-tended gardens when it rang again. He looked. Same number. No idea. He put it back in his pocket.

He was in the tall grass, almost to the woods when it rang a third time. He'd have to answer just to tell the person they had the wrong number. "Hello?"

"Agent Donovan Heath?"

He frowned. Not a wrong number. "Yes." He offered nothing more than the word. The voice . . .?

"This is GJ Janson. I'm not sure if you remember me, but I have some information for you."

21

"You should have called Agent Eames." Donovan told GJ when he got over his shock. "She's the senior partner. I'll give you her number."

He stood in the grass at the edge of the trees, wondering how far he could go before the signal would break and he could just slough off the call.

"I know, but you're the one I was studying." She said it matter- of-factly.

Shit. Had she figured something out about him? He didn't speak, just waited.

"Actually, I have two pieces of information for you. One is just for you." Again, her voice was earnest, but professional.

Shit. Then he looked at the phone. "I thought I had your number. Why doesn't this number log in my phone?"

"I'm on a burner phone."

There were no mirrors nearby but he knew his eyebrows were near the top of his head. "For God's sakes, why?"

"Because I don't know what people know about the case we worked."

To say "the case we worked" was strong terminology for the woman who'd been detained by federal agents through a reasonable portion of it.

"Also," she started in again, "Given the information about you, I thought you might not want your colleagues listening in."

Shit and double shit. His colleagues already knew enough, but he wasn't going to hand her that. "Go on."

"First," Her voice changed then, becoming breathier, as though she were excited. "I was right about my grandfather. He and his assistant, Shray Menon," She took a moment and spelled it out for him, "Write that down. They have been following people with your bone anomalies for about thirty-plus years now. I went through some records he doesn't let me into—" her voice turned wry and Donovan could tell she'd been breaking into her grandfather's secret stashes somehow. "—and the original bones he found, like yours, were over a thousand years old."

Donovan's heart stopped.

Of course, his people were old. The stupid legends of moonlight and howling and ravaging villages were old. But silver bullets required guns, and that limited him to about seven hundred years on that legend. Over a thousand years old? He took a second to force himself to breathe.

As much as the age of the find was interesting, more concerning was the fact that Dr. Murray Marks had been cataloging his species for a handful of decades. "Does your grandfather know anything about what the . . . mutation does?"

Mutation. What a terrible word. It was a small set of dominant genes that lined up through generations. One of them was sex linked, he thought. Did GJ know this? Did her grandfather?

"No, but it's consistent. Once we account for the general stature difference and obvious lack of dental care and proper diet, the bones are identical to yours and the others my grandfather has." She paused a moment. "But I've been studying them as I get the chance—"

"Does your grandfather know this?" he interrupted her, his heart pounding again.

"No. He won't talk to me about it. I've skirted the subject a few times, and he shuts me down. When I have solid evidence, I'll present it to him so he can't ignore me."

Donovan breathed out. So at least GJ didn't know what he could do. Whether that was because her grandfather didn't know or because he wasn't sharing remained a mystery.

"So," she continued, "I was looking at the bones, and the things is, the attachment sites for the tendons and ligaments aren't quite in the right place. I figure the live person would stand and move like a normal person, but also move other ways. Have you noticed anything like that?"

Damn, the woman was forward.

"No," he lied.

"I'm thinking you should be double-jointed, or something like that. A lot." She seemed to ignore his "no" answer.

"Nope," he lied again. "I'm sure it was just an anomaly on that bone set. Clearly, something was off about it."

"No. Not an anomaly. I checked all the bones. Even the oldest set —the thousand-year-old one. It's from the Haryana province in India—"

"Haryana is a state," he corrected automatically. His mother was from the country. He knew little other than what he could find online and the smells of her cooking that had always seemed like home. He shouldn't have corrected GJ, but it had fallen out. He wasn't on his A-game. Straightening up, he set his bag down into the grass and looked out at the blue sky, turning his focus solely to the voice on the line.

"Okay—it was found in Haryana—but it has the same anomalies in the tendon and ligament attachment points. Yours must be like that, too."

"Not that I can tell." He tried shutting her down again. "What else?"

"That's it. That's what I have for now." She sounded disappointed. *Good.* "Honestly, I was hoping you'd say you were double-jointed or something that I could point to as a diagnostic. All I have are the bones. I don't know if it's genetic, or a disease, or something developmental—like the mother ate or did something at some certain point of pregnancy. I was hoping you'd have ideas."

Oh, he did. But he wasn't sharing them. "Is that it?"

"On the bones. Regarding the hospitals in Michigan and Arizona, I have other information."

"Hospitals?" He barked the word out on a laugh. That was a far too kind interpretation of the buildings in their last case.

"Okay, wrong word. So, I went and made myself a volunteer at the assisted living facility where Dr. Benjamin Kellogg is now being cared for. The thing is, Kellogg is a new last name for the family. He used to be Dr. Benjamin Schwartzgartner."

The name hit him like a truck. His A-game was long gone. Where was Eleri when he needed her? He blurted out, "You *what?*"

"Look, my thesis is in shambles, my grandfather is hiding the find of the century from me and everyone else, I was detained by federal agents and only set free without charges because I was helpful. My father thinks I'm wasting my time getting a graduate degree. So I told him I needed a gap year to go find myself." She rattled it off as though everyone had the money and family support to just wander off to a new state and volunteer at an old-folks home.

"So you thought you'd play amateur sleuth on an FBI case?" She was too smart to be this mental. But he'd met people like that, all brains and no common sense.

"Well, I'm getting somewhere. I cracked some of the code last time." She sighed, signaling a stop in her forward momentum. He waited her out. "Is it wrong if I want to consider becoming an agent?"

His head jutted forward in surprise, as though she were sitting in front of him. He was going to get whiplash from this call. "I have no idea what to tell you, other than Agent Eames would clearly be the better person to talk to about that."

Feeling the early stages of a headache, he reached up and pinched the bridge of his nose, then rubbed at his temple. He would have rubbed both, but one hand had to hold the phone for this god-forsaken phone call.

"Okay," she conceded and he wondered if she was done.

She wasn't.

"So, I've been talking with Dr. Kellogg. He's not all there, but he says some things repeatedly. He says he has thirty-plus children. Ben Jr., Bethany, and Bonnie are all names he repeats and the nurses agree those are his three children. I've met Bonnie and Ben Jr. More on that in a minute."

Oh good, she was parsing out the info now. What in God's name did she have?

"But he also lists William, Valerie, Sarah, Peter, Amanda, Roy, Jason, Brett, Chloe and a handful others. The nurses say he's making it up, but he says the same names over and over." She sucked in a small breath. "And I get why they think he's making it up. He some-times says his kids are named Kilo and Echo and Zulu."

This time Donovan sucked in a breath. *Shit.* She was going to be the death of him. Those were names of the kids in the Atlas and Axis programs they'd discovered. They'd been listed on invoices under military lettering codes. "Are you seriously just sitting there and talking to this old man and sifting information out of him?"

He hoped to the high heavens she wasn't doing anything dangerous. Then again, he'd met her. She probably was. She was going to get herself killed. Then him and Eleri.

"That's it. I read to him at reading time; I read to a lot of the patients. Just him more than the others. And he talks. Okay," her tone changed suddenly from defensive to excited. "I got him to talk about some of the kids. He even called them 'graduates.' They have to be Axis and Atlas graduates. Right?"

"Probably," Donovan conceded.

"You should write this down."

"I can't. Text it to me." The headache bloomed across his whole head. His run was shot to hell, and he did not look forward to relaying this call to Eleri. Plus, how was he going to tell GJ that he wasn't writing anything down because he was standing at the edge of the trees, wanting to go for a run in his alternate form because, despite his lies, she was right? He wasn't quite human.

"Texting it doesn't seem safe."

"You're on a burner and I'm on an FBI phone. Text it when we finish."

"Okay," she sighed, "you're the boss."

It was the only reasonable thing she'd said. Now if she could just act like he and Eleri were the bosses, things would be a lot better.

"Well, I met Ben Jr. He's pretty nice. Get this, he's a geneticist like his father. A human alternate splicing specialty geneticist." She sniffed like she was thinking something distasteful. "I played dumb around him. Just a girl volunteering, you know. And I overheard him say he was keeping tabs on several of them."

"What?" That was it. He was going to have to call Eleri and shut down the two days she had with Avery and they were going to have to examine an old case. Part of him was glad. Their Senior Agent in Charge Westerfield had shut that case down quickly. Too quickly.

"Yes, I've tried to look up some of them, but I'm having trouble. I have four names for you. That's why I'm calling."

He couldn't speak. She had street names of some of the graduates of a vicious government program. Then his brain clicked. "First names don't go very far. They all sounded generic."

"I know, that's why I have . . ." She paused, his sensitive ears picking up the sound of paper rustling, "Sarah Vanguard, Chloe Mercer, Peter Aroya, and Jase—"

"*What* did you say?" Donovan demanded, his heart about to pound out of his chest. "What was that last name?"

"You didn't let me finish. Jason Krupp." She sounded offended but holy shit.

"No, the one before it." Blood beat heavily in his ears, his heart working double time, his breathing picked up as though he had made his run after all.

"Peter Aroya. Why?"

22

Eleri bounced into the room with a smile on her face and the lift of hope in her heart. Avery was in town. For barely forty-eight hours, but she threw the front door open wide, enjoying her boyfriend's almost self-deprecating awe at the place. "It's been in the family for generations. I didn't decorate it."

"It's huge," he answered with a breath, his hand in hers.

"That it is." She smiled up at him as Donovan came into the hallway.

The look on his face was enough to stop her cold. "What?"

"Hi, Avery." He held out his hand and she watched as her partner took a deep breath he managed to keep hidden.

"Hey, Donovan." Avery offered a firm, manly handshake in return and a half grin. The two men had never met before, but Eleri had told them so much about each other there was no real need for introductions. "Am I off base thinking that I'm walking through a historical building here?" He said it as though Donovan was a co-conspirator.

"Nope. I've thought the same thing. You should check out the portraits of the ancestors down the hallway." Donovan tilted his head with a wry grin.

Eleri huffed. She'd never thought about it, but it was relatively abnormal to have all your old relatives hanging in full-sized oils down your antique-laden hall. "Sure, laugh it up. Everyone loves having their own wing."

"True." Donovan managed a smile, but it didn't cover that something was bothering him. He said as much in the next breath. "I'm really sorry, Avery. I have to borrow Eleri for some shop talk."

"Is it 'classified'?" Avery grinned as though he was joking.

"Actually, it is." Donovan's response brought Avery up a little short, and Eleri, too. Had the case already picked up again? Just when Avery got here? *Fuck.*

"But if you want, head out the back door and hang a right. There's an old horse barn and Wade's building a flame thrower," Donovan offered in exchange.

"I'm sorry. He's building a flame thrower? Are you serious?" Avery was blinking now.

"Yeah." Eleri finally joined what should have been her conversation from the start. "He's serious. Wade's a physicist and a bit of an engineer. He's trying to reconstruct something from our case."

"A flame thrower?"

"Yes," She forced a grin. "And that's all I can tell you. The rest is 'classified,' as they say."

"Well, then, at least I'll be entertained." He headed out the double doors toward the back. She could see him framed in the old white paint, through the leaded glass that remained from possibly the original builder. His suitcase remained in her car, no talk yet of unpacking or bringing it in, and Avery had already been dismissed.

"What is it?" She could have been mad, but she trusted Donovan. He wasn't underhanded, didn't deal dirty, and he wasn't trying to ruin her break. Something must be up.

"Aside from the ancestors in the hallway?" He hooked a thumb over his shoulder and looked at her as though she should know something. Then he said, "You'll never guess who just called me."

Eleri thought about it for a minute. He looked perturbed. That wouldn't be Grandmere, plus she was more the type for a cryptic note. It wasn't Westerfield, Eleri's phone had stayed silent. She went for a long shot, trying to bring some levity to the situation. "GJ Janson?"

"I hate you." He said it without inflection and for a moment she reveled in her correctness.

Then she realized what he'd revealed. "GJ called you? Whatever for?"

"Because she found a thousand-year-old skeleton like me. And she stole records from her grandfather's journals. He's been studying my kind for thirty-plus years, apparently." His sarcasm oozed. Donovan was *not* happy. "And she also just happened to find another anomaly in the ligament and tendon attachment points—it goes back to the 'super old' skeleton, so it's 'scientific.'" He used air quotes and what she assumed was his best approximation of a teenaged-girl-on-phone voice, though GJ Janson had never sounded like that. "She seems to think I'm probably double jointed or something like that."

"Oh." Despite his obvious irritation, Eleri absorbed the words. "That sounds like a pretty good approximation."

"I don't care. Because she also told me she's been playing amateur FBI agent."

"I'm sorry, what?" Eleri felt her heart stop. Westerfield was going to *kill* them. If they were lucky, he'd have them hanged. If unlucky, drawn and quartered. GJ Janson had inserted herself into their last case, eventually proving herself useful. But their Special Agent in Charge had not appreciated their use of a civilian, regardless of the fact that they would have had to shoot the grad student to keep her out.

Maybe they should have shot her.

"It gets worse, El." Donovan looked around and Eleri worried.

If this was from the Atlas case, then even Wade or Christina or Dana wasn't privileged for it. "What did she do?"

"She went and became a volunteer at Dr. Benjamin Schwartzgarten's nursing home. He changed his name to Kellogg and she still found him. She reads to him and talks to him about his kids. His *kids*, Eleri." This time his air quotes bore a gravity she didn't want to think about.

The "kids" were victims of a cruel government plan. The ends had not justified the means and only a few had gotten out. "Holy shit."

"Save it. We aren't even to 'holy shit' yet."

He went on, explaining the crap GJ Janson had gotten herself into this time. "She found four graduates of the Atlas program. One is Peter Aroya."

"Peter Aro—" Eleri felt her breath suck in as the name came into focus. "You are fucking kidding me."

"Nope. It could be a different one. I notified the analysts and they're digging into our guy's background. If the Peter Aroya who's the son-in-law of our latest victim is the same, we have some serious shit going down."

Eleri's brain began to churn. "Do we wait until we get confirmation from the analysts before we say anything to Dana?"

"Don't we have to? Then we go to Westerfield." His phone rang.

So did hers.

Donovan heaved a weary sigh. "I hate him."

Westerfield always called when they were talking about him. Maybe he should no longer be spoken of by name, Eleri wondered. Maybe that was one of his powers. "Good afternoon, sir."

Donovan looped into the call with a click, "Hello, we're both on now." He almost couldn't keep the irritation out of his voice.

"Tell me about the case. You're on break?"

Eleri took over. Where she and Donovan were concerned, she was still the senior partner. She still considered it her duty to shield him from the crap that went along with the life, at least for a while. She explained about the lack of leads, about Dana putting them on a mental health break after being quarantined.

"What?"

"Sir, she's some kind of bio-psychic. She put her hand on each of us and said our blood pressure was too high and we were collectively headed for a meltdown." Eleri held her tongue and didn't comment that it hadn't helped to be quarantined for a highly unlikely transmissible disease. Then again, had she been in Dana's shoes, she didn't know what she would have decided. Hunting serial killers wasn't for the faint of heart. Being responsible for a fatal transmissible disease getting spread? That would have killed the bio-psychic.

"Wade's building the flame-thrower." She tossed it into the conversation as bait.

But Westerfield didn't take it. "Good. What's this about Aroya?"

Oh *shitshitshit*. Rule one, remember, Westerfield knew everything. "Well, sir, we just got a call from GJ Janson. Seems she's been out sleuthing on her own. She's been chatting with an Alzheimer's patient named Dr. Benjamin Kellogg, previously Schwartzgartner . . . He's one of—"

"Yes, from the Atlas case. And she linked Aroya to this case?"

"Yes, sir." Eleri waited for him to explode. To yell at them for letting a civilian in. To fire her on the spot, terminating her not only from the NightShade division, which she was growing to love, but from the FBI entirely. For a moment, she panicked. Her mouth opened, but words were slow to form.

Westerfield filled the pause. "I've had my eye on her. She's better than we gave her credit for."

Donovan, who'd been listening in and not commenting, now turned sharply to look at her, his jaw suddenly hanging open. *"What?"* He mouthed it at her as he pointed at his phone.

Eleri shrugged. She had no clue. Then again, she never did when Westerfield was concerned. "Well," she flustered her way through it, "that's good to know."

Avery came in through the back door, looked at one of them, then the other, and gestured at her that he would get his luggage. She nodded and watched as he headed past her toward the large, heavy front door. She was seeing her home with new eyes now that there were other people in it. As a kid, she'd not noticed others' reactions.

She spent a few more minutes having Westerfield talk her through what the protocol was if this Peter Aroya was the same one that Dr. Benjamin Kellogg had helped create. Her brain hurt at the implications of that. Mercifully, they were allowed to end the call before Avery came back in.

"Here," she smiled at her boyfriend when he returned. "Let me show you which room to put your stuff in."

Donovan raised his eyebrows at her from behind Avery's back. Yeah, well. She led Avery down the hall to her room and showed him where to stash his suitcase.

He frowned as she opened the huge armoire. "There are no closets."

"Old house." She shrugged.

"I'll say."

Eleri sighed. "I hate to say this, but I think I need to talk with Donovan about the case a little more. Then, after that, I'll hopefully be yours."

He grinned. "I understand. I'm not fully yours either. I have to run —carefully, so as not to hurt my precious play-offs body—and I have to work out and I already gave you my diet and . . ."

"I know. One day. One day, we'll get a real break. Right?"

"I'm sure of it."

With a grin, she headed out into the hall where she found Donovan staring at one of the paintings. "I look like her, don't I?"

"You're more like her than you know," he said cryptically. She was about to tell him to spit it out already, when he did. "You know why Sarah Hale is famous, right?"

He was pointing at the painting.

"She's famous?" No, she didn't know.

"She's a Salem witch."

"Haha. Everyone in Salem was a 'witch.' *That's* your big worry?" Eleri felt the breath she hadn't realized she was holding escape.

"Eleri, she was convicted but not killed. So was Rebecca Eames." He pointed to another picture.

"Yes, Donovan, everyone in Salem was pretty much on one side or the other. Doesn't mean they were actually witches." Jesus, he was running with this.

"And Eleri Llewelyn Hale?"

"My grandmother. I'm named for her. Donovan—"

"Llewelyn is the biggest name in American witchcraft, Eleri." He stared for a moment. "You're a Remy and a Hale and an Eames, and a Llewelyn. I'm beginning to wonder what you *can't* do."

23

Donovan didn't know what to do despite the fact that he'd been told specifically what to do if this happened. He just wasn't positive that *it* had happened. Then again, how could it have not?

This case had taken a massive turn for the bizarre.

It had taken less than a day for the analysts to produce an updated docket on Peter Aroya.

There was a graduation record from a high school in the town of Queen Creek Arizona. The year matched for Peter Aroya's age. His parents were listed as Don and Jane Aroya, both deceased.

It looked legit, but Donovan and the analysts had been trained to read between the lines.

Don and Jane Aroya had died together in a car accident in Tucson when Peter would have been twenty. But there was no record of them having a child. Peter's birth certificate existed, but was issued from a hospital that had closed. Thus, it was nearly impossible to confirm his birth beyond the copy of the certificate the analyst had dug up. Also, using a deceased couple was a great way to create a false identity.

Peter's age at their time of death meant he would never have gone into the foster system, which meant there were no records of him there to confirm his past.

The town of Queen Creek was just over thirty-thousand people in size. It was big enough that it wasn't weird that no one remembered the Aroya family after this kind of time passage. The analysts had checked and not found anyone who did. It didn't mean the family hadn't been there, and it didn't mean there wasn't anyone who remembered them. It just meant that at first sweep, corroboration wasn't easy to find.

The thing that made Peter Aroya seem like a graduate of the Atlas program was that the town of Queen Creek had one high school. It was on East Ocotillo Road, the same road the courthouse sat on. It was also the same road a storm had ravaged in the late eighties— destroying all the land records, deeds, high school reports, everything that one Peter Aroya might need to prove his very existence. That same storm had come through the town just one year before a graduate of the Atlas program would likely have needed those falsified records.

"Eleri!" Donovan yelled it through the house as though his voice might carry far enough to find her. He sounded like an old "I love Lucy" episode and he didn't like it. Then again, he didn't like any of this.

"Are you serious?" She came around the corner, into the airy sitting room just beyond the kitchen.

He'd thought about the layout—the kitchen had to have been remodeled into the place. The original buildings were old enough that the kitchen would not have been part of the structure, but out behind the home. He'd seen evidence of cornerstones in the garden. They were artfully made into part of the grand display, but they were there. This room had been redone to create a kitchen inside the house. And it probably had been redone again to achieve the old-yet-modern look it now sported. The eat-in area and the sitting room he was in would have been part of that.

The windows were almost floor to ceiling, the panes of old glass in small rectangles set into what appeared to be handcrafted framing. He was on a large, comfortable couch looking out at old English-style gardens that were carefully tended to look like they just grew that way. Before him was a coffee table made from a thick dark wood that matched the long table at the eat-in area. He was pretty sure it was reclaimed from something far more important than him. Despite the beauty around him, he couldn't appreciate it.

"I'm sorry. I have bad news." He looked at the pages he'd printed, at the pieces he'd pulled up on his laptop. Another notice had pinged in.

The local branch had sent an analyst out to Queen's Creek. The library was on the same road as the school, thus they had no high school yearbooks either. Not from the years that might have proved Peter Aroya had once been a student there.

Donovan groaned as he read it. He'd wanted Peter Aroya to simply have a coincidental name. He'd wanted the man to be so concrete that he wouldn't have to deal with Atlas at all again.

"Eleri." Donovan only said her name, but he motioned to what was in front of him and sat back on the couch while she read through it and drew her own conclusions.

He put his hands over his face.

Eleri had these beautiful homes. He'd vacationed at FoxHaven— the homes all had names, of course—and at least then he'd enjoyed it. That visit had been cut short by a case. And now, here he was, with woods, fields, farm, and a Virginia tang in the air that he'd never smelled before and wanted to explore and instead he was getting more case information.

"Crap," Eleri said and Donovan looked up, nodding at her as he smelled Avery coming down the hallway. The man's footsteps were *not* light. Then again, he was a professional in a game known for hiring "enforcers." Donovan suppressed his shudder.

"Avery." He whispered it.

Eleri shook her head. "No worries. I'll tell him."

She was standing to do just that, speaking in a low tone to her boyfriend that she needed a few minutes to sort this out, as Donovan's system pinged again. He felt his chest tighten as he started to read. *Shit.*

He didn't realize he'd said it out loud until Eleri and Avery's heads swiveled his direction. Donovan looked up.

"I get it." Avery held his hands up. "Top secret. I'm out of your way." Then he looked at Donovan, "Just give her back to me soon."

"I'll do my best." He shrugged back at the other man. The truth was though, Eleri was needed.

"What is it?" She came back and sat down next to him, her slight weight denting the cushions next to him, her focus entirely on the screen.

"Sara Vanguard and Jason Krupp went to the same high school and graduated within a few years of each other."

"Jesus." She breathed it out tonelessly. "There's no way they all went to the same place and Dr. Benjamin Kellogg just happens to be reciting their names."

Donovan agreed. "They have different graduation years. But all lost in the storm. No records."

"What about the fourth one?" Eleri asked.

"Chloe Mercer." Donovan filled in, then he pushed a paper her way.

Chloe Mercer had died at age seventeen. "But," he added, "Our analysts had no trouble finding Chloe Mercer alive and well. Same social, same everything."

He heard the thump of the final nail in the coffin.

"Not until tomorrow. Nothing will change before then," Eleri told Dana, playing every card she held. Avery was here, and he'd be leaving the next day anyway.

"Not unless a dead body turns up," Dana countered.

"If that happens, then Donovan and Wade and I would just have to turn around and come right back. Except for some massive airline fees, we won't have anything to show for it."

"Fair enough. Leave tomorrow morning," Dana conceded and Eleri had felt the air rush out of her chest. "Now catch me up to speed."

Eleri filled her boss in on the previous case she and Donovan had worked. "We couldn't truly close the case. Most of the few children who 'graduated' the program have disappeared."

Then she was forced to admit about GJ. "We had a colleague who was doing some follow-up work unbeknownst to us. When she updated us, the name 'Peter Aroya' turned up."

"He's one of these 'graduates'?" Dana sounded as shocked as she had a right to be. "Our Peter Aroya?"

Eleri updated her on the rest of the information.

"Well, that's pretty damning. And he's gone missing," Dana mused. Eleri could hear Christina in the background. "What are the chances that the two cases would intersect like this?"

Eleri didn't know, but it was Christina who chimed in. "Probably pretty high. There's a link, we just don't know it yet. What seems random rarely is."

Eleri had to agree with that.

That had been yesterday. Today, she'd left Bell Point Farm. The reprieve had not been as long as promised and it hadn't been long enough. Then again, promises in the FBI were as solid as the air they were written on.

Wade had spent the previous afternoon brushing up on the Atlas case.

They dropped Avery at his airline, giving Eleri only a few short moments alone with the man, before she ran off in a different direction. If this relationship survived her life, it would be a miracle.

The three agents now stood at a private check-in, having badged their way through most of the airport process, when Wade started talking.

"The flame thrower can't be gasoline or even hydrogen gas based. I can't get it to burn hot enough."

"What do you mean? You can't get it to throw fire hot enough, like the pattern we saw, or you can't get it to burn that hot, period?" Eleri was frowning at him while an agent checked her bag and found that yes, she did in fact have the firearm she claimed she had.

"Not unless I make it into a bomb," Wade countered.

Donovan hopped into the conversation then. Eleri couldn't recall when she'd seen him that angry.

"We are in a fucking airport, you two." He was seething. "Can you please stop talking about—" he lowered his voice and the growl almost came through, "—bombs and flamethrowers."

"Oh." Eleri nodded. "Good idea." But then she turned to Wade. "You just couldn't get it hot enough at all or not hot enough and still be hand-held?"

"I'm going to kill you." Donovan sighed. "I'm going to change right here and rip you to shreds."

"You do realize you're issuing death threats in an airport," she countered, but she did really need to stop talking about bombs.

Though the agent at the airport looked at them oddly, she didn't arrest them, and they checked in relatively easily. In fact, the whole flight was so calm that Eleri almost missed when her phone pinged; the analysts had more information for them.

Dr. Benjamin Kellogg, Junior, also a geneticist, had landed at the same airport in Wyoming just two days prior. He'd not been on any other flights using his own name since.

24

Donovan sniffed the air in the small living room and watched as Wade did the same beside him. A sharp nod came from his friend as Wade very quietly announced, "Someone's here, outside."

But Wade didn't say what Donovan knew and there wasn't time to speak it.

The three of them stood inside the ruins of an abandoned house. At least the weather was nice. The power had been turned off almost two years ago. The water had been stopped not much later. On the counter, a scattering of bills and cutoff threats—both opened and unopened—let them know relatively precise dates for the shut-offs.

Donovan had been surprised when Eleri let Wade drive them out here. She'd sat in the backseat most of the time, not opening her eyes to notice just how out of place the shiny rental SUV was. Donovan had watched the trees go by. He'd rolled down his window and let the scents of maples and poplars waft into the car. They were spiking with late spring. They passed an open field with several types of tall purple flowers and lower yellow ones that resembled daisies, but weren't. Donovan didn't know his plants by name, just sometimes by look or by memory of the places his father dragged him. He had no associations with these. They were merely pretty.

He'd been preoccupied with the flowers, with the long drive, with "getting there," and so he'd been surprised when Eleri popped up and put her hand on Wade's shoulder. "Don't turn down the driveway."

When Eleri spoke cryptically, everyone listened. It was only about three more seconds before Wade drove past their turn. They pulled out a map and, at Eleri's instructions, found a route around the back. It cost them nearly twenty more minutes of driving and thirty minutes of hiking.

Now they stood quietly in the Aroyas' house at the end of a long drive. The nearest neighbor was at least a mile up the hidden road. But they'd come in on foot and from the back, no one should know they were here.

Eleri had remembered bug spray, though Donovan and Wade didn't need it. The scent she wafted was repellent to bugs and wolves alike apparently. He scrunched his nose at her as they all stood still inside the house and waited at the sound of a car door from the driveway.

Who could even be here? Peter Aroya? No one had heard from him for over four years. The footsteps were too heavy to be Mina—the information on her said she was tall, around five-nine, but willowy and fine-framed. This was a deep tread. The smell said "man," too. But there was something Donovan recognized, a lingering trace he couldn't place. It had come with the man.

"Fuck it, Peter. Where are you?"

Wade turned his head to look at Donovan, though Eleri seemed oblivious to the man talking outside. She looked at them and shrugged, but it was Wade who made motions, silently suggesting that he go for a run.

Eleri shook her head, but Wade was already peeling his clothes.

"The door!" Eleri mouthed. They'd closed it behind them.

The voice came again. "Peter, you bastard. Where did you go!" It wasn't a question and this time it was loud enough for Eleri to hear.

"Window." Donovan looked at his two partners. There was an open one by the front porch. Though "open" was a relative term. The window itself had been pushed up by some long ago visitor or looter and the screen cut out. Wade could easily slip through it and no one would have to open the door and make noise as Eleri feared.

Wade motioned with his hand, almost angrily, for Eleri to turn around. Donovan did, too. Didn't need to see a grown man naked. Didn't need to watch the strange twists and turns his own body took when changing. Though, for the first time, he began to understand Eleri's scientific fascination with it. With Wade doing the changing, it was simply a thing that was and not a mark of being the sole freak that did it.

Each shift of bone and pop of flesh made him cringe, but Eleri barely seemed to hear it. The man outside did not. He was still cursing Peter.

It had to be Peter Aroya he was talking to, muttering about. Peter Aroya was listed as the last owner on this property. The current owner was the bank, having repossessed the place almost a year ago. The lack of effort put forth to sell the place indicated their belief in the value. Even the "For Sale" sign out front looked relatively hopeless.

At the sound of metal striking dirt, Donovan snapped his head around and looked at Wade as he moved the last few bones in his feet. Wade's fur was brown, the same shade as the hair on his head. He looked as much like a big dog as he did a wolf.

"Go!" Donovan mouthed the word and Wade took off. He was through the hole in the screen before Eleri could protest.

Neither he nor his remaining partner moved. In the light filtering through the windows, he could see the floor was old and uncared for. The chances it would give away their presence was too high.

The second time he heard the noise, Donovan couldn't deny what it was: shovel striking earth. Stuck inside, he couldn't see, but he remembered several holes dug up in the back of the property when they'd hiked in. Though they'd traveled from the side of the big yard, skimming the backs of the neighbors' homes, they'd come around the house and walked in the front door. Plain as you please. He didn't know if Eleri had seen the holes, but he'd smelled the fresh-turned earth, and the slightly older piles. They had taken a while to achieve.

Catching Eleri's attention, Donovan mouthed, "He's digging."

"Digging?" she shook her head, the conversation passing without sound a human ear could detect. Eleri had learned to speak at his level. She could likely barely hear her own voice, but Donovan could hear her. It was speaking back to her that was the problem.

Eleri looked at him, confused, as though she was about to say something else, ask another question, when she gripped the countertop and nearly rolled her eyes back.

Donovan leaped, not caring about the sound, not caring about giving away their position, only needing to be sure that his partner didn't hit her head on the way down.

Only, she didn't go down.

Her eyes glazed, unfocused as her neck jerked up. She appeared to be looking into the middle of the empty room, as though she were watching someone who wasn't there. Her gaze darted frantically. More than one someone.

Seeing that she was okay, if in the grip of something, Donovan focused elsewhere. The best way to keep her safe was to monitor the area beyond. He heard Wade slowly stalking through the trees. He turned his head to look down the hallway, his sense of smell telling him that no one occupied the back rooms they hadn't yet had time to check.

Once, it had been a nice home. Small, just two bedrooms, but plenty of land. It was solid construction. The wooden front porch held two dusty, but originally nice, wicker chairs. In the kitchen, pots hung from a metal grid overhead, suggesting that someone here enjoyed cooking. The couch in the living room wasn't worn, but well cared for. Sturdy. Clean before being abandoned. The TV was large with several pieces of tech hooked up, including wires that led to surround sound speakers. These people had lived relatively well out here. Peter Aroya had commuted quite a distance to his job, but it must have been worth it.

"Donovan!" The hiss of Eleri's voice was too loud. The man outside might hear her. But Donovan was just grateful that she was okay, she was alert and herself again.

He looked up at her and as he watched she let go of the counter and walked up to him, unconcerned with whether her feet made any noise. "That man out there, he's been here before."

Donovan nodded at her once, as if to say, "Go on."

"I almost recognize him. I can't tell you if I ever met him before but he feels familiar." She was speaking in low tones, rapidly doing her best to convey anything and everything she'd gotten from whatever she'd seen. "He came and he argued with Peter and Mina. At least I guess she's Mina." Eleri shrugged.

Donovan understood. They had reasonably recent pictures of Peter Aroya—less than ten years old. The Bureau had dug them up from his work, from traffic cameras, his driver's license. Wilemina—Mina—had been harder to find. She had an old driver's license photo as well, but she must have had it made in Soviet Russia, the pixilation was so bad. It was recognizable only so much as it was of a human female with pale brown hair. It said her eyes were blue, but the picture didn't have enough information to support that.

Unlike Peter, she had a yearbook photo and graduation pictures. Her school remembered her. Her college did, too. But their IDs? Not saved that far back. She didn't participate in any clubs that could be found, nor did she attend parties that had been captured online or in the paper at the time. She'd held a job in Rosedeer, when the couple lived there. But only part time. Only half shifts. Those who remembered her described her as having pale brown hair and blue eyes. Nothing the awful driver's license photo hadn't already told them.

Mina Orlov Aroya had managed to stay out of sight. And her history before she came to the US? Unknown still. Though the analysts were still trying to crack that one wide. It was hard because she and her mother came in under political asylum doctrines.

"He was here," Eleri said, referring to the man outside. "More than once. They argued all the time. Mina was afraid of him.... No. Not of him, but afraid of something he . . . brought with him?" She searched for words, unable to fully form what she'd seen.

"When?" Donovan pressed.

"I don't know. But the house was clean and the lights were on. It was immaculate. Mina was nervous. He made her very nervous." She'd found a good word and latched onto it.

Just then, they heard a sharp bark from Wade, followed by the man's voice.

"Get back!" The sounds indicated he was shuffling around, probably facing off with Wade, given the answering growls.

Donovan moved. It didn't matter now if they gave away their location. Wade was out there and the man had at least a shovel with him. In a fight, it wasn't a weapon to be trifled with.

Donovan burst out the back door, into the area behind the house. Into the thicket of trees that made just enough border to suggest the property line separating this house from the open fields behind it. Eleri stayed hot on his heels. He heard the zip of metal and plastic on nylon and knew she had her weapon drawn.

She managed the words before he did. "Stop. FBI. Put your hands—"

She was interrupted by a burst of swear words and a flurry of motion. The shovel came at her causing her to retreat so as not to get hit. Donovan had jumped in front of her, thinking to knock it out of the way, but he missed. Even as close as he was, he only managed to catch the edge of it with his arm. It hit her in the shin, but she didn't flinch. When she wanted to be, Eleri was all badass.

Even as the shovel clattered to the ground, the man whirled and ran.

It was a bold move with two FBI agents with guns drawn on you.

It was Eleri who dropped her weapon first, who motioned Donovan to put his own gun down. She waved Wade off and let the man go.

Then she walked around the side of the house where he'd disappeared. Then, seeming to change her mind, Eleri began running. She yelled out, "FBI, Stop!" and put a bullet in the ground near the car.

Donovan came around the corner just as she shot, missing in spectacular fashion. "Don't shoot," she warned him, sotto voce. Then she yelled again, "FBI, stop!" and fired again.

Donovan watched as gravel sprayed from the force of the bullet, about fifteen feet behind the car.

"What was that?" He asked her, utterly confused as the car pulled out onto the main street.

"I know who he is." She answered as Wade stepped up beside her, panting.

25

E leri felt her ribs heaving from the exertion of the encounter. She'd not just stayed tense inside the house the whole time, she'd also had that weird vision. Add to that any encounter in which she drew her gun left her dealing with the aftereffects of adrenaline.

Donovan stood beside her, his own breathing rough at the edges. "Why did you miss? You didn't even get his tires."

"Just taking shots." She took a deep inhale and worked on slowing her breathing. "Once I recognized him, I realized I could let him get away. Then I realized that I couldn't let him know I'd let him go. So, I fired randomly to make it look like I was trying."

Donovan looked around into the open space. "Do you think the shots will bring the police department out? —Sheriff's office?" He'd immediately corrected himself.

"Nah." She shook her head. "Out here?" Eleri gestured and realized she was still breathing more heavily than she would like. "I'm sure gunfire is just written off. Also, nearest person should be about a mile away, if not farther. So it may not even register. That's why he could come here and dig up the ground with no one the wiser."

"Who is he?" Donovan asked.

And wasn't that the million-dollar question? "Dr. Benjamin Kellogg—"

"He's in his nineties!" Donovan protested before she could finish.

"Junior," Eleri finished with some satisfaction.

"Oh." Now that she'd said it, he was seeing the similarities in the men's faces. Like father, like son. "So, Dr. Benjamin Kellogg—the one who ran the Atlas program—it was his son who came out to dig in Peter Aroya's yard?"

Donovan sounded incredulous, and well he should. Eleri understood.

"Dr. Benjamin Kellogg, Junior is a geneticist, just like his father. My guess is that he's keeping tabs on Daddy's progeny." She looked up at her partner, "Just in case you were still wondering if this case connects back to the Atlas project. The answer is now unequivocally 'yes.'"

"Jesus." He breathed it out and Eleri recognized the expression, the exasperated sigh, the skyward look as things he'd picked up from her. "What was he doing here?"

"That, I don't know." She didn't want to think about what it might mean. The holes in the back weren't wide or deep, so she was curious what he might have buried here or maybe Peter and Mina had buried it.

"I need to get into the back of the house," Donovan told her and at last she turned around, looking away from the now empty, long shot of the driveway.

"Okay." She almost sighed it. She reminded herself that she loved her job. "Let's go inside again."

They headed back down the gravel drive and Eleri was surprised to see she'd run after the car farther than she'd expected. No wonder she'd been out of breath. She pulled the front door open and waved Donovan inside, noticing the shift in him.

He slowed his steps, lifted his nose a little, breathed slower.

He was scenting and it was fascinating to watch. Donovan didn't stick to the front room this time.

"What did you get back there?"

"I—" He started but then pulled back. "Let me be sure. It's been a long time."

The back rooms stood with doors open, the hallway hooking to the right and around toward the kitchen, toward the back screen door they'd plunged out of at Wade's bark. Eleri stepped into the room and noted that she didn't see Wade outside. Getting closer to the window, she spotted him through a few of the trees, still sniffing around. Nose to the ground, he walked a line, turned, and headed back the other way. He was running a grid pattern, making sure he didn't miss anything. Eleri aimed herself and her thoughts back toward Donovan.

Her partner stood first in the center of the room and turned a full three-sixty. She might not have his sense of smell, but she did the same.

The walls were beige, dulled with age and sun. The windows had been thrown wide and left that way for over a year at least, according to the bleaching patterns on the furniture. A white, metal daybed was pushed into a corner, dust clinging to the bare mattress. Louvered closet doors sat open on an empty space, the rack bare, save for a few mismatched hangers.

Donovan ducked his head and stepped into the closet, sniffing as he went. He walked across the room and aimed his nose at the empty white bookshelf, then the plain wooden desk. He leaned over the bed, checking the mattress in a few places. Then he stood up. "I can't tell for sure. It's still eluding me, but I think the woman was here."

"You think she stayed with Peter and Mina?" Eleri asked.

"I think she *is* Mina." Donovan stared back at her.

"This isn't a couple's bedroom." She shook her head at him then crossed the hall to the other room. "That is a couple's bedroom."

In the other room, a queen bed filled the center space—stripped bare, just like the others. This time the closet held men's and women's clothing, but looked like it had been raked through before it was abandoned. Eleri pulled open dresser drawers and found they held clothes, but Donovan sniffed around.

"It's the same in here."

"The other room looks like a guest room, or maybe an office with a guest bed. You're suggesting Mina slept in there?"

"It happens," he said, and he was right. Married couples often slept in different beds for a variety of reasons.

"You can't pick his side of the bed from hers?" Eleri asked, wondering if she was being dumb for even asking.

"Usually, but not here. Not this long, with the window open—" he pointed to the five-inch gap in the sash of the window leading to the backyard. There was a gray area on the carpet indicating that some-times rain came in and maybe animals. "It's washed the smells out. And from what I can pick up, I'm not sure they had a *his side* and *her side*. I can't pick distinct smells out anymore. I'm not even sure that two people lived here."

"The closet says they did." Eleri waved her hand that way. "And it says only two people." She didn't have to remind him that the analysts were convinced Peter and Mina remained childless. She didn't point out that the house showed no evidence of anyone other than the two of them. "It really pushes Mina as our best suspect."

Donovan nodded.

A bark came from the backyard and the two of them headed down the hall and out the back doorway, the screen slapping behind them. The bark wasn't frantic, it wasn't deep or harsh, and they went willingly if not quickly.

They found Wade, still in wolf form—though she'd expected nothing else—standing in an open spot in the backyard. His right front paw rested at an angle and as they approached, he tapped the spot. Then tapped it again.

He'd found something.

He offered a short bark, pawed the ground hard enough to leave a mark and turned around. Donovan followed him as though he'd spoken pure English and Eleri raised her eyebrows behind their backs. *Werewolves*. Neither man would appreciate the thought. She trailed them, but nearly bumped into Donovan when Wade stopped. They hadn't gone very far.

Another short bark. Wade pointed with his paw again.

She didn't see anything. It seemed neither did Donovan. Wade pushed at the ground again, and this time she spotted a small hole near his paw, about a half inch in diameter. Snake hole? Some small rodent? A big bug?

Satisfied, Wade walked a foot away. He pointed out another one. Then another one. They were odd. Perfectly round. Straight down. Eleri felt her brows pull in. She should recognize this.

Wade walked further away, over toward where several of the holes had been dug. For a moment, Eleri peered down into one, then the other. It didn't appear anything had been removed, but that might be hard to tell. Sometimes people buried cash in their back yard. She didn't know.

Another short bark came from Wade and she realized he was trying to get her to pay attention. "Sorry," she apologized and come over to see he was pointing out more of the same holes.

Then he went back to the spot he'd marked, sniffed the area again and began digging. Eleri looked to Donovan who shrugged and looked back at her. "He smells something."

Though he didn't stop digging, a sharp retort of a bark came from Wade. Even Eleri could understand it. *Yes. He smelled something.*

"Do you smell it?" Eleri asked Donovan even as she scooted to his side, taking advantage of the shade he offered as the sun got warmer. They still had to hike out of here.

He looked down at her, his droll expression letting her know that he knew what she was doing. "Not with this nose." He said it as though she should know that.

They waited a moment, and when nothing happened except that Wade had made a shallow trench in the ground, Donovan offered to help. "There's a shovel over there. I can help?"

The noise he got in reply was clearly a "No."

Eleri stepped back and went to look at the holes in the ground again. As she searched, she found far more of them than just the ones Wade pointed out. They clustered around the dug up spaces and she felt pieces of her brain almost slide into place. "Donovan!"

"What?"

"The holes!" She grinned. "We use them to test the ground. He was using a pointed piece of metal bar to test the ground for softness."

Donovan nodded. "So, he was looking for something buried, either harder or softer than the natural dirt pack."

"Right." Eleri crossed her arms and grinned. She looked around the yard at the holes. They were small. Kellogg had been looking for something he'd lost.

A bark came from Wade as he stepped back, his paws filthy from digging. He looked up at them expectantly, so Eleri stepped forward.

As she looked down, her heart sank. She didn't like what he'd uncovered. It looked like a tangle of tiny roots and a smooth rock. "Shit."

She was pulling a pair of latex gloves from her back pocket before she even realized she was doing it. Wade stepped back as did Donovan, letting her get down on her hands and knees. She was going to be as dirty as Wade.

It took her about fifteen minutes before she was satisfied—though that was probably the wrong word. Leaning back on her heels, she looked around to find her partners.

Wade sat, naked, his arms resting on his knees, clearly exhausted. "Put some clothes on," she told him, but mostly she was berating herself for missing yet another change, so damn close!

Donovan was already leaning over her, looking at what she'd uncovered.

"Oh shit." The words rolled out of his mouth.

"Yeah," she agreed. Wade had smelled it. No one had to be told.

The tangle of tiny roots was hair. And when she pushed and rubbed the dirt out of the way, she'd revealed the round surface and eye sockets of a human skull.

26

Donovan stared up into the bright klieg lights and felt himself sway. This job had gotten infinitely worse today. His only consolation was that the decomposition of the body made it certain that the man had not died on their watch. This one wasn't their fault.

He'd been on the phone calling Dana and explaining the whole thing to her. He usually would have simply followed Eleri's orders, which he already knew would have been as casual as "get us a team. ASAP." Dana's orders however, were more precise. They also included a conversation stating that she'd requested and been given all their paperwork from the Atlas case. To which she told him, "You got shafted on this one. Not even being able to tell the families you found their children. Not getting to really close the case." Then she was regular Dana again, explaining to him how she wanted the scene contained.

Donovan found all that very funny. There was no one out here to contain. Until they set up the lights, no one would have any idea they were even here. Still, he got into the kit they always carried and dutifully tried to roll out yellow tape around the entire perimeter of the house.

Eleri asked him what the hell he was doing. Then he ran out of tape. So he'd limited it to running down the property line at the road side, and staking a wide space around the body.

In a few hours, an FBI team arrived with a cadaver dog—who

ironically kept finding him and Wade. The handler appeared embarrassed, saying, "I don't know why she keeps doing that!"

Donovan just smiled. At first, Wade laughed at him until the female dog had put her nose to the ground, sniffed a neat trail around the yard until she hit Wade's foot, then dutifully sniffed right up his pants leg to his crotch. At which point she sat and alerted.

Donovan had almost bitten into his tongue. The unintentional comic relief of the dog was the only thing making the long night bearable. Though the swarming bugs didn't bite him, they were still obnoxious. He was pretty sure he'd inadvertently swallowed one. There was nothing to eat but water and energy bars and after the fifth, he was convinced they were not giving him any energy. He was tempted to curl up under one of the nearby trees and sleep.

Forcing himself the two slow steps necessary, he planted himself at Eleri's side. "Why are we still here?"

"Because we're in charge." Her voice was as dead-to-the-world flat as his was. She'd been down in the ditch digging up the bones while they waited for the team. She'd brushed at the dirt with a soft broom from a cheap dustpan set. It was her favorite—which he'd learned at one point when he suggested it was so dirty she just throw it away. He was surprised now that he hadn't gotten her black-eyes-of-anger response for that.

He figured they were lucky they hit the skull first. A little off and they might have missed the body. But they wouldn't have. With Wade in wolf shape, his nasal cavity was wide open; he could sniff a decaying body as well as any cadaver dog. And he didn't have to be trained to do it. They wouldn't have missed. Wade might have even been able to tell head from feet when he smelled it and set them to digging in the most valuable place. Foot bones were a bitch to reassemble.

Periodically, the team would call out something. They'd gotten the whole top layer of the body exposed. Two bright yellow strings lay on a perpendicular, staked and leveled, holding court above the body. They existed to orient the photos to north-south and east-west and then to measure down to determine the depth at which different body parts had been buried.

"Come look," one of the experts called over. Eleri popped to life, scrambling to get to the hole and look inside yet again. "What do you say?"

"Same thing I said with the skull. The clothing also supports the conclusion this is a male," Eleri told them, her eyes laser sharp now. "The shape of the skull is non-definitive, but the blonde hair would indicate at least some Caucasian ancestry or that he dyed it."

Eleri lowered herself to her knees and pulled on yet another pair of gloves. This time there was more dirt pushed away in a slurry of mud made as the team kept washing the skeleton. The water helped to clear and clean the bones without damaging them, but the mud was a mess. She put one finger under the upper teeth where the lower jaw had been removed and stored already.

"No shoveling," she reported. "Shoveling" of the teeth indicated ancestry, but it didn't do anything to identify this man as Peter Aroya.

The tech nodded at her, then pointed again and again. "We have a few things. Here—" she pointed to his ribs. "There's a neat hole in the shirt. Looks to have burn marks around it, but it's too old for that to be evidence alone. So now that we've more dug out, I can tell you there's a matching mark on his ribs."

"What?" This time Donovan—who'd been listening only half awake—throttled to full alert and peered down into the hole. He'd been expecting no marks. Whatever Mina Aroya was doing, it wasn't leaving any evidence they could find. So why did this guy have a mark. "Knife?"

A good stab to the ribs was an effective way to kill someone.

"Knife?" Dana's voice startled him. Though he could recall the sound of a car pulling up, he hadn't really registered it. He hadn't really registered any of it until now. Christina trailed behind her, quiet but present. They both looked fresh enough that if he'd had the energy, he would have shaken them for it.

"Nope. Bullet," Eleri said from where she hovered over the body. "And look." She didn't seem at all startled to see Dana and Christina here.

Hail, hail, the gang's all here. Though when he looked around, he realized that Wade had gone to sleep in the passenger seat of their empty car. He didn't know if that made the man smart, lucky, or what. Donovan only knew he was jealous.

His thoughts pulled back to the hole in the ground and dead body in the hole.

"See the side here?" Eleri again pointed to where the techs had most of the skull unearthed. It sat on a pedestal of dirt, the rest carved away, giving it a creepy, floating look. "That's another bullet hole. And back here—" she moved to the other side, almost to the back, but Donovan could see the damage through the empty eye socket. "That's the damage of an exit wound. I'll want to do a full report, but that's a bullet to the brain."

"That's a cause of death," Dana mused confusedly. Her confusion seemed to make techs wonder. In the regular world, this was all normal. Bullet to the brain was a reasonable cause of death, and honestly, if you were going to bury a man in someone's backyard, your having shot him in the head was a good reason to do so. But in the NightShade world, in the world where this woman was running around with a damn flamethrower killing people out of fear and nothing else? Then a bullet to the brain and a normal backyard burial were very confusing, indeed.

Donovan was about to declare himself beat, but Dana made his morning worse. Or better.

"We need to get out of here, team. They can finish this up."

Eleri started to protest and Donovan understood. It was her body. It was probably hard enough on her to not be doing the digging herself. But she didn't get a chance to say anything, Dana gave out even more startling news.

"We have Dr. Benjamin Kellogg Junior in custody."

Eleri woke to her phone ringing after just barely two and half hours of sleep. She was supposed to be afforded four. So she ignored it.

Her phone rang again. Either someone was dead or someone was dumb. Her hand slapped out at the nightstand that was always right beside the bed in these hotels. She'd slept more nights away than in any of her own beds in . . . well, since her Senior Agent in Charge Westerfield had called her at the mental hospital over a year ago and told her she was getting out, that he had a case for her.

The face of the phone was too bright to register in the near total darkness in the hotel room. The Bureau favored certain chains for lodging for their soundproofing and blackout curtains. Eleri thought about the fact that this was the first one they'd managed, since this killer seemed to favor victims in small towns. Eleri counted them lucky if there was an hourly motel nearby.

As her eyes adjusted, the horrid noise came again. The ringtone she'd once thought was sweet was going to have to be changed lest she throw the phone across the room. The blurry letters came into focus as her brain did and she scrambled to work her thumb while at the same time coming fully awake.

"Hey, baby. Good morning." Avery's voice came through the line, sweet despite his stupidity.

"It is neither good nor morning. Why are you calling so late?" She stuttered and corrected herself, "So early?"

"It's seven a.m. on the west coast. Unless you're in Hawaii, it's morning."

"What?" She barely got the word out before she looked at the phone again and saw that he was right. "Shit."

"Sounds like I woke you. I'm sorry. I really thought you'd be up."

"No, it's okay. Normal people would be awake." She was sitting up now, but not fully alert. This was the life she'd agreed to. Hell, it was the life she'd chased down and handcuffed and read it its Miranda Rights.

"Did you see the game last night?"

"No." Her heart turned. She'd promised to watch. If she could. Shockingly, she hadn't been able to. "I'm sorry. Dead body."

It was all she could tell him and even that was probably too much.

"You get that many live bodies in your line of work?" He chuckled.

"Sure, but good point, we don't call them 'bodies.'" She changed the subject. "Did you win?"

"Yes."

"That's fantastic!" She was truly excited for them. They were in the playoffs. A first for the relatively new team.

This time it was him changing the subject. "You said normal people would be up by now. But you're not normal, are you?"

"What?" Maybe she wasn't as awake as she felt like she was. Her brain turned it over until it made sense. "No. I'm an agent, we work all hours and nothing is overtime. I'm sleeping because I was on site until four a.m. uncovering a body. I don't know how to be normal."

She was satisfied with her answer, but her senses were pinging her. There was something in his tone that was ominous.

"That's not what I meant."

"What *did* you mean?" This time she asked it with deep concern.

She could feel herself starting to distance from the conversation. Was he done with her?

He sighed, heavy and long and dejected. "I'm not as dumb as I look, Eleri."

"I never thought you were dumb. What's going on, Avery?" Her blood was thinning, running cold. She was sitting stock still, waiting, tense, fully awake now, her eyes glazing as her focus turned inward, ready to curl up in defense. She told herself she did not need this now.

But Avery had other ideas. "I heard your partner talking to you about your family. In the hallway, at Bell Point Farm. He said your ancestors were witches. Why would you hide that kind of heritage from me?"

"Jesus, Avery. If you're going to listen in, do a better job of it. I didn't know." She immediately regretted snapping at him. "I'm sorr—"

"How could you not know?" He pushed over her apology.

"Why should I? What did *your* grandparents do for a living?" Apology be damned. She'd had no idea. First Donovan, now Avery? "My parents told me the pictures were of great-grandparents. I don't even have to look up their names—they stared down at me in the hallway every day when I would go to school."

"All you had to do was google it!" He countered.

"Why would I? Have you googled *your* grandfather? Or for that matter, your five-times-great grandfather?" She huffed out a breath she hadn't meant him to hear. There was nothing like a fight in the morning that shouldn't have been morning. Not yet anyway. "I'll bet I know more of my ancestors' names than you know of yours!"

There was a deep pause and she wondered if this was the end. She shouldn't have told him she'd been up with a dead body. It was a breach of Bureau classified information.

"You're right," he conceded. "I don't know my great-great-grandparents' names or jobs or much about them."

Good. The thought went through her head followed closely by the thought that she'd won, but at what cost?

"Are you a witch?"

"What?" She didn't even get time to process it.

"Eleri. You have to look these people up. Your partner is right. Your great ancestors were witches who were tried in Salem and disappeared before being hanged. Not just one. *Several* of them. And you have a grandmother—that's not that far back, Eleri!—who's a *Llewelyn.*"

This time when the name came back at her, she understood. She'd looked it up when Donovan shoved the details in her face. It was disturbing how many tangled chains of American witchcraft coursed through her father's side of the family. Grandmere had been right. Her mother had run from Grandmere's roots right into just as big a mess. Only she didn't know.

"Eleri." He said it as though he'd said it several times already. "You know what that makes you?"

"It doesn't make me anything," she countered, tired again.

"It does. You are literally the granddaughter of the witches they could not burn." He said it with a conviction that shot through her. Something she had not considered before. She wasn't a strange girl with strange hunches. She wasn't a psychic. She was the product of her ancestry, a lightning bolt of heritage she could not escape.

"Eleri," he pushed again, "Are you a witch?"

27

Donovan was sitting at yet another conference table in yet another branch FBI office when Dana's phone rang. The look on her face said it couldn't be good. Her eyes closed and she glanced away, her hand coming up to shield her face as though if she couldn't see the bad things they couldn't see her. Donovan might have felt worse for her if she hadn't been his boss and if she hadn't been about to share the bad news with the rest of them.

He heard the voice on the other end of the line.

Another murder. Pretty sure it was linked. Only this time, the body had burned while alive.

"The DNA came back—the preliminary work," Eleri said as she looked up, unaware of Dana's bad news. She said it as though everyone at the table already knew that preliminary was all there could be at this time. "The body in the yard was Peter Aroya."

"They did an ID already?" Christina was leaning forward, also unable to hear the conversation on the phone.

"No, but I have enough evidence." Eleri pulled out a page and with half his attention, Donovan watched her slide the familiar letter across the table. "The body was sent into CODIS and AFIS and local sites, and no matches. But the general genetic test we rushed through a for-profit clinic, generated this letter."

Christina picked it up and scanned it. "Who are Las Abuelas?" She mangled the word, just as Donovan had the first time he'd encountered it.

"It's a group out of Argentina, searching for missing kids. The genetic combination that triggers that letter is pretty specific." Eleri was almost cheerful in her explanation, glad for the match. But she was making it harder for him to listen in to Dana's conversation. Had his boss not been warned that he and Wade could hear everything? Even if she turned away and went into a corner of the room?

Christina waved the letter at Eleri. "So, are they coming for him?"

"No, it's not like that. Las Abuelas—and some other groups—have an arrangement. The letter is generic. The DNA testing company agrees to send it to anyone who matches, but they don't alert Las Abuelas. It's up to the person who gets the letter, to decide if they want to reach out."

"But this is unique enough to ID Peter Aroya?"

"I wouldn't sign the report yet, but I'd write it. This is pretty damning," Eleri continued on, listing out the same pieces Donovan had linked himself. "Also, this body was found on Peter Aroya's property. The decomposition indicates it's been there the right amount of time to be the missing man. Dental should confirm that soon—I'll do that as soon as the films come in." She was talking about the dental x-rays. Most people hardly called them "films." "And this letter links him to the Atlas project. I'll be shocked if that's not Peter Aroya."

She didn't mention camel DNA or what the body's full genomic profile would look like. They'd ordered it to help ID the man, but Donovan wasn't ready to explain what had happened at Atlas.

When Eleri opened her mouth again, Donovan waved a hand at her to get her to shut up. For the first time, she looked at him and frowned, finally catching on that he was listening to Dana's phone conversation.

Her eyebrows lifted in question, and he returned a grim shake of his head.

"Another body?" she mouthed the words, her voice coming through low to even his own ears.

He nodded this time, noticing Christina frowning at both of them. It occurred to him that he and Eleri had developed the kind of shorthand couples did, or partners. It hit him that he'd never had that before. Not the best friend in school, not friends in med school, but Eleri was already frowning at him again.

Dana had turned off the phone and looked at the group. "We have two new bodies."

"Two?" The word flew out of his mouth before he could catch it and stop it.

She nodded then looked at each person at the table. If Wade had managed to hear the whole conversation, he wasn't giving it away.

When a chorus of nods came back to her, Dana started in, "We have a male, . . ." She seemed to have lost the information she needed already. Then she looked at her phone and plowed ahead. "Dale Wallis. Another truck driver. The decomposition on his body indicates he's been dead about two days."

"No one found him?" Wade asked. "These fires seem to be a signal. Wouldn't the neighbor see it?"

"Nope, super contained, even more than at Gennida Orlov's apartment."

"What's the connection to the previous bodies? If there is one," Eleri asked and the whole group hung on Dana's answer as if she was the teacher. Well, they were going to be tested on the material, Donovan thought.

"Nothing. Just that he's a trucker, like Leroy Arvad."

"So we think Mina Aroya is on some kind of killing spree, getting truckers to pick her up along with her flamethrower?" Wade asked as though he were genuinely confused. He was the crime scene guy, not the psychoanalysis guy. "Then she's killing off . . . what? People that pissed her off? Like her husband?"

"Don't know about that," Dana answered smoothly, "But this trucker guy looks like another source of transportation that she just removed."

"That's cold." Donovan heard the words out of his mouth. He'd grown up with an abusive father who had the mother of all secrets. He'd seen the man kill in fits of rage. But he'd never seen the kind of crazy that would lead someone to cover up a ride in a truck with murder. The truckers probably picked up all kinds of hitchhikers. At least, Donovan couldn't fathom that this woman was the first they'd ever given a ride to. "So then are we assuming the other victim was her target? Or was this just another person in her way?"

That worked from the theory that Mina Aroya had offed her husband—somehow with Dr. Benjamin Kellogg finding out and looking for the body. Though in Donovan's mind that made sense. GJ said that Dr. Kellogg Junior was keeping tabs on the Atlas graduates. If he'd been keeping up with Peter Aroya, then the man went missing, and there was a newly turned lump of dirt by the property line . . . well, it added up to Dr. Junior coming out with a shovel periodically and trying to find some evidence.

"So Mina and Peter meet, they get married, they live in Casper, then Rosedeer, Wyoming," Donovan recited it to the table at large. "They don't have any kids, live a relatively quiet life in the middle of nowhere with Mina mostly as an at home wife with very part time work. Do you think she just snapped?"

Christina opened her mouth, but it was Dana who beat her to the punch.

"Maybe. The second victim has to be the target here—Dr. Benjamin Kellogg Senior."

"*What?*" The sound came from his vocal chords and Eleri's in unison.

Dana nodded sagely, then added more, "And he didn't just die. He burned. Alive. The ring of fire around him was a joke. He was on fire in the middle of empty, unburned space."

"Holy shit," Wade muttered. Donovan could tell Wade was getting squirrely. He'd left NightShade, unable to or not wanting to deal with what they saw. Maybe something particular had happened. But he'd gone back to his first love, physics. Now here he was again and the thought of people getting burned alive was bothering all of them.

"Dr. Kellogg's dead," Eleri said it with reverence. All the physicians and scientists who'd worked on the Atlas project were now gone. And good riddance, Donovan had thought. Kellogg had led the brigade. Donovan didn't like the way his thoughts turned mean, but they did. *He deserved to die that way.*

They were absorbing it when Dana said, "The body is still warm. We are wheels up for Phoenix, A.S.A.P."

Everyone was standing, gathering whatever pages, tablets, and laptops they'd brought. Everyone but Christina and Wade.

Wade spoke up. "Are we pegging Mina Aroya as our killer?"

"For now." Dana shrugged. "It's not shoot to kill yet because we have no real evidence against her, but yes."

Donovan looked at his friend still sitting there, needing a minute to digest the happenings. So while Wade thought, Donovan threw another log on that fire. "I want to revisit the flamethrower. I think it may be . . . supernatural."

"You really think that?" Dana asked him, the two of them standing, poised to leave, but having this conversation instead.

"I've thought about it all along. We rejected the idea because there was no reason to think it was supernatural, but now there's enough information leaning that way. How would she carry it around? Hide it? Also, think about what the five of us can do. A real pyromaniac isn't that far a stretch." As he laid the cards out one by one, he was becoming more convinced.

"It's possible."

"I think it's more than possible," Donovan countered, gathering strength behind his idea as he spoke. "Look, Wade can't duplicate it. We can't get that heat, or that range, or that portability. And if he can't do it, how could she?"

"Um," Wade spoke up. "Maybe she's better than me. Maybe she knows about an alternate fuel that I don't."

Eleri stared at the two of them, then turned to Wade. "What do you think the likelihood is that she's actually better at this than you are?"

Wade blushed. "Statistically, that's actually pretty small."

Eleri turned to Dana, her lack of words standing up for Donovan's idea as much as anything she could have said.

"Wait." It wasn't loud but it was firm. Christina still hadn't budged from her seat. "I didn't get a turn to tell you what I found out."

Oh. Donovan realized she'd just been quiet, like she often was. They hadn't even asked.

"I found the redacted parts of Gennida and Mina Orlov's history in Russia." All eyes were on Christina and she began talking. "They are from Rakhya—a small city just beyond the railroad from St. Petersburg. Though nothing has been proven, there are rumors that there's a government outpost just outside the city where they do testing. Sometimes on the citizens."

"Shit." Donovan heard himself mutter.

"It gets worse." She reached into her bag and pulled out a black and white satellite image of a relatively barren area despite the patches of green. "That's Rakhya," she pointed, "and that's an unnamed set of buildings that have no designation in any publicly available paperwork except that they're government."

"So there's a little backing to the story?" Donovan asked her.

"Oh, there's more. Mina and Gennida traded their story for asylum." She looked up at them now, the information flowing. "It seems the government liked Mina for testing. She had something. In Gennida's testimony—which I finally got my hands on—Mr. Orlov was a piece of work and he knew the government wanted his daughter so he *sold* her. But first, he held out and drove up her price."

Donovan wanted to vomit.

"He died later—not sure if Gennida offed him or not."

"So there might be a family history of removing an unpleasant husband?" Eleri asked incredulously.

"Maybe." Christina shrugged. "Gennida Orlov begged the Russian government for her daughter to be returned and she sold everything. Eventually the cash disappeared and her daughter Mina came back. No idea if her mother bought her back, if the daughter escaped, or if the money was used to hire a specialist to break her out. Next they escape Russia and come here." She took a breath then. "But Mina's testimony is worse. Drugs injected into her. Trials, near death. And it all failed. She had no powers, just a history of horrible, involuntary drug use. There's still more that's redacted, but that's a lot."

"So, maybe she had some skills before she was taken by the government. Maybe why they targeted her. But we don't believe she got out with no after-effects of the drugs," Dana clarified as Donovan rubbed the back of his head, trying to put it all together.

He sighed heavily. "Not anymore we don't."

28

E leri sat in the very back of the minivan again. It was a different vehicle—different make, different model, even a different color —but it was basically the same car. The big SUVs the FBI favored weren't useful for hauling five of them around. Not unless they wanted to squish three adults across the back seat.

Donovan had given the front passenger seat to Christina, leaving him and Wade in the middle. Not that Eleri noticed much, she was staring out the window at the passing country. It felt a lot like going to the Aroyas' house—just the same landscape over and over. Only this didn't have the fresh tang of wildflowers and she had the threat of Avery's new knowledge haunting her.

"El? What's going on?" Donovan was practically hanging over the back seat. It looked casual enough that—unless Dana had managed to get the back of the new minivan bugged—it just appeared the two of them were chatting.

"Nothing." She tried to get away with shrugging him off but wasn't surprised when it didn't work.

"It's not nothing, El." Donovan prompted as though somehow he was the new king of talking it through.

She didn't answer as the dry landscape passed her by. She'd been glad not to be back in Arizona. Her file said "no children." The FBI knew what she'd been through as a kid. Her sister had been kidnapped literally behind Eleri's back. Though she'd been ten at the time and couldn't have been responsible, she'd felt responsible for it all her life. She'd joined the FBI, and became the best at it that she could be, hunting killers and seeing the kinds of things that kept people up at night. But that wasn't what kept her up.

The landscape had been sandy and the heat rose off the ground in waves. It hadn't been that long ago they'd been out here chasing down a lead on Atlas. While the Atlas progeny weren't kids anymore, they had been. *No children*, she thought.

Though Eleri knew her sister was dead, her mother and father didn't. Grandmere had told them often enough that they should have listened. Grandmere wasn't being mean, she was trying to help them let go. Instead Nathalie and Thomas Eames had called her a crazy old woman and gone on with their hunt for a girl who would have become a woman but wasn't there to find. Eleri imagined her sister buried in the dry dirt out where the landscape blurred, beside the Atlas kids that hadn't made it.

Eleri should have been able to handle the stress, but it was piling up. She wanted to tell Las Abuelas that their grandchildren had been found, but she'd been shut down from higher levels. Eleri knew first-hand what it was like to live with a missing person.

"Eleri?" Donovan prompted again, not having moved from where he hung over the seat, facing backward to talk to her. "What is it?"

"Everything."

"Go on."

Wade had also turned around and was making himself part of the conversation. Maybe that was good. Maybe the burden would be lessened to share it with more of them.

"I want to tell the families about the Atlas kids. I know we can't, but I'm carrying it. I shouldn't, but I can't shake it."

"We'll go back to Westerfield," Donovan assured her though she knew Westerfield wouldn't budge. It would be a governmental nightmare to explain what had happened. But Eleri was trying to come up with a workaround.

"It's weird being back here in Arizona." Donovan's gaze darted out the window. "I can't say I'm sorry Kellogg's dead, though."

"Me either." She let her mouth settle into a grim line. "Couldn't have happened to a better candidate. I'm just curious what he did to Mina to have her make his death the worst. That has to be a clue in itself."

Donovan didn't fall for her redirection though. "What else?"

"You really want to know? It's personal."

"Bring it." It was such an un-Donovan-like phrase that she almost laughed.

"Okay. I've gotten alerts on three new bodies found this past month. None turned out to be Emmeline. But . . ."

"After Grandmere's note, you're really on edge. You aren't just sorting anymore, you're expecting it." He'd seen Grandmere's beautiful note card with the words "Emmaline will be found soon" on it. Each of these new notifications of a body found of the right age and state of decay strung Eleri tighter than ever before.

She nodded in return. "And it gets worse. Avery overheard you ranting about my ancestors and asked me flat out if I'm a witch."

"Oh, shit, El. I'm so sorry." He didn't even correct her that he hadn't been ranting. He hadn't.

"I'm sorry, that's not on you." She shrugged. "It's on me. I should have looked. I mean, my parents told me about my ancestors and I didn't care about knowing more. We're a first family of Massachusetts and a first family of Virginia. Llewelyn is just my grandma Eleri's maiden name. I never thought it was good for much other than a security question to my bank account. I never looked further."

"Me neither." Donovan shrugged.

"I don't know any of my family history beyond the people I've met." Wade chimed in for the first time. "You thought you did. So why would you look into it? The question is, how is Avery taking it?"

"I have no idea, because I didn't have an answer for him." She was looking vaguely past them, but now she focused on each man in turn. "I mean, *am I?*"

"I think so. It's the only explanation that makes sense," Donovan added as Wade returned to his usual participation-via-shrugging.

"Should I start trying spells?" She was at a total loss. "What do I tell Avery? Even Grandmere doesn't do this!" Her center felt like it was unraveling. She'd finally gotten a handle on her "hunches" as she worked with NightShade. Compared to Donovan and Wade, she seemed almost normal, but now . . .

"I don't think you need to invest in a cauldron just yet." Donovan thought he was funny. Eleri wasn't so sure. "But you can look into it, see what fits."

The last part at least made sense, but then he kept talking.

"I think you should show Avery what you can do. Maybe a little of it."

"Oh, that's nice," she retorted, not sure where the bitterness was coming from. "You're giving out relationship advice now?"

He ignored her attack and conceded that he probably wasn't the best for that. Turning to the other man, he asked, "Wade?"

Wade didn't laugh or make a snarky comment like Eleri might have expected. Instead he got quiet for a moment. "I told Randall that I can do something. That I'm odd. And I told him I could smell that he'd been out at the bar. I even told him which one."

"Randall?" Eleri asked.

"I've been dating him off and on for a year." Wade gave a half-shrug, like *what are you going to do?* "*On* because I really like him. A lot. *Off* because I can't tell him the truth."

It hit her then. She could tell Avery. She was only herself. She wasn't giving away anyone's secrets except her own. Should he run off and tell the world, at worst people would think she was crazy or a little psychic. But Wade and Donovan, with every person they told, they didn't just out themselves but an entire group that had kept their secret for generations. Their safety depended on it. Before she could say anything, Wade spoke again.

"I've considered changing and letting him catch me in wolf form. See if he figures it out. Recognizes me."

"That one works." Donovan nudged Wade. It was how Donovan had found his current girlfriend, if she could be called anything so formal. She'd been stalking him and figured out that Donovan and the wolf were never seen at the same time, a la Clark Kent and Superman.

Shit. Eleri breathed in and realized that she did feel better. Lighter.

"We'll find Emmaline. And you hand those files over to me, too. I'll help." Donovan said it so matter-of-factly that she almost cried. It had become too big a burden to carry on her own. Especially knowing that the end of a decades-long hunt was almost over. Grandmere would be proven right, Eleri knew.

"Okay kiddos," Dana announced to the van at large. "We've arrived." Here being the assisted living facility where Dr. Kellogg had died. "We have the younger Kellogg in custody still. He's being transported here. He doesn't yet know about his father. The two daughters live near here and I'm concerned the son may be a target, too. Does everyone have a good eye out for Mina Aroya?"

Shit. Eleri pushed her brain back toward the case. She hadn't pulled her head out of her ass long enough to consider that "the body was still warm" meant the killer was likely still in the area. Or at least couldn't have gotten too far. She had to stay focused. Pursuing the recovery of her sister's body would wait until after they brought in Mina Aroya. For a moment, Eleri wondered how hard it would be to prosecute the woman for killing Dr. Kellogg. His history made some of the Nazi scientists seem nice by comparison.

Dana was checking them out. This time they were going in armed. With handcuffs. Loaded, with one in the chamber. Safeties off.

For a moment as Eleri checked herself, added a clip-on holster at her waist for her extra magazines, she considered they were headed into an old folks' home, fully armed. It was almost laughable until she considered that the man had burned to death and bullets were useless against fire.

She exited the minivan, crawling out of the way back like the badass agent she was, fully on alert. A series of soft head shakes between them indicated no one saw anyone who was or could be Mina Aroya in the parking lot or surrounding areas.

They headed into the facility, casually in formation. Dana flashed her badge, all of them following suit. Their badges all had the small diamonds at the ends of the border lines, indicating that not only were they FBI, they were NightShade. No one else knew this, but Eleri noticed it each time she looked.

Her heart picked up pace ever so slightly as they passed the front desk, Donovan and Wade already sniffing the air. Eleri kept her hands at her side, loose, casual looking, but ready.

She caught Donovan's eye and he took another sniff, nodded, and tapped Wade on the shoulder.

"She was here?" Eleri whispered at them.

"The woman was," Donovan returned. "Whether that's Mina Aroya remains to be proven."

Good point.

But this was confirmation of the same killer. Eleri forcibly relaxed her shoulders. The group wound their way closer to the victim's apartment, their very presence confusing to the residents.

The director of the facility herself showed them to the room, her face drawn into a grim countenance. She was used to death, but not like this. "No one saw anything. We've begun our own questioning."

The body had cooled while the agents were airborne. The staff had been questioned despite the FBI request that they not speak to each other. Local agents had come in and started to secure the scene, knowing the special team was on their way, but even they hadn't been able to stop the gossip, the sharing of stories.

Eleri waited while Dana inspected the place, but only from the doorway. She couldn't very well go in and touch the body in front of the other agents. It would look too odd, too far out of protocol. So she just glanced inside. One by one, they stood in the doorway while the others stood guard.

It was as bad as Eleri feared. The smell of seared human flesh was overwhelming. What had once been Dr. Kellogg was now curled on the bed, charred and shrugged into a "pugilist's pose." Common among burn victims, the body pulled into a fighter's stance as the muscles contracted with the heat. It had not been an easy death. The clear ring of unsinged quilt surrounded him, in case there was any concern this wasn't linked to the other killings.

The father of the man who'd been digging in the prime suspect's yard yesterday now lay dead, but the psychology didn't add up. That was Eleri: forensics with chemistry and some psych. It was how she'd wound up in the analysis unit following her hunches and attracting the attention of the NightShade division.

Before she could say anything, she was interrupted by a shrill voice.

"Who would do this to my father!" It was a demand for justice more than it was a question.

"And you are?" Dana asked as politely as she could, though it was clear it was one of his daughters.

"Bonnie Kellogg."

Dana only nodded. It was the right response—waiting. It took only a few seconds before the woman broke down. "I should have followed him like Benji and Bethany did. I should have gone into genetics." Tears rolled down her face as Eleri went on alert.

"Both of them followed him?" She asked. They were *following* his work?

"Yes. I was the black sheep. Elementary school teacher." She shrugged. "Bethany is on her way here. She's his favorite. She's the one who understood him best."

Eleri asked a more precise question. "She's following in the work he started?"

"Yes." Bonnie sniffed and wrapped her arms around her waist. "My Dad was a pioneer in genetic research. He saved so many lives."

Eleri begged to differ, but her job dictated that she not say so.

"Tell us exactly where your sister is." Eleri put her hand on the woman's shoulder, jolting at the grief coming through the connection. She yanked her hand away but continued, "We're sending an escort out to her. She may be a target."

29

Donovan looked between the two interrogation rooms, Dr. Bethany Kellogg sat in one, her brother, Dr. Benjamin Kellogg waited angrily in the other. Donovan stood in the central holding room than had a two-way mirror into each of the other two holding rooms. Dr. Bethany Kellogg was pissed as hell, and with good reason.

Her father had clearly been painfully murdered. She wasn't allowed to see him or her siblings. All she knew was that she had been met by an FBI envoy and brought here to the FBI local branch building. She was both a suspect in the case at large and a possible target. She knew none of this.

Dr. Benjamin Kellogg was being held in the other room, directly opposite his sister. While Donovan could see out windows on either side of the central observation room, Benjamin Kellogg couldn't see straight through to where his sister sat less than thirty feet away facing him.

He wasn't pissed. He was scared, though he was trying desperately not to show it. *He should be pissing his pants*, Donovan thought. They'd caught him digging in a yard which turned out to contain a dead body within a few feet of where he'd been searching. The FBI had chased him off and shot at him. While Eleri had been trying to miss, he couldn't have known that.

This was Donovan's least favorite part of the job. The best inter-rogators were people-readers. They were sociable, making idle chitchat and gleaning information. The first third of the "interview"—because "interrogation" was so harsh a word—was about getting to *know* your new friend. Once you were friends, they might tell you how they chopped up all their ex-girlfriends and fed them to the alligators. Or why their dad had just gotten so annoying he needed to be shot. Donovan understood this on an intellectual level. He simply had none of the required skills. The only thing that saved him was that he could usually tell when people were lying. They sweated a little; the thing the polygraphs picked up? He could smell that. Usually.

Christina was with him, the others stayed at the retirement home —at the crime scene. Though Dana was apparently a fantastic interrogator, she was also waiting to touch the body. Dana wanted one nose at the scene and one here. The boss lady had also decided that Eleri's skills weren't from touching people, usually from inanimate objects, thus she wanted Eleri at the home as backup to Dana's skills. Donovan had observed the same thing or he would have argued Dana's choices.

"I got nothing," he sighed to Christina. He didn't know who he wanted to interview and his current partner was being her usual quiet self. How was she going to question somebody? "You choose."

"Let's be mathematical," she offered. "What's the likelihood they'll open up more to someone of the same gender or opposite gender?"

He barked out a laugh. "They'll both react better to a female. Her because my size is threatening—"

"As is your general expression," she tossed out in a rare moment of sharing.

He didn't disagree. "—and him because he'll relax more. He probably thinks he's smarter than either of us, but he'll see you as less of a pissing contest."

"So you choose me to do both?"

Yeah, actually he did. "Wait. Screw them. Especially him. He can wait. He was attempting to dig up a body. Let him stew in it. Let's both interview her first. You talk. I'll sniff. I'll give you a thumbs up or down under the table where you can see but she can't."

She nodded, agreeable as usual.

"Wait." He put his hand on her arm as she started out the door. Like him, Christina was probably less anxious to get going as she was to just get it over with. "Will you override her?"

"I don't know what to show her to make her talk."

"Can you look like her sister?" His brain churned with the possibilities.

"Sure, but I can't answer like her. It would be so suspicious. Plus, how long before she sees her sister again and her sister says she was never here?"

All good points. He nodded and followed her out the door.

He did the introductions, told Dr. Bethany Kellogg they were recording the interview and had her state her name, address, and other pertinent info for the record.

It wasn't a long interview. She didn't want to become their friend, no matter how hard Christina tried or how understanding she was. Dr. Bethany Kellogg was angry.

"Why can't I see my sister? I thought my brother was on the way. He was supposed to fly into town last night." She looked back and forth between them, making her demands before either of them could get a question in edgewise. "Is my brother a suspect?"

"No," Christina answered, using the assumption that the question was about the elder doctor's murder and not in a larger framework Dr. Bethany didn't even know about. "Please tell us about your work."

"What does that have to do with anything?" She was bewildered.

Christina tried to tie it back into something more reasonable for the woman to understand. "We understand that you were continuing your father's work."

"Oh God, did someone target Daddy? Is this about his research?"

Um. Yeah. Donovan thought it but didn't say it. With what the elder doctor had done? How could it not be?

Christina answered it better. "We can't know for sure until you help us figure it out. Please, tell us about your research."

Finally nodding in agreement, Dr. Bethany Kellogg started talking.

She did viral vector research—which she had to explain in detail to Christina. Basically, she took viruses, gutted them, and made them deliver human or engineered genes into human cells. It was already in use in Cystic Fibrosis patients, in therapies for some cancers. The problem was it only worked where the virus went. She was working on delivering it to all cells as well as targeting ovaries and testes.

She was excited now, talking about her work. It seemed for a moment she'd forgotten what happened to her father. But that was a normal coping mechanism. "By targeting the reproductive cells, we don't change anything for the person who gets the treatment, but we can help their offspring."

Donovan let her talk even though her comments churned his stomach. He wasn't against gene therapies in general, but her work was walking the line of developing a God complex. He'd just seen what that God complex could do. He'd dug up the bodies of the victims of it. Her smile wasn't infectious. He faked it.

Her smell indicated she was telling the truth and that she wasn't nervous about her work. She didn't seem to even understand that she should have some moral dilemmas about it. Maybe she'd had them once and convinced herself it was okay. Or maybe she had a better heart than her father and was simply naive about the way her work could be used. But Donovan didn't think the second one was it. She was too smart, too enthusiastic, too ruthless sounding to be that naive. She just didn't care. Shades of her father.

They exited the room and turned their attention to her brother, Dr. Benjamin Kellogg.

Eleri touched the bed, trying to pick up something. She touched the unburned half of it first. The fire ring around the body was neater than the previous ones. This time it was a complete and perfect oval with the inside untouched and the outside burnt as black and crisp as the body.

She didn't study arson, but she hazarded a guess. "I'd say the fire hit two-thousand degrees."

Dana looked at her questioningly.

"See where his lips pulled back? That doesn't tell us much except that we can see his molars. They popped. That takes high heat."

"I thought they could burst at lower heat," Dana added. Neither of them were fire experts, though they clearly needed to learn.

"Crowns and dental work, yes, but that's his untouched tooth. High heat." Eleri pointed with a gloved finger. It had been a hard find, because his mouth was clenched shut, so the tooth hadn't popped and disappeared, but remained held together by the force of the jaw. She'd spotted the telltale crack only because she'd been looking.

Eleri pulled her glove and put her bare hand on the bedspread, hoping she wasn't destroying any evidence. Dana was behind her doing the same thing on the body. Eleri tried to ignore her.

At first, the clean bedding gave up nothing. The quilt looked handmade, but even shades of the person who stitched it weren't coming through to Eleri. She moved around, putting her hand softly, flat onto the burned surface.

Her breath sucked in.

Flames engulfed her and she almost jerked her hand back. Though she felt the heat and saw huge bursts of orange, yellow, and blue dancing around her, she could also still see and feel the room as it was.

Keeping her hand firmly on the destroyed bedding, she turned to survey the room. The entire circle lit up and in the middle, she could see Dr. Benjamin Kellogg in his last moments of life. He didn't run, though he did scream. Whether that was in pain or just a consequence of contracting muscles, she couldn't tell. He took a step then bounced back toward the middle of the circle almost as though stopped by an invisible barrier.

Was this why they all died dead center?

As fast as it came, the image disappeared. Eleri moved her hand. Then again. It didn't come back. She closed her eyes, stripped her other glove, and placed both hands flat onto the burned part of the bed. Nothing.

She tried the blackened wall. She tried the antique desk—the wood still held heat, though the fire department had doused it. Maybe they'd been looking for something to do in a room that should have been their domain, yet by all reports it was completely put out before they even arrived.

Eleri wanted Donovan here, but she couldn't ask him because he was at the branch interrogating the children of the deceased. Despite having a five-member team, they were spread too thin.

Wade was off sniffing his way through the hospital and trying to acquire the surveillance/security footage from the time of the last murder up until the current afternoon. He was also scoping the place out—by smell and sight—to see if Mina Orlov had hung around to check out her handy work.

When the visions didn't come back no matter what she did, Eleri turned to Dana and waited until the other agent lifted her hand from the body. She disappeared quickly into the restroom, presumably to wash something away. Despite being a forensics specialist, Eleri didn't want to think about what might have gotten on Dana's skin. Eleri didn't bare-hand any of her subjects. That was gross.

When Dana emerged a full minute later, drying hands she'd clearly thoroughly washed, Eleri asked her, "Anything?"

Dana shook her head. "No, actually too many things. Alzheimer's —which means I see the things he sees. Such as, he truly believed elves were moving his keys. I saw him giving kids shots and working with cells in the lab. If I hadn't read the file, I'd have thought he was some kind of pediatric specialist."

"That's one way to put it," Eleri said wryly.

"He had a tumor in his liver and arthritis and bone spurs. He lived in a lot of pain—"

"Good." Eleri spoke it without thinking, but she didn't disagree with her immediate assessment. She didn't like herself for it; on the other hand, she couldn't muster up kinder feelings either.

"There was a lot in his brain, and it muddied things, but this was just him burning to death." Dana reached outside the doorway and threw her paper towel into the biohazard bin that had been set up to collect such things. "Are you ready?"

Eleri nodded and they headed out front to meet Wade. It took another fifteen minutes to get a preliminary set of the day's video of the people in the hospital.

"I'm sorry." The man behind the counter looked genuinely upset. "I can't get further back than that without getting someone higher than me to unlock it. I think Marsha can't, either." He referred to the woman who ran the facility. Since the place was part of a bigger conglomerate, Eleri didn't find that odd.

Wade nodded at him and passed over yet another business card— they'd been handing them out like Halloween candy. "Call me by this evening, let me know when to expect it."

The young man nodded.

They headed out to the parking lot, having handed the scene back over to the local agents to process. This time, a big black SUV awaited them. Dana must have wanted to look more FBI-like. They did, once again, weapons not drawn but at the ready, hands loose at sides, in case Mina Aroya should present herself. She didn't and they climbed into the SUV, closing the doors firmly.

Eleri spoke first. "I think Donovan is right. The fire is definitely not made by a flamethrower." She looked into the back seat. "I mean, Wade can't duplicate it, and now? The fire has a perfect edge. I saw it. It happened all at once, the flames were everywhere. The person who can do it, can probably also move freely inside the fire without getting burned."

That just made Mina Aroya a hell of a lot more dangerous.

30

E leri peeled her gloves for the umpteenth time that day. She was hungry and both physically and emotionally exhausted. Three different times she'd contemplated calling Avery and coming clean, just saying, "yes, I think I'm a witch" and explaining what she could. All three times her break had been interrupted. The case was too crazy to do anything personal, to have any time for anything other than hunting the killer. Eleri wondered how other agents had families.

She'd done the autopsy on Peter Aroya's remains. Donovan, a former medical examiner, had done only a little of the work, because Donovan was used to weighing organs and taking blood and tissue samples. This body had none of that. In his medical examiner days, it would have gone the same way—initial scan by him, then determination that it belonged in the hands of a forensic anthropologist or one of the new breed, like her. Not anthropology, but human forensics as the base. She had far more hard science under her belt than most forensic anthropologists, but she lacked the history component. Still, she preferred it her way. She'd been glad when Donovan had declared his part done and left her alone.

Well, alone with a dead body and a full report to write by herself. The only important part had been the "by herself" part. The work had been a breeze, given that she could breathe more easily, doing one job she was familiar with, even though it was behind a cloth filter mask.

Still, the work had been long. She'd written the report, filed it, printed it, and was walking down the hall with it now. It was nine p.m. and she'd had no dinner and couldn't remember lunch. She'd had a handful of crackers and a candy bar, if she remembered right.

She hit the conference room to the smells of hot cheese and baked dough and nothing had ever smelled so good.

"Pizza?" she asked breathlessly as she walked through the doorway. It must have just been delivered, she could feel the heat and see her teammates just starting to serve themselves.

Donovan nodded. "Didn't you get my text?"

She pulled her phone and, sure enough, she'd missed it.

"I ordered what you like on it. We didn't want to interrupt you." He smiled and handed her a glass, an actual glass, with ice and what had to be coke.

"You are a god among men," she told him and grabbed a paper plate. Real glasses, paper plates, cheap napkins with the pizza logo pressed into them. She didn't care.

No one spoke for probably ten solid minutes. The only sounds were ice clinking, chewing, and stomachs settling. Donovan, then Wade, then Christina each got up for second servings. Eleri had gotten herself three pieces and an extra can of coke before she even sat down. She was not getting up again. As she contemplated the fact that her good diet had gone to hell in a take-out hand basket, she poured more coke over the ice. She did it every minute or so, topping off her drink, keeping it cold and fizzy. About the fifth time, Dana finally addressed the group.

"I hate to be the one to say it, but we have to work this out."

"That's okay," Eleri conceded, "I feel five hundred percent more human after pizza. Thank you."

Dana smiled at her—a real smile—and Eleri offered one back. "So where do we start?" She asked it as though she was serious but lifted her third slice of pizza and went in for a bite. She wasn't going to stop eating just because Dana wanted to talk. Thankfully, no one seemed to expect it and everyone was still chewing, drinking, and wiping their faces periodically.

"We need motive. I can't figure it out. We think—relatively confidently—that our killer is Mina Aroya." Dana laced her fingers, resting her elbows on the table top. "But I can't figure out why. Why would she kill her own mother?"

"Because her mother let the Russian government experiment on her?" Donovan offered up.

"Sure," Christina countered, "but there's far more evidence that the father sold her into that and the mother protested. Her story says the mother tried to run away with Mina and her father brought her back. Mina would have been early teens maybe, at the time. She would remember her mother trying to protect her. And her mother was the one who ultimately got her out of the program and out of the country."

Eleri had wondered that, too. "There must be bad blood. We don't have any kind of record of them visiting her, do we?"

The analysts had done a preliminary check on finances on everyone the team was looking at. Then they went back and combed through years of back taxes, credit card expenditures, everything, to see if they could put anything together.

Christina shook her head. "They didn't visit her, but there's every indication that she visited them. Every year. She had flights and debit card use in Wyoming, in both Casper and Rosedeer when the Aroyas lived there. No hotel charges, either. So she was either staying with them or other friends who happened to be in the exact same cities as her daughter and son-in-law. Not seeing them doesn't make sense. The money trail says she went to them. It looks like they weren't estranged. Not fully."

"What about the other murders?" Dana asked. "Any theories on why she would murder a schoolteacher and a geneticist at another lab and an at-home mom?"

"I got the geneticist, too." Christina spoke up. Her pizza was getting cold. Eleri stayed quiet and kept eating. "I missed it on the first pass. The police report from his friends says Burt Riser was dating a new woman—Willa."

"So?" Wade asked it, but Eleri watched as it dawned. "She's Wilemina. We think he was dating Mina? Then she killed him?"

"When were they dating?" Donovan asked Christina.

"Just before he died. The friends say he was wild about Willa and they were all waiting to meet her. One friend said he thought he remembered Burt saying his new woman was Russian," Christina added.

That was pretty damning. Eleri finally put down her slice and wondered if she'd get to pick it up again. "That fits with my best guess of decomposition on Peter Aroya. I need a forensic botanist to be sure, but the body had a few decent-sized tree roots going through the ribs and around the skull. I think it was there at least two years, maybe longer."

"So she offs her husband, takes up with Riser, and offs him, too?" Dana asks.

Wade hopped. "Kellogg tortured her husband. That one's relatively obvious. Until you add in that she offed her husband. Why would she both kill him and avenge him?" He took another drink of orange soda.

"Right," Dana replied, "That doesn't make sense."

"Maybe it does." Eleri took a deep breath. "I want Wade to check my work, but the bullet wound trajectories suggest Mina didn't kill him. She's too short."

"So . . ." Dana frowned. "Benjamin Kellogg?"

Eleri nodded. "His height is consistent with the angle of bullet entry." She didn't like to draw conclusions from non-proof evidence.

"Then why wouldn't he know where the body was buried?" Wade asked the table at large.

"It's possible he killed Peter Aroya and left Mina to clean up the mess," Donovan suggested.

"Why would she do that? Why not report it?"

Eleri fielded this one. "Did you see their records? They were practically hermits. They either hated people or they were hiding something. Aside from Peter going to work, and her just occasionally getting out of the house, they didn't do anything. But more than that, calling the police would mean that she had to say she knew who did it. She would have to admit to some kind of relationship between Dr. Benjamin Kellogg Junior and her husband. If she outed Atlas, she'd probably be killed for it. She probably was afraid."

"So she went on a rampage using firepower she got at the hands of the Russian government?"

Eleri shrugged, she really didn't know. Those pieces didn't all fit yet.

Dana's next words were world weary and didn't even have to do with the case. "How did the two of them find each other? Both of them tortured by government experiments. They wind up married to each other. Jesus."

Eleri fielded this one, too. As far as she knew, she was the only one in the room with any psych background and any profiling experience. "People with like experiences find each other. There have been experiments on it. For example, if you put two sociopaths in a room of a hundred people they'll find each other and be best buds within an average of five minutes."

"Seriously?" Wade asked, yet another slice of pizza hanging limp in his hands at his shock.

"Yes. In fact, if you tell them they are the only sociopath in the room, they'll find the other one faster." Eleri shrugged. The science of it was disturbing, but understandable on a certain level. "People see something when they find a like soul. I'm honestly not surprised Mina and Peter Aroya found each other. They were probably the only ones they could each trust with the truth about their pasts." The more she talked the sadder she got about what they'd lost. "So maybe Benji there shot her husband and she went on a murderous rampage."

"Maybe." Dana sighed again. "Either way, we've got to bring her in." She turned to Wade, "What was on the nursing home video?"

"A whole lotta crap. That's what." This time he set down his pizza and picked up his notes. A smudge of red sauce got on the margin but he didn't seem to care. "It's a weekday, so even though school just let out locally, not too many visitors. Seven visits to the whole complex that day before the murder. Three separate women at least in their seventies. Any of them could be Mina, but each stayed in the lobby or the restaurant and didn't go down the hallways. One older man, the same. Two younger, lone men and a single gaggle of teenage girls left the lobby, but none of them work."

"Explain," Donovan pushed.

"The video is too rough for faces. It's pretty much the crappiest thing I've seen. Honestly, if this place gets robbed, the video will only prove that they got robbed." He shook his head. "Mina could have disguised herself as a man—but these guys are taller than she is. Also, each person coming in went face-to-face with the guy behind the counter, so while getting past the camera was easy, getting past him would be hard. He didn't remember anyone he didn't recognize coming in."

Wade took a breath and continued. "Both the men, alone and at separate times, went down the other hallway—away from Kellogg's room. There are no cameras in the halls for privacy, but there are cameras at the outside entrances at the end of the hallways. So those men didn't loop around and come back in the other way. And the girls were teenagers—again, nothing odd from the guy at the desk. They are clearly all chattering with each other like teenagers, and they do go down Kellogg's hall, but I don't buy any of them as the killer."

Eleri nodded. "It would mean that one of them killed Dr. Kellogg while the others watched, or snuck away and did it, then returned, hoping her friends would leave before the charred body was found. Plus, how would Mina come and make friends like that? Fit in with the teenagers so easily and pass the clerk without him recognizing her picture at all? No way. It's has too many problems. She's not on the camera."

"No one came in any of the end doors, either." Wade sighed. "Unless she went in three days ago and hid out, she didn't come in the normal way."

Eleri felt all the energy drain out of her suddenly. The case had stalled. They had Benjamin Kellogg and his geneticist sister in custody. The schoolteacher and her family were at home but under FBI surveillance. Agents were combing the assisted living facility. Agents were combing the Aroyas' home. Agents were still combing the other murder sites where necessary. But no one knew where Mina was.

Eleri looked around the room. Everyone looked as tired as she did. She spoke to Dana. "I have to get some sleep."

"We all do. Let's wrap it up."

Just as they stood, all their phones went off.

Shit. Eleri looked down at the message, stunned.

Dr. Benjamin Kellogg Junior was dead. Burned crisp in a ring of fire just like his father.

31

Donovan arrived at Benjamin Kellogg's motel room as close to a panic as he'd ever been.

Dana broke land speed records getting here and he didn't even want to think about how Eleri had been thrown around in the back of the minivan. At one point, a cop had popped his lights and run his siren and Dana simply flashed her badge out the window at him and kept driving.

As they pulled up, Donovan watched her approach the officer who'd followed them. She held her badge out as she explained. Donovan pulled his wallet, flashing his own badge as he went by. They had to get in.

Apparently, the two agents arriving for shift reported that the agents they were to relieve were missing. The unguarded body was burned to a crisp in the middle of the room.

Donovan and Eleri pushed inside first, shoulder to shoulder in the narrow doorway. Neither budged, somehow comfortable wedged in like they were. The room was empty except for the fresh smell of burned human flesh. A human—whether it was Benjamin Kellogg junior or not remained to be determined—was burned to a dark char in the middle of the cheap comforter.

The Bureau often brought detainees to rooms like this. No one expected the FBI in a cheap motel. With only one door and one window, and often constructed of brick, they were usually good places to store witnesses.

Two agents stood on either side of the open doorway in the dead dark of night, watching their six. Dana, done with the police, came up and nudged her way in to see between them. That meant looking over Eleri's head and getting in front of Donovan.

"Holy mother of God." She breathed it out reverently.

This was their second charred body in twenty-four hours. No one had been burned like this before. Donovan shook his head. Was Mina angrier? Upping her game? Or was she simply mad at these two men specifically? Donovan had no idea.

He turned to Dana. "Can you touch him?"

"If he's cooled down," she replied before muttering, "Not that that's a problem I've ever had to deal with before."

Eleri moved to the background with Wade and Christina, their huddle illuminated by the sodium light at the back of the parking lot. Donovan didn't blame Wade or Christina for not looking. It wasn't for most people. He stepped back, as it was, no one should be setting foot on the carpet or in the scene. They didn't want to contaminate what the techs might find. He looked at the agents standing by.

"Did you enter the room?"

They both nodded but only one spoke. His appearance screamed "FBI Agent" with his dark suit and neatly cut hair. But that's what Donovan had looked like the few times they'd sent him on detail before he was officially inducted into NightShade. It was how they were supposed to look. "We arrived, checked the body and the room to be sure no one was still inside—alive. Then we left and stood guard."

Standard protocol. Someone had to go into a scene. You couldn't assess death just from looking through the doorway, even though sometimes you actually could. If the man on the bed had been alive, the kind thing to do would have been to shoot him. But, knowing what they were dealing with, Donovan was almost certain he'd been dead before Mina Orlov left the room.

"They're safe!" Christina announced.

When Donovan looked at her, confused, she followed up with, "The two agents who were on first shift. They're almost here."

She'd understated it as the first car pulled up just then and the woman climbed out, her badge glinting in the dark as she flashed it. "What's going on?"

Her eyes darted from one of the agents at the door to the other. "Who are you?"

The man on the left glared at her. "Next shift. Protecting the dead victim you abandoned."

"No." She shook her head, managing to look both frightened and stubborn at the same time. She, too, was in a suit and white shirt. Overkill for the heat of the day, but enough to make it clear she was a federal agent.

Dana pulled her aside and put a hand on her shoulder. Donovan wondered if she could feel the woman's emotions. He was pretty certain he was smelling them—the cold fear that spiked adrenaline, the confusion that started the churn of stress and cortisol, general sweat and anger that her charge was dead.

"Please, tell me what happened." Dana stayed soft, steering the agent away from seeing the scene.

"We checked him into our custody at three-twenty-two p.m. My partner—he's on his way—and I arrived early, at about three. We did a thorough sweep of the whole building even though we've used it before. We swept the room for bugs, both electronic and organic, braced the windows, checked our weapons. We followed protocol. Then we waited until the two agents who were bringing him dropped him off and we assumed custody until nine p.m." She took a deep breath and Donovan waited along with Dana. "At about six-thirty our relief team showed up. Early. So we called the Bureau. It was perfect protocol. It was strange, but we called it in. *I* called it in. I checked badge numbers, looked at pictures, faces, my partner ran his finger along the ID card to see if it had been tampered with. The branch confirmed everything. They'd been sent to relieve us. They wanted us on shifts at twelves and sixes, so they were relieving our rotation then. I went in, introduced them to the charge and we left."

She looked back and forth between them and kept talking. She had to know they were waiting her out. She had to know, but she kept rambling. She was very shaken up for an agent. Then again, she was accused of abandoning her post and letting her charge get brutally murdered. "I left in my own car and my partner in his. There he is."

She pointed to the car coming up, and Dana sent Donovan to intercept him.

Fifteen minutes later, as he saw Eleri escorting the crime scene techs into the room and following them dressed in her own paper booties and hair cover, he returned to Dana. He'd stashed the partner in the car as had Dana with the woman. "It's a match. Not entirely perfect, but excellent corroboration. He says she called in the badges. He checked them for tampering—there was none. He says he heard the voice on the other end of the call and that it sounded like the Bureau. The agents seemed like agents."

"Get this," Dana raised an eyebrow at him. They stood apart from the action at the door to the room, and could talk a little more freely. "Christina?"

Christina popped herself into the conversation then. "I called the local branch, *their* branch, and double-checked the story. She called in, but hung up as soon as the receptionist answered the phone. The Branch secretary called her back five minutes later and asked if everything was okay, as per protocol for hangups. She said everything was fine."

"Pull her phone." The words tumbled out of his mouth, though Donovan knew they didn't need to be said.

"I'm all over it." Dana walked to the car and asked point-blank for the agent's phone. She handed it over easily, along with the unlock code.

Within about thirty seconds, it was clear that she had called the local branch at about six-thirty. And hung up less than two seconds after connecting. A return call from the branch occurred five minutes later and lasted less than thirty seconds. Dana marched over to the car where she confronted the agent, who shook her head vehemently.

"No, I didn't hang up." She was bewildered. "It was a long call. It should show that." When she reached for the phone, Dana let her take it back. They'd already captured screen shots and plugged in a backup, so no one could tamper with the data.

"Oh shit." Her voice wavered. "It does look like I hung up. But I swear I didn't."

Dana, Donovan, and Christina took the phone back and walked away.

Dana sighed. "That agent is exactly who she says she is and has been assigned to the local branch here in Arizona since she graduated from Quantico. I'll bet you a hundred dollars, she arrived home right on time—the GPS in the car will confirm it. I'll bet she walked in the door and didn't smell like smoke or charred flesh or anything."

"You think she didn't do it," Donovan said. She was the logical choice. Kill her ward, then lie about another agent.

"She has already provided solid alibis for other dates—like when Mina's mother was killed. She was in training in Quantico two years ago when Leona Hiller died. How would she have even made that happen? Leona Hiller died on a Tuesday. That training session never had a Tuesday off." Dana was aggravated and frustrated at the number of dead leads.

Christina spoke up, albeit quietly. "She said two agents came to the door to relieve them. Have her meet with the sketch artist to draw them. Have her partner do it, too. Unless they planned this out with serious detail, they won't be able to fake it."

Dana was nodding. "And if they did see someone, we'll have two eyewitnesses to confirm it."

"If one of the women looks like Mina Aroya, that will help, too," Donovan added, getting on board with the plan.

In just minutes, Dana had called two sketch artists to the scene. Wanting to keep the agents in her sight, she brought the sketch artists to them.

Donovan helped Eleri catalog data once they were cleared to touch the body. Eleri even managed a preliminary ID. She'd met Benjamin Kellogg just the once, but she had his wallet and other pictures she could reference.

She looked up as Donovan stood in the doorway pulling on his own paper cap and booties. "It's him. I can't write the report yet, but I'll be shocked if it's not."

"What do you have?"

"Ring." She pointed with her pencil to one curled hand. "Shape of skull. General height and weight. No dental records, but the office reported a few fillings that should be easy to find. Two color-matched composite and one silver in the back molar. All match. Plus, these look like his clothes. We just saw him wearing them. I say it's a match. This is him."

Donovan looked around. "Where's Wade?"

"Out in the woods sniffing around, seeing if he can catch a scent."

Donovan frowned, hard. "Not as . . ."

"Nope. We'll have to leave, let one of you change, and bring you back to make that happen. And we should do it soon." She looked up at him. "I'd rather not wait until the scene is cleared and the trail may be old, but it's up to Dana."

The last part was stilted, as if she'd forgotten for a moment that she wasn't the senior partner on this. Donovan nodded and got to work helping with official identification of the body and any clues left at the scene. Shockingly, there were none they didn't have from every other scene.

One of the techs informed them, "We have hair. It doesn't belong to either agent nor the victim. As long as the room was vacuumed before use, this is a lead." She headed back inside the van and back to work.

Dana put Christina on making sure the room had been thoroughly cleaned per protocol before Kellogg was kept there. Then she began pulling records from the Aroya house, calling the team stationed there for information, checking for hair samples from the Arvads' home, from Mina's mother's apartment.

Then, an hour later, after Donovan's stomach began growling, Wade reported back that he'd followed the smell around the outside of the building but not much farther. Though he'd checked the bulk of trees separating the hotel from the strip mall next door, he'd gotten nothing. However, he did get a hit at the restaurant across the street. He smelled the woman at the doorway, and he'd freaked out some customers asking if he could check their booth. He'd eventually flipped his badge to explain why he was crawling through it and making them get up out of their seats. The vinyl held the smell well.

Then Christina made an announcement that made Donovan's stomach flop.

"The sketches are in, and they match."

32

E leri looked at the pencil drawings and felt her blood pressure rise. There were four total drawings, done in pairs by two separate sketch artists. Neither of the women were definitively Mina Aroya and neither weren't.

It was clear that the agent they were calling "A" and the one they called "B" matched with the two sketches. The A agent—the one who'd stood on the left—was blond. The other was brunette. There were minor differences in the eyes and such. The sets of drawings matched closely enough that it was clear the Agents who were supposed to be watching Kellogg weren't lying about seeing these two.

Eleri handed the sketches back to Dana. "Maybe they were paid to leave? That phone call doesn't make sense. She hung up!"

Dana shook her head. "I got nothing but the nasty smell of burned flesh in my nose and the squidgy feeling that I'm never going to wash it off my hand."

"Ew." "Squidgy" was not a word Eleri had ever expected Dana to utter.

The next words out of Dana's mouth were a surprise, too. "We are heading out to eat." She told an agent from the local branch and left him in charge of dealing with the crime scene. Mostly this meant telling the motel owner—who'd showed up on site in the middle of the night—that, no, they couldn't just clean it up and get the room ready to rent out again. Eleri wondered if she could hand him a couple twenties and shut him up, but she wasn't going to jeopardize the case.

She wondered when Westerfield was going to issue a kill order on Mina Aroya. How many bodies did the woman have to burn before he did? Then again, they had circumstantial evidence against her, nothing more.

Dana was informing the agent she was leaving on site that, after they ate, they would come back with a dog. He nodded as though it were no big deal and within a few minutes they were back in the minivan like a big family and off for food.

Of course, they didn't eat at a restaurant like civilized people. Eleri sighed her frustration, though she knew it was the right thing to do. She wanted someone to bring her a coke and keep it full. She wanted to have a cloth napkin or even real pressed-alloy silverware instead of plastic. But she smelled a bit too much like burned body to be welcome in a restaurant. And they needed a place to let either Wade or Donovan change.

At least if they ate carryout at the hotel, she could take a shower.

Forty-five minutes later the sun was up, she was clean—though she could still smell death in her nose—and fed, and it improved her mood a lot even though her plastic fork had been nearly worthless and she hadn't slept at all in well over twenty-four hours. She was running purely on fumes and food and was grateful that her boss seemed to notice that.

Dana sent her with Donovan to be the "dog handler," and tasked Eleri with gleaning information from Wade while Donovan changed. Then Donovan was thumping his tail at his door and they left with him walking down the hall directly at her side. He was far too big to keep people from being nervous, but the idea of putting him on a leash left Eleri with the belief that she wouldn't have all her limbs intact if she did it.

There were three cars for their group and Eleri had the keys for the SUV, which gave Donovan enough space to sit in the back. He pushed past her and climbed across the driver's seat into the front.

"Uh-uh." She shook her head at him. "You can't wear a seat belt. Back seat."

He stared at her, deadpan, and didn't need words to tell her what he thought of that.

How had they not had this argument before? She wondered. "If we have to stop suddenly and you go into the dash and break bones, I will not be responsible." He still glared. She wasn't having it. "Fine. You stay there. If you do break bones and *can't change back*, then I'm taking you to the nearest hospital for treatment and explaining everything that's going on. If that doesn't work, I'll take you to the *vet*."

He growled low is his throat but hopped down and let her open the door to the back seat for him.

Jesus. She climbed in and started the car, heading first to the strip mall. They passed the hotel and saw a crew loading Kellogg's body into a waiting ambulance for transportation to the morgue. At the strip mall, they climbed out and walked the length of the sidewalk, going into the small convenience store where Donovan scented the woman.

They caught the clerk just as he was opening up for the day. Eleri held up the sketches and asked the man if he'd been on shift the evening before. He had been, it was his store, and no, the two women in the sketches had not come in. This answer came only after she explained there were four sketches but only two women—a concept he had problems with. She didn't know if that was because he didn't get it or because she couldn't explain it well, having not slept at all the night before.

"No, no one like that came in here. Not two women. Not in suits."

After a few more minutes, Eleri had his name down in her notes, his contact number, and his store info. She also had that he'd been working the cash register off and on since noon, but swore he paid attention to everyone who came in because he had alcohol in the store and didn't really trust his afternoon help. She asked for the security video. He shrugged and said the camera had been broken for years. Eleri fought a sigh.

They hit the restaurant across the street and got other information.

Donovan beelined for the same table Wade had described. He'd not told Donovan. The dual "hit" made her pretty confident Mina Aroya had sat there. But Donovan only put his paw on one seat and shook his head at the other.

In a booth like that, it would mean only one person sitting in it. Eleri suddenly hated her life. She talked to the manager, who said the waitress who'd waited that table was already home. So Eleri tried her damnedest to conduct the interview over the phone. The waitress only recalled one woman alone around that time. She ate fries and soda and nothing else.

Eleri asked a few more questions, then the woman said, "Is she wanted for something? Because my cash came up shy yesterday for the first time in years, honey."

Eleri wasn't one much for being called "honey" but the information brought her up short. She asked a few more questions while Donovan sat dutifully at her side. He wasn't allowed in the restaurant at all, and only her badge had made it happen. In the end, the waitress was missing the same money as the cost of a large plate of fries, a soda, and the tip the woman had left. It had struck her as odd that she would be shy exactly the ten dollars that had been left on the table. It was her only ten-dollar table on the shift.

Thanking the woman, Eleri hung up the old cordless phone the manager had handed her, then went about handing out her card again. The sheer number of cards she'd handed out could fell a forest, she thought, but shoved it away. They had to catch Mina before anyone else died. Anyone they liked better than Benjamin Kellogg, that was.

Her brain fried, she packed them back into the SUV, with Donovan no longer trying for a front seat. He must be as dead on his feet as she was. Back at the hotel, she debriefed Dana, jealous that the others had gone to sleep, but respecting her new boss for waiting up for her.

Donovan came around the corner just then. He'd walked the hotel hallway in jeans and a t-shirt but no shoes, but no one could muster up the energy to care. He'd gotten dressed—as it were—to come talk to them, then he was likely to strip and fall into bed face first. An act she planned to duplicate for herself.

"No," he interrupted her. "There was no smell on the other seat that matched anything at the motel or at the strip mall. She could have been there with someone else. But if she was, that person left."

Eleri had nothing to add; all she could muster was a shrug.

Finally, she was sent off to her hotel room to sleep. There was nothing more to do. Before they made it out the door, Dana spoke up. "We have new information, but it will keep for a few hours."

Donovan stretched. Sitting in a conference room chair now, his muscles felt used and not fully recovered from changing. In his morgue days, he couldn't shift to sniff things. There were cameras on his work, on him. If he came in as the wolf, it would have been on film. Here he thought he'd have more options. And he did, but he wasn't as in control of his shifting as he would have liked. Though he couldn't get a good sense of smell on things at his old work, at least at home he shifted when he wanted. Now, he was a command cadaver dog and bloodhound. He was nose to the ground, working. He wanted to be running. If he ever caught up on sleep, that was.

They'd gotten Bethany Kellogg into protective custody inside the Bureau building. She was now in the room just down the hall from the conference room he sat in. Every ten minutes, someone got up and opened the door to be sure she was still in there and still safe, despite the fact that she had no bathroom, no windows, and nowhere to get out or in. She was not a happy camper.

Bonnie and her family had been moved to a more secure location too, though the agents were still holding out hope that she wasn't a target because she hadn't engaged in any of the research.

Benjamin Kellogg's wife and two young daughters were in tight custody as well but again, the agents were holding out hope that they weren't the target. Eleri had thought to send in a therapist. The kids had lost their grandfather and father in short range and unexpectedly. The mother knew both men had been killed. They had to be terrified. But Donovan hadn't thought of it. Only Eleri.

It was his turn now to get up and open the door and check on Bethany Kellogg. He knocked, per protocol, swung the door open before there was an answer and was met by a glare of epic proportions. He wanted to ask if anyone was hiding on the far side of the bed, but instead, he walked in and swept the room himself. No one was there. Her glare intensified, but she didn't speak.

That was why they were rotating that duty.

He closed the door behind him and returned to the table with his fellow agents around it. It was covered in papers, tablets, laptops, and some box Dana had yet to open.

Dana was walking around the table, maybe having had enough sitting and spewing out information as though she were a computer generating random numbers. "The hair from the last burn matches hair found at the Aroya house."

"That doesn't mean much." Eleri managed to say it before he did.

"Well," he countered, "It means something but it's not like a DNA match."

"True," she conceded and Dana started in again.

"It also matches hair found at the Arvads' home in Louisiana, and hair at Gennida Orlov's apartment there, too."

Donovan felt his eyebrows go up. "Does it match anyone living in those places?" He pretty much already knew it shouldn't. Long, caramel colored hair wouldn't. He'd seen LeighAnn Arvad. Gennida Orlov had lived alone and had salt and pepper hair.

Dana shook her head. "Of course, the residue on it changes. We think different shampoos and stuff. But it could be one person staying in hotels." She shrugged. "The big kicker is what turned up at the Aroya house."

Dana turned and put her hands on the table on either side of the box. "This was found under the floor boards."

She pulled out a pocket knife and began cutting the tape. "It's a baby book. Peter and Mina Aroya had a daughter."

33

E leri stared at the box, not sure if she was hallucinating. She'd slept less than four hours so it was possible. That was all the time Dana had allotted them. It was fair, except her body had disagreed with the concept of rest. She'd woken up in a damn pentagram again. This time socks made the star points. White, balled-up sock pairs on the floor around her. With a few other pieces thrown in, it was too perfectly spaced to be anything else. So now she didn't trust her eyes any more than she had when she'd woken up.

The baby book was thick and heavy, the cover purchased and the pages added. Before she knew it, Eleri was on her feet, crowding Dana for a better look. Luckily, the senior agent didn't seem to mind.

Carefully, Dana unboxed it, pulling out three loose pages. They weren't baby book pages but rather information the agents at the site had added. They showed the layout of the house and a mark where the book had been pulled from beneath the floor boards.

"Did she die?" Eleri asked. When Dana shook her head, Eleri added, "Because there was no evidence of a child in that house. None. No pictures, no toys . . ."

She looked to Donovan who spoke up in agreement. "You would think there would be something. A piece of clothing. A picture, even a framed ultrasound. People do that. El's right. There was nothing."

Dana flipped through the pages quickly. "It goes right up to about age . . ." She checked inside the front cover, then back. "I can't tell.

There's no birth date. No hospital pictures. No dates. Anyway, the girl looks about thirteen? Fourteen?"

"So possibly not dead." Eleri looked over Dana's shoulder and checked the picture. The girl looked a lot like Mina Aroya. Just lighter hair, like her father.

Dana found a good page and read out, "Grace Faith Aroya."

"That's a little heavy for a woman who came from an atheist country . . ." Wade commented off-handedly.

Christina turned to him. "Maybe she found God. She was here a long time. Lots of people here want to help you find God."

"Good point," he conceded.

Eleri picked out more loose pages from the bottom of the box. As she flipped through she became more appalled. "Under the floor-boards" had been the wrong term. There was a trap door in the floor of the closet; the photos were clear. A staircase led downward into a room that resembled a storm shelter. Inside it were toys. Bean bags. A bookshelf with children's books. A rack with clothing. Her stomach churned.

"Looks like the storm shelter where they kept the records at Atlas," Donovan said from where he'd been looking over her shoulder. She hadn't even heard him come up behind her.

"I was thinking the same thing." Silently, she passed the photos to Dana, who'd been engrossed in the baby book.

"They hid the daughter," Dana marveled. "Completely hid her. Like Anne Frank in the attic. Only under the floor."

"I was thinking the same thing," Eleri repeated her words of a moment ago.

Dana looked at the photos for another full minute, carefully soaking in the images. Then she passed the book to Christina and Wade. "You do that when you're hiding a person from someone or something. But what were they hiding the daughter from?"

Eleri looked to Donovan only to find him looking back at her. She took a deep sigh. "Atlas."

"What?" Dana asked.

"Atlas," Eleri repeated, feeling like she was doing that a bit much. "Peter Aroya is one of the program 'graduates.'" She said it though the word made her want to shudder. "Any child of his would be of partic-ular interest to the project."

"You think Dr. Kellogg was following his 'graduates' around and waiting to see if they had kids?" It was clear Dana was trying to process all of it.

"I'm confident of it." Donovan spoke before she could.

Eleri agreed. "I'd hide my kid from him, too."

"Shit." Dana let it out like a low whistle. Her phone gave a subtle beep and she pointed at Christina. Her turn to check on Bethany Kellogg.

They all stayed silent while Christina left the room briefly. Whatever was happening, whatever Mina was doing, they weren't letting her get at anyone else.

As the door closed, Dana turned to Donovan. "Could the daughter be the woman with Mina? Would they smell alike?"

Wade sat up straighter at the table and Donovan leaned back, letting the other wolf field this one. "No. We'd be able to smell the family line probably, but they wouldn't smell like the same person."

"So maybe Mina just uses her sometimes. Like when she needs an extra agent," Dana mused out loud. "Maybe the daughter went in to buy the stuff at the convenience store."

Donovan shook his head. "She would have smelled different. And I smelled those two agents who stood guard the first time." Eleri watched as Wade nodded in agreement. "I smelled one woman in the room."

"The daughter could be pretty tall by now," Dana added.

"Sure," Donovan agreed. "But she'd smell different."

"Shit, I don't know." Dana leaned back, not down for the count, but out for a moment.

Eleri looked around the room. "I think the big question is: If Mina's out killing people, where is her daughter now?"

Eleri fought the urge to sink to the floor, sit, and put her head in her hands. She'd been standing in this hotel room hall for three hours and she had three more to go. She was wearing a full suit, a wire in her ear, and the bored expression of a federal agent standing guard.

The devil on her shoulder told her to sit down. She was going on fewer hours of sleep than meals in the day and, besides, there was another agent on the other side of the door. His name was unimportant, his stance was solid if a bit arrogant. He liked this. He liked being the badass in his black, tailored suit. He liked being ready to take down the room service clerk if he looked a little too sketchy.

Eleri, on the other hand, had had enough of this shit.

The problem was that the last set of agents hadn't included a NightShade agent. It hadn't included one of their team. Thus a pair of women, posing as agents had managed to jack that up and murder their charge. The two agents who'd gone home had been thoroughly interrogated. They'd been put through polygraphs. And despite the physical evidence against them, they were coming up clean.

Plus, they'd been thrown together for the detail. That was common. One shady agent would have a hard time working through an unknown partner on an assignment like that. So, while they had met each other for the first time about fifteen minutes before their detail started, they told identical stories about what had happened. And in spite of hours of interrogation, guilt, and hunger, neither story had deviated. But there was no call into the branch to check badge numbers and names on the replacement agents. Just the one call that hung up, and the return call five minutes later. Analysis showed that call had been picked up while the female agent had been in her car. She hadn't mentioned the replacement agents, because she thought she'd just talked to the center about them. And Dr. Benjamin Kellogg's watch had been checked, despite extensive damage, one of the techs managed to re-align the hands. This put the fire that killed Kellogg stopping the watch less than fifteen minutes after both those agents were proven to have left the scene.

Eleri felt her teeth grind.

She couldn't sink to the floor. The angel on her other shoulder told her a life was at stake. The devil reminded her that life belonged to Dr. Bethany Kellogg, who had proven to be no better of a person than her father or her brother. So Eleri reminded herself that other lives were at stake and if they could catch Mina Aroya, they might be able to save them. She thought of Dr. Bethany as bait and kept her knees straight.

The rest of the team was back at the motel gleaning whatever clues they could. Not much was coming in after the preliminaries; Eleri knew this because she was getting updates on her watch. Mostly, they were things like further analysis showed the hair had matched most of the locations. She found that to be interesting but certainly not damning. Hair was like blood type, circumstantial, but hardly proof.

She fought a yawn as a couple went into a room closer to the elevator than where she stood. By using a room farther down the hall, the Bureau managed to keep the surrounding rooms clear. No guests, no staff, just FBI agents.

No word had come in from Bonnie Kellogg's safe house, either. Nothing other than that nothing was happening there. Maybe being a schoolteacher would save her.

Bored out of her skull and desperate to keep from falling asleep standing up, Eleri started patching the pieces together. The existence of a secret daughter changed the playing field.

A hidden child would be homeschooled. The birth date of the daughter wasn't listed, but later gaps in Mina's own medical and work history seemed to reveal a year in which the child could have been born. It would make the daughter about fifteen if she were still alive. Eleri did the mental math and matched it up to Dana's assessment from the pictures.

Could Leona Hiller have maybe watched the daughter? Leona Hiller had died in a fire and, aside from living in Rosedeer, Wyoming during the same time Aroyas did, she had nothing in common with them. Her husband had not recognized either Peter or Mina Aroya's pictures. There were no checks made to Leona Hiller from either of them. But if they were keeping their child from having records, they would pay cash. And Leona Hiller's off-the-books daycare would have been perfect. Would Leona Hiller have had some kind of records? The house had burned, but someone needed to ask Mr. Hiller to search and search hard. That record could make the difference. He could get closure on his wife's death.

That scenario would have meant they hid the daughter at home, but maybe not out and about. That would be odd. Eleri still couldn't put together why Mina Aroya would kill a woman who watched her child. Would the drugs from the childhood experiments have made her crazy?

Eleri had been thinking that they were dealing with a calculating woman. What if they were dealing with one who was batshit insane?

Her other thought was that if the three Drs. Kellogg were all in the same field, then maybe Bethany was the only one left alive who knew anything that had been going on with Mina and Peter Aroya.

A jolt startled her as her wrist buzzed with a new message. Jesus, she might have been falling asleep. That shouldn't have startled her. Tipping her wrist slowly up, she read the incoming message from Donovan.

"On my way."

She checked the time and, holy shit, her brain had been wandering for the whole three hours. Nodding to her erstwhile partner, she said, "I'm going in for check. It's almost time for me to change out."

He nodded back but said nothing.

Eleri turned the knob and found Dr. Bethany Kellogg reading in a chair. Judging from the puffiness around her eyes, her reading hadn't pulled her attention from the loss of her father and brother.

"Just checking on you, ma'am," Eleri stated it coldly, then swept the room, the closet, and the attached bath. All were clear. She was getting ready to walk out when she changed her mind. "Dr. Kellogg, I have a feeling you know far more about Peter and Mina Aroya than you've been willing to tell us. Your father is already dead—"

"Because of your incompetency!" She started up out of the seat, but Eleri glared at her and the woman immediately sat back down.

Her eyes hadn't gone glassy black, she knew, she could feel that this was just general "Bad-Ass Bitch" mode and not the surge she'd felt the last few times Donovan had mentioned it. Pushing down her odd thought of "I really am a witch," she tipped her head. "No. Our agents have been proven to have followed every protocol. We are on better alert now, but you need to be aware of just how knowledgeable and cunning your father and brother's killer is. If you can help, you might save your own life."

The woman snorted, so Eleri bit back a "suit yourself" and left the room.

When she walked out, the other agent was at guard, and Donovan was striding down the long hallway toward her. He looked sharp in a pressed suit and earpiece. He probably had the volume turned down to nothing.

Holding her tongue, because it wasn't the time nor the place nor the company, she didn't tell him how tired she was or that he finally looked like a real agent. She simply nodded a thank-you and let him take her post.

She was waiting on the elevator, too tired for the stairs and barely holding herself upright in the manner befitting federal protection, when she heard the scream.

Her head snapped to the right, only to see Donovan and the other agent rush into the room. The door looked to be open before they turned, and her feet were pounding the hallway carpet before she consciously made the decision to move.

Grabbing the edge of the doorway with one hand, she used it to swing into the space and see what was happening.

Dr. Bethany Kellogg stood screaming in a ring of fire. The room blazed as the other agent put it out and Donovan moved with sharp precision around the empty spaces, checking for anyone there.

Eleri started to enter the room when she felt someone bump her shoulder, but no one was there.

34

Donovan watched as his partner of less than one minute doused the room with white foam. Having checked every corner with his eyes, his gun, and his nose, he declared the space safe and went back to grab the screaming woman. She hadn't quit yet.

He didn't care. Donovan simply took her by the arm and hauled her toward the front of the hotel room, into the hallway, as per the protocol they'd designed in case someone got in, in case there was fire, in case the woman survived the encounter.

Eleri was there; he smelled her before he saw her standing in the door to the hallway. He told Bethany, "I've got you."

They walked directly across the open space and into the room straight across from the one still a little bit on fire. Eleri stood with her face toward the elevator bank and her back to Donovan and his still-screaming charge. Each time the woman quit, it seemed she was just taking a breath to let fly again.

"I checked it," Eleri added. She'd swept this room before coming back for him. Protocol. Teamwork. The other agent was in the other room and would stay there until the fire was out.

It wasn't the time to say so, but there was no one Donovan would rather have at his back than Eleri Eames.

Later, he would admit that he'd manhandled their charge, just a little. He would also admit he was sharp with her. But at the moment, he didn't care. "Shut. Up."

She smacked her jaw shut hard enough for him to hear her teeth click.

Eleri came in behind him, closing the door behind her just as hard. She'd looked tired before, but now she was wired. "You'd better start talking."

"*Was that staged?*" Searing anger oozed from every pore of Bethany Kellogg's body, but Eleri didn't react.

"No," she said. "It wasn't. You just got a taste. We have no idea what you're up against, but I think *you* do. Start talking."

The doctor glared at her.

"Fine, but I can't stop this. For all my skills, whatever that was got into a closed room guarded by two federal agents." Eleri shrugged. "It's your funeral."

Maybe it hit the woman then, that she'd be going to her father *and* her brother's funerals very shortly. She could be added to the mix if she didn't change what was happening.

Donovan reached in his pocket and pulled out his recorder. He carried it with him all the time, a habit borne of being an M.E.

The woman shook her head. "No record."

"Record. Or no protection." He didn't think he had the actual clout to refuse her FBI agent guards at this point, or even NightShade investigation, but he tried it.

She crumbled. "My Dad is a pioneer."

That was not the word he would use, but he fought the urge to vomit and held his tongue. For a moment, he waited for Eleri to leap on her in a rage at the reverence the woman held for the monster her father was. But out of the corner of his eye, he caught only a nod of "go on." Eleri was playing poker like a champ.

Dr. Bethany Kellogg continued, "He created genetic programs that would eventually save the human race. He ran trials at local universities in Arizona. Students signed up because he paid handsomely for their participation in his trials."

Donovan fought the wide-eyed blink at the complete and total falsehood of that statement. Was she lying to protect her father, or did she not know about Atlas?

She looked between them, then continued. "They got some of the early forms of breakthrough gene therapies. A handful of students graduated his program, having stuck through the entire therapy regime." She waved a hand. "Do you know how human trials go?

They can opt out any time or just not show up for the next appointment." She explained it as though they were agents with no idea what she was talking about. Donovan not only understood human trials, he understood that what her father had done had not met one whit of FDA guidelines. Nor moral ones. He pushed a blank look on his face and nodded.

He watched as Eleri looked to the doorway, then turned to meet the other agent, keeping him in the hallway as a guard again. Was the thing going to come back? It had smelled like a woman, but Donovan had only started to recognize that scent when he heard the screaming. And there had been nothing there.

Nervously, Bethany Kellogg told them how her father had stayed in touch with many of the subjects of his trials. When he'd retired, Benjamin, her brother, had taken over. That had been some time ago. She looked away at the floor, then back up at the two of them.

"Benji dated Mina for a while. She was Mina Orlov then. I don't know what she wanted from him, but I always got the impression that he was her meal ticket for something. I thought money, but then she dumped him for Peter Aroya." She looked up at Donovan, then Eleri, then back to Donovan. "I swear, I have *no idea* how she even *knew* Peter Aroya. He didn't have money, but she threw Benji right over for him."

"Threw him?" Donovan asked, not sure what she meant.

"Dumped him. Big time. Next thing I know, she and Aroya are married."

She was getting worked up, so he turned to get her a glass of ice water only to find Eleri standing there with it. It almost hurt to serve this bitch, but it had to be done because she knew something. She knew a lot.

The younger Benjamin Kellogg had dated Mina?

There was a warrant to search his home. Donovan was praying the man kept a diary that he told all his teenage girl secrets to. Or maybe he went full Watergate and thought his ideas so were grandiose everyone would want to hear his recordings.

Donovan was opening his mouth, when Eleri tipped her head slightly, assessing the woman. "You can drink it. I'll get you more."

"I want water around in case that bitch shows back up." The ice clinked against the sides of the glass from the way her hand shook.

This time Donovan didn't have to ask a pointed question. Bethany

Kellogg was already talking. She'd calmed a little at first, telling about her brother, trying to help them catch whomever was doing this. It had been about five minutes and the only updates buzzing in on his watch were the same ones he saw Eleri trying not to roll her eyes at. Nothing. The agents had fanned out around the hotel.

No Mina Aroya. No fifteen-year-old girl who might be Mina Aroya's daughter. Nothing. It was as if she'd vanished. It was time to ask the most pertinent question.

"Tell me what happened in the room," he pushed.

"You opened the door for her!" Bethany Kellogg accused. "Then she came in and set everything on fire." The ice clinked harder.

"Who?" He asked as calmly as he could. He hadn't seen anyone.

"That bitch."

"Who?" He needed a name and he hoped Bethany caught on before he had to say specifically that.

Her mouth opened and shut. Her eyes darted as her anger turned to confusion. "I don't know."

"You know her but you don't know her name?" he asked. "Can you work with our sketch artist and give a description?"

"I—" she started then started over. "I— don't know her name, and I can't see her face. It's almost like it wasn't there."

He tried a different tack. He'd been trained in this and was discovering it was easier to interrogate someone he hated. "Can you tell me what she was wearing?"

"I—" She huffed out her breath and shook her head. "I can't see her. In my memory."

"Do you know her?"

"*How would I know?*" Her confusion turned to anger. "She was there. But I can't remember *any* of it. I can't see her, but that bitch tried to light me on fire."

"You know it was a woman?" he asked again, his own frustration growing. It seemed she had more information before she opened her mouth. It was supposed to go the other way. Get them talking, get them accessing the memories and the information started to flow. But no, this was damming her up.

"I—"

Good God, another stilted, lost answer.

Eleri tapped his shoulder. "Can we talk?"

"Don't you leave me alone!" Though the words were angry to the very core, Dr. Bethany Kellogg reacted this time with fear. She clutched the glass of ice water in two hands. The water shook until it sloshed.

"We won't," Eleri reassured her, even as she headed for the door. Eleri was definitely better at reassuring than he was. He wanted to yell at the woman. Tell her what her father had really done. Tell her why Peter and Mina Aroya hated the Kellogg family so much. Eleri thought the same things he did. She just hid it better. Must be all that Southern Belle training.

She brought the other agent back into the room and waited while Dr. Kellogg negotiated with him to bring the fire extinguisher with him while he stood guard. Donovan didn't point out that it had already been discharged. He let that part of his mean streak stand. Eleri was pulling him into the hallway and into yet another room they had charge of before he could say goodbye to the woman huddled in the chair. Eleri had her weapon drawn and he found that his own hand had already reached for his Glock.

Without a word, Eleri nodded at him and pushed the door open. In perfect unison, they swept the room, finding nothing. He watched as Eleri pushed her foot into the seat of each of the chairs. As she waved her arm into the shower curtain checking with her hand as much as with her eyes. He wanted to ask her about it, but she was holstering her weapon and turning to face him.

"Donovan, what happened back there?"

He shrugged. He truly didn't know.

"She said you opened the door," Eleri stated. It wasn't an accusation and she managed to make sure he didn't feel that it was.

"I didn't."

Eleri shook her head at him as though trying to make some of the pieces fall into place. "But the door was open."

"What?" He leaned forward.

"I heard the scream and turned to look from the elevators. From where I stood—" She shook her head again, her eyes darting toward the floor as she remembered what she saw. "—it looked like the door was already open. You were turning to go inside but the door was *open*. Who did that? How did you let them?"

He thought back and realized that the door *had* been open when he went through. He pointed toward the other room, trying to remember the other agent's name, but Eleri was already on it.

"He says he didn't open it. And he remembers that when the two of you turned, the door was open already." She paused. "Bethany? Did she do it?"

Donovan shook his head. "We would have noticed."

"Then who opened the door, Donovan?" She asked him, pushing him to recall something. Still not accusing, but needing an answer. Then she floored him. "And who brushed past me as I ran inside?"

35

Eleri had never seen Dana so mad. Then again, she hadn't known the woman long. She did, however, see her new boss hang up the phone after talking with Westerfield and fight her own instincts to throw the phone into the wall. Eleri knew that feeling.

Right now, though she was confident they were going to get yelled at, Eleri stayed serene. She could get used to not having to be the one to explain to their Special Agent in Charge that apparently their suspect was invisible. She could not only stash her daughter where no one could find her, spark a fire around or even on a person, but she was also invisible. Ya know, like in Scooby Doo.

Eleri was still trying to wrap her head around it.

"She can't fucking be *invisible!*" Dana yelled. The conference room was soundproof, supposedly.

Bethany Kellogg was back to being housed at the FBI branch building. This time she was in a double reinforced room. The external keypad entry system needed two agents with different codes to open it, and the furnishings were fireproof.

Eleri's brain tweaked with the unkind thought that the room may be fireproof, but Bethany Kellogg wasn't. She fought to keep her mouth from tweaking along with it.

Dana put a stop to that. She slammed her hands down on the table, startling them all and making all the tech they had scattered on the surface bounce. "The door was open. Please explain that."

She was staring at Donovan and Eleri wanted to answer for him, but she couldn't. It wasn't her place.

"I can't explain it." He shrugged, but it was out of lack of information, not shrugging off the problem.

"There were only three of you there. Two agents and Dr. Bethany Kellogg. Who opened the door?"

"I—"

Dana didn't let him finish. "And if she did, then how the hell did you not notice?"

"I have no answer for that. I didn't notice anything until she screamed." He looked beaten up. Eleri understood. No one liked Bethany Kellogg, but the failure to protect her was a personal one for Donovan, nonetheless.

"How did you not notice?" Dana was looking at him. "Were you tired? Asleep on the job? What?"

This time Eleri did jump in. "He wasn't tired. I was. He was on point. When I heard the scream, I was already somewhat facing that way."

Dana looked at her as though she couldn't possibly be getting in the way of anger at Donovan, but that's exactly where Eleri was. Dana was being thorough—at least that's the decent answer Eleri spun for herself—but enough was enough.

"The door was open before Donovan even turned to run in. He and the other agent were facing into the hallway, so it's conceivable that Kellogg did open the door very, very subtly. It's insanely unlikely, but it's possible." Eleri stood her ground. "It would, however, mean that Dr. Kellogg knew the killer was coming. Because if she did it, she opened the door and left it that way while she went back into the room to sit in the chair. She was petrified of whomever came in, so I doubt she opened the door for them. Maybe she was expecting someone else?" She paused. "Option number two, Donovan did open the door."

"Hey!" He protested, but she steamrolled him.

"That would mean that he did it right in front of the other agent. And they each swear the other didn't open the door."

Dana deflated. She sank into the big conference chair, her head lolling back. "This case sucks buffalo dick."

"Yes, it does," Eleri conceded, noting nods from Christina and Wade.

Christina was leaned over the table, her shoulders tight, her gaze steady. Wade, on the other hand, was looking into the corner, steadily squeezing and releasing some disturbing stress ball with pop-out eyes. To someone who didn't know him it would look like he didn't give a shit, but Eleri knew he was thinking.

Christina offered up a solution. "If we can get the daughter, we can control Mina."

"The daughter could be in Wyoming, or here, or anywhere." Eleri hated to be the devil's advocate on that, because she'd love to get her hands on the daughter, too. "Where would we start?"

"She's here," Christina insisted. "There were two female agents at the motel. *Two*. That means Mina had someone with her."

"Could be someone she picked up off the street and paid," Eleri countered. "Easy money."

"Nope." Donovan was the one who came back at her that time. "You can't just find anyone off the street to play agent. Maybe knocking on doors? Yes. But they fooled two federal agents who had orders to stay another three hours. That's serious business right there."

Eleri had to concede that point. Agents were specifically trained to project that walk and attitude. It was part Law Enforcement Officer, part intellectual arrogance, part badass. "You're right. Anybody off the street would have stuck out like a kid playing dress-up in a suit."

Shit. Every time she found an angle, it got dismantled. Though they were all playing that "you got jack" game.

For a while, no one said anything, and finally Dana sat herself upright and looked around. "Do you want the weird news?"

"It's not good?" Eleri deadpanned. Good news would be good. Then again, Dana wouldn't have held onto good news this long. She wouldn't have tried to pin the open door on Donovan if she'd had actual good news.

"Sure," Christina offered it up, almost jolly. It was an odd state for her, out of her usual quiet, thoughtful norm. Then she topped it with a little more. "I mean if the case is gonna suck buffalo dick, why not suck *weird* buffalo dick?"

Oooohhhhh-kayyyyy. Maybe the other agent hadn't slept at all.

Dana interrupted her musings. "So, Kellogg has been singing. At least this put the fear of God in her that we can't protect her. She said Benji had an affair with Mina."

Eleri and Donovan already knew that.

"After she married Peter."

Whoa. That was not the original story. Eleri felt her eyes pop.

"He thinks the daughter may be his."

Holy shit.

"So at first, she said Mina Aroya shot her husband. But when we pressed her with the forensic evidence—Thank you, Eleri—" Dana offered a short nod her way, "—and suggested that said evidence pointed at Benjamin—"

Eleri didn't interrupt. They all knew her evidence was simply "not likely Mina" because it had been someone taller. Bethany Kellogg didn't need to know that.

"Kellogg copped that her brother had shot Peter Aroya. Accidentally, of course."

"*Twice,*" Eleri piped up. "Some accident."

Dana nodded, a smile coming onto her face. "She said they got into a fight over the kid, there was pushing, and Peter got shot. She said Benji panicked and shot him again, since he couldn't leave the man injured."

"Peter got shot?" Eleri questioned that. "It sounds almost as though she thinks Peter Aroya magnetically attracted a bullet at high speed. Benjamin Kellogg had to have brought the gun, and at least been holding it. Jesus, I hate these people. I can't believe Bonnie is allowed in a school at all."

Dana gave a conciliatory nod at that one. "In other news, we've been showing the sketches of the two women around at all the crime scenes. Everyone says 'maybe.' No yeses. No nos. Just 'Maybe.'"

"That's weird." Wade finally looked at the group. "I was thinking—"

He didn't get to finish, cut off by the simultaneous buzzing of all their phones. Almost as one, they looked down, pulled them out of pockets, then began accessing the secure servers on the tablets and already booted up laptops on the table.

Eleri didn't read the accompanying text, it was the picture that grabbed her eye. Churned dirt, lumps in it, then the lumps out on a table. Knobs of long bone and some teeth. Human parts. What was left after a harsh burn.

"Where is this from?" She blurted the question out before her brain could tell her to read the report.

"In the crawlspace of the Aroya house," Donovan told her, having apparently read the attached notes. "What's the time of death?"

"Given the seasons, I'd guess more than a year. I can't see fresh burn marks in the dirt." She sighed. "I hate pictures. I'll want to see the scene."

"While we've got Mina Aroya running around here, killing people?" Dana asked her.

"She's only trying to kill Bethany Kellogg," Eleri countered, though she suddenly felt like a terrible person for saying it.

"Later," was all Dana seemed willing to commit to. "Look what they found near it."

Eleri searched through the other pictures and found her breath sucking in. A child's bones.

"Is that a boy or a girl?" Christina was asking.

"Can't tell," Eleri spoke without looking up. "Skeletons don't show sex until puberty."

"What about the adult?" came the next question from Christina.

"Hard to say. Pictures make it worse. But looking at the one piece —" she flipped back until she found what should be the base of the skull, then again to a sliver that was the upper part of an eye socket. "—preliminary, and very bad guess, is female."

"They're running DNA tests," Dana told her. "To match to Peter and Mina Aroya, if they can."

"Tell them to test for Kellogg," Donovan added and Eleri nodded along. If he thought he was the father of the daughter they couldn't find, might he also be the father of this child?

"Are the bones from two more kids?" Christina was asking. "Ones who didn't make it?"

Eleri was shaking her head, trying to analyze the bigger skeleton from the pictures of limited, burned remains. She would only be able to give a very wide age bracket. Eleri opened her mouth, only to be stopped by a rush of noise in the hallway beyond the door.

Not that soundproof, she thought as she pieced it together. Feet. Running toward her left, behind her in the hall. More Feet. Yelling. *Shit*. That's where Bethany Kellogg was.

Eleri's own feet were pounding the hallway, her gun sliding out of its holster even before she realized she'd moved. She was surprised to see Dana was in front of her, having reacted faster despite being farther from the door. Christina passed her, but it was mere moments before all five of them were part of a throng of agents—mostly in suits and ties—crowding the door to Dr. Bethany Kellogg's holding cell.

It took Eleri only half a moment to realize what was bothering her. She heard no screams. Bethany Kellogg should be yelling her foul head off.

But she wasn't.

Eleri pushed her head inside, smelling what she realized Donovan and Wade must have picked up down the hall.

Dana was pushing her way through the crowd, using her elbows, refusing to let go of her weapon. "This is my scene."

In a ripple, the agents who'd gone in first rolled back, allowing Dana—and Eleri right behind her—to see the still smoking corpse on the bed. The covers were barely charred.

"Shit! Shit! Shitshitshit!"

Shockingly, the sound was from Dana's mouth and not her own. Eleri looked again, this time aiming not to see that there was in fact a dead, burnt-crisp body on the bed, but to identify it.

Stones from rings and a diamond necklace looked like Bethany's. It could be someone else, but that would be damned hard to pull off. Dana looked to Eleri for confirmation. Probably she already knew but was holding out hope that Eleri might say that it wasn't Bethany, or that some switch could have been made. Eleri shook her head. They'd lost their charge.

In the FBI building. Under protection of multiple agents. Again.

Feeling her shoulders fall, Eleri turned in time to see Wade and Donovan still out in the hallway. She was wondering if they could smell Bethany's scent even through the burn. It would be a faster identification. She was opening her mouth to ask when she saw their heads pop up in unison. Leading with their noses, both men took off at a run.

36

D onovan followed his nose down the hallway. He smelled *her.*
Wade tucked in close behind him, his own nose confirming
Donovan's unseen diagnosis of the situation.

Whoever she was—Mina, the daughter, or maybe someone they
hadn't considered yet—she was here. She'd been in the room with
Bethany Kellogg, and she had moved down the hall past him, though
he couldn't recall her name or face. At the time, he'd thought she
must be another agent, there were so many in the throng. Then his
nose caught her scent and he followed that.

He saw her duck out the door at the end of the hallway, one of
only three entrances into the building. The guard nodded at her with
a smile as she left. Not invisible at all.

Donovan pushed through the agents all rushing the opposite way.
They'd been breached. Their charge was dead, on FBI property. Only
a few of them were hustling his direction. Not so few that her passage
seemed odd by any stretch, but enough. It was part of the job. If all
the agents went one way in the event of even a full-scale catastrophe,
then it would be easy enough to create a diversion. It was still easy
enough for someone to slip out.

Pushing past the guard with fewer pleasantries than the woman
had exchanged, Donovan heard Wade stay behind.

"Did you know her?" Wade asked the guard and Donovan could
only guess that Wade was pointing out the door. Donovan's own eyes

were scanning for movement, looking for people, and specifically for *her*.

The surrounding area was covered in small hills and low scrub. If she knew the area any better than he did, she could easily hide. Donovan had to admit he didn't know the area at all. It hadn't occurred to him to scope it out. Surely someone in the office—or even many of them—were very familiar with the surrounding area. There was a convenience store almost caddy corner. A busy street between. Another street if one went through some scrub and came out the other side. But Donovan had just exhausted his knowledge.

He didn't have time to go back and ask; he just hoped Wade was on his A-game.

Trailing out the doorway, he put his hand on his weapon. He'd reholstered it for the run down the busy hall. It wasn't appropriate to wave it around here in the open. Cars went by on the street. People crossed the intersection to the convenience store. His eyes scanned for cars in the parking lot just pulling out. Women. People who looked out of place.

He didn't see anything.

As long as she hadn't gotten in a car and driven away, he could follow her trail. It was nowhere near as fast as spotting her and running after, but it would have to do.

"You got a bead on her?" The voice over his shoulder was Wade's. A little out of breath, it was clear his partner had come up behind him.

Donovan shook his head.

"Then let's get to work," Wade told him, leaning into the Phoenix air and lifting his nose for a quick inhale. Donovan did the same. The low wind was perfect, enough to aim a smell toward them without scrambling it or ripping it apart.

Crouching low so he couldn't be shot, Donovan occasionally lifted his head and checked over the tops of the cars. He wasn't sure if he really believed she'd shoot him, but given what the woman had done to her last two victims, he'd almost prefer a gunshot wound. He'd truly prefer that she didn't see him at all.

He caught her scent again at the side of the parking lot. Just as he was turning to ask Wade if he smelled it, too, he saw the other man nod softly. They walked in lock step several feet forward, then paused, sniffed, and kept going.

Her scent was here. It was fresh, but not current. She wasn't close by. Or if she was, she was somehow masking her trail. Donovan didn't think she'd ever done it before—not that they were aware of. She didn't even seem to realize she had the equivalent of dogs on her trail, so there was no reason to believe she was doing it now.

The two men inched forward, then moved faster as the trail got stronger. It took them out the end of the parking lot, as though the woman walked right between the parked cars and kept going. They followed.

Up and over a sandy dune held together by scrub brush, they traced the trail. It headed back into a section of streets that held small industrial buildings. Donovan fought the flashbacks the landscape brought on. The Atlas building had been set into land much like this. Farther away from society than this, but the plants were the same, the small rolls in the land were the same—strip away the diesel and the smell was the same. He kept walking.

They were up and over two of the hills, the scent having scattered a little when they spotted movement.

"Get down." His own voice barely below human threshold, Donovan knew Wade would hear him but the woman wouldn't. In unison, they crouched slowly then popped up together.

Two voices in sync yelled, "Hands up. FBI!"

She turned slowly, her own weapon raising up.

Donovan was glad she was listening to them, he'd had no idea she was armed. She wasn't one third of the way turned to face him when he started swearing, "God-dammit! Sorry El."

She heaved a sigh as Wade apologized, too. "At least I know I'm heading in the right direction if you two are out here."

Relaxed now, no longer worried about her own partners shooting her, she let her weapon drop to her side. Donovan kept his eyes darting around. "I can smell her, Eleri. It's strong. She was here."

"Really?" Eleri looked between them. "Do you know which way she went?"

He let Wade keep lookout while he walked a tight circle checking for direction. "I'm not sure, but I think this way." He pointed in between two of the small dunes, back toward a squat building that housed some kind of mechanical shop.

"Then you two head that way and I'll try the other way." She was walking off before Donovan could answer.

But she was the senior agent. "Where should we meet back up if we don't find anything?"

She sighed a moment but didn't look back at them. "I guess at the office. See you there." And she headed off in search of Mina Aroya.

Wade and Donovan followed the trail farther. Until Wade growled.

"Son of a bitch! We just made a loop. She looped us."

Donovan was feeling the lead weight of missing her in his chest and tried another ten minutes to find where she exited the loop. But they came right back where they'd been before. After three tries, he gave up. "The scent's too scattered."

"I'm not surprised." Wade shook his head, clearly as disgusted as Donovan was. "The wind kicked up a little. There's only scrub here to hold the scent. I mean, I can catch it, but I can't tell which way it goes. If I was in full wolf I could do it, but I don't see any way to do that now."

"I guess we admit defeat and head in." He tried not to let his irritation take his guard down. His eyes darted one way then another, the way he'd been trained. At the time, he'd thought all of the FBI preparation a violation of his Hippocratic oath. He hadn't meant any of it. He'd learned how to shoot, roll, fight, and follow leads along with his Quantico cohort. Though he'd taken the physician's oath more as fact of training than ruling of his heart, he'd never thought either of them would stick. Yet here he was with a gun in his hand, ready to shoot, and beyond hopeful that the good he did far outweighed the harm.

Wade fell into step beside him as they headed back toward the branch building. They'd come around far enough to head in the side door on the opposite end from where they'd exited. This meant the guard wouldn't immediately recognize them. They stayed quiet, one of them always watching—and more importantly listening—behind them.

They entered the building and had to check in. Donovan flipped his badge open and passed through security like the pro he'd somehow become. It hit him then, maybe the need to entertain himself while security ran his badge, or maybe just that he'd been wanting to know. "Wade, why did you come back for this case?"

"You haven't figured it out yet?" Wade almost grinned as he flipped his own wallet open, showing his badge, waiting while security ran a finger over the surface and checked the numbers.

Donovan shook his head as he was waved through.

"You don't get to leave unless Westerfield says you can," Wade told him, his own information clearing the system. "He can call me back whenever he wants and I can say no, but that can be overridden."

"Is that all of us?" Donovan asked, frowning now as he headed down the hallway, taking turns that would lead them back to where the charred corpse of Dr. Bethany Kellogg was waiting.

"Some more than others." Wade shrugged.

"But you've seemed more involved in this case. You ran from L.A. as fast as you could. You're happier on this one."

Wade nodded. "A few things at play. I've been under investigation for building bombs before. I cleared, but I'm one of a few people who probably could have devised what we found on an old case. I knew what those bombers could do, and I didn't want to be near it. I didn't want to be accused." He sighed. "But also, Randall."

"Randall?" Donovan asked, remembering Wade had said he was dating the man off and on. Not telling him the truth about what he really was.

They took another turn and Wade continued, "He said when I told stories about my time with the Bureau, I sounded excited, alive. I like physics, but the grant-writing is killing me. I'm considering coming back."

"We'd love to have you." Donovan clapped him on the back, offering a one-armed hug and wondering when the hell he'd started reaching out and touching people. Living people. Lord.

Another hallway and another corner and they were facing the throng stuck at the bottleneck of the doorway into the vault their witness had been stored in. Christina hung out at the back of the crowd.

Donovan came up behind her, making his presence clear. "Did Eleri get back yet?"

"No," She responded. "This case is killing me. I take it you didn't find anything?"

"Well, not after we lost the trail."

"You had a trail? How far?"

He frowned, growing worried. "Out to where we saw Eleri. I mean after that, it looped. She should be back by now."

"What?" Christina asked him. "After you saw Eleri? She headed to the lab. The bones from under the Aroyas' house arrived."

"No. She was out there." Donovan pointed out the door that was now visible at the end of the hallway, just beyond the small security checkpoint. "Beyond the parking lot."

"Donovan, what are you talking about? She was here until five minutes ago." Christina stared at him like he was nuts.

Turning to Wade, he saw the understanding register on his friend's face at the same time.

37

E leri set the last tiny piece of bone aside. They were crumbs really. Burned to a black, ashy consistency, not unlike charcoal. The small pieces were sometimes hard to catalog.

The size and curve of the piece would determine that it was part of the shaft of a long bone, but whether it was humerus or femur, right or left, would take more work. She'd set it aside.

It was the skull pieces that she'd sorted out first. Laying them out, she tried to put the facial elements in position by where they belonged, creating a sinister looking template on the large paper she was using. Eleri thought the face calming rather than terrifying. The person had burned. They deserved closure at the least. Determined to find it, she assembled the back of the skull the same way, though it was as much gap as bone.

Ignoring the rest of it, she focused on the small pieces she had. Normally, she'd take calipers and get a series of specific measurements—distance between the zygomatic arches, specific markers on the forehead to the base of the skull, width of the eye sockets, and so on—to feed into a computer program. While it gave no definitive answers, the program analyzed the results and told them who the skull most likely belonged to: man or woman, some ancestry, maybe age. She had none of that.

Limited to the tiny fragments, she picked them up one by one. The eye socket piece she'd noticed in the picture was her first stop.

She set it back down, then checked the width and curve on the small piece of jawbone she had. She checked the sutures at the back of the skull last and concluded that the skeleton was most likely female. Most likely in her thirties to forties. The sutures she'd checked were late to seal. These hadn't quite fully fused, but were close.

There were a few fragments of the hip girdle, which were thicker and harder to burn. Eleri found she was impressed at the thorough job done on this skeleton. Most people didn't know that even a crematorium generally left a few pieces of larger bone incompletely burned. Those would be ground to dust by hand and put back in with the ashes given to families, and crematory fires ran hot. Very, very hot. These pelvic girdle pieces were near crumbling as she touched them. They'd burned hot and long. They also indicated that the human had been female. There was no way to tell if she'd given birth or not—not from such an incomplete skeleton.

On a whim, Eleri pulled out all the records she had on the bodies associated with the case. She was carrying the big file around, much of it on paper, some of it in x-ray film that had been sent by the dentists and various hospitals the Bureau had drawn records from.

In a separate spot on the table, she set the stack and pulled the first one off.

Leona Hiller's file was set aside. Her body was found intact. Then Eleri had a thought and picked it back up. What did the report say? So many times, bodies were identified by the fact that they matched relatively well and who else would have been there? Errors in identification were rare, but could happen. Eleri double-checked it.

Husband had IDed her at the morgue. Tattoo matched. Necklace matched. Even Eleri could look at the pictures from the autopsy and match them to Leona Hiller. Eleri ruled her out and went to the next.

Marcy Davis, the school teacher who was a possible victim. Watch, bracelet, photo ID, no family confirmation. Dental records. Eleri pulled them out and held the small film up showing the molars. In the bones, she had two molars, one almost intact and one with a set of three roots, though the crown was gone. Neither matched anything in Marcy Davis's mouth. Eleri set that file aside, ruling it out, too.

She'd been part of the team IDing Gennida Orlov's body, so this wasn't Mina Aroya's mother. Eleri set that file aside, as well as all the ones of the men. The last one she had was Mina herself. Though Eleri was sure Mina was up and alive and torturing the Kellogg family, she couldn't mark it off on that belief alone. If anyone asked, she needed to say she did an official rule-out.

Picking up her pen and noting yet another comparison in her notebook, she grabbed the two sets of dental films they had for Mina. The x-rays had been taken almost ten years before. So not finding a match didn't mean anything unless Eleri could prove that the tooth she held was the same position and side as one in the old picture and that it didn't match. That's what she was hoping.

She held the small film up to the light and picked up one of the teeth.

Of the three roots, one twisted oddly. It was good to have anomalies like that. Made a rule-out easier. Tooth roots didn't just change and twist, those things were permanent, unless the tooth was pulled or knocked out or such.

Eleri froze. She picked up another film, an even older one. But there it was. The twisted root. It showed up better on the second film —it had simply been taken at a better angle to spot it. Eleri set down that tooth and picked up the other. This one was relatively easy to identify. It was tooth number twenty-nine. All teeth were numbered according to an American chart. This one was on the lower right side and different from the others.

Though the films were trying to catch the molars from that side, about three-quarters of this tooth was captured in the picture.

Eleri stopped breathing.

It matched.

It wasn't enough to declare that the bones she held belonged to Mina Aroya, but it was more than enough to try to extract any DNA that might still be there. It was more than enough to start considering that Mina Aroya had been dead for a while. No, Eleri had enough to *believe.*

She snapped the gloves off and was walking out the door when she had a second thought. In their last case, bones had been stolen from an FBI office. She wasn't letting that happen now. So, while she wanted to tell the team what she'd found, she first packed up her files, checked the pictures she'd taken, then laid the bones back in their padded and disturbingly small box. All that was left of Mina Aroya fit in a box the size of a binder.

She tucked it under her arm with new reverence and headed

down the hallway to Dana and the team. Her burden was heavy, both physically and mentally.

Two minutes later she was on the other side of the building, back in the stupid conference room that looked like every other conference room in any FBI branch. The only difference was, this one held her friends.

Though they'd been talking, they all looked up at her as she entered the room full tilt, plopping her bag unceremoniously onto the end of the table. She held up the small box of remains just as Dana asked, "You've got something?"

"This," Eleri announced, "is Mina Aroya."

"What?" Dana's head popped forward in disbelief.

"Well," Eleri conceded, "there's not much here and I wouldn't swear on it in court, but . . ."

"But?" Dana prompted while the others stayed cloyingly silent. Eleri focused on her boss.

"But she was found under the Aroyas' house. Estimates put her time of death after Peter's and right around the time the bills stopped getting paid. This set of remains also has two teeth intact enough to do a comparison. While I can't declare that this is definitively Mina Aroya, I do have more than enough information to try to do DNA matching or look for more history on Mina to find adequate proof."

"If you had to call it now," Dana pushed, "what would you say?"

"It's Mina." Eleri set the box on the table surface, only then realizing she was standing at one end while the others clustered far away. The table was made for more than they had.

Eleri left her things farther away than she would like and headed to the other side of the table. There was a counter along the side of the room. It sported a sink and cabinets and even a small fridge. The FBI expected their agents to be holed up here for a while. She opened the fridge to find sodas and in the cabinet, she spotted snack size chips. She grabbed one of each and was popping the bag and the top on the soda when she realized they were looking at her oddly. "What?"

"Donovan and Wade ran into you out beyond the parking lot, looking for the woman." It was Christina who said it. Both the words and her voluntary participation felt odd to Eleri.

"No. I wasn't there. I've been in the lab." She shook her head. They must have seen someone else and made a mistake. She popped a chip. Chewing, she caught their stares.

"We spoke to you, Eleri," Wade said as Donovan nodded. "You said we should split up to find her."

"No. I wasn't there." She didn't get it. "How could you speak to me when I haven't left the building?"

Donovan turned to Dana and said, "She wasn't there."

Eleri narrowed her eyes at them. It was a question?

"Eleri, it wasn't a mistake. We saw you, you spoke to us," Donovan pushed the issue.

Wade chimed in, "Although you were less . . . educated sounding than you usually are."

"Also, the agents outside Bethany Kellogg's room are on video opening her door," Dana added much to Eleri's surprise. "They lean down, laugh, and take turns punching in the code."

"What?" Eleri asked, maybe the lack of food or surprise over Mina Aroya's bones was making her brain not function.

Dana nodded. "When questioned—separately—they said they were playing video games. Though they have no idea why they were doing that. They know they weren't supposed to do anything other than stand guard, but they both played video games."

"Except they were unlocking the room." She was getting it now. "Who else is on the video?"

"She is." Dana's tone was ominous. "She's slim, has amber color hair, and shows up on film if not memory."

Dana pushed a printed picture across the table at Eleri and she was picking it up when Christina spoke. She'd seen the woman before but couldn't place her.

"I think she's like me." The words were soft, breathy, almost apologetic. "I've never met anyone like me before."

Dana's voice cut through again, throwing information at her faster than she could quite process it. "The infant at the house—"

"I have it," Eleri mentioned that she was now in possession of those remains as well.

Dana nodded. "They got enough DNA from the bones to run it."

Eleri nodded. Those bones had been buried, not burned. That made sense.

Before Eleri could say so, Dana spoke. "It links to Mina Aroya by a one-half match."

Eleri knew that math and she latched onto it as something that made sense in this mess. "That means parent, child, or sibling. Child is the only one that makes sense."

Dana nodded. "And it also matches one-quarter to Dr. Bethany Kellogg."

"Grandparent, grandchild, niece or nephew," Eleri filled in. "Niece or nephew." She confirmed as her brain clicked into place.

Again, Dana nodded. "The infant was Mina and Benjamin's child. Barring odd circumstances."

"Odder than what we're already seeing?" Eleri snorted the question in a most un-professional manner.

Donovan shrugged. "I talked to you out beyond the parking lot, Eleri. I know what I saw and I know what I remember."

She nodded. He'd been duped, but his next words shocked her.

"It means that every witness on this case is unreliable. It means everything we have from witnesses is complete trash."

"Holy shit." She thought about all the people in Florida who'd seen nothing. Eleri turned to Christina, "Could you override all the people at Gennida Orlov's apartment building?"

The other agent nodded softly. "It wouldn't be my simplest task, but 'I wasn't here' is actually relatively easy. Replacing it with specifics is hard."

Eleri's brain was only half listening. She was thinking about LeighAnn Arvad and her truck driver husband. Had she seen anything? Eleri thought about everyone at Gennida Orlov's apartment. Leona Hiller's husband and kids. The man at the gate at Burt Riser's house and all the neighbors.

Eleri's head snapped up. "I know where I saw her before."

38

D onovan stared at Eleri trying to figure out what might have been different when he'd seen her out beyond the parking lot.

Had it been her shirt? No. That had been the same to the best of his memory. He could have told a witness at least the color and that she wasn't wearing a suit jacket. He could have picked that shirt out of a line-up to say it was what she was wearing today. That wasn't it.

Was it her face? Had something been off there? He shook his head as he thought it through. It had been Eleri. He would have asked if she'd looked a little off. Despite his friendship with Wade, and the fact that he was now working with more partners, there were only two people in the whole world he trusted on sight: Eleri and Lucy. Lucy wasn't here.

Though he admitted he had no reason not to trust the Eleri he saw, or to think it might not be his friend, he had trusted her implicitly.

Eleri was looking at him oddly, and she should be, he'd been studying her face. Looking for clues. Clues he hadn't found.

"I saw her before." Eleri pointed to the picture.

"That's not a good shot," Dana said. Though the woman's face was captured head on—the FBI didn't dick around with their security cameras—it was still aimed downward. Even though no one had reacted, she'd averted her head a little.

Donovan looked at the picture that captured her profile. Maybe she hadn't seen the extra cameras and didn't know to avoid them. No one questioned the woman covering her face.

It took him a moment to figure it out. No one had seen her. No one had noticed that she was averting her face. Only the video had caught it.

"I saw her in profile," Eleri was saying. "One of the cars on the way into Burt Riser's house the night he was killed. She was in the back seat."

Eleri pushed the picture back toward the middle of the table and went on eating her chips as though she hadn't been hijacked and her partner played. Wade scrambled to get to the picture, even though he'd looked at it before. He'd said he didn't recognize her.

"Oh my god," Wade said now as he held the picture in two hands. "She could have been at Dr. Kellogg's nursing home."

"What?" Dana was asking. No wonder, they'd all looked at it and said it could be Mina Aroya—hard to tell from the profile taken when she was bent over, chatting with the agents at Dr. Bethany Kellogg's door. "There were no cameras in the room."

"Right," Wade agreed, blinking as his memory came clear, "but there was a group of four girls at the front desk, who went down the correct hallway where we lose camera coverage. She could be one of the four girls."

Christina was nodding. "We dismissed it because we were looking for Mina specifically. How would adult Mina have made it seem like she was just one of the girls as she walked in? How would she have gotten in so tight with a cluster of teen girls?"

Wade was following right along. "Because one—she *is* a teen girl and does fit in and two—she overrode them to make them think she's their friend just like any other." He turned to Christina. "Can you do that? Make the whole group think you belong?"

She sighed and Donovan knew what she was thinking about before she said it. He just wondered if she'd told Wade the same story. "I did it all through high school. Changing someone's mind about something is on the easier scale. For example, you're my friend, you're my boyfriend, you don't like that other girl you actually do like."

Donovan fought the urge to wince. Surely, she was describing what she'd done. That sucked.

"That's her." Wade finally relinquished the photo back to the center of the table.

Dana leaned forward, looking at each of them in turn. When she got to Donovan, he felt it like a physical weight. Only when she had everyone's undivided attention, she spoke, "We have to crack this. She's dangerous. She might be done—which could mean she's in the wind—but we won't know. We have to find her."

Heads nodded around the table. Not that this was news; this had been their job from the moment they opened the file and were assigned the first murders. But now there were no teams to call in for backup on a killer who could make you think you were talking to your best friend. She had been horribly evasive and maybe they had a lead now that they knew what she was up to, but had they found it all? Or was there another piece in store for them?

Dana took a deep breath. "Is she Mina and Peter Aroya's daughter?"

Wade sighed and pointed to the picture. "She looks a damn lot like Mina Aroya. But that's not enough to conclude that she's the daughter."

There wasn't an immediate answer.

Donovan took it upon himself to start the conversation they needed to have. After all, they'd been chasing a dead woman for a while now. What if they were wrong again? "That's the best guess. We need DNA to confirm her relationship to Mina and Peter. Where do we get that?"

They discussed getting fingerprints, both for analysis and for DNA, but she hadn't touched anything in the Bureau branch. Not that they found on the video.

Eleri spoke up, bringing in some of the science he should have thought of. "Bethany Kellogg thought the daughter might be her brother's. So, when we get this DNA, we need to test it against both Mina and Peter Aroya, but also against Dr. Benjamin Kellogg."

Donovan looked to Dana for the next bit. "What do we have from the warrant for his place? Is there anything that ties him to the girl?"

Dana surprised them all by saying, "We have a ton of stuff from his place. We have file cabinets full of notes from his father. I read through them a little. I'll say this, I used to be a breast cancer researcher, before NightShade. I understand the science he used, it's old now. But what he did with it? I had to quit reading. I was going to vomit."

She looked to Eleri and Donovan. "This is the case you two worked before this?"

Eleri nodded solemnly and Donovan found he didn't have to answer.

Dana sniffed in through her nose, as though her stomach might still turn just thinking about it. "I'm having a hard time being upset at any of the Aroyas for killing any of the Kelloggs. Benjamin junior knew what his father had done. Bethany might not have, but the son definitely knew."

"Do you think those experiments are why the daughter is . . . The way she is?" Christina looked around. "Not just angry, but her skills?"

Holy shit. Donovan didn't say it out loud, or he wasn't sure if he did. But yes, it had to be. "Her mother was experimented on by the Russian government and her father by ours—"

"—if she's Peter's child. Dr. Benjamin Kellogg seems to think she might be his," Eleri speculated. "But that would actually make her *less* special."

"Oh, I think she's special enough," Wade murmured. Still everyone heard him.

"So," Donovan started playing out scenarios. With Peter and Mina Aroya both dead, there was probably no one left to say what had gone down at the Aroya house. "The infant under the house was Mina Aroya's and Benjamin Kellogg's, right?"

There were nods from Eleri and Dana, who both easily remembered the math on the DNA match. Christina and Wade didn't answer.

He asked another question, "And it would be younger than this daughter out walking around? Faith Grace or whatever it was."

Eleri nodded again.

"Which means," Donovan continued, "That Mina Aroya *did* have a relationship of some kind with Dr. Benjamin junior. Did her husband know? Is that how he wound up dead by Dr. Benjamin Kellogg's hands?"

"You think he found out and they fought and he died?" Dana asked him.

"I think it's possible." Donovan shrugged. "The problem is that we had a narrative we were working from. That Benjamin Kellogg was keeping tabs on Peter Aroya and wound up killing him, thus sending Mina on a rampage of revenge. But that didn't entirely work with the mother and it sure doesn't work now. If Mina was having an affair with him, then why would she kill him?"

Eleri looked away. "Maybe it wasn't an affair. Bethany Kellogg was our source on that one. And she seems to have—had—an idealized view of her father, too. One that doesn't hold up to facts. Maybe this story doesn't, either."

"You think he raped her?" Dana asked.

It was only a shrug that answered at first. "Or coerced her. Bethany seemed to think Mina thought he could cure her. Maybe he told Mina that he could. Maybe he made her . . . sell herself in exchange."

"That's disgusting," Christina replied.

"But it happens," Dana added.

Donovan picked up Eleri's thread. "If the daughter had any inkling of this, and if she saw him kill her father, then most of this story gets a rework. Those skills she has? And being a child with a child's view? This starts to make more sense."

"The grandmother?" Dana asked about Gennida Orlov. "If Grace Faith Aroya is our killer, then Orlov is her grandmother."

"Maybe she blames her for the mother's problems in the first place." He shrugged. It fit better than Mina killing the woman who'd saved her. "Maybe she's a horrid old Russian grandmother who never makes cookies."

He'd meant it as a joke but it fell flat. The woman was dead, after all.

"Burt Riser?" Dana asked.

Donovan threw another dart at it. "Mother's boyfriend? We don't even know." He'd lost it. He'd tried and this didn't fit any better, but the narrative was important. He hadn't thought so as an M.E. He hadn't thought so when he started Quantico. Then he'd learned. When you were hunting, the narrative gave you aim. A direction to follow. They needed that now more than anything.

"Hey." Wade threw the one word out to the table. While Donovan was hoping for a rescue of his idea, Wade took it another direction. "We can see her on the videos. She can fool us, but she can't fool the cameras."

Right. Donovan had been thinking about that thread for a while.

He'd been pulling at it but it hadn't unraveled until Wade spoke up. "We need body cams."

"Yes." Dana latched onto the one actionable idea they'd had. "I'll get those for us right away." She paused, "And get cameras and a feed on Bonnie Kellogg's family, too."

"Also," Wade added, "I was wondering what you all know about hypnosis. Can we hypnotize the witnesses to figure out what they actually saw? Like a video. Is it really in there? Did you ever do that, Christina?"

She shook her head vehemently. "No, it never occurred to me that someone might be able to pull that information up. Huh."

"We should start with me. Then Wade if he wants." Donovan looked to the other man. Before they wasted time on the people in Florida or on LeighAnn Arvad, they might as well see if the idea had promise. He thought about that for a minute. Then he turned back to Christina. "Does this mean that she studied Eleri? To know what she looks like, to override us and think we saw my partner?"

He wasn't prepared for how relieved he was when she said, "No."

"I don't think so. I can make you see your grandmother. I don't have to know the person, I just have to know what they are to you."

"So if I don't have a grandmother, you'll be in trouble?"

Christina nodded. "Exactly, but if I do know that you have a grandmother, I can make you see her. Now I get in trouble if she's in a wheelchair and I make her run or something like that. The more I know the better, but I don't have to know the person. Just like I can make you think I'm your best friend, just as me, I can almost as easily make you think I'm your best friend, whomever that really is. But if that's a guy and I walk into the ladies' room, there's a problem. See?"

He did. At least he felt better that this teenage bitch wasn't stalking his partner. Probably.

"There's something else," Christina said with an air of resignation.

But she didn't get to say what it was as the entire perimeter of the room burst into flame.

39

E leri jerked backward as the flames rushed up around her. By force of will and years of training, she stood calmly and kept her breathing shallow. It wouldn't help to breathe in smoke.

Crouching low, she looked around for the fire extinguisher. She wasn't certain it could put out a fire that she could clearly see was supernatural in origin, but her brain was racing. She had two alternate thoughts for the red canister. One was to aim the spray at the Aroya girl, if she could find her. Startling her might stop her. Two was to bean her on the head with the heavy extinguisher. She didn't want to hurt a child but for fuck's sakes, the kid was trying to burn everyone.

Unfortunately, Eleri's plans didn't matter. The fire extinguisher hung within easy reach on the wall of the room. So it was engulfed in the flames that surrounded them. Now, instead of devising ways to use it, she was worried about it heating too much and exploding.

She searched the room, watching as Dana looked up where the flames were spreading across the ceiling. Christina was motioning frantically to everyone and Donovan and Wade were crouching and making hand gestures to each other.

They circled just behind Dana, pushing her a little out of their way to avoid the flames. As Eleri watched their motions, she realized they were heading toward the door, even though it too, was behind a blazing wall of yellow and blue.

She was considering rushing for the fire extinguisher. Noting that the sink was behind the wall of flame, too, which meant she couldn't douse her jacket or herself for protection, at least not without first running through the fire.

Donovan and Wade were approaching the door and Eleri had no idea what their plan was when Christina smacked the tabletop with both hands.

Eleri's heart—already beating about a hundred miles a minute—jolted to a dead stop for a second. Her whole body jerked at the noise and her head whipped around to look at the only one of them not fighting the flames. The out-of-character move by Christina was her first warning.

"Breathe!" the other agent yelled. "Just stand up and breathe."

Eleri didn't at first and then her heart began pounding again. Her lungs sucked in air at the relief even though the flames continued around her.

Standing, Eleri put her own hands flat on the table top and faced Christina. For once, the other agent looked fierce and even angry.

As Eleri watched, the others caught on and came back to the middle of the room. They stood around the table and looked at Christina who wasn't even breaking a sweat.

Breathing deeply, if not normally now, Eleri took stock. The air felt warm but was clean. There was no soot. When she looked at the walls, they weren't charring. Though it felt like she'd been trapped in the burning room much longer, it was most likely less than a minute. Even so, the walls should have cracked and begun peeling by now. They were intact.

Wade stuck his hand slowly out toward the fire. "Will it burn me?"

Christina shrugged. "I don't know. I think that depends on how much your mind believes the illusion."

"It feels hot." However, Wade must not have thought he was in too much danger because he stuck his hand directly into the flame. He pulled it back and looked at his palm, either not caring that they were all watching him and awaiting the results or not noticing. He stuck his hand in again. After a few more passes, each lasting longer than the one before it, he held his hand out to the four of them. "Not burned."

The air in her lungs felt hot, Eleri decided, but she didn't feel the smoke. She'd been in gas training houses—where officers threw OC and CS gas bombs in and practiced putting their masks on and off in the gas. She'd been in smoking houses. Hell, she'd been in Gennida Orlov's apartment not that long after the woman died and the smoke in the air could still be felt. It made her think of something. "Christina, the other places really burned."

"I know. This is all override." She looked around until she got their attention, Wade the last to look up as he'd returned to testing the "fire."

Eleri turned to Donovan and Wade. "You two met up with her and didn't know it. She pushed you into believing you were seeing your friend. You bought it."

That sounded harsher than intended, Eleri thought.

Christina continued before Eleri could self-correct. "Any of us could have run into her before. Even multiple times. Just because we know about this one doesn't mean we didn't see her before. She could have been at the Arvads' house. Or at Orlov's apartment and we may have talked to her and not known it."

The words hit Eleri with the force of a sledgehammer. It hadn't occurred to her—even after knowing that Donovan and Wade got taken in—that this didn't have to be the first time.

"We would have smelled her," Donovan said.

The words comforted Eleri, but only a little. She wouldn't have smelled jack.

"We would have smelled her on you if you'd interacted with her," he added, maybe catching Eleri's concerns.

"If we didn't touch her? If you were in human form? If we bathed afterward?" Christina asked, clearly not quite buying the "we are safe" ideas Donovan wanted to believe.

The two men looked at each other, then reluctantly shook their heads almost in unison. Eleri would have laughed, except for the part where she wanted to cry. Behind her, the fire raged on.

She asked the question as it was starting to form in her mind. "Christina, you're having this whole conversation, but I haven't seen any real changes in the heat or quantity of the fire. Can you do both at once? Easily?"

The other woman nodded. "Once it's established, holding it is just a matter of a small amount of work to keep you where you believe."

Just then, the fire at the door surged, reaching out for Eleri, the heat pushing her into the table. She jumped, even though she knew it wasn't real. When she took a deep breath and looked at the others around the table, she saw Donovan, Wade, and even Dana all looking sheepish. Apparently, she wasn't the only one who bought it.

Then, just as quickly as it came, the fire receded. Turning to watch, Eleri saw as it seemed to shrink back into the corners of the room, almost as if it were a gas getting sucked out. The heat left with it, the standard temperature feeling almost cold in comparison.

She turned to Christina to comment, but Christina was gone.

Instead, around the table stood Donovan, Wade, Dana, and... Dana.

The two Danas were dressed identically. Their looks of fear that changed to perturbation mirrored each other. Even their curls bounced the same. Eleri was at a loss. She tried to reason her way through it. Dana had been on the right of Christina when it had been clear which was which. So, was the one on the right still Dana?

"Okay—who's the real Dana?" The Danas asked.

Shit! They both moved their mouths in perfect unison.

Then they both looked shocked at that.

"How did you do that?" Wade demanded, almost sounding angry. Eleri knew him, though. There was some strange science afoot. Wade wanted to know how it worked.

This time no one's mouth moved. "I make you see the same thing in both places. Sometimes I put Dana's image onto me, like now when you shouldn't see anyone speaking. And sometimes I put something else onto Dana, like when you saw both of us speak."

"That's not okay!" Both Danas protested in mirror image.

Eleri thought she might be actively experiencing a brain bleed.

The Danas grabbed hands and moved up against the wall. Unfortunately, it wasn't obvious which one of them was pulling the other. "Come, figure it out."

Eleri, Donovan, and Wade circled the table until they stood in the space in front of the two Danas.

Eleri turned to her friends. "How close do you have to be to smell the difference?"

"In human form?" Wade asked.

"That's the best answer. I mean, if you're already wolf, you're better and you can tell. The problem is your human nose. So that's what we need to plan for."

Donovan nodded as he and Wade slowly approached the Danas,

sniffing at the air. They were a few feet away when Donovan then Wade lifted a finger and pointed at the Dana on the left. "There."

Eleri couldn't tell.

"Good," that Dana—definitely Christina—said. Then Eleri's eyes blurred. She couldn't distinguish anything. The Danas were moving. She blinked, trying to clear her vision, but nothing worked.

It disturbed her that, even knowing what was going on, even knowing what Christina could do, she'd wondered why her eyes were blurry. Her first thought was still that something was wrong with her instead of that she was being tricked and the answer was outside of herself.

This time the Danas called on Eleri to make the distinction.

Looking rapidly between them, she took three fast steps forward and pushed one of them sharply in the shoulder.

Both women were trained Bureau agents, so the lack of verbal "ow!" and the immediate readiness to fight back weren't a surprise. They also weren't what Eleri was looking for.

The woman she hit rolled with the move, her curls shook backward, and her expression flinched ever-so-slightly. The other Dana flinched in surprise, in a move that was decidedly un-Dana-like.

Eleri pointed to one, then the other. "Christina, Dana."

"Good," the Christina one said. "What did you see?"

"You didn't react like Dana would, and something flickered in your expression. You looked like Christina for maybe half a moment."

The Christina-Dana looked at Eleri for a moment. "I didn't know you could break the facade by startling me. I don't do it much and I never did things like try to look like someone else. I guess I've always used it defensively as an agent." She took a deep breath and looked to Eleri. "Your turn."

Eleri thought she'd had her turn and wasn't prepared for Christina to mimic her.

"Ohhh." Her breath whooshed out of her as though she'd been hit. Another Eleri stood in front of her. Her skin tone—darker than white, but lighter than the ebony she'd inherited from Grandmere— suddenly seemed to be a color, rather than just "self." Her hair was redder than she imagined, not a carrot color, not bright, but deeper in hue she found as she examined this other version of "Eleri." Her eyes were greener than she thought or else Christina was doing a bad job.

Turning to look at Donovan and Wade, she checked out their

reactions. Before she could say anything at their puzzled looks, Christina grabbed her and scrambled them.

It was a test. She had to play along. They had to learn. Otherwise, they'd never be prepared and more people would burn. So Eleri stood still and looked from Wade to Donovan and back.

Donovan looked directly at her and said, "That's Eleri."

Wade nodded.

Dana was given a chance. Christina mimicked Donovan then Wade. They all tried Eleri's hit-one-of-them process, finding it worked. But then Wade put a stop to that. "We have to be able to tell even if we can't touch them."

They all nodded. And the job got harder.

It was much easier for Eleri to tell two Donovans or two Wades apart than two Danas or two Christinas. They all decided that their past bonds were making a difference and that if one of them told the others who was who, they would have to go with it.

When Eleri struggled with one set up, Donovan leaned over and said, "Try looking a different way. You have these skills in there somewhere. Time to tap them."

She hadn't even thought of it. To her, the hunches and visions were things that came to her. She didn't call them, let alone control them. Donovan was suggesting an entirely different avenue than she'd ever considered, but she took a deep breath and tried to see the difference.

It took five tries. Five agonizingly slow and pointless attempts before she relaxed and managed to set her brain right. "Christina!"

She almost shouted it out. It was hard to hold, but she saw Christina.

They tested her again and again. Though she was easily fooled if she was startled or didn't specifically look, Eleri found she could take a deep breath and see through the disguise. They tried it with the fire and she found she could make the visions recede if only for a moment.

It wasn't much, but it was something.

Her stomach growled just as Dana's phone rang. *Figured.* All she'd had was a coke and a bag of chips in how many hours? The lack of sleep meant she needed more food, not less.

Eleri was at the side of the room pulling drinks out of the fridge for everyone, then going after the chips—they had to eat—when Dana looked up.

"I've had the team install cameras as many places as they can. On our cars, at the Kellogg's safe house, and more. The officers with Bonnie Kellogg's family are wearing body cams and so will we."

They all nodded in response. That had been the plan. So why did Dana look upset?

"When we decided that Bonnie Kellogg hadn't been part of the bigger genetics plan, we decided that she wasn't a target. There's nothing definitive yet, but the agents on her house are reporting small things moving. Missing memories. And someone showing up on footage hours later."

Dana looked grim. "We were wrong."

40

Donovan sat in the back of the SUV with Eleri for once. His legs were cramped and it felt like his knees were under his chin, but he wanted to see the video she had on her tablet. They were on their way to the Kellogg family's safe house. Since Bonnie was the only Kellogg sibling left, she was the next presumed target. According to the video, it appeared they were correct.

Eleri tucked herself in the middle, between him and Wade. Jealousy ran through him that the other two seemed to fit without contorting or wishing their femurs were shorter. Every turn of the car swayed him. He tried to ignore it and lean over to look at the screen Eleri tried to hold at a reasonable position for all three of them.

He cranked his neck. "Play it again?"

She hit a few buttons and the video started over. It showed the young woman from the FBI hallway, the one on the video who was present when the agents guarding Bethany Kellogg's room unlocked the door. When they'd thought they were playing video games.

On screen, the same young woman walked up the sidewalk to the safe house, turned up the front walk and headed toward the door. But she didn't go up the steps. She aimed to the right, and began openly casing the house. She stood on tiptoe and peered into windows. She pushed on frames, checked to see if things were locked. Then she headed for the backyard.

"Look." Eleri pointed. "She's moving the potted plant so she can climb over the fence."

"So?" Wade asked, but Donovan was watching the young woman's motions more closely.

"She can't unlock the fence, at least not with any special powers. She has to do it by hand," Eleri pointed out. "Whatever she can do, moving the lock is not easier than actually climbing a six-foot wooden fence. That's at least something she *can't* do."

That was good, but Donovan kept watching, looking for a break in her cover. Something more they could use against her. Even though it tugged at him that she didn't appear to be too far out of childhood.

He watched her traipse through the back yard, where she went boldly up onto the porch and turned the knob to see if it was locked.

It was.

Good for them, Donovan thought. Locking it was FBI protocol, but the number of families who didn't believe it was necessary or who simply "forgot" was much higher than one might think. Unfortunately, in this case, the lock probably wouldn't stop her. She looped back to the front of the house, opening the opposite gate from the inside, and sliding along the narrow strip that separated this big house from the equally big house next door. They lost visual for a moment.

Then, right on cue, she appeared around the corner, headed up onto the front porch, and tried that knob, finding it locked, too. Again, he breathed easily. Then he didn't.

"How old is this footage?" He aimed his question toward the front of the car.

"Three hours," Christina answered back, logged in to some other device in the front seat.

"How do we know she's not there now?" He asked. Three hours was too long. "How do we know the family is still alive?"

"The guys in the car out front are still checking in regularly," Dana assured him, but he wasn't assured.

"Every thirty seconds?" Because anything less than that was enough time for the unseen girl to get into the house. "They didn't see her when she did this, right? And they were watching the house the whole time. Right?"

"Yes," Dana answered solemnly as she took the turn maybe a little too fast for the big vehicle, but not fast enough for the situation. She was running a little too calm for his tastes.

Eleri joined in then too, "What were the agents guarding the house told? Do they know what she can do?"

"No," Dana answered and the car went silent for a moment.

This was NightShade.

Donovan took a deep breath. He hadn't considered this aspect of it before. He'd always thought they were special. Few. Unique agents using what they could to help solve the difficult cases, like the cult he and Eleri had started on. Even the odd ones, like the bones found in Michigan. The ones that were so time sensitive that any extra boost was needed—like in L.A. He'd not considered they'd be hunting those with abilities similar to their own. He didn't know why it hadn't occurred to him before, but it hadn't.

What chilled him was that they weren't after a criminal with abilities similar to their own—they were after a criminal who was far superior in skill and willingness to kill. That put them at an unbelievable disadvantage.

Dana stopped the car about four blocks from the house.

Though he wanted to unfold himself, Donovan asked his question first. "What are the agents doing to protect themselves and the family from her?"

"They're watching the loop at three minutes." Dana opened her car door and climbed out as though the answer was reasonable. The tone in her voice said otherwise. She was at least as upset about that situation as he was.

He felt the anger rolling off Eleri even before he climbed out of the car and heard her words. "They aren't safe. Are you going to leave them like that?"

"Not my call," Dana replied calmly enough that she appeared to be fighting her own anger on it.

Donovan only managed to look at her oddly before she answered his unspoken question.

"Westerfield."

Donovan's only real consolation was that, according to the video, there was no evidence the woman knew she was being watched. Just as his brain tripped over the thought, Christina put it to words. "Are we going to call her Grace when we meet her? Are we confident enough to do that?"

He wasn't. He'd even been thinking of her as "the woman" ever since they'd realized they were wrong and it wasn't Mina Aroya. He was glad he hadn't come face to face with her and arrogantly called her by the wrong name. Doing so would tip their hand that they didn't know as much as they wanted to believe they did. However, he did know who to ask.

"Eleri?"

Startled, it took her a moment to catch on that he was ready to rely on another of her hunches. This killer was too much for them. For anyone. She'd murdered repeatedly without leaving a trace. It had taken this long and this many deaths in rapid succession for them to even get a handle on her. They needed to throw everything they had at her. Psychology was a valuable tool. Speaking to her as a person and not a suspect could go a long way. Using the wrong name would be just as bad.

Eleri took a deep breath and stared at the small trees separating one yard from the next. Donovan looked at them too, as though he might see the answers in them. He didn't.

"Yes. She's Mina Aroya's daughter. She's Peter Aroya's daughter, too."

He was taking it as the answer when Eleri spoke again. Not to the group, but this time to him. "Do you think that's the problem?"

"What?" He didn't understand.

"That her mother was the victim of government testing and so was her father. Do you think it's a genetic fireball?" She almost laughed to herself, but the situation was too grim for it to bloom. "Literally."

He could only nod. The Atlas graduates had been fed into the general population, into the fabric of daily life. They knew what they were, but could never come forward. He wondered for a moment where the others were, but Dana interrupted his thoughts.

"Cameras." She handed out packets to each of them.

Donovan pulled his out and inspected it. A small clip for his lapel. It looked like a tie tack, but he wasn't wearing a tie. The wire fed from the pin, down behind his shirt to a transmitter. He had two spare batteries for it. A note on the pack told him it would begin to vibrate regularly as the battery got lower, so he should wear it somewhere he would feel it. He pushed the extra batteries into his pocket and looked up. Eleri's looked like a small brooch. Dana's like a flag pin. Christina's was a pair of glasses. Wade was using a pocket knife to poke a hole in the back of his shirt pocket to run the wire. His looked like a pen.

"But we can't see the images," Donovan only noted the futility of it then.

"Tablet." Dana held it up. "I can see. I'm going to be your eyes and ears. Tomorrow we all get glasses that will project the camera image directly in front of you in real time. But they aren't here yet and she is."

One by one they acknowledged the futility of the situation. It didn't appear the girl was there now, but Bonnie Kellogg's family was in danger. And Bonnie hadn't even done what the rest of her family did. They had to protect her, even if it meant getting in the way.

Even though they were probably also targets themselves. It was a sobering thought. Grace Faith Aroya was a killer. She took out the people who'd harmed her family. But she'd also taken out a few people who—at best guess—had helped her. Surely the five FBI agents were already on her kill list.

It took five more precious minutes to plan what their route inside was. To get earpieces in—at least they were tiny and wireless and non-obvious. They spent time contacting the guard agents at their various stations around the house, letting them know the team was in place and would be coming in.

Dana spoke into her comm—attached to her collar and very secret agent-y looking. "I don't think she's here now. But you have to watch for any strange movement. She's unbelievably crafty."

"*Crafty*," he repeated as though the word were in any way adequate. The agents guarding the family had no idea what they were up against, but to tell them would blow the NightShade division wide open.

"Copy," Dana replied, though none of them knew why.

Donovan changed his channel just in time to catch the last snippet from one of the guards. "—wife is opening the front door and looking around. I don't know why."

Now, Donovan understood. From the looks on the others' faces, they knew, too.

"Shit!" Dana yelled it as they all took off running. They were four blocks away. Parked where they wouldn't be spotted from the house.

Though they'd successfully remained out of sight, they might now be too far away.

The agent responded to Dana's swears and Donovan heard the exchange over the pounding of his own feet. He heard it over Eleri beating a hard path beside him and Christina coming up in the back. Wade had shot off in a different direction, but Donovan had no time to worry about that now.

"What do you want us to do?" The agent asked, staying calm even though none of the rest of them were. Then again, he'd only seen someone open a door they shouldn't have. He didn't know why.

"Nothing. Just nothing." Dana's voice was remarkably calm considering that her feet ate pavement at a startling rate.

Though he'd pulled ahead, Eleri yelled to him, "Donovan!"

He didn't slow but put his hands up. He could hear her. She knew it.

"Wade went to change. You do it, too."

He had a better shot with that nose. He had his best chance in that form. There were just enough trees behind the tiny playground to give him cover. There would be no Eleri holding a bag for him this time. There was no guarantee no one could see him.

But Bonnie Kellogg and her family were in imminent danger.

He was peeling his clothing before he even hit the shade of the trees.

41

E leri came through the front door like an avenging angel. To the Kelloggs, seated together in the family room near the back of the house, she must have looked more like a bat out of hell.

The first one to breach the shell of the house, she finished her initial visual sweep then pulled up short. Nothing was happening to the family.

Was it possible the mother had just opened the door to look around? Would she even know?

Suddenly, the race hit her. She'd flat out run four blocks and though she made a point to stay in shape, you were never ready for the adrenaline kick. She still wasn't out of it. So, taking a harsh breath, she forced her vocal chords to work.

"Why did you open the door?" She was looking right at Bonnie Kellogg. She expected a pointless answer, but she had to ask.

"I thought I heard one of the agents knock." Bonnie waved it off. "Why? Did you come in here because of that? We're okay."

Eleri only wished that was truly the case. It might be, but she had no way of knowing. Not yet. Then the idea snagged something in her brain. "Why did you think it was an agent? Not a neighbor or something?"

"Well because—" The first two words came easily, but the sentence, and even the thought, seemed to hang up at that point.

Bonnie started again, "Because—" Finally, she shrugged. "I don't really remember, but I did. No one was there, anyway."

The family was starting to ignore her, to go back to reading, playing video games, the oldest kid was poking away at a phone screen. Dana burst in behind her, startling them all over again.

Eleri turned with her palm out, suggesting that Dana stay her questions, thinking they should keep the family as calm as possible. Dana nodded back. Eleri spoke again in an even tone.

"I'm going out back to meet up with the other agents." She had to tell Donovan and Wade not to come crashing through the door.

Eleri was turning toward the back door when Christina entered through it, gun first. She swept the room. It was smart to do it for herself, though Eleri and Dana were clearly not in a state of active alarm. Unfortunately, none of them could really trust what they were seeing. Waiting until Christina finished, Eleri offered a quick introduction.

"I'm Agent Eames, and these are Agents Brantley and Pines." She gestured, open palm, to each of them in turn.

"Lady Agents," the husband said, amused as he looked up from the video game he played with the oldest daughter who was decked out in a soccer uniform she wasn't getting to play in today.

"Agents." The correction was out of her mouth and accompanied by a smile before Eleri could think that she didn't give a shit what he thought. She was already past him and out the back door.

"Wade. Donovan." Though her natural inclination was to hiss the names, she was trained well enough not to do it.

A low growl came from beyond the back fence. They could scale it if they needed to, but instead she tried to make short work of a board. With the heel of her shoe, she gave several good kicks and managed to wedge it to one side. It was wide enough for them to squeeze through if they needed to.

Shit. She hadn't checked first. "Dana, is the backyard clear?"

It took a near eternity for Dana to reply, but eventually it came. "Clear. Move around? Give me camera view."

Eleri complied. Dana was watching five feeds . . . Or maybe just three. The men had to have shed their cameras when they changed.

Just then, Donovan growled again and began pushing his way through the open hole in the fencing.

"You don't have to—" he was through before she finished the

sentence and Wade was coming close behind him. "—we didn't find her."

But Donovan was already cutting across the lawn on a beeline for the back door. Eleri had closed it behind her when she came out, in hopes that if she was followed Grace would have to open the door and she might see at least that, or recognize that it was open when it wasn't before.

Trusting Donovan and Wade, who clearly saw or smelled something she didn't, Eleri bolted across the lawn just behind them. It would be easier and better if she opened the door.

She touched more of the steps up the way up to the deck than either of them, but she made it. Seeing her coming behind them, each had split the doorway. Though they were out of her way, neither was taking his eyes off the knob. They wanted in and fast. Eleri was turning the knob when Dana's expletive burst through her earpiece.

Donovan saw her when he entered the house with Wade hot on his heels. Thin and nearly blonde, she startled him first by her age—she was definitely younger, teenaged. He couldn't let that sway him though, she was a killer. Her eyes darted one way then another, probably trying to figure out why Dana was swearing, why everyone was here.

For a moment, he was surprised she hadn't covered herself for him, but then again, why would she? What would it matter if the dog could see her?

Dana was looking frantically around the room, her eyes darting one way then another. She swore a little more under her breath and then gathered herself in a manner that was clearly forced.

Stopping as abruptly as he entered, Donovan looked away and made a low, rumbling noise, hoping he communicated to Wade not to charge her. They had the advantage as long as she didn't make the effort to override them.

The father was staring at Dana. "What is going on?"

"I tripped," Dana lied back to him, as she obviously knew that Grace Aroya was here. "We're here to keep you safe."

"Well, you don't need to swear in front of my kids." He was flustered and angry and probably put out by a threat he hadn't seen and sadly, never would. With a huff of undeserved irritation, he sat back down and resumed his game with his daughter. The daughter handled the exchange with better grace than the father had.

Donovan trotted off to the edge of the room as nonchalantly as he could. He hated playing "dog" but playing "spy" was actually pretty okay. The movement must have finally caught the attention of the father again, because he jumped up and yelled, "You can't bring that dog in here!"

Eleri was close behind him and seemed to be trying to communicate with Donovan, but the interruption had to be dealt with. "Sir, they're mine and they're a valuable part of your protection team."

"You need to take them out of here."

"I won't," she answered, placid as a still lake.

"You have no right to bring such big animals around my family! I didn't ask for this." He was turning red, shaking, angry. Donovan could smell it on him. He wished he could speak. That would make the man shit his pants, but he listened to Eleri while Donovan made as casual a scan of the room as he could.

"I'm sure you didn't ask for it. Need I remind you of why we are here? Of what happened to your in-laws? A dog or two is something a nice hepa filter can take care of," she pointed into the corner, "and you'll be alive at the end of the day. You're welcome." She said the last words with a finality that Donovan appreciated.

"Donovan." She said it to him at a low decibel as he realized somehow they hadn't set what she should refer to them as. His head perked to her. *Good dog*, he thought.

Her eyebrows lifted at him with questions. In response, he kept his eyes on her, but aimed his nose toward the girl standing in the corner of the room. He whined ever so slightly.

How long did they play this out? Grace Aroya was standing there probably ready to light up the place. He didn't know. She didn't look like she was having any crisis of conscience about there being kids here. She just looked like she was watching and deciding when to make her move. Luckily, she'd dismissed the dogs.

The family had no idea this young woman—the very same one who'd killed their relatives—was is the room. Donovan didn't put anything past Grace Aroya; she'd already checked the windows, tried the doors, climbed the fence. She was inside. What more did she need to do when she could make them all think they hadn't even seen her?

Sure, she could walk out and try again another day. And maybe she would. After all, she'd just discovered the FBI was watching the house, trying to keep the family safe, from *her*.

As Donovan watched, Dana made what looked like a routine sweep of the house. Her eyes twitched and he could tell she knew the girl was there. Why had she sworn before? Probably, she'd seen something on that monitor of hers. The glasses would be incredibly helpful, he knew, not that he could wear them when he looked like this . . . He saw Dana glance at the tablet and try not to give away what she saw. Good, she had the girl at least located. And it didn't appear that the girl knew what the tablet signified, that she could be found.

Wade stood next to him, probably watching her without looking like it, just like Donovan. She hadn't overridden him, and it didn't look like she'd overridden Wade either. Christina had parked herself by the front door and was taking slow breaths, though Donovan couldn't figure out what she was trying to do. She couldn't see the young woman, that was obvious, but she was trying to casually find her. Eleri had also planted herself by the back door and was centering. As Donovan watched, he could see her breathing rate and probably her heart rate slow. She held her gun loosely in her hand, not threatening, but ready. He'd seen how fast she was.

As he watched, her eyes lifted and she scanned the room.

It was just a subtle shift in her breathing, but he caught it. *She saw!* Eleri could see the girl. Whether it was plain as day or just a shimmer of the atmosphere that told her where Grace Aroya was, he didn't know. Eleri saw her.

As he looked across the room, he saw the young woman's eyes narrow. Whatever she'd been waiting on, she'd had enough. He had only a split-second warning before the room burst into flame.

He scooted from the edge, forcing himself to stay calm, but the problem was that it wasn't like Christina's fire. It wasn't just an exercise in pushing back an override. He could smell the smoke and the paint charring off the walls. The screams as the family raced to the center of the room and huddled together were ringing in his ears as he thought, *this fire is real.*

42

Eleri felt the heat lick at her skin and she stepped away from the wall. The family huddled in front of her, the daughters yelling, the father screaming his fool head off and the mother, Bonnie Kellogg, somehow keeping it all together. Her arms wrapped around her family as they clustered close despite their hysteria. Was she calm because that's what she was? Or because she'd seen this coming? Did she know what this retribution was for?

Even Eleri wasn't quite sure.

The flames behind her reached out as they began pushing everyone to the center of the room.

Looking up, Eleri could see her. There was a fuzziness to Grace Aroya—as though Eleri's eyes were blurry, but she was there. As best Eleri could tell, she was seeing a vision of what was there over top of what Grace Aroya didn't want her to see.

"Turn it off, Grace!" she yelled. As the teenager startled, her cover slipped for a moment. Then her eyes narrowed once more and the fire flared hotter and brighter than before.

Grace was a bitch.

Donovan and Wade raced past her then, flying at the girl, mouths open, long teeth ready to do damage. Eleri flinched. She'd not seen Donovan kill like this. A low-level fight was all she'd witnessed before.

For a split second, an old image formed in her brain. She wasn't supposed to know it, and Donovan didn't know she'd seen it, but she'd been privy to a vision of his father killing his own boss one night late at work. The transformation and the rage had been scary to watch. Just as scary was seeing the way the man treated Donovan. It was hard not to find shades of his father in Donovan's attack now.

Before the thought could fully form, fire burst from nowhere and Donovan flew backward, then Wade beside him. The noises they made as they hit the ground tore pieces out of her heart, but she didn't have time to take them into account. Nor did she have time to deal with the father, screaming at the top of his lungs, "*What the fuck is going on?*"

Eleri strode toward Grace Aroya, feeling something well up inside her. She hadn't known it before, but now it felt like generations of power and she pulled it up higher and higher. Donovan would tell her that her eyes were black. She believed it now. The way Grace Aroya was looking at her, they would all believe it.

"Turn it off, Grace!" She yelled it with enough force to send the young woman stumbling back as though hit with a massive punch. Grace flew into the wall, the fire winking out behind her as she hit, keeping her from being burned.

Eleri wasn't sure who was more shocked at her burst of power, Grace Aroya or herself. She was also startled at Grace's control over her own fire. As surprised as she'd been at getting seen and hit, she should have flown into her own mess and started to burn. That she'd managed to turn it off, and to not blink out the entire house from being startled, that she'd done it in such a controlled area, was impressive. And scary. Grace Aroya had far more control over her powers at age fifteen than Eleri had at thirty.

There wasn't time to ponder their skill sets, though. Grace Aroya was back on her feet and mad as hell. She pushed her hands out in front of her and Eleri watched as a wall of fire sprung up between them.

Her startled gasp made her suck in fumes and high heat. She could feel her lungs sear and she could feel her own power blink out at the surprise. *Shit.* She couldn't see Grace.

She was shaking her head, backing up as the heat licked out at her when Donovan rushed up, but skidded to a stop. The heat was too great.

Eleri took a deep breath, feeling the temperature in the house was getting too high. Someone had to get the family out. She turned and yelled at them, "Get out. Out the back door."

"We'll burn!" the father screamed at her, though if he was angry or just pissing his pants, Eleri couldn't tell.

"You'll die if you stay. *GO!*" She screamed it back at him, but her scream was one filled with rage. Anger at him for holding his kids in place while he babbled in hysterics. Anger that he wasn't pushing forward. Her only consolation was that he had no clue.

It was Wade and Donovan, no longer able to get to Grace Aroya, who began tugging at the family members, pulling them toward the door, toward safety. It was Bethany and the daughters who started moving even as their home blazed around them.

Eleri tried again to take a breath and re-focus, find Grace Aroya in all this hellhole of a mess. But even as she felt things start to shift inside her, she felt a flurry of air beside her.

Dana.

A massive kitchen pot in one hand and the tablet in the other, Dana looked at her device while she made an epically strong move with one arm. She threw the water where she knew Grace Aroya to be, even though she couldn't see her.

Dana herself was wet. She must have run into the kitchen and doused herself—which would have meant running through the fire first. Eleri didn't see any damage, though she was sure Dana had to have it.

A roar of anger came from Grace Aroya as she came into view only briefly. Then she winked out again. Her voice hit the air with a burst of rage, though. "Stay back! Do not come get me!"

Had Eleri been anyone other than herself, had she not had her training, had she not been ready to fight this slip of a monster, she would not have moved forward. Instead, she and Dana headed where they'd last seen Grace.

Dana was wet.

Eleri was not, but she used her anger to push the fire aside, her own voice welling up with rage.

The screen on Dana's tablet cracked from the heat, and as she took a few more steps forward, the picture blinked out. Eleri could see Grace Aroya again, but now Dana couldn't—she was advancing blind.

Then, she flew backward.

Her hands clawed at her neck, but there was nothing there.

Out of nowhere, a soaked Christina came at Grace from the side. With expert moves, she slid one arm under the girl's chin and up the other side, taking advantage of having a superior height.

"You will *not!*" She yelled it into the ear of the young woman she now had in strangle hold.

"You can't stop me!" she managed to scrape out.

"Turn it off, Grace," Eleri yelled while Dana still clawed at her throat. She was already turning blue, so Eleri dove for the other agent, reaching up to her throat.

Dana had stumbled to the floor, her only focus on finding air. Her hands raked down her collar bones, one over the other, but caught on nothing. She tapped, flat handed on her chest, almost pointing at herself. She couldn't get air. Eleri's own hands reached for Dana's throat but found nothing.

Looking up at Christina, frantic, Eleri yelled, "Kill her!"

"Stay back! You can't get me!" Grace Aroya yelled again. The very sound of her voice, scraped as it was, indicated that Christina had not yet found the right hold on the hellcat.

Christina adjusted and yanked backward.

Eleri looked up, shocked to see that Christina fought empty space.

Eleri's eyes darted, searching the room to find the back door open, the family out, Donovan and Wade out with them. They'd probably all suffered burns. The family would tend each other, but who would tend her friends?

It was a thought that blinked in and out of existence too rapidly to hold.

Eleri was running her hands all over Dana, trying to find anything she could do to help, but there was nothing physical on there.

The chokehold was taking too long. But as she glanced around again, Eleri saw that the fire had stopped advancing. Christina's hold changed, indicating she was supporting more weight as Grace Aroya started to fade.

But Dana was still choking.

With a deep breath and a gathering of power, Eleri let fly. She screamed at Dana, as though that might break the strangle hold. She pushed the woman to the floor and tipped her head back as though her airway was simply closed and needed to be opened. She tried mouth to mouth, as though she could force air the other way when Dana couldn't get it herself.

But the airway was closed. Nothing opened it.

Christina leaned forward, yelling at Eleri as the invisible weight she held slumped in her arms.

Dana's eyes met Eleri's and she grabbed at Eleri's arm, her grip death tight. With one last contraction of her lungs that yielded nothing, her eyes rolled back and she slumped to the ground.

She was out, but she wasn't dead yet. Eleri looked around frantically, finally running into the kitchen. She grabbed a sharp knife that was too big for the job and the thermometer she found as she scrambled through the dish drainer.

She opened the plastic container, dumping the thermometer as she jumped or leapt over still burning furniture. She stayed low when she didn't have to clear something as the smoke was becoming overwhelming. Windows were opening, letting some of it out, but she paid no attention.

Sawing at the closed end of the thermometer casing she worked until she hacked it off, never looking at her friend. Dana lay still. Eleri didn't have to check to know that.

Once it was cut through, she had a semblance of a tube, oddly shaped but good enough. She clutched it in one hand and knelt beside Dana's unmoving form. She rubbed her fingers along the front of Dana's throat, finding the Adam's apple, moving down and about a centimeter to one side. Then, with no fanfare or skill, she pushed the knife through her friend's skin, feeling the sharp kitchen blade pierce epidermis and then the rings of cartilage of the trachea. *Success!*

She pulled the knife out, bloody and used. The area was now a mess and it was harder to see. She felt her way around, found the spot opposite her cut and plunged the knife in again. With no touch to orient herself, Eleri simply rotated the blade and made a crosswise cut joining—she hoped—the two side cuts she'd made.

Running bloody fingers across the thermometer tube she located the cut end by touch and pushed the other, smooth end through the hole she'd made.

Dana did not suck in air through the jagged and amateur tracheotomy Eleri had just performed. Eleri didn't sit back on her knees though. She'd been leaning low, but now she had to sit up enough to push on Dana's chest. She counted.

Not "Another One Bites the Dust" by Queen, which worked for rhythm, but "Staying Alive" by the Bee Gees. That was what Dana needed. Eleri couldn't sing it. She could barely breathe in the air that was now too black to even see Christina through.

So she sang in her head as she began compressions on Dana's chest.

onovan tried not to breathe as he raced back into the house. The smoke was real enough this time. The fire raged on, blistering his skin more than it already was, but he had to get to Eleri.

"She won't leave!" Christina cried it as she hauled the limp form of Grace Aroya out of the house. The girl looked smaller than she had before, when she'd been in a murderous rage.

Donovan—fully human and upright now—wore only pants. He and Wade had gotten the family out of the house and bolted for the woods. Pants were the only thing they spared the time for and hardly that. They'd made forward progress, running back toward the burning house while they zipped and snapped.

His arms bore welts and blisters, as did his hands. No one escaped that house uninjured. Except maybe Grace Aroya. Though he knew she was a kid, though he knew it made him small, he wished her the most severe injuries of all.

Wade—ever the physicist—started them opening doors and windows. "Relieving pressure on the system," he said. He yelled at the family to stay back.

Donovan should have been tending their wounds, being the only physician in attendance, but he couldn't do it until he knew that Eleri and Dana were safe. Eleri, mostly. He was man enough to admit that he was more than attached and that he was frantic that Christina and even Grace Aroya were out, but his partner wasn't.

Christina was pulling the limp girl unceremoniously down the stairs, with his nose clogged he couldn't smell if she was alive or dead. The roar and wail of the flames drove him forward into the house.

Wade pushed past Christina, coming up after him. There were two people inside to bring out. Christina grabbed Wade as he bolted past her and yelled over the roar of the fire, "I'll make it easier, but stay low. It will look and feel clear for you, but it isn't."

Already over the threshold and feeling the blistering heat pick at wounds he already had and working to make new ones, Donovan was amazed to watch the air and fire clear. He breathed in a clean feeling, and he could see Eleri across the room, working on Dana. Blood was everywhere and Eleri was performing CPR.

Wade pulled him down to the floor, reminding him of Christina's words. Together, they raced to the two women and Donovan grabbed at Eleri, pulling her off Dana.

"No, I can't stop. She's not breathing!" Eleri scrambled against him.

"The fire—" he was telling her, but she interrupted.

"Is gone!" She scrambled to get back to her post, but Wade was already hooking his hands under Dana's arms and pulling her backward as he headed for the door.

"It's not." Donovan dragged Eleri though she fought. It was the one and only time he could think he'd ever used his superior physical strength against her. Then again, she could do that black-eye thing and lay him flat probably, so he kept talking. "Christina overrode us so we could see. It's still on fire. Listen."

He could hear the crackle of the flames, but it didn't matter, Eleri was now bolting for the door, knowing Wade had Dana. Probably she'd figured out for herself that they couldn't save Dana if they didn't get her out.

He grabbed at her shirt, missing and getting only the waistband on her pants. "Stay low. The smoke."

She ducked and chicken walked out the back door, screaming as her sleeve caught on fire from a source she couldn't see. Still, she grabbed his hand and pulled him through the small opening. Eleri dragged him behind her as his bare feet stumbled across the deck. He was pretty sure they fell down the short staircase and onto the grass.

Only then did he feel the pain. It flared out across his skin, his scalp, the bottoms of his feet. As he sucked in what he now knew to be clean air, he felt his lungs sear from the smoke he'd been breathing.

Eleri grabbed him and they rolled in the grass. She even hit him on the head once and when he frowned at her for it she said in the raspiest voice he'd heard, "Something was burning and stuck in your hair."

He didn't know why but he laughed at her. He told himself the tears running down his face were from the smoke.

They were okay.

He looked around, first spotting the skin on his arms and noticing his right arm was red and blistered to the point of not being recognizable. As he looked at it, it began to hurt, a deep, sharp pain that nearly made him scream out. But he clamped his teeth and pushed it back. Only then did he feel that the pain was only around the edges of the burn. He'd seared all the nerve endings, the skin was burned dead. It meant third degree. A skin graft. It meant . . .

He didn't dwell, he just looked farther.

People littered the lawn, many of them in firefighting gear. One of them tried to put an oxygen mask on his face and Donovan pushed the hand away.

Then he realized he probably needed it. Trying to speak through the flow of oxygen, he explained that he was an agent and needed the paramedic to follow him around. Only his voice didn't work. It had quit on him, ravaged by fire and smoke, the same as the rest of him. He tapped his chest, looking pointedly at the young woman trying to treat him. "I'm an agent."

Nothing. No sound. He breathed in, his eyes scanning through the throngs as he spotted another paramedic doing the same to Eleri. She pulled out her badge and flipped it open, getting instant recognition. But he was only in pants. He started patting his butt, surprisingly happy to discover he'd left the wallet in them. Of course he had, he and Wade hadn't stopped to put things neatly away. He flipped the badge open and motioned, now making the paramedic follow him around.

Except the first step killed him.

His knee collapsed underneath him at the pain shooting up his leg. He spotted Eleri who was looking at him and then back at Dana.

Dana was flat on the ground with three people in jumpsuits working frantically over her. All Donovan could see was her feet and a shock of curls spread on the grass, but at least she was being taken care of.

Eleri was following a group out through a chunk of the back fence that had been cut to let them all escape the backyard without having to pass close to the burning house. Ironically, the board Eleri had moved remained on the other side of the yard.

Heavy hoses were dragged into the back yard as Dana was loaded onto a stretcher and two firefighters stripped their jackets to help Wade put his arms over their shoulders. They lifted him away, obviously in pain. Donovan quickly found himself on a stretcher then in the back of ambulance.

With nothing he could do—Eleri and Wade and Christina were safe, he couldn't tell about Dana—he dozed. When his head jerked up, he found he was in an ER bay with Eleri sitting in a chair beside him and staring at him.

She had pieces of her clothing cut away. Bandages adorned various parts of her body, with her skin showing in other spots. Mostly it was clean, though the rags of her shirt were not. She smiled at him. "Welcome back."

Blinking a few times through a thicker than normal haze, he squinted at her before looking at himself. His right arm was bandaged from above his elbow to his wrist. He spotted smaller squares of gauze all around his torso, held in place with a long section of tube gauze. He remembered it well from his ER rotation in med school. Never expected to be wearing it himself, and certainly not this much of it.

He found a bandage around his head—held in place by a thin strip of tube gauze. His arm wore a sleeve of the stuff. At least his bare feet had been given actual socks, though the lower part of his left pant leg was cut away and a larger bandage was held in place by yet another sleeve of tube gauze. He should have bought stock in the stuff.

"Wade?" he asked.

"Looks a little better than you," she rasped out, then smiled and leaned back, yanking the curtain open between the bays. The reveal showed the other man reclined on a bed with a drink in a dinky plastic cup with a straw.

"Christina?" This time he felt the small tears and burns in his throat as he spoke. As he watched, Eleri pushed a button.

"She went to get some vending machine food. She's been sitting with Wade," Eleri whispered as she motioned to the empty chair by his bed. "We're all together."

All. That was only four.

"I fell asleep?" He asked as a nurse showed up and Eleri ordered him a drink, then stood and walked a few steps, clearly exhausted.

"They bandaged your arm and you screamed. They sedated you." She looked grim.

"Not very manly of me." He lamented even as her eyebrows already rose.

"Nope. Horribly indecent of you to run into a burning building to save your friends." Her sarcasm was as dry as her throat sounded. "Even though some of the firefighters had already arrived."

He hadn't seen them.

"You sustained the only third degree burn of any of us." She sat back down, looking more somber. "Scream away."

He didn't. He did something worse. He asked, "Dana?"

There was a long pause before Eleri just shook her head.

Donovan closed his eyes. Christina arrived then, pushing through the curtains that kept their little group closed off from the rest of the ER, if only visually.

One of the doctors came in then and explained what they'd found, what Donovan's options were.

"My foot?" Donovan asked. When he'd stepped on it, it had screamed in pain, his leg collapsing underneath him. "How burned is it?"

"Shockingly little," the doctor said while looking at the chart, and for the first time he realized what an obnoxious physician he must have been. Good thing he'd worked with dead people. The woman continued on, "You had a shard of glass wedged in the sole of your foot. That's what you stepped on. We removed it, cleaned it, you have deep sutures as well as surface sutures."

"Monocryl? Four-point-oh?" He asked, making her finally glance up at him.

She caught on and started talking shop, at which point she was very animated. Until he asked about his friends and then asked if they could leave.

"You have a third degree burn over a portion of your arm," she intoned cautiously.

"How much?" He bantered back and forth with her. Though he

never convinced her that he could care for it at home—it would eventually need skin graft surgery, with eventually being preferably soon —he at least convinced her that he knew what he was talking about.

"If you leave, it will be against medical advice."

"I'm a physician. I've got plenty of medical advice." He grinned to cover the fact that he was done with this place.

Eventually, she made him sign out of his own accord, muttering how "doctors make the worst patients," then muttering more when he asked about the morgue.

It took thirty minutes to get down there. He needed a wheelchair —the medical team insisted because of the cut on his foot and that he was still on hospital grounds. But at last he, along with their badges, got the four of them down to see Dana.

He stood on one flat foot and the ball of the cut foot. He hurt everywhere, but maybe not anywhere as bad as the center of his chest. Donovan told himself it was from smoke inhalation as he pulled back the sheet.

He blinked as he spotted the plastic coming out of her throat. "I forgot you trached her, Eleri."

"I tried." Though her voice was relatively calm, he could hear how hard she fought to keep it that way. "Obviously, I did it wrong."

"No," he hopped and grabbed gloves, then hopped back. Feeling around the cuts Eleri had made and the makeshift tube she'd put in, he asked, "Is the other end chopped like this?"

He didn't want to pull it out. He'd be pissed if someone played with a body in his morgue like that, though Dana would be shipped to an FBI location for a more formal autopsy.

Eleri shook her head. "The other end was already open. It was smooth, so I put the raw end up. Didn't want to cut or snag anything inside. Not that it helped."

He looked at his partner. "You did it right."

Then he decided, *screw it*. He was going to claim this body, anyway. Any FBI medical examiner could ask him what he'd done, and he'd tell them. Let them come at him. He pushed on her chest. Nothing. He grabbed a scope and looked down her throat. Nothing was out of the ordinary.

He looked to Christina. "Could Grace have overridden Dana's thoughts enough to make her think she was choking? And Dana believed it enough that she died?"

Christina shook her head. "I can't. I mean, I can make your skin feel like there's a fire, but I don't think I can do more than you can do with your own brain. I don't think so!"

He hadn't meant to make her so distraught, but he'd needed to know. Hopping over a bit, he put the scope down the jury-rigged tracheotomy Eleri had devised on the fly in a burning house. She'd done it well. He'd be proud if he wasn't standing over Dana's body.

He stood up. "Her lungs are completely collapsed."

Christina started crying in earnest. As he watched, Eleri put her arms around the other woman, but Christina's sobs didn't lessen. Her voice wasn't even scratchy when she spoke—which Donovan chalked up to the fact that she'd been standing right behind Grace Aroya, probably the cleanest air in the house. But it was Christina's words that haunted him.

"I was overriding her. I don't know how she did it. Because I was pushing her to let go of Dana. Even after she passed out, Dana still couldn't breathe. Whatever she did, it was more than I can do."

44

They'd driven out here into the middle of the desert. Wade drove. Christina rode in the back with Eleri, even more silent than she usually was. Eleri wondered if she was plotting revenge, or at least regretting that Grace Aroya was still alive.

For Eleri, the drive reminded her of heading out into the desert looking for the Atlas compound. Strangely, the case wouldn't seem to let them go. This girl was the odd result of the Atlas Defect and whatever the Russian government had done to her mother. The only thing that kept her from sinking into bad memories was Donovan.

"Stop it," she told him. "You can't take the bandage off. It's a third-degree burn. It might get infected."

Jesus, the man had the letters M and D after his name. You'd think he'd know that.

"I know." No, he didn't. "I just want to look at it, though. It's not third degree anymore, Eleri."

She'd seen it that morning. There had been a package waiting for Donovan when they arrived back at the hotel the night before. Though comfortable, the hotel hardly qualified as the home she was desperately in need of. Dana's death was weighing her down. On the one hand, it should—her boss and partner had died. On her watch. On the other hand, she couldn't afford to have her mind distracted. Eleri had looked at the box and recognized it, handing it to Donovan to open.

Christina and Wade had nearly knocked it out of his hands. They started in on *what if it's a bomb?* and *we have no idea who it's from!* But Donovan recognized the writing as a return address of sorts even if there was no formal one.

"It's from Grandmere!" As though she was now his Grandmere, too. Eleri decided she didn't mind sharing.

Wade and Christina had still gone through the standard procedures, only to produce a small, recycled plastic pot with a slightly foul-smelling brown poultice in it. Though the pot had originally belonged to some face cream, that clearly wasn't what was in it now. Grandmere had scrawled in sharpie across the white cap "ARM." Donovan hadn't waited any longer, he'd sniffed it hard, pulled his bandage off, and slathered that crap on. He rebandaged it and then told Eleri she should stay with him, in case it made him hallucinate or something.

She was pretty sure he just didn't want to sleep alone. Neither did she. So she'd headed back to her room, changed, then returned and fallen on the other twin bed, comforted by his already steady breathing, and she'd passed out.

She'd woken to the harsh reality of Dana being gone, but also to Donovan's excited cries about his arm. Though his burn had technically walked the border between second and third degree, he was now calling it a light second degree burn. He said it hurt like a motherfucker, but he smiled when he said it. Eleri assumed it must feel much better.

She reminded him to keep it sterile, then rolled her eyes because he'd just rubbed a random, slick, gross-smelling sludge on it. Who knew if it was sterile anymore? He'd declared, "I love Grandmere!" and gotten on with his day. So she had, too.

Eleri now saw the small, squat, square building come into view through the front window of the SUV. Armed soldiers stood guard at the door. One stood on the roof, too, constantly scanning in all directions. The building had a Faraday cage built into it and the frequency was hopefully jamming any mental signals the girl was putting out.

As they parked and piled out of the car, Donovan putting only ginger pressure on one foot, Eleri asked, "Christina, are you okay with this? You won't be able to override her."

Though Christina nodded in response, Eleri kept going. "We can turn the Faraday cage off while we're in there. Wade and Donovan can smell her, I can find a way to see her. If you want to try it."

"Why?" Though the other woman spoke this time, Eleri didn't find the sound comforting. "I did it yesterday. It didn't work. I don't see what the point is of letting me override her if she can still kill my friends."

As Christina visibly got herself back together, Eleri saw that she and Dana had been close. They were partners, had been long before Eleri and Donovan had even met. While Christina hadn't spoken much, she and Dana had a strong bond. Eleri had lost a boss and someone she respected and worked closely with; Christina had lost the equivalent of Donovan. Eleri couldn't fathom it. Even having lost her sister, she'd still *seen* her sister in some form. Emmaline had visited as she'd grown. Dana was dead.

At the hands of the small killer in the cell.

Eleri nodded her understanding and led the way in. With Christina in the early stages of grief, and Wade only a temporarily reinstated agent, she was now the ranking officer. This clusterfuck was now her dog and pony show. Somehow Dana had handed it over with the suspect in custody. All Eleri had to do was figure out how to keep Grace Aroya incarcerated and put a bow on it.

She breathed out. She needed this interview.

Inside, they looked through the two-way mirror and found the girl handcuffed to a table with thicker than usual cuffs. The kind reserved for the most dangerous escapees. Electing herself and Wade to go into the room with Grace while Donovan and Christina observed and stayed in touch through comms, Eleri girded herself. She wasn't looking forward to this.

As she walked into the room, she watched the young woman perk up from her abject boredom by a little bit. Eleri was starting to introduce herself, when Grace Aroya spoke.

"Let me go."

"No."

"I'll let myself go." She shrugged, her expression as deadpan as if she were in detention for not turning in her homework.

"You can't get out," Eleri told her, not liking the disturbingly placid calm behind the girl's eyes.

"Watch me." Grace Faith Aroya, took an audible breath, but not a big one and blinked up at Eleri. Then she looked at the bar that held her right handcuff to the table.

As a high security suspect, she was cuffed separately to two separate bars welded to the table top. Her feet were cuffed to the chair which was welded to the floor and also to the leg of the table. The furniture was designed to be too heavy to move with any ease. Certainly not for a person of Grace Aroya's size.

But as Eleri watched, the point where the bar contacted the table surface began to spark and melt. Grace Aroya stared at it harder. Then she yanked up with her wrist, trying to bend the hot bar. It didn't work.

"It's steel, honey," Eleri said it as calmly as she could. She was wearing fire retardant clothing, no sprays or other products in her hair, but this girl could probably still set her on fire. Eleri could only hope the precautions would work. "You'll have to get the bar molten enough to pull the cuff through. I don't think you'll get that to happen. Or get it to bend."

Nothing here was standard issue. Including the suspect.

"Can we talk?" Eleri asked, pulling out the other chair—it was nowhere near as heavy as Grace's—then waiting while Wade did the same. She listened to the slight hitch in his breath, but he didn't give her the signal.

"Sure. It'll give me something to do until I break out." Grace Aroya offered a small shrug.

"Why did you kill Dr. Benjamin Kellogg?" Eleri left it open.

"There are two of them," Grace Aroya stated as though she were talking about cars or toys. "The older one tortured my father when he was kid. The son tortured my mother—"

"How?" Eleri interrupted.

"You really want to hear this?" It was the first time Grace Aroya even looked interested in the conversation. "Fine. He told her he could cure her."

"Of what?"

"All the bugs and glitches in her system from the experiments done on her as a kid. She still saw murders as they took place. She knew who was molesting their kids. Everything bad? She saw it. She had to live with all of it." Grace Aroya leaned forward over the table top as though sharing a secret. "He told her he could cure her. Then he forced her to have sex with him as some sick payment. It went on for years. And he never fixed her. He didn't do shit. Then he threatened to tell my Dad."

Eleri felt her eyes narrow. "You're fifteen. Your mother's been dead for at least three years, how do you know all this?"

"She's been gone for barely a year!" The young woman snapped back.

Eleri reacted with feigned surprise. She'd been looking for a more exact date. Grace didn't seem to catch that she'd been duped. Eleri nodded at her as though understanding.

"I had to stay hidden. When we were little, we got to go to daycare and have teachers come. But when we moved, when the good Dr. Kellogg started coming around, we couldn't even have that. They kept us in a room under the floor. There could be no toys, no trace of us in the house. We had to stay hidden so that monster didn't find us. Who knew what he'd do if he did? None of it mattered. In the end, he found us anyway."

That matched what Eleri remembered from the small house. There was no trace of a child at all. She nodded along at the story, trying to look like it was all news to her. She zeroed in on one part. "Us?"

Grace huffed slightly, her wrist tugging at the cuff inadvertently. There was a beat. "I had a sister. She died very young."

The baby had been a girl. "Was she Dr. Kellogg's baby?"

"Maybe." Grace shrugged. "She was my sister."

So she had some feelings about some things, Eleri thought. "Did you kill the baby?"

"No." It was fast and clipped. *A lie.* Grace flipped her hands palm up, as though to show she had nothing in them.

"Did you kill your mother?"

"No!" Another lie.

Holy shit. This girl had killed her infant sister and her own mother.

"Did you kill your father?" Eleri didn't add "too," didn't want the girl to know they knew she was lying.

"No. Kellogg did that." She sat back. "Dad came home and found him coming after Mom. Though he didn't see the worst of it. He and Dr. Kellogg fought. Kellogg hit him, pushed him. Shot him, then shot him again, just to be sure he was dead." Her jaw set.

"You sound like you saw this."

"I did. We came out of hiding at all the noise. He told Mom she had to help him bury Dad." She made a move as if she would cross her arms but the cuffs stopped her.

Eleri nodded and switched subjects. "Burt Riser?"

"He was an asshole." She looked between them, waiting until she seemed to catch on that they wanted more. "My Mom went out with him a few times. He made a move on us."

"On you and your baby sister?"

"Sick, huh?"

But it didn't ring true. It wasn't that the information wasn't right. It *was* sick, and Eleri knew it could happen. There was something in Grace's intonation; it was off. But once again, Eleri nodded. She threw out another name.

"Leona Hiller?"

"She was a bitch."

Well, it wasn't an out-and-out confession, but damn, Grace Aroya was a killing machine. "How did you know her?"

"She watched us."

"So you killed her? How?" Eleri saw that her questions were now irritating the girl. She seemed to have more emotion over being questioned than she did over killing a man her mother dated.

"Strangled her. Burned the house around her. You couldn't figure that out for yourselves?" She turned to Wade. "What? You don't talk?"

"I talk." He smiled softly, again inhaling. Eleri wondered if the girl had figured out what he was doing. If she had, she was Oscar-worthy, she didn't show it.

Grace Aroya shrugged. She seemed irritated, but not like she'd caught on to Eleri's tactic of questioning her on things they already knew, trying to gauge how much the girl was lying.

Seeming to have had enough, Grace Aroya made her demand again. "I talked, now you let me go."

"I can't do that, Grace."

"I'm going to get out." She stated with the confidence of the young.

"I don't think so, honey." Eleri tried smiling, but Grace was already lifting up out of the chair.

"Let me go or I'll kill you all."

Wade had sniffed the air and was signaling frantically. Grace Aroya was going off. The room was heating around them.

Eleri hoped that Donovan and Christina had seen Wade's signal from behind the glass. Her life depended on it.

45

At the hotel again, Donovan threw himself back onto the bed as though he would relax, but he couldn't. Eleri was pacing in front of him, washed but still wet.

They'd all known the plan. Wade would sniff, look for that hint of hydrogen that seemed to indicate Grace Aroya was about to light up. He would signal if he found it.

The girl had answered Eleri's questions calmly enough until the end. She'd started getting antsy. It had been a game of chicken then. Get enough answers but don't push so hard Grace explodes in a fireball. Make sure Wade is on his game, and that Donovan never blinks while watching for the signal.

Then, Wade signaled.

Donovan didn't think his heart had raced as badly even the day before with the house fire. Though the fire had started unnaturally, fire itself was a normal thing. This was not. This would be an explosion. The split second it had taken the system to deploy had stopped his heart for an eternity. He and Christina should likely be safe behind the bulletproof glass, but he didn't doubt Grace Aroya's power. He was not ready to have saved Eleri from a burning house one day only to watch her die the next.

But the sprinklers had come on.

To call it a sprinkler system would be to call a tornado a light wind. The intent was to douse everyone in the room with freezing cold water, making it harder to light them up. Grace had clearly shown she was capable of burning human flesh directly. It was also designed to be a deluge that would blur Grace's vision, making it more difficult for her to identify her target. Also, it should give Eleri and Wade the half-moment they needed to dive for the door and get out.

They'd made it. Soaked and shaking, but alive.

Grace Aroya had stayed shackled to the table, screaming as the water came down. The floor had drains, but still it puddled around her sneaker clad feet.

The four of them had bolted the room shut, checked the Faraday system, checked in with the armed guards, and gotten the hell out.

Eleri and Wade had sat in the back seat, dripping wet but not complaining, the whole ride back. Once back at the hotel, she'd showered and Donovan had laid face up on the bed, willing his heart to slow down.

She'd come out, dressed but still with wet hair, and started pacing.

"It's wrong, Donovan." She shook her head to herself.

He watched her, wondered what Christina and Wade were doing, and listened. He'd love to pace too, but the deep cut in his foot wouldn't allow it. He considered checking in on his burn, but Eleri was in need of a sounding board, so he sat up and tried to participate. "About killing her mother?"

"Yeah, did you think so?"

He nodded. The answer had been too pat. The snarl behind it had been a 'bitch had it coming' and not the same outrage she'd had when talking about her father's death. "Same with the baby sister."

"The baby sister bothers me," Eleri said, but he couldn't untangle it.

Did it bother her because she'd lost her own sister at a young age? Did it bother her because it was a cruel act of a probably sociopathic mind? Or what? He added his own two cents. "I think she did it."

"Yes, that part sounded true, but there's something I'm missing."

"You didn't ask about the grandmother," he prompted.

"Picking my battles." Eleri shrugged, pacing more but not talking. She'd made about three turns when her phone rang.

"Avery?" she answered with some joy.

Donovan paid only half attention, able to hear both sides of the conversation as he rolled up his sleeve to check his burn. Peeling back the tube gauze and the pads that covered the gooey mess of burned skin and ugly salve, he examined it as he heard Avery press Eleri about her history.

Was she really a witch? Had she really not known? What could she do?

He heard her breath hitch and thought about getting out of the room. But he didn't walk well, and she was in between him and the door. He stayed put, tried to be quiet.

"I don't need this now, Avery!"

Oh shit. He was here for a fight.

Avery asked something else that Donovan blocked, but he wasn't able to block Eleri yelling back at her boyfriend quite as well. "My boss died on me yesterday, though I tried to save her. I was in a burning house and I almost died today when—"

She cut herself off before revealing classified information in the middle of a fight. He heard her breath suck in. He could almost hear the tears welling in the corners of her eyes.

"Eleri." Donovan heard Avery's voice, both the plea and the anger behind it.

Maybe Eleri didn't. "I don't need your inquisition or your damned witch hunt right now!"

She hung up and threw the phone into a chair where it bounced and tumbled to the floor. She didn't look, but Donovan did. It didn't break.

Heavy breaths moved her shoulders as she stood there holding it in. Her hands braced on her hips in angry fists. He could practically hear her counting in her head. Three. Four. Five. The phone rang again, lighting up the screen with Avery's face.

Donovan made a move to fetch it, but she shook her head at him.

With a nod, he waited, sitting back down, getting the pressure off his injured foot. He fiddled with the bandage on his arm so as not to pay attention to her and to give her what space he could. The burn looked better, he thought, though it was hard to tell from the edge. Grandmere was a voodoo genius, and there was no telling what powers coursed through Eleri's blood. Just apparently not any that would allow her to speak calmly to her boyfriend.

She looked at him then, square in the eyes even though they shimmered with unshed tears.

"I've got it."

He listened, grateful for the change of subject.

"When the Aroyas lived near Leona Hiller, Grace was young. She said, 'she watched us.' But the baby wasn't born until much later. Those bones aren't that old. Leona Hiller probably never met the baby."

Donovan was frowning at her as a heavy pounding started at the door. Though he was standing, Eleri was already across the room. He was wondering if he could put Grandmere's healing salve on his foot, too. If he ran out, would she know to send him more? He figured she would.

His odd train of thoughts was interrupted by Christina barging through the doorway, shaking her tablet. She'd taken up Dana's mantle of collecting all incoming information and distributing it to the team. Now her eyes were wide.

"We fucked up." The words were even harsher coming out of her so often quiet mouth. She was not only yelling it, she was shaking.

Donovan agreed, but it was Eleri who put her arm around Christina. They had fucked up. They'd saved Bonnie Kellogg and her family, but they'd done it by offering themselves up as targets instead. They'd lost Dana in the process.

Christina shrugged her off and Wade came running into the room through the open door. Everyone was now in Eleri's hotel room—and "everyone" was now one person less than it used to be. Donovan's heart pinched at the thought and at Christina's obvious distress. He pushed it aside.

Ignoring Wade, Christina growled at the two of them, "Remember we said Grace Faith was a stupid name? Well, it is!"

Donovan was nodding, applying his training and the "let them get it off their chest even if it's dumb or just venting" portion of his communications courses both from med school and Quantico. But Christina wasn't bitching about the stupidity.

"It's *two* names." She waved the tablet. "We got the warrant to read Dr. Benjamin Kellogg Junior's will. Remember Bethany said her brother thought he might be the girl's father? Well he left them something in his will. *Them.* Faith and Grace are twins."

Donovan felt his jaw drop and his heart stutter as his brain clicked. The split in the path that he and Wade had smelled outside the Arvads' house. Two kids had been walking down the street before

Burt Riser's murder. Of the four girls at Dr. Ben Kellogg's nursing home, the desk clerk could ID only two of them.

"Us!" Eleri shouted, joining Christina's previously one-woman fray. "She said 'us' but the baby wasn't old enough. That's what she lied about. She didn't kill the baby, her sister did."

"Or they did," Donovan added in. "Either her sister or they together killed the mother—Mina Aroya—too."

His heart sank. Christina was right. More right than she could know. They'd fucked up.

"Eleri?" He asked her because she was the most educated in this area, though they'd all had some training. "You called her a 'little sociopath,' did you mean that as something mean to say or as a real diagnosis?"

"Real diagnosis. Not that I'm qualified to make it, but yes. And maybe even psychopath, depending on how you want to define it. Why?"

He understood her question: why was this important when they had one in custody but not the other?

He asked that next. "What's the likelihood that the sister is also a sociopath? Or psychopath?"

With a gulp of breath, Eleri fell backwards into a seated position on the end of the bed. In the background, Wade tapped frantically at the tablet he'd brought.

"High." Eleri's voice was flat. "Given the way they've been working together. I mean . . . if we're very lucky, Grace Aroya is the sociopath and she's been forcing her sister to do all these things and Faith Aroya will disappear now that her sister's in custody."

"How lucky would we have to be for that?" he asked. In the background, Wade pulled out his phone and made a call.

Eleri looked at him solemnly. "Luckier than we have ever been."

"So, assuming the sister's out and about. We have one of them. We have the one who controls the fire—you smelled it, right, Wade?"

It took a moment and re-asking the question to get Wade to nod "yes" and Donovan's thoughts started cranking through the options again.

"Or they both have that skill," Christina added.

"Shit." That had not occurred to him. "How do we even figure out which girl has what? Or if we even have Grace and not Faith?"

"Names don't matter as much," Christina told him, "Remember

when I caught Grace at the safehouse? I had her and she kept saying 'stay back' and 'you can't get me now'?"

It clicked in his head as it clearly already had for Christina. "She was talking to her sister, not us."

Christina nodded. "And the sister, the one who's out and about, she can do the override. I don't know if this sister can—"

"She can't," Eleri interrupted with conviction. "She didn't even try to override us to get out of there. I don't think she can. She only tried to burn her way out." Then she looked confused. "The other sister has the override?"

"She has to have it. Dana was still completely unable to breathe even after I'd overridden the girl I had the choke hold on. Dana died after the girl I held was unconscious, because I was fighting the wrong sister."

Donovan heard a short sniff of breath, a soft sound bordering on terror from Wade across the room. He looked up at the other man to see Wade's eyes wide and his chest heave as he worked to get the words out.

"I've tried five different people. No one can get contact from the outpost."

46

Donovan smelled it before they arrived at the compound. The scent was strong enough to blow in from miles away. He took a deeper breath trying to sort out the components. With each passing second it became clearer as Eleri drove them over the smoother-than-it-looked road out into the desert.

"Building's burning," He said it calmly, as though he were saying how much two and two was.

"The agents?" She asked as she went hand over hand on the steering wheel around the next turn.

Wade was in the front seat next to her and shook his head before Donovan could answer.

"Fuck," Eleri muttered as though that might help or change things.

In the back, beside him, Donovan kept an eye on Christina. She didn't even flinch at the mention of the burning building. He reached out with the back of his hand and touched her on the shoulder. "We need you on your A-game."

Turning, she faced him without blinking. Her expression was blank enough to look deadly. Her eyes, no longer red, were focused and sharp. "I am on my A-game."

He shouldn't have said anything. He'd thought she was sad and grieving. Maybe she would feel it later, but Christina was past tears. She'd moved through the pissed-as-hell stage of grief and directly into the revenge stage. Faith and Grace Aroya didn't stand a chance.

They bounced around another curve and Eleri silently pointed out the front window. A wisp of black smoke curled up in the distance where the compound was. Or had been. He knew it was gone now. Despite the fact that it was fire retardant, it was burning. That had to be one hell of a fire Grace Aroya put on that place. Or had Faith Aroya done it? How much did they look alike?

The agents were walking into a shitstorm. But if anyone was still alive here, this NightShade team was their only chance.

Christina took a short breath and faced forward. Then she started talking. Maybe more words than he'd ever heard from her at once. "I've been walking back through the scene at Bonnie Kellogg's house. Given what we know now, I've come to several conclusions. Correct me if I'm wrong, question me if I don't have all my facts."

The SUV bounced again, but it didn't seem to affect Christina. Maybe it was enough that they weren't stuffed in because they no longer had five agents on the team.

"One, there aren't three of them. There isn't a third sister. We have only two names, and Benjamin Kellogg Junior wasn't aware of a third child." She waited a beat until no one contested her. "Faith Aroya—the twin we didn't capture—doesn't have any fire skills. When I started the chokehold on Grace—the twin we captured—the fire stopped growing and then didn't flare at all. I can only conclude that Faith would have added to the fire in the attempt to kill us if she could."

This time Donovan spoke up. "What if she was afraid of burning her twin?"

"Then she doesn't have a real fire skill. Grace Aroya kept a clean, clear area around herself—and probably her twin—at all times. She had no burn marks when we had her in custody," Christina countered. Donovan had to agree.

"Grace Aroya has no override skills," she started again. "If she did, then she would likely have tried them on us in the compound when we interviewed her."

Eleri shook her head. "We had the Faraday cage."

"That Faraday cage was crap," Christina countered. "I made her flip her hands over several times. I made Donovan scratch his head."

"Hey!" The reaction was immediate and not what he'd been trained for. "Why me?"

"They were interviewing. They needed to not be interrupted.

After I did you, I did the girl. She didn't seem to know she was being overridden."

"Why didn't you say something?" Eleri fought a small measure of anger. Donovan could hear it in her voice.

"Because, it worked inside the cage. No one inside could override the people outside. Or vice versa." This time the sigh was packed with emotion, but she stuffed it back down. He smelled it, then it faded. "I didn't say anything because I thought she'd probably tried it on the men outside and it didn't work. I thought she'd given up and wasn't going to do anything more. I didn't want to let her know she could do it to us. Then . . . I didn't say anything because I wasn't at my best. I am now."

If it was an apology, it wasn't outright, but it was solid. Donovan nodded softly at her as they pulled up closer to the compound. The smoke was carrying up—a blessing, if it could be called that.

The agent that had been on the roof was nowhere to be seen, but Donovan climbed out of the back door and looked up anyway as though he could see through the thick, spiraling haze. From the smell, it seemed the agent up there was still on the roof. The two who had flanked the door still did, though they were neither upright nor moving.

Eleri ran out of the car, leaving the door open. She dug her fingers under their gear to feel for a pulse. Donovan could have told her there was nothing to find, but her actions were faster than his words.

He drew his weapon, keeping it aimed at the ground and stood guard around Eleri. In less than a moment, Wade had joined him, the two of them watching over their boss as she turned the bodies, presumably checking out the scene. It was now a forensic scene, and whether it appeared as one or not, it was a murder. Her specialty.

Donovan breathed steadily in and out, controlling the situation rather than letting it control him. It took forty breaths before Eleri made a pronouncement, "It looks like they shot each other."

Shit, he thought it but didn't say the word.

Eleri continued, "The door looks like it wasn't forced. The security is so tight I don't know how it would be."

She stepped up to the door, into the smoke even though most of it was being carried away by the light wind. She coughed several times, but continued to push buttons. "It looks like the agents here were the last ones to access it. The duress codes weren't used."

Of course they weren't. Donovan tried not to blink. He couldn't afford to miss anything.

"That's Faith Aroya." The words came from Christina who was starting to creep around the corner of the building now that Eleri was coming back to join the small group.

"Come back," Eleri told her, firmly, clearly, and with a touch of fear. "None of us can afford to go out there alone. If Faith Aroya overrides you before you get to her, you're toast. If Grace Aroya burns you before you can override her—"

"You're *literally* toast," Donovan finished the sentence for her and watched Eleri and Christina acknowledge that with a raised eyebrow and a tip of the head from each.

Christina pulled back. She spoke to Eleri without taking her eyes off the surrounding landscape. "We need to check."

Donovan turned to Wade, who hadn't participated in the conversation yet. Wade was staying tight, but checking out the place with his nose to the ground as best he could in human form. "What do you have?"

"She was here." Wade knew he was confirming what Donovan had picked up, but that was as important as anything. Either of these girls could likely kill any or all of them on a whim. If the twins stuck together, it was possible even the NightShade team couldn't defeat them. And they stuck together.

Wade turned his head side to side, then shook it as though disgusted with himself. "I can distinguish two scents now that I'm trying. They use the same soaps, wear the same clothes, have the same physiology. It's almost like they're trying to hide the separate scents."

"Or maybe they're teenage girls who share everything." Though Eleri's voice sounded like she was chatting at a cocktail, her expression was focused on the seemingly empty land around them. Her stance was deadly.

Donovan couldn't smell the distinctions yet, just that "she" had been here. Then again, he didn't have his nose to the ground, he had his head up.

Eleri's voice came low, but clear. "Let's move."

They followed Christina in a tight formation. For a moment, Donovan thought it might be funny if he were watching it on TV or such. But he wasn't. He was here. Possibly so were Grace and Faith

Aroya, which meant he could wind up dead in a very short time. Dana had not expected to die before the end of this case.

He took his steps carefully, placing one foot over the other. Gun out, ready, aimed downward, he scanned the horizon looking for shadows rather than people. He trusted his nose more than his eyes. He wondered if his hearing would pick anything up and he strained to sort the sounds coming from far away.

Nothing.

He watched as Eleri, taking the lead now, steadied herself with a deep breath as she reached the corner. She set her shoulder against the brick, tipped her head, moved her hands. In position now, her gun was up and ready, and she rotated. Donovan knew she was using the corner as cover and getting just one eye and the tip of her gun around the edge to see. She could shoot someone center mass, but she would only be exposed at part of her head, one eye, and part of one shoulder. It was an excellent mathematical trick of angles that defied every TV cop show he'd ever seen.

"Clear," she breathed out, not hiding her relief as she slipped around the corner, using the brick at her back for cover. Though things in the building still burned, the brick and stucco was designed to be fireproof. The smoke vented out the top, and though the wall was hot to the touch, this was still the safest place to be.

One by one, they slipped around the corner, Donovan the last to go, still aimed backward, waiting for Grace and Faith Aroya to take advantage of his momentary solo status. They didn't show, and he quickly joined the others on the side of the building, trying not to whoosh out his breath in relief that he was still whole. He wasn't safe yet.

At the back corner, the smoke had billowed and eddied. The wind was blowing the other direction and Eleri turned the corner again, one hand, one gun, one eye. Only this time she pulled back.

"Smoke's too thick. We'll have to cut it wide to go around to the other side." She stepped around again, now scanning far and wide, then stepping out into space. The others followed faster, Wade and Christina in between, Donovan only a step behind.

It was more dangerous back here. The brick couldn't conceal a person, but Grace or Faith Aroya could be hidden in the smoke. Could Grace control it? He tapped at Christina, never taking his eyes off the path behind them.

"Could Grace control the smoke so they could breathe clean air in the middle of it?" He tipped his head toward the dark shadows they walked around. He had no doubt that Faith could conceal them there. He scanned again for shadows and shimmers, but saw nothing he could discern. He inhaled, checking for scent, but caught only a lungful of smoke.

"Yes," Christina answered him matter-of-factly after a hesitant thought. "She kept a clear area for herself in Bonnie Kellogg's house. So I would expect it."

"Shit."

Christina nodded in response to his swear word but he heard Wade muttering. Though the others probably couldn't hear it, Donovan picked it up clearly.

"If I get out of here, I'm going to tell Randall everything. If I get out of here . . ." He repeated it like a mantra, and for a moment, Donovan found a smile. It made him think of Lucy, his quasi-girl-friend. She was ex-special forces, this was probably a Sunday at church for her, but he was about to shit his pants.

The smoke forced them to take a wide berth around the third corner, but it cleared out a bit after that. Despite the acrid air, Eleri had them hugging the building again.

He wondered if he only *thought* he was hugging the building. He tried a trick he knew for anxiety—three things I see, three things I can touch, three things I smell. He even tasted the air. It all matched. All he could do was conclude that he was really here, really hugging the too-warm brick and watching as his partner, the very best friend he'd ever had, was being her bad-ass self and lining up to take the last corner.

47

E leri took a deep breath. Just like each time she did it, she regretted it. The smoke was searing her lungs, probably causing permanent damage. But not breathing caused much more permanent damage, much faster.

Dana.

If flitted in and out of her head with traces of irritation and her own irreverence, anger that Dana was gone, and fear that it had been too easy for two girls to kill Dana.

Holding her arms straight, she used the corner of the building as a pivot point and carefully traced a small arc with her feet. First the road came into view.

Clear.

Then the SUV. She lingered, looking for anything obvious—huge bomb under the carriage? Faith and Grace Aroya inside the car?

Nothing.

She took another step, and another, until she was out in front of the squat building, having come full circle. Eleri wanted to drop her gun to her side and cry. No one was here. No one but the two dead agents on the ground, their blood soaking into the dry dirt, their families unaware. Was it even safe to send a team out to clean this up? Probably not yet. But if they didn't, animals might get to the bodies. There was no good answer here.

She didn't drop her gun or her stance. There was no room for error, and Faith and Grace Aroya might get the better of them even if they didn't screw anything up. Dana hadn't, and now Eleri was in charge. This sucked.

Turning to Donovan and Wade, she asked, "Are they still here?"

"I didn't smell anything," her partner said it and her old friend confirmed it.

She still didn't sigh. "Let's get out of here."

It was as much of an operation to get into the car as it was to circle the building. Though the girls had never used radio trackers nor built bombs—that they knew of—Eleri would feel stupid if she got in the car, turned the key, and felt it blow up around her.

They looked into the back seat. Then they touched it. They looked into the trunk space, then touched it, too. Then the engine, the undercarriage. Nothing went unchecked. At last, they all felt confident enough to climb in and head home. Eleri clutched the steering wheel, unsure if she'd rather be in the back where she could relax more or if she was better off in control.

The road was a worn path through the dark, dry silt out here. It wound between plants and what might be creosote, Eleri wasn't sure. She didn't have the mental energy to figure it out. She just knew they were twiggy and rough-looking and she didn't want to hit or even scrape one with the car.

Without taking her eyes off the path, she opened the conversation she didn't really want to have. She wanted to avoid it, but she couldn't. "We have to figure out where they'll be next."

"At their next target," Wade offered up as he looked out the window. Eleri wondered if he was enjoying the scenery, or if he thought the girls would fly up beside the window like super-villains.

"What's their next target?" Eleri asked as she stopped at the edge of the dirt before turning onto real road.

"We are," Christina said it from the back. She said it with no emotion, no inflection at all. It was hard to argue Christina's correctness. They had hurt the girls more than Bonnie Kellogg's family had. Eleri was sure the bullseye had shifted squarely onto her own back.

Despite all the tension, they made it back to the city, back to the hotel, hearts heavy. They didn't speak as they headed inside. They touched each other, Donovan and Wade sniffed, they asked odd questions standing there in the hallway. It was all a strange attempt to confirm they were all who they appeared to be.

Donovan and Wade had already run into Faith Aroya once, and they'd believed she was Eleri. They'd captured Grace Aroya, and Faith had freed her sister. The team needed both girls. Caught. Together. Without a kill order from Westerfield, it was their only chance of ending this. But it was hard to know if the person in front of them was really who you thought they were.

Eleri let herself into her hotel room, closing the door and bolting it, feeling her brain start to shut down with the small sense of peace that offered.

They were ten stories up. The bolt was activated from the inside. She flipped the metal stopper—much more effective than the old chain-style lock. The windows were made of a thick plexi, to stop people from committing suicide out of them. It would keep angry teenage girls out as well.

Before she fell onto the bed and into a long overdue oblivion, Eleri showered. If she didn't do it now, then when? Though she could turn the water off and on, she couldn't do the same with her thoughts. Her group was falling apart. They were united between them; Dana's death had solidified that. But inside, each of them was cracking. They were tired—four days straight with very little sleep. They were grieving—no matter how well they knew or liked Dana, she was gone, and it was hard to take. They were failing—Dana's death was a personal error for each of them. They were broken, battered, and outgunned.

With everything they had, they were still not the superior creatures in this battle. That scared the shit out of Eleri.

In the past, she'd felt that she had control of at least of part of it. If she played her cards right, she could come out the victor. Now? She thought she might play all her cards right and still lose. She could lose her friends. She could die a painful, fiery death. There was no reason to believe she would win, and little reason to believe she even could.

She only knew she had to keep going. It was who she was.

Wrapping the hotel towel around her and appreciating its softness as only a person contemplating a painful death could, she grabbed her phone.

Quickly, she shot off a text to Avery.

—Sorry about the other day. We lost a team member. I haven't slept. Terrible case. I don't know what I am, so I can't hide what I don't know.

She hit send. Was that enough? Was it right? Partly, she wanted to apologize for being so short with him. Partly she wanted him to understand that she'd told him she wasn't available to be a "real girl-friend" when she was on a case. She started onto the next message.

—You'll have to decide if you still think you can deal with all this.

She left it at that, set the phone aside, and started to crawl into bed in the towel.

With her knee on the mattress, Eleri reconsidered. She wanted to turn off the phone so she could avoid a reply from Avery. She didn't have the energy to deal with the case, let alone the boyfriend. She wanted to curl into the bed and sleep, but that wasn't an option either. Not yet.

She got dressed: pants, socks, bra, shirt, she even put sunscreen on her face. Everything but shoes. She would be ready to get up and go if she needed to. Somehow, she didn't doubt it would happen.

Only then did she lay down.

She felt her head hit the pillow and watched the world go black.

In moments, her feet hit the soft padding of leaves that littered the forest floor. The air was fresh and clean and she walked along the path as her shoulders released the tension of the day. She couldn't remember what had made her so uptight.

"Eleri." Her name floated on whispers of a voice she knew well though it had never existed in her reality.

Emmaline, arrested for years at age seventeen, stood in front of her. "Come with me."

Eleri nodded and followed.

"It's close," her sister said, her smile sad. Eleri couldn't tell why Emmaline would be sad that things were close, but she didn't say anything. She only nodded and followed the path her sister cut for them.

Expecting the square house with the corner door—the one she always found in these woods—Eleri was surprised when Emmaline turned onto busy streets. Though it was night, strings of lights hung above them. People walked on covered sidewalks, keeping off the roads, though only the occasional car went by. Music filtered from some of the houses, and while it was upbeat and down home bluesy, it soothed Eleri and she smiled.

Emmaline turned a corner, her hand trailing along the building as she walked. Following, Eleri did the same. She watched as rough brick passed under her fingers, the colors were each different, yet somehow all the same. Then, when she blinked, the brick became black bars. Wrought iron fencing marked the side of the cement walk now, and as Eleri looked through it she saw mausoleums, raised tombs, headstones, angels and more. The sea of white, gray, and black-faded marble was beautiful, repeating and changing as she looked out across it.

Only when she stopped, when she held the fence in front of her, did she feel the cold seep in. Gasping, she turned to find her little sister had gotten far ahead of her.

"Eleri."

She moved to catch up, the chill coming after her in tendrils and wisps. She passed a building with blue siding and bright shutters, and another with white and black paint before she was confident she'd left whatever stalked the graveyard behind.

Emmaline stood in front of her, at another wrought iron fence. Eleri peeked cautiously through, only this time the fencing led into a courtyard. The floor was dirt, shrubs and even trees had been planted between pavers. Roses grew in the gaps, climbing wildly up the walls. In the back, a large tree with a gnarled trunk provided shade.

"You have to enter. It's coming soon," Emmaline said as the gate opened.

Eleri put one foot inside and felt the chill coming again. When she turned to look at her sister, she saw for the first time the blood dripping from Emmaline's fingertips. Only Emmaline didn't seem to notice. "You have to go in."

Eleri stepped backward and followed instructions, turning to look once more over the beautiful secret garden her sister had led her to. Only this time—up close—she saw that the pavers were edged with pieces of dull white. Through the dirt, bones pushed up, pieces peeking here and there. Eleri knew them all. Recognized instantly that they were human. She saw hands, pelvic bones, sacra, and under the tree, facing almost sideways, a skull.

Backing away, she made it all the way to the fence, only to find that it had closed and locked behind her. Emmaline was gone. She was stuck and her heart began to race.

Not afraid of bone, Eleri looked again. This bone was bad. The chill that was seeping inside her came from these remains. They changed each time she looked, each time more confusing, each time more frightening.

"Eleri!" The whisper came from the back of the garden.

From behind a climbing rose, Emmaline had opened an old-fashioned, arched wooden door. Her sister beckoned as Eleri picked her way through, careful not to step on human remains. Once out the back, she was in the forest again. As Emmaline closed and locked the door behind them, the cold receded and the heat of the summer woods began to wrap her in safety.

In no time, they were at the house Eleri had originally expected. This time Emmaline followed her inside. They walked to the back room but did not find Aida Weddo stitching spells in her rocker. Instead, a bed, draped in white netting awaited.

"Sleep," Emmaline told her and Eleri complied. She climbed in, crawling under sun-warmed covers as her sister sat in the rocker to watch over her. The feeling of safety and love and hope was something she wanted to hold onto, but it slipped through her grasp as exhaustion set in.

She slept for hours in the white bed.

Luckily, she was rested when Emmaline touched her shoulder. "Eleri, you have to wake up now."

From beyond her sister, Eleri heard a new voice. Another young woman.

"Echo, did she really sleep through all that?"

48

Eleri breathed slowly, keeping her muscles as relaxed as she could force them to be. It had seemed silly, training to appear to be asleep. That had been years ago, when she'd been at Quantico and she hoped she not only remembered all the tricks, but that she could pull them off.

"Look at this. She hung her stuff up in the closet. It's cute."

She let out her breath and offered a twitch of her shoulder as her head lolled to the side. Shifting a little, she heard the two girls still as she did it, but then she settled in with a sigh.

"Where's her gun, Ember?"

Eleri couldn't distinguish their voices—not one from the other. But she could hear the voice in her own head. *Under my pillow, bitch.*

She almost hadn't done it. Almost crawled in without checking, she'd been so tired. But she had done it, and with the recent shifting she'd done in her so-called sleep, her right hand was creeping up under her head, getting close enough to grab it.

Her hips were squared and so were her shoulders, making her a smaller target. Because she now faced the edge of the bed, it also gave her the easiest position to spring from. She tried not to tense.

They'd been here for approximately ten minutes, going through her things. Or at least that's how long she thought it was. One, she'd woken up and they were already here, so it seemed they'd arrived not too long before that. Two, she couldn't tell for sure because she couldn't open her eyes and check any time pieces. There was nothing that ticked to count off, nothing that beeped or buzzed on any regular basis to give her a sense of passing time other than her own internal clock.

While pretending to sleep, she'd learned that the two girls called each other "Echo" and "Ember," names that made a surprising amount of sense. They seemed to think it was James-Bond-like in some way.

In that same time, she'd figured that she was an idiot. Sure, she'd made certain that she was ten stories up, but there were stairs and elevators. She'd made certain that the bolts were all thrown, but the hotel managers had to have a way in. And these two girls could get the managers to do anything they wanted, such as giving them the master keys, or just coming up here, opening all the bolts, and then promptly forgetting they'd ever been here.

No one knew they were here. Anyone who'd seen them would forget.

Eleri wasn't sure what time it was, though she suspected it was very early morning. Unfortunately, no one would miss her for a while. She was the team leader, she was the one who would call the meetings, so no one would have to check on her for being late. She was on her own.

In the time the two had been in her room, she'd been listening to them as they went through her things. She'd come to a conclusion, one she didn't doubt now. They were psychopaths.

The way they spoke of the people they'd killed, these two young women didn't think of them as human at all. Even those who'd picked up two hitchhiking young women and helped them on their way were discarded as easily as a fast food wrapper. Eleri had given them the benefit of the doubt—she'd harbored a concern that Leroy Arvad had picked them up and made a move on them. They were young, attractive, and hitchhiking. It was an easy conclusion to come to: revenge for his poor behavior.

Eleri was shocked how hard it was to keep to herself, to steady her breathing into the long, slow slides of sleep when they discussed what he'd done. He'd done nothing bad. He'd helped them. Fed them. Offered them a place to stay.

"I think she's the bitch that figured out that truck driver gave us a ride," one of them stated. The girl was behind her, which made

Eleri even more nervous, but there wasn't much she could do about that.

"Should've killed the wife, too." The tone was that of someone lamenting a missed opportunity. "Should have made it look like a murder-suicide."

Eleri fought the churn in her stomach.

She didn't have time to wonder if they'd been abused, if maybe that was why they'd killed their mother and their sister. Or if maybe Mina and Peter Aroya had found themselves in the same situation as other parents of sociopaths—with a kid that couldn't be reached and couldn't understand that other people were living things with feelings and needs that mattered.

Eleri had worked NCAVC—the National Center for Analysis of Violent Crime—through the Bureau for a while. She knew her sociopathy test, and these girls were passing with flying colors.

Unfortunately, sociopaths had a strong evolutionary advantage: they just didn't care. They weren't beholden to social norms, or the belief in life as sacred. It meant Eleri was the severely handicapped player here. Also, she was one against two with no backup on the way. She took another slow breath and let it out with a little sound, rolling her shoulders again.

She'd been playing a long game here. Her fingers touched her gun and she couldn't resist. Another low half-moan, half-breath, another small squirm as though she were still sleeping deeply. She knew they were watching her, waiting, but Eleri now had her hand firmly on the butt of her gun. She settled back in to feign deeper sleep and wait for her best chance. She only hoped she didn't feel the stab of a knife or the burn of a bullet first. She had no idea what weapons they were holding. No idea if she'd even feel the heat before she burst into flame.

Their next words told her that—unfortunately—her thoughts were right on target.

"Is she ever going to wake up?"

"Let's just get it over with."

"No. I want her to hurt."

"Trust me, Echo. If she wakes up on fire, she'll hurt."

"I want her to see us. I want her to know that *we* did this." There was a brief pause, then a tone that belied the teenagers they were. "I want people to know they can't fuck with us and get away with it."

"Oh, I think they know. I just want to be sure she burns."

"You and that fire. You get to kill all of them."

"You get to do all the other fun stuff. Like convince people you're an FBI agent!"

"That *we're* FBI agents."

"True. Do it. Wake her up. Let's get this show on the road."

Eleri felt it pulling on her brain like a tide. *Wake up.* She wasn't asleep, so she couldn't actually wake up. She fought it.

It came again, stronger. *Wake up.*

Unable to fight it completely, she took a deep breath and made a noise. It released some of the pressure, some of the overwhelming desire to sit up, rub her eyes, and look at them. It sounded like they were standing at the foot of her bed. They were no longer speaking.

Eleri's hand gripped the gun, hidden and ready to use. It was loaded, one in the chamber, and she couldn't remember the last time she'd been so glad she slept with it ready.

Wake up.

She let her eyes flutter. In those brief flashes of light, she saw them. Two girls—on their way to being women, but truly just girls—standing at the end of her bed. Identical faces. Sweet. Beautiful. They looked like their mother.

Eleri made a noise as though she were confused and blinked again. She didn't pull her hand out from under the covers, though she'd shifted the gun, they couldn't see. If one of them could read her mind, she was screwed. But so far, neither had shouted, "Gun!"

She started to focus on their faces, thinking about how she could bring them in. She'd kill them if she had to, but she didn't want to. They were kids. Facing them, she wanted to believe they could be saved.

"Do you want to burn her first? Or play with her?"

Eleri blinked her eyes wide. *Okay, fuck them.* She wasn't waiting for a kill order from Westerfield. Not anymore. She focused on one, then the other. "Hello, Faith. Hello, Grace."

The shock on their faces told her she'd gotten it right. They thought she could tell them apart. Eleri kept her expression bland, but it had been a flat-out gamble.

As she watched, they faded from view.

Fuck.

She was fighting ghosts.

A laugh came from the corner of the room. The curtains swayed, caught fire and slowly burned out.

They're flame retardant, you idiot, she thought it, but looked at the curtains as though she were puzzled. But that might not be the right way to play it. They knew that she knew what they were. She'd called them by name.

The curtains flared to life this time. Not just one spot, but the entire window, the whole length of the room. The heat pushed at her. Eleri ignored it, scooted her hand a little closer.

Despite the thick carpet, she heard them—little flutters here and there that betrayed that they'd split up. She fought the need to turn her head and look.

The tide in her head turned. No longer was she being urged to be awake, but Eleri felt them trying to make her afraid. They weren't just doing scary things to her, they were overriding fear itself on their victims.

Her heart raced, her adrenaline—already high—started to slide from her control. Eleri fought to both act afraid and not actually be afraid at the same time.

She hadn't done this with her eyes open before and it was harder this way. Taking a long, shallow breath, she tried to flip the switch she'd found, the one that could turn the override Faith Aroya was using on her.

Nothing.

Shit.

A deeper breath this time. A sharper focus.

Eleri fought the urge to blink. She could see them. One of them—presumably Grace—was standing on the side of the room that was catching fire, one item at a time. Eleri's head swiveled to look at her but then she kept moving past as though she hadn't seen. She'd already played one card, that she knew which was which, Eleri didn't want to let them know she could see them.

Despite the error, Grace went on lighting things on fire. The small pad of paper on the bedside table. Eleri made sure to jump a little, even as she clenched the gun harder. Her shirt, hanging in the closet burst into flames. Eleri again pretended to be afraid instead of angry. She was glad that her first thought was, *That was one of my favorite shirts, bitch!*

From the corner of her eye, Eleri caught sight of Faith. She was walking around the bed, staring at Eleri and it was hard not to stare back.

She sighed. If she waited any longer, the smoke would overtake her. It was hard work, fighting the override Faith had put on her.

Now or never.

Eleri scooted her left hand back under the pillow as though she was leaning back, afraid. She looked at the fire and whimpered while she calculated their positions. She shuffled her legs under the covers and gasped as her suitcase caught on fire, too.

Without a deep breath or even a blink as warning, Eleri shot out of bed, a gun in each hand. Two feet planted firmly on the floor, she looked from one girl to the other, staring them directly in their damned surprised eyes.

Her right hand came up holding her Glock, aimed on Faith, standing right next to the bed, and her left held her backup piece pulled from under the pillow. Eleri leveled it at Grace, standing near the closet. She didn't want to shoot until she had to. Deaths weighed heavy, she knew that.

"FBI. You are under arrest. Put your hands on your heads." She said it in the voice she'd been trained to use. The one that brooked no questions, allowed no rebuttal against her authority. The one she'd trained on harder than anyone else, because she was tiny, red-headed, and somewhat oddly colored. Authority didn't follow her like a puppy the way it did with some.

Faith roared at her. Angry, raging against the fact that her powers weren't working on Eleri.

Eleri felt it, the takeover of something—something beyond adrenaline, something beyond the normal—as she felt her own primal growl coming on. "Do. It. Now."

Neither girl moved, but Eleri felt her hand grow hot. Aiming in Grace's direction with her left hand, she shot.

The recoil was stronger without her other hand for support. The noise deafened the room for a moment.

Then Grace laughed. "You missed."

"I meant to. It was the only warning you'll get."

They laughed in unison this time, and Eleri felt the tide pull her under as she watched Faith's face transform from beautiful, if haughty, young woman to human monster. The edges of her vision crowded with sparkles chased by blackness.

Eleri pulled the trigger as shapes and light disappeared.

She shot three more times into the empty space in the room, firing on instinct, all sight gone.

"Eleri!" Donovan's voice came from the doorway as he stepped inside. But she'd already pulled the trigger again.

49

Donovan froze as he waited for the white heat of the bullet to hit his system. It took a moment, he knew. The body rejected all feeling at first because the pain was so great.

"Eleri!" He yelled it, afraid to take a step forward, afraid he would collapse as he felt the sting in his shoulder.

Just his shoulder.

He breathed a sigh of relief as his brain offered up some humor to diffuse the situation. *It's only a flesh wound.*

As he thought it, he was hit from the left, thrown into the wall by hands he couldn't see. He smelled them then, two distinct but very similar signatures.

Grace and Faith.

He heard them. Yelling, angry as they ran down the hall, and he heard bullets chasing them. Frantically, he looked around the room at the fires. The curtains were burning out. Eleri's shirt was dripping in flaming shreds onto her suitcase in what had been a neat closet until it burned. But they weren't flaring up. The smoke was billowing into the corners—neatly missing the sprinkler heads.

"I'm blind," Eleri yelled out, but he watched her lower her guns. At least she wasn't shooting into nothing anymore. No wonder she'd shot him.

"Are you okay, Donovan?" This time, it wasn't about information.

It came through in her voice, the stress, the threat of tears. "Did I hit you?"

He already had his hand reaching around to his shoulder blade, where he pressed against the wound for good measure. But when he pulled his fingers back, all he saw was a spot of blood. He looked down at the front of his shirt as the gunfire from the hallway ended. The fabric wasn't even torn. He'd only been nicked by something flying through the air. Thank God. He'd been injured enough on these cases. "No, El. I'm fine. You didn't hit me."

"I missed!" Christina called from the hall beyond the door he'd opened and that the two girls had run out. Christina had unloaded her weapon down the empty-looking hall and hadn't hit anything.

"I don't think I got anything either." Wade backed her up. They both must have come from their rooms when they heard Eleri fire.

Donovan had arrived at Eleri's door, ready to knock when he saw it was open. Hearing her voice, he wanted to push his way in, so she could see him. Something in her tone was so intent, he hadn't done it. Then he'd heard the other voices.

Turning quickly, he now looked behind him and saw the hole in the drywall. That made his heart stop. It was so close. Too close. Eleri had almost shot him.

"We need a better plan," he hollered to her, too loud. His ears were still ringing from the gunshots.

"FBI!" It wasn't said with force, but with authority—Christina's voice. Though the rest of it garbled, he could make out that she was talking to someone from the hotel. Shooting up their establishment tended to bring them out in force.

He heard Wade's voice, more garbled words, mashing their way through the tone that now sounded like someone had struck a tuning fork on his skull. At least he knew the phases and that meant it would be fading soon.

"We're heading out," Wade yelled. "Follow when you can."

Donovan understood. It didn't matter if Eleri and Donovan were bleeding out or on fire. Follow when you can. *If* you can. Wade and Christina were doing the job. The girls had to be caught.

Grace and Faith Aroya had just run away. They might even still be in the building.

"Donovan, get me the comm!" Eleri, still blind for some reason, was now sitting on the bed, patting frantically at the table.

Even as he crossed the room, he could see how close she was, she knew where it was, she just didn't know exactly where *she* was.

"Here." He thrust his device at her, knowing she could feel the buttons even if she couldn't see them.

He breathed in, smelling the overwhelming scent of powder from the guns Eleri had fired. Looked like she'd gone at it two handed. No wonder she'd missed. But it was smart, facing down two of them, powers like they had. Two guns was the only way to do it.

Donovan waved a hand in front of Eleri's face as she flipped the phone around and tested the buttons by feel. The staticky beep of connection came through.

"Wade! Christina!" Eleri yelled it.

Donovan watched as her eyes failed to dilate or contract. She didn't focus on anything. She was blind. He was just as concerned that she wasn't that concerned. She should be pushing her fingers at her sockets, trying to see if there was something physical she could do to restore her sight. She wasn't. She was frantic, but it was her words that did that, no concern for her eyes.

"Yes?" Christina's voice came back, followed immediately by, "Go for Wade."

"They call each other Echo and Ember. Grace is Ember, she's the firebug and Faith is Echo. She has the override."

So Christina had been right, he thought. He wondered if that was all the information Eleri had to share, but it wasn't.

"You have to know, they are sociopaths! They'll stop at nothing."

His blood chilled as Eleri kept going, frantically.

"They said they should have killed Leroy Arvad's wife so we wouldn't have traced them so fast. That's their justification. Leroy Arvad was good to them and they killed him anyway!" She was spilling it all, frantic. "I know what I'm talking about. I know that psychopath test! And they fail it. They aren't even human, I'm telling you! They're monsters. I'm issuing a kill order in Westerfield's stead."

Donovan was desperately trying to keep his heart in his chest. What havoc could these two girls wreak if they truly had no respect for human life? He was breathing faster now, worried about Christina and Wade and what they were running into without him and Eleri as backup.

Eleri pressed her button on the phone again, still far more disturbed by what she was saying than by the fact that she couldn't see. This was the longest, deepest override Faith—Echo—had perpetrated to date. At least that Donovan knew of. The fire had faded when Christina put the choke hold on Grace. Dana's inability to breathe, her death, was caused by the fact that Faith was nearby and none of them even knew to look for her, let alone to stop her.

Eleri hit the button to make it beep at Wade and Christina again. Through the comm line, which they were keeping open, Donovan heard the systematic sweep of the area. If they'd gotten near the girls, they hadn't known it.

"I still can't see!" Eleri yelled into the comm, frantically. "I. Still. Can't. See."

She punctuated it with a sniff and a vocalized gasp. Donovan's first thought was to hug her, she was so distraught. She held the phone to her head with one hand, and as he looked at her, he realized something was more off than just that her eyes stared into nowhere.

Her right hand, not holding the phone, tapped a finger on the gun she was still holding. Though it was laid on the bed right beside her, Eleri's hand still wrapped around the butt. Her first finger, her trigger finger, tapped at the trigger guard as she issued another overly-panicked sniff of fear.

Donovan almost caught the signal too late.

She *still* couldn't see.

Faith, or Echo, wasn't known to override anyone from a distance. If Eleri was still blind then the girl was—

He sniffed the air.

Dammit!

He'd missed it. The smell of gunpowder, the ringing in his ears, he'd just not been paying attention to Eleri's very un-Eleri like ranting. Donovan only prayed that Wade and Christina understood that *she still couldn't see.*

He looked at Eleri for a sign, but she couldn't see him. She truly was blind, but she signaled him anyway.

"Donovan?" She sniffled her way through the word as though she was upset.

"Yes?" It was all he could say. They were here. At least Faith was. If he said anything more, he would let on.

It turned out, Eleri wasn't signaling him, she was locating him. Making sure this time.

Without warning, she pivoted on the bed, braced both hands on the bed and shot into her closet.

A scream erupted as well as a yell of fury. Even before he could turn to confront the intruders she'd located, he watched as her eyes focused again. She shot into the closet another time and Donovan lifted his own gun and aimed as he watched the two girls blink in and out of his vision.

He didn't let the gun waver.

One girl held her arm, still screaming, the very noise seeming to set off new fires around the room. Ember, then.

Echo grabbed at her sister—from what Donovan could tell in the snippet of vision he was seeing—and began to drag her out of the room. Piecing the frames together and using scent, he rushed to the door and stood in their way. When he lifted the gun, it was a scant inch from Echo's nose.

She stopped dead, her still screaming sister bumping into the back of her. It had all happened so fast that Eleri was still yelling "F.B.I. Stop where you are!" and Ember had only begun to drip blood on the carpet. It oozed between her fingers, there was plenty of it, but it probably wasn't a fatal shot. Damn good job by a blind woman though.

"Stop," he told them, his voice deep and menacing. After all, they were just teenagers.

He saw it before she did it. The deep breath for some primal scream. If Echo loosed all her power, she might liquify their brains. He was reacting before he even realized he did it.

His lower jaw stretched out, his head rolled side to side, pushing the frontal bones forward, repositioning his zygomatic arches to make his face longer. His arms he held tight, his hand still gripped the gun, but he rolled his shoulders and his hips at the same time.

He was a tall man, but standing there, actively transforming, he arched up onto his toes and filled the doorway. He let loose a roar of his own, and Echo stared at him in abject terror.

She backed away, into the room, taking Ember with her. Ember still bled through her fingers, still shed flames around the room through her tears. Only this time the sprinklers came on, surprising all of them.

Eleri had her gun up, but was at the side of the girls, almost across the room. It wasn't a good shot. He wouldn't take it if she were the one standing here. He didn't count on her taking the shot. He leaned forward, pushing Echo and Ember back into the room, back into the gathering smoke.

He leaned forward and growled again, but never expected the hit he took.

50

E leri watched in awe as Echo—Faith—pulled back and punched Donovan in his changing face.

It wasn't a hard enough hit to do real damage, but it was enough to startle him. He jerked back.

Echo yelled, "Now, Ember!" and yanked her sister around him and out the still open door.

Donovan's hand came up to cradle his jaw as his eyes blinked. Whether that was from the sting of the hit or the sting of the smoke that was rapidly filling the room, Eleri couldn't tell.

The chair was on fire, the remaining tatters of the curtains caught again. The bedding smoldered and burst into flame behind her, propelling her forward. The coffee pot in the little alcove beside the door started to melt, then the glass pot exploded.

Leaping backward at the sound, she was unable to avoid all of the flying glass and took stinging hits on the side of her neck and arm. Even as she jumped forward to get out of the heat of the flames she'd nearly jumped into, Donovan jerked away too, indicating some of the flying glass had gotten him. He made a noise of dull pain and shook his head until his face returned to normal, until his teeth looked less like fangs, and his jaw less like it would tear a man—or teenage girl—to shreds.

"We have to get out—" The last word was lost in a coughing fit, as Eleri ducked her head into her arm and pulled her shirt over her nose. She had only to glance up through the thickening smoke to see Donovan do the same. She was two steps from the door when it burst into flame.

There was nowhere left to run, nowhere but—

She grabbed Donovan's sleeve and tugged at him. The bathroom was tile. Cold, hard compound for the vanity. Porcelain for the toilet and tub. She hopped in and turned on the shower. Cold.

She pushed Donovan under the spray, though he'd already caught on, and just as quickly traded places with her. In a moment they were doused, water went everywhere in the bathroom but that was hardly their concern. Eleri grabbed at towels, shoving them under the spray even as she opened them. Donovan did it, too, the two of them working in perfect sync.

They could have just run through the fire wet, but the towels would afford extra protection, something thick and cold to breathe through. But the precious seconds it took was costing time as the room blazed hotter beyond the bathroom door. Eleri didn't know if they'd made the right decision.

They stared at each other, wrapped a towel around their heads, protecting their hair and scalp. They threw the largest towels around their torsos and held smaller ones—maybe washcloths—over their faces.

Holding hands to keep track of each other as much as for comfort, they ran. Eleri let Donovan lead. He had sharper senses than she did, but she didn't know if he could use them with all the smoke clogging the air.

Her feet fell on uneven ground as she stepped on broken glass, something fabric, and then a fallen chair. Her ankle twisted under her, but Eleri didn't stop. Donovan was pulling her anyway, it wasn't an option.

They stumbled together into the hallway. The smoke was pouring out here, the noise of the fire alarms deafening. She hadn't noticed it in the room with the fire crackling around her.

Just as Eleri pulled the towel down from her face, she caught sight of Wade at the end of the hallway. His feet pounded down the overly bright carpeting, chasing the closing doorway to the stairs.

"Come on!" He yelled it as he motioned with his hand. It didn't slow him down.

Despite her somewhat twisted ankle, Eleri found herself running down the hall after him, peeling the wet towels as she went. She leapt over the ones Donovan threw aside, no match for his superior speed. He was a runner, had been since track in high school. She couldn't keep up, but she could have her weapon ready.

She checked the chamber, put a hand to her hip, feeling for her extra magazine, even as she chased her partner down the hallway.

51

E leri was the last to arrive in the stairwell, the huge fireproof door swinging heavily closed behind her. It was taking its sweet time so she ignored it, instead focusing on the scene in front of her.

There was carpet at the landings, nothing plush like in the hallways, but something. Otherwise the stairs were utilitarian, metal covered in some kind of concrete substance to provide traction. The railings were painted metal, the walls cinderblock. The perfect place to face down the firebug on the landing a half floor below.

Christina was partway down the steps, her weapon aimed, when she yelled, "F.B.I. Stop!"

For a moment Eleri wondered why they kept yelling it? It clearly wasn't working. But when she shot a teenaged girl, she would sleep better knowing it wasn't a surprise. Knowing that said teenager decided to not stop when told. Decided to ignore the authority of the Federal Bureau of Investigation. Eleri had dealt with people raised to mistrust the government, this was not that situation. The cold stare in each girl's eyes was not about mistrust, it was about calculating how to take out four F.B.I. agents because the agents were in the girls' way.

Wade was heading down the steps behind Christina, though he didn't add his voice, he added his bulk and his weapon.

Ember screamed up at them, her hand still on her arm, the sleeve now red with her blood. Eleri wasn't sad that she'd winged the girl.

They needed to be stopped. She was considering what she could do to knock them out, when Ember screamed again.

With the scream, the air in front of her heated as Eleri watched. It formed in a yellow-orange wave, then shifted into a curved front of fire. It didn't swirl and crackle, or consume some flammable object to survive. The girl had literally made fire out of thin air.

The thought—the awe of it—was fleeting as the fire surged on a pulse of air so strong and hot that it blew Christina and Wade backward.

Eleri had still been harboring thoughts of saving the girls. Finding a way to lock them up. As Wade and Christina lifted off their feet, those thoughts fled. With the fuel of adrenaline, her thoughts now raced.

Echo and Ember couldn't be stopped other than to be killed. They couldn't be held, not in any way the FBI could guarantee. They'd already seen that. If the Bureau only managed to hold onto one of them, the other would pry them loose soon enough. Together, and even separately, they were killing machines.

She wanted to feel bad for them. Kept in the alcove under the trap door in the closet. A mother who may have been crazy and may have had skills of her own. A father they spoke of adoringly but who'd been killed in front of them. None of this changed the fact that they'd made FBI agents shoot each other dead. How would that be explained to those agents' families? They'd killed Leroy Arvad and hadn't even bothered to make him look like the bad guy in their own story. They'd killed the truck driver in Peoria—probably with the same story.

It happened before Wade and Christina hit the ground. Eleri lost the last shred of compassion she'd held so tightly. Her hands opened, her gun hit the floor where she dropped it. Her feet left the stucco style tread and she ran head-long into the fire.

Her hands stayed out in front of her as she leapt over Wade and Christina. She was unsure how hard they'd hit, if they were even okay or still alive, but there was no time to stop and check.

Echo and Ember saw her coming. Still angry, still fighting, they began to retreat, down the staircase, around the corner. They were attempting to get out of sight, but Eleri didn't let them.

They stopped on the next landing and Echo looked frantically around them for something she could use. It was Ember who screamed again and Eleri saw the fireball coming for her. This time, it was hotter blue-white fire.

Donovan saw Eleri disappear around the corner after the girls. Later he would take a moment and recall this and decide if her feet had actually touched the stairs. Right now, he was stooping to pick up the gun she'd dropped.

She clearly didn't need it, but he wanted it in hand if she did.

He was regretting the decision as he heard the air crackle for a second time, only this time the fire was hot enough to make the entire hallway sizzle. He breathed it in and ran forward anyway, leaving Wade and Christina where they had fallen. There was no time. They wouldn't survive at all if Echo and Ember got away.

The scream he heard and saw was Eleri's. It was rage, pure and simple. These two had killed and killed again. They'd killed Dana despite Eleri's valiant attempts to save her. And they were trying to kill all four of the remaining agents in the hallway. Eleri's rage was founded. Donovan could only have her back.

He watched as she leaned into the scream, standing on two separate steps, she used the angle to reach her face toward the two girls aiming back at her on the landing below. The scream seemed to work against the fire. He watched as, in mid-air, the fire pushed forward and Eleri pushed it back.

He was raising his gun when Echo looked at him, and suddenly the gun was lifting, aiming away from her. He felt his muscles do it. Just like it unlocked something in Eleri, the primal fear had tapped into something in the girls, too. This was not him envisioning waffles while making oatmeal. This was his own body disobeying him. The muzzle of his gun was coming around toward his face.

He felt the buzz in his head and ducked away from his own aim. Glancing down the stairs, he saw Echo snarl at him and growl with her frustration. Probably mad that he didn't die as quickly as the others they'd targeted. He would not make it easy.

He pulled his shoulders and pushed his face, watching her as he did it.

Let her be afraid of what he was. He'd never wanted to use it that way. Never wanted to inspire the fear his father did. Until now.

The gun wavered as his shoulders changed. Then it wavered again. Echo's gaze flew to a point beyond him, behind where Eleri and Ember faced off, the air between them simmering with power.

Christina appeared beside him and he wanted to be relieved, but there wasn't time. She was reaching to her ankle and pulling at something. He couldn't look, couldn't take his eyes off the girls, didn't dare stop fighting the overwhelming urge to eat the barrel of his gun.

He felt what Echo wanted him to do and he knew it wouldn't kill him. Not the way she wanted him to do it. Must have been something she saw on TV, because it would only blow off the side of his face and leave him partially paralyzed. He'd seen it. His muscles strained against it as much as his brain did. The worst of it was that part of him *wanted* to do it. She had the power to not just move him, but to make him *desire* the taste of the metal in his mouth and *feel* the oblivion of a death he knew he wouldn't even achieve.

Clamping his teeth together so he couldn't put the gun in his mouth, he was shocked to see Christina holding a hunting knife in her hand. She tossed it to the ground at Echo's feet as the fire between them folded and turned back. Not by much, but Eleri was gaining a little ground.

Why had Christina given them the knife? She'd handed them another weapon. He didn't even know if the girls could make it fly through the air or not. He wasn't confident they couldn't.

The fire fought back—pushing itself outward again and he watched as Eleri gasped for breath and took two steps back before aiming herself at the flame between them again. This time he saw that tears were rolling down her face. Even as he felt the pressure to get the gun in his mouth fade, he saw the black in Eleri's eyes and the pain in the tears she was shedding. But she didn't let up.

Aiming his gun again and wondering at the change he looked down into the stairwell. As he watched, Echo picked up the knife and screamed. Then she stabbed her sister.

Eleri fell forward, almost tumbling down the stairs as the fire lost its force. Barely finding her footing, she kept from going head over heels into the very flames she was fighting.

The fire was yellow again, the blue-white heat having dialed down. The flames crackled, fading in places and Eleri could see the two girls in the stairwell.

As she watched, Echo stabbed Ember. First awkwardly in the arm. The knife stuck, maybe having struck bone. Echo yanked on it until it came free. She pulled back and yelled, *"Noooooo!"* at the top of her lungs as her arm came down in an arc, this time the blade found a home between ribs.

The fire Eleri had fought disappeared with the scream of pain that peeled forth from Ember's lips. Almost dizzy with nothing to push back against, Eleri shook her head for blood flow and spotted Christina.

The other agent stood just behind Donovan. Her hands hung loosely at her sides. Her expression was blank. She stared straight ahead, but there was no doubt this was her work.

Whether Christina willed it or not, another scream—this one in anger—came from Ember, as she pushed against her sister. But this time, Echo's clothes caught fire.

Still she pulled at the knife. She cried as she rocked the blade back and forth to make it release. Blood was flowing out both her sister's arms now. As she reared back, sobbing, she stabbed again, even though her shirt was now fully engulfed.

Eleri felt her hand clench.

She didn't have her gun.

But she heard the bullet as it whizzed by her, feeling as though she was in slow motion and she could watch it spin past her on the way to its mark. Her mouth fell open as she heard and saw the second bullet.

Wade.

He was on the steps behind her, and by the fourth shot—she didn't know how she was keeping them sorted in her mind—she realized some of the bullets came from Donovan's gun.

Both men stood braced in classic shooter stances. Each unloaded a full clip into the stairwell as Eleri watched the world go black and fall away.

52

Donovan closed up the stitches in the second, small identical body. They were crap stitches, as one does in an autopsy. No need to worry about a scar. These bodies weren't even going to a funeral home.

He'd pulled more lead from them than he could count. Some of it he left intact, finding and identifying it by x-ray. It felt odd, examining a body that he had killed. Or at least, helped kill. It still wasn't odd enough to not do the job.

Pulling out a chair, he sat in the corner and typed the report himself. Normally, as a medical examiner, he'd dictated his reports. But who would he dictate these to? His skin wanted to crawl, as he typed with his back to the only two bodies in this room with him.

They were dead. They weren't coming back.

If Christina's turning them against each other hadn't worked, his and Wade's bullets would have done it. Though honestly, given the burns on the one body, and the organs pierced by the hunting knife on the other, the bullets had been a mercy killing.

A mercy killing with at least twenty-plus bullets apiece. By that count, Wade had reloaded and kept firing without missing a beat.

Echo and Ember were dead.

Bonnie Kellogg and her husband and daughters were alive. They had minor burns, but no more. He'd talked to them a little as they were debriefed and sent home to start to put their lives back together.

Bonnie bugged the crap out of him—and Eleri, too—he could tell. Her defense of her brother and sister and father let on that she had some idea what they'd been doing and she wasn't fully against it. She was not the sweet teacher she'd seemed to be. Donovan had harbored fantasies of pulling his weapon, shooting her between the eyes and taking the last of the Kelloggs off the grid. Instead, he'd recited the Hippocratic oath in his head while she prattled about "those people" and he'd gritted his teeth and forced a smile he hoped didn't look too "big bad wolf." Then again, he hadn't cared.

Hitting send on the report, he stood and stretched. He'd peeled his gloves to write up that neither girl had showed a single physical anomaly that would indicate the powers she had in life. The blood-work had come back. The girls matched ninety-seven percent human with traces of some animals but a clear match for several camel genes.

Donovan could only wonder—though it didn't go into the report —if there had been unknown ramifications of the elder doctor Kellogg's work. Maybe this crap hadn't all come from their mother. Or maybe the powers did, but the sociopathy came from the paternal side.

He wouldn't likely ever know. He just wanted to get the hell out of the desert. He needed to run out his own back gate and onto Carolina National Forest land. He needed to call Lucy and tell her what he'd been up to. Peeling the paper gown, he looked over at the bodies making shapes under white sheets. Someone else would put them away, ship them wherever Westerfield wanted them. Donovan was done with them.

He headed down the hallway, taking several wrong turns. The morgue was almost always in the basement of the hospital and through a maze. With the gown off, the urge to scratch at his arm was almost overwhelming, but he remembered the fight to keep the gun out of his mouth and this seemed easier.

The itch meant it was healing. The salve was working miracles. He'd asked Eleri about Grandmere marketing the stuff and Eleri had only raised an eyebrow. She'd fainted on the steps that afternoon and Donovan had raced to her side. His heart pounding, he'd been afraid that even in death, Echo and Ember had stolen something else from him.

But he'd quickly found a steady pulse, checked her head for

obvious injuries, and seen she wasn't bleeding anywhere. He'd picked her up, carried her up the stairs and laid her out on a bed the hotel managers provided when Christina and Wade flashed their badges. She'd been heavier than he expected. More to her than met the eye, he thought. Or he'd just been exhausted. It had been a weight he'd been happy to bear. She would be fine.

And she had been. She'd sat up soon enough, wanted a Coke and Cheetos, of all things. Then even mocked him when he started a simple enough conversation about arm salve.

"Do you really think it's the herbs that are healing your arm?" Eleri shook her head at him. "She'll kill herself if she exerts that energy for everyone. Grandmere loves you." She'd smiled, eaten a handful of Cheetos and frowned at him.

"Have you smelled it?" She asked.

No, he hadn't. Burns did not smell good.

She shrugged. "Honestly, it's probably pesto."

That had been it. Eleri had been Eleri again.

They'd avoided the finality of the case for a short while, then filed paperwork on the bodies they'd left in the stairwell. Eleri was currently at the branch office, packing up the bones from the Aroya house to send to storage.

Christina and Wade had taken care of having Echo and Ember's bodies transported, and calling in an F.B.I. cleanup crew to smooth things over with the poor hotel that had more than one burned room, a trashed hallway, and a stairwell that had seen an epic battle that left it with scorch marks and blood spatter.

His phone rang as the elevator doors opened.

"Lucy!" He felt himself smile. It wouldn't hurt to see her again. He had to go home, but then he could go to L.A. for a while.

He blinked in the sun as he hit the front doors and tried to process what she said.

"You what?" He asked as he stopped dead under the pick-up awning. An orderly ran into him and Donovan stepped to the side to listen.

"Your agent in charge? Westerfield? He and I have talked about a few things. He's used me on other cases, you know."

Donovan did know, but that wasn't what she was talking about.

Her voice grew more excited. "He wants to send me to Quantico. To get trained as an agent!"

Holy shit. He didn't say those words, though. "That's amazing!" Donovan blinked in the sunlight as her words soaked in.

"He wants to start some new division under NightShade. Something for us normals."

He almost laughed. Lucy was anything but normal. She was the Terminator. She was epic in a way he'd never be. What Donovan said was, "Of course they want you in the F.B.I. You'd be amazing at it."

Then more words fell out of his mouth. "I should come to L.A. soon to celebrate with my girlfriend."

"Your girlfriend?" He heard the surprise in her voice and felt it in his chest at the same time.

"Too soon?"

There was a pause when everything in his chest fell a few feet. But then her voice came again, "Nope. It's good."

After a sigh of relief, a little planning and more congratulations, he hung up and started toward the car again. He was just thinking how Lucy—a.k.a. Walter Reed—would be in the F.B.I. probably within a year, when his phone rang again.

This time the number made him sigh with exasperation and he ducked under a tree for shade while he fielded this next disaster. "Hello, G.J."

"Hi, Donovan. I have an update for you!"

Of course, she did. She didn't know when to quit. He hated to ask, but it was going to come out anyway. Better to get it over with faster.

"What did you do?" He hadn't meant it to sound that way, but it was out now.

GJ didn't notice. "So, you know how I found Peter Aroya? And you know what they did to him, when he was a kid, at Atlas?"

"Yes." Donovan knew. He'd been there.

"Well, you also said you couldn't notify the families, that your Special Agent in Charge wouldn't let you. That it would incriminate the US government or something. Well, I don't work for the government."

"What did you do?" He wanted the families notified, still he didn't quite trust GJ.

"Sooooo," she drew it out sounding like a kid. But she thought like a scientist and a bit like a genius at times. She was also capable of being obnoxious as hell. Donovan waited. "I traveled, I found them, befriended them—"

He rubbed the bridge of his nose. He didn't want to know, but he did.

"—and I encouraged them to get genetic testing."

"You what?"

"Befriended them and convinced them to get genetic testing. I have one to go. Three of them have already gotten letters from Las Abuelas. I told them to respond." She had a smile in her voice, proud of herself.

His heart beat stronger. She'd done what he and Eleri wanted to do. With no strings.

"Oh, and I've found seven of them now. One was already deceased, but I met his kid and she's getting the testing done, too!" GJ was excited. For once, Donovan figured she should be. Then, she turned more somber. "I wanted to do something for you and Eleri. I know you wanted to get this done, but your hands were tied. Mine aren't. Consider it a thank you."

He sucked in a breath and only then realized he was leaning against the tree. It probably had scorpions climbing on it, but he didn't care. He was wiping away tears he hadn't known he was losing.

GJ was right, he and Eleri had fought to tell the victims. The children had been stolen, people waited for them still.

Someone walked by in the parking lot, but it was a hospital. It wasn't all that odd to see a grown man crying with his phone to his ear. When the passer by looked at him questioningly, he said, "Good news."

"Congratulations." The other man nodded, smiled, and headed on.

Donovan still hadn't said anything to GJ. He pushed the words out. "Thank you. Thank you for this."

"Of course. You and Agent Eames fought for me."

"I don't know what Agent Westerfield will say when he finds out, but I won't be the one to tell him. It's your call." The tears were still falling. The relief he felt was a weight he hadn't known he was carrying.

GJ surprised him again. Though he didn't know why she still could. "I already told him."

This time, he said it, "Holy shit. What did he say?"

"Actually, he offered me a spot with some division he runs. NightShade?"

For a second Donovan felt like the ground had spun beneath him then snapped him back into place. "He what?"

"He's building a new section of his division. He said if I can pass Quantico, he'll put me in. I'm looking at start dates . . ."

Donovan didn't hear the rest of what she said. It went in and out his ear in droning noises. He managed to congratulate GJ on her success and even agreed to relay the information to Eleri.

He headed to the car wondering if another call would come in. If something else would rock his world. Instead, the phone stayed silent and he started the engine while he made plans.

Head home.

Run.

Go to Los Angeles and see Lucy.

Check in with Eleri.

Take a moment and be free of the weight he'd carried. Then, take a moment and come to grips with the fact that he had GJ Janson to thank for that.

He pulled out of the parking lot and into a future he was less sure of than ever, but happier with than he'd been in a long time.

53

E leri sat at the old wooden table at Bell Point Farms.
It had seemed the right thing to come here. She'd wanted to
go to Patton Hall, their family home in Kentucky. The one her
mother stayed at most of the year in the decades since Emmaline had
disappeared, but Eleri couldn't go there with her mother in residence.

Though she wanted to walk the ground Emmaline had disappeared from again, she wanted to come back as an agent. She wanted
to saddle one of the horses and ride the woods they hadn't found her
sister in. She wanted to search for clues that might have somehow
stayed hidden through the years. She would come back as a trained
expert, not as a ten-year-old terrified she'd never see her sister again.

If she did, she would have to deal with her mother.

While Grandmere's special brand of talents seemed to have
skipped Nathalie Beaumont Eames, Eleri's mother had a way of
making her talk. Especially when she wasn't ready.

She wasn't ready.

Eleri looked out at the dark night, framed in the old panes of glass
set in the double doors. The farm was vast. The night wide open with
possibilities, but Eleri was afraid.

In front of her on the table sat something she'd never seen before.

It was a file on a set of bones found in New Orleans. For the first
time, Eleri held a report that she couldn't rule out. For the first time,
she wasn't sure that the skeleton they'd found wasn't her sister.

Something in her own bones told her Grandmere was right.
Emmaline.

Look for other novels by A.J. Scudiere.
Available in bookstores, online, and at ReadAJS.com

ABOUT THE AUTHOR

AJ holds an MS in Human Forensic Identification as well as another in Neuroscience/Human Physiology. AJ's works have garnered Audie nominations, options for tv and film, as well as over twenty Best Suspense/Best Fiction of the Year awards.

A.J.'s world is strange place where patterns jump out and catch the eye, little is missed, and most of it can be recalled with a deep breath. In this world, the smell of Florida takes three weeks to fully leave the senses and the air in Dallas is so thick that the planes "sink" to the runways rather than actually landing.

For A.J., reality is always a little bit off from the norm and something usually lurks right under the surface. As a storyteller, A.J. loves irony, the unexpected, and a puzzle where all the pieces fit and make sense. Originally a scientist and a teacher, the writer says research is always a key player in the stories. AJ's motto is "It could happen. It wouldn't. But it could."

A.J. has lived in Florida and Los Angeles among a handful of other places. Recent whims have brought the dark writer to Tennessee, where home is a deceptively normal-looking neighborhood just outside Nashville.

For more information:
www.ReadAJS.com
AJ@ReadAJS.com

Printed in Great Britain
by Amazon

84613681R00195